MAJESTY

The Sorcerer and the Saint

By

D.W. Murray

Majesty
by D. W. Murray

Printed in the United States of America

ISBN 1-59781-804-6

www.xulonpress.com

Dedication

*T*o my children, Wesley, Brandon, and Sophia, who asked for a bedtime story, and were the first brave travelers to enter the realm of the Nohr World. And to my wife Mary Ellen, who encouraged me to write it all down.

Table of Contents

Majesty

The Sorcerer & the Saint

*T*he goblin's job was simple. "Keep an eye on the child."
It was only a human child and a little girl at that. How
hard could it be? But this was no ordinary child, for she had
a guardian and that made all the difference in the world.

CHAPTER ONE

Something in the Closet

*N*othing unusual ever happened in Somerport. It was a quiet little town, with pleasant sunsets, white Victorian houses and front porch swings. Normally, the weather was quiet as well, but the rumbling of thunder over distant hills was a sign of things to come.

The old weathervane atop the Campbell house pointed due west and hardly moved in spite of the strong gust of wind that blew through the trees. A weathervane that resisted the weather was a peculiar sight, but not as peculiar as the horrible little thing that sat atop the roof of the Campbell home. The tiny gray creature rested its lumpy back against the cold steel of the old weathervane and looked up with yellow eyes as an icy rain began to fall.

The pointy horned imp hated the light of the earthly realm and even this gloomy half light was more than it could bear. The grim urchin was barely twelve inches tall and grumbled as the rain drizzled down its bony face. Then with a shudder and a chill, it quickly disappeared from view to set about its dark purpose.

The house itself looked drab and dreary, nothing like it

did years before, back when there was the laughter of children and the white haired old woman with her worn out old Bible used to pray. It was then that a light surrounded the quiet little home, a pure golden light that shone like a beacon from heaven. Of course no one ever saw the light or even knew it was there. Yet, from the chimney to the basement, the front door to the back fence, the Campbell house glowed like a lantern and by night it grew even brighter.

But now that the old woman was gone and no one prayed for the children any more, a living darkness had descended on the house, and all that was needed was a willing heart for the watchful creatures to set their dark plan in motion.

The boy sat in his room and glared at the sheet of paper. He had said the strange words over and over again, countless times, and still nothing had happened.

"What good is a magic spell if you can't use it?" Jack sneered and stood to his feet. "It's not like I didn't try!" He yelled at the empty space around him. Then with hands trembling and his face twisted into a snarl, he gripped the piece of paper and tore it right down the middle. Jack gathered the two halves together and ripped it again and again and when he was done, he tossed it into the air. The bits of paper drifted down like snow, but before they could settle, Jack whirled around and kicked his chair. He shoved his desk and knocked over his lamp, which shattered the bulb with a pop. He staggered and stumbled and tore through his room, kicking books and boxes and piles of clothes like so much trash.

When he was done, the room resembled a garbage heap and hardly looked any different. Still, he felt better about himself and stood in the center of the room, with his chest heaving up and down. But before he could catch his breath, he thought he saw something. In the dim stillness, something moved. Jack leaned forward, and peered at one of the tiny pieces of paper on the floor. He blinked and rubbed his eyes as the thing stirred, then leapt off the ground and flitted back and forth, like a moth trying to find the light. He looked here and there as every fragment of paper, every shred down to the tiniest speck came to life. They hopped over things, swirling around in a sudden flurry. There was no wind, or even the slightest hint of a breeze, as Jack stared in disbelief and the bits of paper fit themselves back together, without the slightest care that the boy was watching them perform their magical task.

In a matter of seconds the old sheet of paper was back and rested itself on the floor as though nothing unusual had happened. Jack reached down with hands trembling and picked it up. He flipped it over several times to check the front and back, but aside from its yellowed tattered edges, there was no sign of damage or the slightest tear.

Jack suddenly stiffened, as though he sensed another presence somewhere nearby. Then, with the paper in hand, he turned to face the closet that lingered in the shadows across the room. He stared at it reluctantly, and regarded it with a new found respect. The closet was where he had found the old sheet of parchment and it was from behind that door where he knew its power had come.

"Okay... I'll do it," he said. "I don't know how, but I'll try." Jack whispered softly, a dark and solemn oath he would never forget.

Katie Campbell sat watching the rain streaming down her window. She drew her knees up in front of her and listened to the distant thunder as the rain began to fall and showed no sign of letting up. Dad would be late, but even with the dreary weather to contend with, the window seat was lined with pillows and she was comfortable.

"I have learned to be content in whatever situation I find myself." Katie smiled as she remembered what her Nannah used to call her, "pearls of wisdom." They were words from the Bible which the old woman used to read to them when they were little. Now in the quiet moments, Katie missed her dearly. Ever since Gramme Nannah had passed away things were very different. Katie couldn't say how, they just were. Even when she wasn't thinking about it, she could feel it. And sitting there, alone in her room, she could feel it now, with the rain trickling down and the steady patter against the glass.

She listened for a while until she heard another sound, a peculiar knocking. At first she thought it was the wind or a branch outside, rapping against the shutters, but then turned around to see a tall shadowy figure standing in the doorway of her room. It was her brother Jack. At thirteen he had grown considerably and was an ominous figure lurking in the dark. She watched him for a moment and was about to say "Come in" when she realized that he wasn't looking at her at all. Instead he was tapping on her door very lightly and inspecting it with great care, as though it contained the knowledge of ancient secrets that were his to find, if only he knew what to look for.

After a great deal of frowning and nodding, Jack finally stood back, took a deep breath, rubbed his hands together as he had done so many times before and started to chant.

"Dig a who, big a who, bah lah, boo gia." Jack said in a low voice, much deeper than his own, like he was pretending to be someone else. When nothing happened he began to say the words faster and louder. The silly sounding words made Katie giggle.

"Quiet!" Jack said, and continued to chant. "Dig a who, big a who, bah lah, boo gia." He repeated the words with greater insistence, as though he wanted the door to do something.

"Dig a who, big a who, bah lah, boo gia!" He said and flicked his fingers at the door, like he was counting by tens, when Katie finally interrupted.

"What are you doing?"

Jack dropped his hands by his sides and stared in defeat. He had done this to every single door in the house and each time, it was the same.

"I'm trying to cast a traveling spell on your door, but it won't work." he said with a look of disgust.

"Oh," Katie said and tried not to sound totally disinterested.

She didn't really understand why Jack felt her door should have a traveling spell and didn't think her door particularly needed to go anywhere. But since she was ten and Jack was her older brother, if he was willing to waste his time, she was willing to watch.

Jack pulled the sheet of paper from his back pocket.

"I don't get it." he said. "I wanted a transformation spell so I could do stuff. You know, like turn pennies into gold, and they send me this traveling spell that doesn't even work."

"They?" Katie asked.

Jack ignored her and stared at the piece of parchment. At the top of the page in very fancy writing were the words,

"Gellzoowin's Sorcery and Wizard's House of Magic."

Just below was Jack's name next to the words "Traveling Spell." The magic words were clearly written in the middle of the page. At the bottom were the instructions that told you how to perform the spell. They were written in Old English. Jack made a funny face as he looked at the words for the ump-teenth time and read them aloud.

"Set ye door at the Nohr World's sliver of a splinter's eye to ye dwelling place then rest ye brow at the spot."

Jack paused then shouted, "What on earth does that mean?!"

"Why don't you pretend to be something else?" Katie asked. "Being a wizard doesn't look like very much fun."

"What do you know?" Jack huffed and didn't like it

when his little sister talked to him like he was the baby.

"BEEP! BEEP!"

Katie spun around to look out the window and saw the car pull into the driveway. She jumped up and ran past her brother who just stared at the sheet of paper, pondering the riddle in his hands.

"Daddy's home! He's home from work!" Katie shouted and dashed out the door. Now that the show was over, as far as Katie was concerned, Jack would have to figure it out on his own.

Downstairs there was a frantic jumbling of keys at the front door, and a fair amount of fumbling at the door knob. When the door finally swung open, Dad stumbled in, and looked as though he had just walked through a car wash. He stood there in sopping clothes, with briefcase in hand and tried to maintain some sense of dignity as he adjusted the package tucked under his arm, then cleared his throat and forced a smile.

"Honey?!... The garage door..." He called out with the rain still dripping down his face, but before he could finish, a voice called back from somewhere in the house.

"I turned it off!" It was a sweet voice that was obviously busy at the moment.

Dad frowned at the answer and the lack of any reasonable explanation.

"And why would you do that?!" He asked, trying not to sound too upset, since an open garage door, or at least one that was switched on, would have saved him the aggravation of running through the rain and getting his clothes soaking wet.

"The table, sweetheart, remember?" The pert little voice called back with a cheerful and happy note, as though it all somehow made perfect sense.

"Oh, of course," Dad said, even though he didn't know what a table had to do with a garage door that wouldn't open. But since he was already wet and dripping on the carpet, he decided he might as well surrender when he heard someone coming down the stairs.

Katie was moving fast, bounding down two steps at a time, and before Dad could move, she hit the ground running and jumped into his arms. It was an open field tackle that made him drop everything to catch her. Katie squealed as she hugged him and clung to his neck like a trained monkey. Although his days of college ball were long behind him, and he was a little thicker around the middle, he was still fit enough to take on a ten year old girl even if she did have a death grip around his neck. Dad stumbled back and pushed the door closed behind him.

"Alright, alright I give up!" He chuckled.

When Katie finally looked, she giggled and pointed at his hair which was wet from the rain and stuck out in weird places.

"What?!" Dad said, pretending not to know what was wrong, which only made him look sillier.

"What did you bring me?" Katie asked, grinning from ear to ear. This was hardly the normal reception, but then tonight was special. Dad glanced down and Katie's eyes lit up. On the floor were his briefcase and the package, slightly dented from the fall. It was wrapped in crinkled brown paper, neatly taped at all the corners and marked "Express Mail."

Katie jumped down and tore through the postal package, like a crazed animal. Before the last piece of paper could hit the floor she yelled, "A kite! A Dyna-flow Rainbow flyer! Just like the one I wanted! I can't believe it! Can it really do tricks?!"

"If you're good enough. It's even got dual lines and control handles." Dad said.

Katie gazed down at the picture of the kite in its shiny new box, her mind soaring in the clouds with dreams of the toy she could hardly wait to fly.

"Thanks!" she said.

"You got an "A" and a promise is a promise." Dad said, then backed away to hang up his coat and nearly bumped into Mom on her way by. Mom was a small, slender woman who had managed to keep her figure and her sanity while raising three children.

"Comin' through." she said, with oven mitts and a steaming hot bowl of rice. "I bought the antique table for the study. It's in the garage. I didn't want you to hit it. How was your day? Wash your hands. It's time to eat." Mom said, and was gone before Dad could even open his mouth. He smiled then picked up his briefcase and set it beside the door.

Seated in the dining room, just down the hall, perched atop her high chair was baby Sophia, tossing sugar frosted crunchies everywhere. At nine months old, this was great sport.

"Hey Fia! How's my little chubby bubble?" Dad said and waved.

But the baby was too busy looking for more cereal to empty onto the floor and couldn't be bothered with cute little nicknames at the moment.

"Oh, Sophie," Katie said then shook her head as she went to help her sister.

"Hey, Jack!" Dad yelled upstairs just in time to get a glimpse of the boy going back to his room with his face buried in the sheet of paper.

Jack mumbled something, more of a muffled grunt than a word. Still the message was clear. "Whatever Dad. I can't be bothered right now." was the gist of it. And with that, he slammed his bedroom door behind him.

Dad turned to Mom who was on her way back to the kitchen.

"Tonight is the night we settle this." Dad said with a look.

Mom answered with a reluctant smile. "I'm ready when you are."

This was a terrible start for a wizard's apprentice and Jack knew it. He sat on his bed, with the paper in hand, and stared at his closet as he thought back to when he first heard the voice. It was four months ago to the day, right after Gramme's funeral, and he had been seated in the very same spot. The voice only spoke to him once, the voice of a man that whispered two words, two words that still echoed in his mind, "vaulted verses." When he first heard it, they meant nothing and made no sense. But the more he thought about it, the more mysterious and magical the words became. He said them over and over again and when he could think of nothing else, he knew there would be no rest until he found out what they meant. That was when he began to study.

Jack brought home stacks of books and devoted himself to learning everything he could about wizards and magic. The more he read the more he wanted to know. Jack read about the elder arts of sorcery and spellbinding. The books spoke of ancient mysteries, legends and hidden powers, but nowhere did it mention the two words he was searching for.

Jack had looked everywhere, until one day when his mother had finally given him the dreaded task of cleaning up his room, starting with his closet, which now looked more like a cave. The closet door was swung wide open and had not been closed for months, due to neglect and the overflow of tangled objects heaped in front of it. Jack waded into the mountain of clothes that had been gathered there. At first it looked as though he might be gobbled up by the clutter of clothes, toys, empty soda cans, and candy wrappers. Jack dug his way through, complaining all the while, and flinging things here and there as he went. The more he dug the more there seemed to be.

"I'm going to need a shovel," he thought, and when he was completely inside the closet with clothes dangling all around him like vines in a jungle, something caught his eye. It was a glint of metal in the shadows. He moved a few more things aside and there, shoved against the wall, near the back of his closet, was a silver chest, the size of a shoe box. Kneeling there in his closet, he stared at the thing with great curiosity, then brought it into the light to get a better look.

The little chest was finely polished with a swirling silver pattern, carved into its surface. Jack tried to think if he had ever seen the silver box before, but knew it was highly unlikely, since he would have remembered such a thing. "Then how did it get here?" He wondered. Surely no one in his family would have hidden it in his closet.

After much thought, Jack knew there was only one explanation, and as a newly self appointed wizard's apprentice, he was sure of it. The silver chest was obviously not of this world and had magically appeared by itself. Jack settled down in front of the mysterious box and smiled; pleased with the explanation, even though it was fantastic and impossible.

There was a silver latch on the front of the chest, which Jack slid open easily enough. When he was ready, he placed his hands on either side of the box and lifted the lid. The inside of the chest was lined with red velvet and contained nothing more than an old yellowed piece of paper, which was neatly folded. Inside was a message hand written in large letters which looked like some sort of spell.

"How in the world?" he thought to himself, and was suddenly a little more suspicious about his discovery, since the spell seemed to support the idea that the box was indeed magical. Jack glanced around to make sure he was quite alone and when he had regained his nerve, he read the instructions more slowly. He read them again and when he was sure he knew what to do, he placed the note back in the box and set it in the closet. After a great deal of effort, he cleared away all the junk, then closed the closet door, stood back and said the magic words.

"Sumelkim Otcalf!"

A second later Jack thought he heard something that sounded like the fluttering of wings, on the other side of the door. He reached for the door knob then remembered that the instructions specifically said to keep the door shut until dawn. As curious as he was, he decided to wait.

The next day Jack opened the door very slowly, half expecting something to fly out of his closet. But aside from the usual clutter, everything seemed normal. The silver box was right where he had left it. Jack pulled it out, and when he opened the lid, he found the same piece of paper. At first he thought nothing had happened, until he unfolded the old piece of parchment and was amazed to find something else written on it. In addition to the magic spell were four new words, "How are you today?" The words were written in the same perfect handwriting.

Jack scrambled to find a pencil, cleared off a space on his desk and wrote very carefully, the letters F- I- N- E. "Fine," it was a simple response. With that he folded the paper, placed it back in the silver box, said the magic words and closed the closet door. Again he heard the fluttering sound and stared at the door, but dared not open it for fear of breaking the spell, or even worse, letting what was ever inside get out.

The following day when Jack opened the door, he looked inside the silver chest and to his surprise, the old words were gone and had been magically replaced by new words. The note simply said, "Very good, is there something I can do for you?"

Jack could hardly contain himself.

He wrote back, "Who are you?" then put the silver chest back in the closet, said the magic words again and listened. Jack heard the flapping sound fade away, as though there was a great space on the other side that led far beyond the walls of his closet.

The next day Jack took everything out of his closet,

which impressed his parents greatly. "Now that's what I call house cleaning!" Dad exclaimed.

When the closet was perfectly empty, Jack stood inside and looked around. It was a small space, only five feet wide and six feet deep. He knocked and banged on the plaster walls which were bare and obviously quite solid. When he was satisfied that there were no secret openings or hidden passageways, Jack just scratched his head and read the note inside the silver chest. They were the same words he had written the day before. "Who are you?"

Jack wondered if he had forgotten to say the magic words then decided that if he was going to send the letter back, there was a much better question he wanted to ask. He erased the first message and wrote, "What are the vaulted verses?"

All things considered, it seemed to be a logical question. After all, if the box was really magical, sent by means of magic, one would think that whoever sent it should know the answer to the question, since it was indeed a question of magic.

"At least it was worth a try." Jack thought.

He put the box back in the closet, closed the door and said the magic words. There was the usual flutter of wings and the note was on its way. The question was, where to?

The following day Jack opened the silver chest and found the same words on the note. Again there was no response. He erased the words with some concern and wrote, "Hello. Are you there?" then put the note back and closed the closet door. He said the magic words and heard the usual birdlike noises coming from within. This time he was more concerned about the message and hoped there would be an answer.

The next day Jack was surprised to find a new message. It read, "How about a nice traveling spell?" Jack was so overjoyed he held onto the note for the whole day and read it every chance he got. Then when he was really able to give it some thought, it occurred to him that he didn't know what a traveling spell was and honestly had no interest in one. If he had his choice he knew exactly what kind of spell he wanted. Jack finally wrote back, "I'd like a transformation spell, please." He folded the paper, placed the note back in the box then closed the door. As usual, he said the magic words, "Sumelkim Otcalf," but what he did next even surprised himself.

Jack quickly grabbed the door knob, gave it a twist and flung the door wide open. And when he looked inside, floating near the floor, just above the silver chest, was a tiny creature, a little man, eight inches tall, as shiny as metal and as black as coal. It had the face of a cat and shielded itself from the light with leathery black wings. The thing whipped its tail, bared its pointed teeth, and glared at Jack with eyes that turned red as fire.

As quickly as it could, the hideous little creature opened the silver chest, grabbed the note, then looked back one last time, hissed like a snake, and dove into the misty darkness of another world, through the back of the closet wall. Jack watched it until it disappeared, then took a step back and slammed the closet door in horror.

It was several days before Jack found the courage to move his bookshelf and furniture away from in front of the closet door. When he did, he was armed with a flashlight, a baseball bat and wearing his catcher's mask. With the closet door swung open and his bat held ready, Jack looked around to make sure the little monster was no where in sight. When he was sure it was gone, he found the silver chest, and read the new message written on the piece of paper.

It said, "The creature is my servant. It's afraid of the light. Don't do that again. Now, how about a nice traveling spell?"

The voice of reason whispered. "Turn back now!"

But it was only a vague warning, drowned out by burning curiosity, and a desire to know what secrets lay within the shrouded world beyond his closet door. Then without any concern of the dangers involved, Jack scribbled the words, "A traveling spell would be fine."

Moving carefully and cautiously, he put the silver box back in the closet, closed the door and said the magic words. Jack shuddered when he heard the thing inside, flutter away and again the horrible creature had come and gone. But since most servants usually stayed with their master, Jack was relieved to know that at least the thing didn't actually live in his closet.

The following day he received just what he asked for, a genuine traveling spell fit for a wizard. This particular kind of spell was to be cast upon a door. He had managed to figure out that much, but nothing else, and there were no further messages. That was nearly three weeks ago.

Jack sat there staring at his closet, contemplating the mystery of it all, when another thought popped into his mind. It was like an alarm had suddenly gone off in his head. He jumped up and looked around suspiciously.

"Something's wrong!" Jack thought. "Wizard's intuition, that's it!" He had read about it and even tried to practice it a little, and now that it actually seemed to be working, he found the sensation rather thrilling. When it occurred to him that if it really was working, it meant that there was really something wrong and he needed to be worried instead of excited. He felt an urgent need to leave, to get out of the house. But, before he could finish the thought, there was a knock at the door.

"Jack...dinner." Mom said and peeked her head inside the room.

"Wash your hands before you come downstairs." she said then took one look at the mess and closed the door.

"Now what?" Jack bit his lip and paced back and forth.

He thought about climbing out the window but it was still raining and a two story drop down to the bushes below would break more than his fall. Jack tried to calm himself and stared at the door. Whether or not it was wizard's intuition, he absolutely didn't want to leave the safety of his room and wished there was something he could do, something that could help him. What he didn't know was that something was already there and had been watching him the whole time.

Jack sat at the dinner table dressed in black: black T-shirt, black pants, black socks and black combat boots. As usual, the clothes made a statement. Jack was never prepared to say what that statement was exactly, but it was clear his clothes had become a kind of uniform. He was also the only one at the table with black hair. Everyone else had hair that was brown and rested on their head in a normal fashion while Jack's hair stood straight up. Aside from that and the earring which Mom and Dad were thankful was in Jack's ear and not somewhere else, Jack looked relatively normal.

Mom and Dad smiled at each other and tried not to stare. Katie said grace and blessed the food, while Sophie sat in her high chair and provided plenty of entertainment. She pounded her spoon in protest and as dinner progressed she squished handfuls of creamy vegetables between her fingers and plastered globs of it on her face.

"Very good." Mom said when the baby managed to actually get some into her mouth. Katie laughed at the mess she was making while Jack winced and did his best not to look.

The conversation was light. There was talk of the day's activities, what Dad had done at work, the antique table Mom bought at the store, Katie's "A" on her spelling test. Jack watched them all suspiciously and waited.

Just then, Sophie stopped wrestling with her food long enough to point at Jack with her sloppy spoon and laughed.

She laughed so hard she chuckled and snorted, then looked Jack straight in the eye which made his hair stand up even straighter. It was as though she knew what was happening and that no amount of magic or wizardry could possibly get him out of this situation.

Jack glared back at her then looked around the table. Whatever was going to happen, he would just have to sit still and ride it out. Then in the middle of a second helping Dad made the announcement.

"Well, I've got something to tell you." he said.

"What is it?" Katie asked excitedly.

Jack looked at Katie from the corner of his eye. It was all he could do to keep from reaching over and putting his hands over her mouth.

"Is it the picnic? Is it?" she said and could hardly sit still.

Jack frowned and thought, "Don't be silly. This is about me, not some stupid picnic."

"... Maybe," Dad said then smiled and leaned forward to look at Katie with a raised eyebrow. "How did you know?"

Katie jumped out of her chair.

"I knew it! I knew it!" she yelled. "Tomorrow is Saturday and it's going to be warm and sunny. It'll probably be the last good day of the year. Can we have the picnic tomorrow?! Please?! It'll be great! I promise!"

"Last good day of the year, huh? What do you think, honey?" Dad said.

Mom nodded as though it might not be a bad idea.

"I guess so." Mom said. "You could even try out your new kite. Unless of course you've got other plans."

Dad suddenly looked surprised and disappointed. "You don't have other plans do you?"

Katie smirked then grinned at the question while Jack just stared.

"That was it? All that worrying for nothing? So much for wizard's intuition." Jack breathed a sigh of relief and finally relaxed while they talked. Now that dinner was over, all he had to do was wait to be excused. Jack sat with his chin propped on his hand, and looked away at the blue lamp with the pink shade on the side table. The lamp was a rich dark blue, the perfect color for a wizard's robe. The pink glow of the lamp shade reminded Jack of what was commonly known as "wizard's fire"; the glow that came from a wizard's hand when he successfully cast a spell, which was something Jack had not yet managed to do, nor had any other human since the days of Merlin.

"Jack!" Dad said for the third time.

The boy jumped and was a little annoyed that he had to come back to their boring conversation.

"What?" Jack said.

"The picnic?" Dad asked as though Jack should have an opinion, since they had been talking about it for the last five minutes.

"Oh, yeah... cool" Jack said, sounding totally disinterested and just nodded while Dad stared at him and frowned. The moment of truth had come and Jack hardly noticed. There was a rather lengthy pause, during which time Dad looked at Mom. Mom smiled at Dad and Dad nodded. Mom nodded back and Dad raised an eyebrow to which Mom shrugged and frowned back. Jack looked back and forth at the two of them like he was watching a tennis match. But since this wasn't nearly as much fun, he pushed his chair back and promptly asked to be excused.

"Wait!" Dad said.

Mom and Dad suddenly looked frantic, blinking and nodding back and forth, this time with a little more English and top spin. Katie had never seen her parents act so strangely. They snarled and grumbled like two spoiled children, fighting to get their way.

"Mom?... Dad?" Katie said, but her parents only ignored her.

"You... No you...No you... No you!" is all they said with
their blinking eyes, jerking heads, and twitching lips.
Although they had both agreed that the time had come to
talk to the boy about everything: the books, the magic, his
fascination with wizardry, and all the junk in general, neither
one could bring themselves to even say a word. The two
were hopelessly engaged in a grueling contest of face making and head jerking with no end in sight. And so with that,
Jack simply left the table, plodded upstairs and retreated
back to his room.

When he was gone, Mom and Dad stared at each other
dumbfounded, like partners in a doubles match, who had
just watched an ace go right down the middle.

"You..." Dad said, pleading with his arms outstretched.

"Me? I thought you..." Mom said in her own defense.

The two were hopelessly confused and although neither
one could even begin to explain what had happened; there
was in fact a very good explanation. But since it involved
unseen creatures with supernatural powers that had invaded
their home to steal their children, neither one of them had a
clue.

While Mom and Dad were still glaring at each other, the
baby sat in her high chair, perfectly still with food on her
face and her eyes fixed on the ceiling. The infant hardly
blinked. Her gaze was so intense Katie looked up as well,
but saw nothing.

The baby stared unafraid, at the tiny demonic creature
floating near the ceiling, peering down at them from its
nonexistent perch. The mischievous spirit was no bigger
than a wrinkled old shoe and looked just as pitiful. It sat
with its arms drawn up in front of it, with eyes as black as
polished marbles. It was this wicked little imp that had
brought fear and confusion, and helped Jack to escape.

Now that its job was done, it no longer paid attention to
Katie's Mom or Dad. Its eyes were fixed on the children.

The devilish creature was afraid and nearly trembled. Not because it was unveiled and could clearly be seen by the infant, but because the imp absolutely hated children that glowed.

The thin layer of light that covered Katie and her sister, radiated from their bodies and shone brightly through their clothes. The creature peered at the light and trembled, for every minion of darkness knew that any child who glowed was a child of God and that meant there was a guardian nearby. When the imp had seen enough it wasted no time and quickly turned aside as though it had been called away, then dove through the wall to escape. Once it was gone, Sophie thrust her spoon at the ceiling, flicking bits of food into the air, then turned to Katie, wide eyed and yelled, "Dah Bah!" which meant "WHAT WAS THAT?!" The baby stared at her, waiting for a response, but Katie got goose bumps instead and shivered.

CHAPTER TWO

What's So Big About Magic?

*J*ack rushed to his room, then closed the door behind him, and breathed a sigh of relief. It was a narrow escape and he smiled to himself, totally unaware that he was still being watched. Without a sound, a dozen little creatures crept through the walls like living shadows, invisible monsters, black hearted imps and pointy horned urchins. They hunched under withered wings, and gathered around the demonic little creature that had returned from the dining room.

"It saw me! It saw me!" The tiny imp squeaked and trembled as it chattered on nervously, when a tired and reluctant voice moaned from the shadows.

"Who… saw you?"

The imp cried out. "The little one and the child! They glowed! They glowed! We dare not leave this chamber or it will find us!"

The demonic spirits huddled together under the watchful gaze of their leader, the only one who didn't seem the slightest bit worried, a green eyed, hook nosed goblin that stood

31

three and a half feet tall. The goblin, Numlock, sat atop Jack's bookshelf in plain view, looking as defiant as ever and glared at the boy as Jack went about his business. He hated this place, and the task he had been given. In short, the goblin hated humans and was not afraid to say so.

"Humans, bah!" he snarled through pointed yellow teeth.

The imps and urchins stopped their seething long enough to listen.

"What are you afraid of? These bottomless barrels? Bags of bones? Worthless wonks the lot of them, no magic in them, no magic at all, what good are they?" The goblin snarled.

The imp fluttered up on bat like wings and cried out.

"But the guardian! The guardian!" he screeched.

"Hang the guardian!" shouted Numlock and swiped at the tiny imp.

The creature quickly darted back into the shadows, panting in fear. Numlock turned his back and rubbed his stubby beard as he observed the boy. Jack was chanting again, sitting cross legged on his bed, and happened to be flicking his fingers at something on the floor. Numlock groaned and could barely be bothered. He climbed down off the shelf and made his way across the room. There was so much junk scattered around, the goblin didn't know what Jack was looking at, or what he was trying to do.

Amidst the clutter was an old book. It was worn with a tattered cover and Numlock guessed that was it. Since it was his job to encourage the boy and keep him happy, the invisible goblin reached down and gave the book a gentle tap.

The book barely moved but Jack's eyes lit up in utter amazement, even though it was not the focus of his attention. The truth was, he was trying to move the object next to the book, an old baseball with ragged stitching that was brown with age, but when the book moved instead Jack focused all of his efforts on that. He hopped off his bed, lit a candle and hunkered down over the book in the flickering light, then strained as hard as he could to use his magic powers, but it was hopeless. Numlock had done his duty and the book would not move again.

The goblin watched the boy with growing resentment, and thought back on the events that had led up to him being sent here. It was still fresh in his evil mind, like it was only yesterday. Numlock growled at the memory.

The order had come from Marplot, great high sorcerer of the wizards' grand council and most powerful wizard of all the Nohr World. At two thousand, nine hundred and forty two years of age, Marplot was also the oldest wizard in the Nohr World and quite a pathetic sight. He was so thin and worn; his long gray beard weighed more than he did. Too frail to walk, the feeble old wizard floated from place to place like a ghost, in his grand council chair, with his little goblin servant chasing after him wherever he went. Still no wizard dared challenge Marplot, for his power was too great.

When his eyes failed and Marplot was blind, he trained his hands to see and used his magic to read the ancient scrolls by mere touch. Although the doddering old wizard was nothing to look at, he was really quite famous. It was widely known, that when Marplot was a young wizard and had risen to power, he conspired with demons and joined in a plan to wage war against God. In that day the battlefield was Earth and the Son of God had dared to become mortal and stood before man, alone and without his angels.

The wizards and demons joined forces and used their powers to turn the minds of men against the Lord of Glory. And when they had put the Savior to death, Satan and his demons rejoiced to see the Son of God, betrayed by men and hung on a cross, but the battle was not yet won.

Marplot was only one soldier in the army of darkness, but still he remembered the day the angel came down from Heaven and stood atop the empty tomb to proclaim that he who once was dead was now alive forever more and had saved all mankind from certain destruction. The angel's words were like a hammer that smashed the gates of hell, and declared the glory of God.

With the victory won and the Son of God seated upon the throne, Satan and his demons were defeated and the wizards of the Nohr World were all made to look like fools. That was over two thousand years ago and Marplot could not forget the past which haunted him. He toiled in bitter envy, seeking revenge, but he would have to wait upon the Lord. He would have to wait until Christ's return.

The problem was no one knew the day or the time. Marplot searched his books on sorcery and went through his entire library. He searched the writings of the early mystics, writings on ancient history. He even searched the Holy Scriptures which was a difficult thing for a wizard to do. To a sorcerer, the word of God was like a dagger in the flesh, but Marplot would bear any pain to learn the secret of the Lord's return.

Try as he might, the answer was nowhere to be found. In truth, it was a secret that God kept well hidden which made Marplot all the more determined to find it. He did, however, manage to stumble across something fascinating.

The Holy Scriptures mentioned the word, "children," nearly two thousand times. It seemed that God had a special interest in children and that alone was enough to make Marplot suspicious.

"Why was God so concerned with children?" he wondered.

Did they know something about God no one else did. If so, perhaps one of them held the answer to the secret he was searching for. Century after century, he studied the minds of children, and discovered they did indeed hold special knowledge. He also discovered that the knowledge faded with time, which he felt had something to do with innocence that went away as children grew older.

Over the years Marplot learned many things from the children. He learned that God loved daisies more than any other flower. That's why there were so many of them.

He learned that your smile was connected to your heart. If you had a good smile you had a good heart. If you had an evil smile you had an evil heart. Anyone with a good smile and an evil heart was truly wicked and would be found out eventually. Since Marplot had no smile at all, he chose to ignore this information entirely.

One child knew that dogs could see angels and barked because angels were so bright and shiny. What that had to do with God the wizard didn't know. There was a lot of this kind of information which Marplot considered useless, but every once in a while he came across a child who knew something really interesting. For instance, one child knew that angels could indeed be tempted. The wizard made a note of that.

Another child knew that goodness was stronger than evil. Marplot disagreed but made a note of that as well. Then there was the infant who smiled all the time. Her parents called her, "a happy baby." The truth was, the infant remembered Heaven and could still see it clearly from the comfort of her crib. Her parents never suspected.

Another child knew that every single person believed in God even if they didn't care to admit it. This kind of information was interesting but hardly what Marplot was looking for. Then there was the rare instance, when he came across a child with really incredible knowledge, things that were truly astounding. These children were one in a billion.

Marplot remembered the little five month old baby who knew exactly what the throne of God looked like and what it was made of. A hundred years later there was an eight month old infant who knew why God made the universe so big. The baby understood it with perfect clarity but the matter was simply beyond the wizard's ability to grasp.

Fifty years later he came across a child who knew the

purpose of dreams which the wizard found very interesting. Marplot had to wait another one hundred and thirty five years before he met the child who actually came close. It was a little boy who was only two years old and he knew why God was going to judge the world. The problem was he didn't know when. Still Marplot was encouraged by the information and kept searching.

He continued to search the minds of children for another four hundred and fifty seven years without so much as one piece of interesting information. Then one eventful day, the wizard Marplot came across a peculiar little girl. At four years of age this child knew the names of the twelve apostles and could recite the Ten Commandments. Admittedly, this information was readily available to anyone with a Bible, but this child knew such facts about God at an age when most children were more concerned with their toys. This caused the wizard to look more closely and when he did he shouted.

"Kaaaaay-teeee Cam Bull!" the feeble old wizard announced to the grand council in his quivering voice. "I have found you at last!" he yelled. "She is the one. She knows the way... Find her! And you will find Majesty!"

Of course, at the time no one knew who or what Majesty was until Marplot explained.

"This is the key!" he croaked from underneath his matted beard. "The horse of power and glory will bring the Lord of hosts back to reign over all the kingdoms of all the worlds. Find the horse and we will have power over Heaven itself. We can stop the Lord's return!"

The girl was considerably older now and since her innocence was slipping away, there was a fair amount of debate as to what to do next. There was talk of sending an army of ogres to fetch the child, but the council decided on a more subtle approach, since an army of ogres walking the earth would attract more attention than they needed. Not to mention, the child would most likely be guarded by an angel. With that in mind, the grand wizards set about the task of studying the girl to learn everything they could about her. Most felt it was all useless, really. The little girl was far too old. At ten years of age, what little knowledge of God, left inside of her, was less than a glint in her mind and fading fast. Indeed, they would have to move quickly if they were to get anything out of her at all, but even this was a delicate matter. The knowledge of God was a very dangerous thing and getting it would not be easy. Like a serpent trying to avoid the sharp quills of a porcupine, it called for great skill and cunning.

They found it peculiar that such a special child of God should be born to average people like Scott and Elaine Campbell, two powerless humans with no particular interest in God or His kingdom. But it wasn't until they discovered the boy that they considered his curious mind and were able to devise a plan.

For the most part they argued about the best way to use the boy, and what sort of trap to lay for his sister. Then they argued about the wrath of God to come as a result of it all, and spent a great deal of time on that. That's when Numlock's master stepped forward and offered a suggestion. "Perhaps it would be better for all, if the child came to us." He said.

The council approved the idea and placed the matter entirely in his hands. And thus, before Numlock knew it, he had been thrust out of his world and sent to Jack's room with the instructions to stay there until the job was done. And here he was, loathing every minute.

When Numlock looked at the boy he was sitting on the floor staring at the book in a sulk. The goblin wagged his head then growled and turned away. It was time for him to see where the girl was. The imps and urchins watched the goblin cross the room then shrank back when he passed through Jack's door like a vapor and ventured into the hall. Numlock leapt into the air and crouched on the upstairs banister like an ugly cat. He glanced around nervously, then raised his head and sniffed. There was an essence of something, a sweet fragrance in the air that he recognized.

"Yeeaak!" he belched.

The guardian was nearby and he could smell him. Numlock snarled. He hated his master for making him do all the hard work and hated him even more for putting him in such a perilous position. Still, guardian or no, he would stand his ground and do his job.

His fiendish green eyes peered downstairs as he watched the child of God. Katie was all aglow, as she hugged her Mom and Dad. They kissed her golden face and spoke to her with soft reassuring voices, full of love and caring. It was all too sickeningly sweet for the goblin to bear, and when the little girl turned and started up the steps toward him, Numlock glared at her in surprise, rounded in horror and retreated back to Jack's room. Once inside, he poked his head through the door to see where the child would go.

Katie walked to her room and when she opened the door, Numlock pulled back, shielding his eyes from the blinding light coming from within. The goblin watched as Katie went inside and closed her door, without any care for the light beaming all around her, then when the hall was darkened once more, Numlock gripped his dagger and growled; for the light that came from Katie's room could only have been made by one thing, a ministering spirit, a defender of the throne, an angel of the Lord. Numlock sneered and knew he had found the guardian.

Katie's room was nicely decorated. It was brightly colored. There were dolls and cute stuffed animals. It was all neat and pleasant, with the exception of the seven foot angel, standing in the middle of her room radiating light like the sun. The angel floated off the ground and took up so much space, his head scraped the ceiling and his wings barely fit inside her room. His silver eyes were aglow as was his entire body. The angel was lovely to look at, but if Katie could have seen this warrior of God draped in white robes smiling down on her, she would have been absolutely startled out of her wits. The fact that he was a protector of the innocent, sent by God to keep her far from evil would have brought little comfort especially with a host of imps, urchins and a hook nosed goblin living in the room, just down the hall.

Katie took her seat by the window and the angel turned to watch her. His wings cast silvery sparks as they swept through the walls and he gazed down upon the child. He could feel her emotions stirring. The strange goings on at the dinner table had left Katie feeling unsettled and out of sorts, and the more she thought about it the more it disturbed her. Then there was her brother who was acting stranger than usual and this upset her as well. Katie had to admit she was having a lot of thoughts lately that were upsetting. Then she remembered something her Nannah used to say.

"When troubles start to come your way, wait to worry and start to pray."

"Wait to worry and start to pray, more pearls of wisdom," Katie whispered then climbed down off the window seat and got down on her knees. She folded her hands, bowed her head and closed her eyes as the angel knelt down beside her and folded his huge wings behind him.

The only official prayer Katie knew was the Lord's Prayer and the twenty-third Psalm. Aside from that she usually just talked to God and told him what was on her mind. Katie had to think a moment and when she was ready she spoke softly with a tenderness in her voice that was both sweet and respectful. It was a simple prayer, from the heart of a child, which made the angel smile.

Then with a polite, "Amen" she hopped to her feet. Katie tended to keep her prayers short and to the point since she figured that God was busy and had far more important things to do. Still, she was so confident in the power of prayer she simply had to go see if Jack was any different. The angel rose quickly to get out of her way and watched Katie march to the door.

When Katie reached Jack's room, she peeked inside. It was darker than usual. Katie's first thought was, "Maybe I should have prayed for Jack's room instead."

She knocked and wished she hadn't. It was a weak little knock that tried not to attract any attention to itself. Katie could see Jack hunched over his large play table that was shoved in a corner. The boy glanced over his shoulder then turned back around, which was the usual greeting. Katie wouldn't have minded a bit if Jack had actually gotten up and helped her across the room, but she knew that was too much to hope for.

The room was watching Katie and she could feel it. She stiffened slightly and tried to find the courage to tell the room to, "Mind its own business"; but it was hard enough just walking across the darkened floor that was littered with clothes and other things she could hardly make out.

The ugly goblin glared down at her from on top of Jack's book shelf. Katie could feel his icy gaze as she passed by and looked around her. The moment she took her eyes off the floor she tripped and stumbled then paused to see where she was going. When she did, the devilish imps crept out of the dark to surround her like a pack of wolves. They gloated with hungry eyes and licked their pointy horns with long black tongues that curled out of their mouths like shiny ribbons. Red claws clicked and glinted in the dark as they threatened to devour her delicious innocence. The fiendish creatures were still churning with hideous delight and wicked pleasure when the huge angel walked in behind Katie and filled the room with light.

The perfect light of God was the last thing the little monsters ever expected to see in Jack's room. With a shriek and a howl, evil scattered in every direction, like cold water splashing out of a hot pan. It jumped into books and ducked inside boxes. Imps and urchins darted back and forth; bumping into each other then dove through the walls like terrified shadows.

The light hit Numlock so hard it knocked him off his perch atop the bookshelf and sent him crashing to the floor. One look at the guardian and the goblin scrambled to his feet as quickly as he could, lunged head first and slid under a pile of clothes, where he waited and trembled.

The evil creatures made lots of noise fleeing for cover, but none of it made a sound to human ears, nor did Katie or Jack see the light of the angel. The room was just as dark as ever, but with evil in hiding and the invisible angel towering over her, Katie felt much better.

She crossed the room and came up behind Jack. In front of him was what used to be his train set. Now a medieval landscape took up the entire surface of the table, miniature and perfect to the slightest detail. There were hills with miniature trees and bushes, and a miniature stone castle, wonderfully constructed, in the middle of it all. Below it was a stream of real water that flowed under a little stone bridge that Jack had made. The pump was well hidden and the water flowed around tiny rocks that looked like boulders next to the little castle.

In the dim blue light of his desk lamp, it all looked quite real. The castle was called Baithenwar, a name Jack found in a book. Baithenwar meant "refuge" which seemed to fit, since he spent so much of his time sitting there, dreaming about magic and fighting magic battles.

Below the stone bridge was the black knight with grim mace held high. He was trapped by a dragon perched on a ledge just above. The monstrous beast was poised, reared back on its hind legs, with wings spread apart, and huge jaws gaping wide. The black knight's armor would offer little protection. One blast of the dragon's fiery breath and the dark warrior would be reduced to ashes.

Katie peered over Jack's shoulder with some interest, but all she saw were toys. The knight was a little plastic figure painted black. The dragon was twelve inches long, made of rubber, with cloth wings. Katie watched, as Jack reached across ever so slowly and moved a little bronze wizard into position behind the dragon. The bronze figure was no bigger than a chess piece and finely polished. Then with his thumb and forefinger on the little wizard, Jack prepared to make his move when Katie asked, "What are you doing?"

Jack cringed. The question affected him as always, like fingernails on a chalkboard. He paused and spoke slowly, never looking away from his toys.

"... I'm about to cast a spell." he whispered.

Katie just stared. By the looks of things her prayers had not been answered. But since she had already come this far and managed to brave the cruel darkness of Jack's room, she decided she might as well see what she could do on her own.

"So what's so big about magic? None of it's real, you know." Katie said.

Jack winced again and tried to speak as calmly as he knew how.

"Why don't you just go back to your room? Okay kid?" He said smugly just to show her who was boss.

"And there's no such thing as wizards either." Katie added.

Jack finally turned and glared at her.

"What do you know? You're just a girl!" Jack said, jeering at her.

Katie shrugged, determined to make her point.

"I know that wizards and dragons don't exist and magic isn't real. It's all just a bunch of phony tricks." she said, sounding very sure of herself.

"Oh yeah? And I suppose that God and his cutesy angels and all that stuff you read in the Bible, is supposed to be real, right?"

"Of course." Katie said. "Everybody knows that."

Jack rubbed his hand across his face.

"That's it!" he said, then grabbed his sister by the arm. Jack walked across the room, with Katie stumbling and bumbling along behind him, and when they reached the hall he placed her outside then slammed the door in her face and locked it. Thinking that was that, Jack turned around and stood toe to toe with the warrior of God, a seven foot angel that could hardly be described as cutesy. The glowing guardian glared down at Jack with fiery eyes that had seen the defeat of the Persian army and the fall of the Roman Empire. The angel sneered at the boy's rude behavior, looked away then stormed out of the room, taking his light with him.

As soon as the angel was gone, Numlock crept out from under the pile of clothes to see if the coast was clear. Jack had already gone back to his table, when the rest of the devilish creatures slowly came out of hiding. They looked around rather sheepishly at first then began to elbow each other and nod their approval as one of the creatures came forward.

"He did it! He sent it away! This one will do well in our world!" The imp said and squealed with delight. The devilish minions and urchins clapped and cheered for the human boy, but Numlock remained silent and his eyes turned cold.

"It is the child of God they want. This one will never survive in our world. The boy is only human." the goblin sneered.

Outside of Jack's room there was a sign on his door that read,

"Keep out!" Another sign, scribbled in red marker, was exactly the perfect height for Katie to read, and shouted its message loud and clear.

"NO BABIES ALLOWED!" Katie just pouted at it.

"Katie? Are you all right?" Mom called up from downstairs.

"Yeah Mom!... I'm okay," Katie said with a sigh. This was not the first time she had found herself in the hallway outside of Jack's room and stood there, thinking. Her prayers had not worked out the way she wanted them to. Then it came to her, a thought that was more of a question, and standing there in the hallway it was begging to be answered. Katie asked herself.

"What does Jack like more than anything in the whole world?"

"That's easy," she told herself. "He loves magic."

She remembered how Jack would go on and on, whether she wanted to hear it or not, about every mythical creature imaginable. He talked about fairies that could see into your heart. He talked about trolls, that could build anything as fast as you could think of it, or ogres that were too stupid to build anything at all. Ogres were mean and big as bulls. They carried tree stump clubs, rusted axes and wandered through the woods, without enough sense to get out of the rain. "You'd be mean too if you were that stupid." Was Jack's conclusion.

Her next thought was directed to herself.

"What do I like as much as Jack likes magic?"

It was a good question and the answer came to her as quick as a flash.

"I like God."

She didn't know as much about God as Jack knew about magic, but that was okay. God made her just as happy. That's when it occurred to her. Jack wasn't happy at all, not in her opinion. She couldn't even remember the last time she saw him smile. Perhaps that was the answer. Jack knew everything about magic, but as far as she could tell, it didn't make him happy. In fact, lately he was looking pale and sick with worry.

The more she thought about it the more obvious it became to her. If Jack was going to get better, something had to be done. Katie glared up at her brother's door with her invisible angel standing behind her, taking up a ridiculous amount of space in the hallway.

"God is more important than magic." she declared. "And I'm going to make sure you understand, whatever it takes.... whatever it takes." Katie said with a frown then plodded back to her room.

By the time she climbed into bed, she was feeling much better about everything and with her head nestled on her pillow; she closed her eyes and went to sleep. The angel stood next to the bed and put his hand on the hilt of his sword. As an angel, his presence was enough to make Katie's room a stronghold, a tower of strength against evil. Even Jack had only been able to get as far as Katie's door and no further. But with Katie's own words, she had issued a challenge that would lead her straight into danger. As her guardian, he could protect her, but had no authority over her free will and in such matters could not interfere. Standing there, he could sense the powers of darkness growing in the house and even in the world around him. The angel looked down on Katie. For now she was safe in her room then with one last look around, the guardian disappeared into a speck of light and was gone.

CHAPTER THREE

The Chase

$\mathcal{B}$y nine o'clock Saturday morning, the family was in their little gold van and on their way. They drove through quiet neighborhoods where people mowed their lawns, trimmed their bushes and read their papers on shaded porch swings. Along the way, a baby pointed from his stroller. A dog barked and ran circles in its yard; and a curious flock of birds gathered overhead, attracted by the supernatural being that was gliding just above the trees. Aside from that, the guardian angel went completely unnoticed as he followed the van.

Soon they were driving along narrow roads, winding through the hills of Somerport. The ride through the countryside was relatively peaceful. All except for Jack's grumblings, which were typical for any ride that lasted longer than five minutes and involved having to sit next to his sister; who at the moment happened to be staring at him as though he were on a shelf in a museum.

"What's the matter with you?" Jack snarled.

Katie just smiled and wondered when she should tell Jack about God, but judging by the look on his face, she could tell that now was not the time. Jack's anger continued to prowl around inside of him and the presence of the angel above only made matters worse.

An hour later, they arrived at the camp grounds early enough to find a perfect spot, overlooking the bay. Dad spread their blanket in the shade of a big oak tree, while Katie unpacked the picnic basket.

When all was done, Dad put Katie's kite together then showed her how to hold the control handles and use the guide lines to make it do tricks. Then just like that he handed it over. "Wait for the wind." he said.

With a gust of wind and a pull of the string, Katie watched in amazement as the kite rose into the air.

"That's it, Pumpkin! You're doing great. Now you're on your own, sure you can handle it?"

"Uh-huh," Katie said gazing up at the rainbow kite, with a jerk of the shoulder and her tongue curled at the side of her mouth.

Jack however was not as impressed and followed Dad with his head down and hands jammed in his pockets, as they headed to the paddle boats. Meanwhile mom chose a quiet moment to settle into her lawn chair, and read a book in the shade of the tree. After a while, she looked over at Sophie who was sitting on the blanket, surrounded by toys and staring up with the most peculiar expression. The infant watched the man who was glistening like a shiny new coin, draped in white robes with his giant wings folded against his back. The angel stood next to Katie, watching the kite soar high above and seemed perfectly content right where he was, until the baby pointed at him and yelled.

"DAH- BAAH!"

Mom looked up at the invisible angel standing right in front of her and smiled up at the sky. "Yes sweetheart... kite." she said with a pleasant smile, and went back to her book.

The angel looked at the woman and the infant then

glanced around. There were other babies on other picnic blankets staring and pointing. There was even a Cocker Spaniel yapping noisily. But the dog fell silent, and shied away when the guardian spread his enormous wings and rose into the air, higher and higher, until he was so far above the park he was little more than a speck. From there he could watch Katie just as well and not attract any attention.

Dozens of kites sailed above the windy hilltop. Some were larger and went higher. Some had long fancy tails that twirled like windmills. Some looked like caterpillars dancing on air, but none of them were as colorful as Katie's and could do fancy tricks. Katie didn't mind showing off just a little and even made her kite fly sideways which impressed the other kids nearby.

"Woooaaah!" They said, and were sure that Katie was some kind of expert, that is, until she pointed her kite straight down, pulled back as hard as she could and plowed the nose of the kite into the ground like a dart.

"It's time for a break." Katie said, then dropped the control handles and walked away with her head held high, as though she had meant to do it. When Dad returned with Jack, it was time to eat and there was plenty of food. There was chicken and salad, chips and fries, burgers and hotdogs. But, even with a picnic on a beautiful sunny day, Jack could think of nothing but the traveling spell that wouldn't work.

"Can we go home now?" he whined.

"Nope!" Dad said with a smile and patted the boy on the back as though it was a good try, then handed him dessert; Mom's cherry cheesecake with strawberries, and whipped cream swirled on top. Even Jack couldn't resist that.

After lunch they played games, had quality time and family time and just when Jack thought they were done, Dad rubbed his hands together and grinned.

"How about we do some fishing?" Dad said with a wink and grabbed their fishing poles. Jack gave a weak smile, like it was absolutely the last thing he wanted to do.

"You boys have fun." Mom said as the two plodded off together.

With the sun high in the sky and another slice of dessert, Katie laid down for a nap and fell asleep next to the baby. When she awoke, nearly two hours had passed and the setting sun peeked through the shady trees across the lake. Katie sat up, rubbing her eyes and Mom looked up from her book.

"I was beginning to think we were going to have to carry you to the car," she said.

Katie looked around to see other families leaving as well.

"Is it time to go already?" Katie asked, and took a nice long stretch.

"C'mon and help me clean up." Mom said then placed a book mark in the page where she was and started clearing off the blanket. Katie grabbed a few things and happened to notice the title of the book. She tried to sound out the big words.

"The ex... exploray..."

Mom smiled, "The Exploration of Revelation."

Katie repeated the title.

"It's one of Nannah's old books I found in the attic." Mom said.

"What's it about?" Katie asked.

"Well..." Mom paused. It seemed to be a tough question.

"It's about the last book in the Bible, which talks about the Lord and His return."

"What does it say?"

It was another hard question that made Mom stop to think.

"Well, it says a lot of things, like... Jesus is called The King, and He rides a beautiful white horse."

It was the image of the white horse that stuck with Katie. She smiled to herself as she tried to picture the animal and

wanted to know more about the story, but the park was closing, Jack was grumpier than ever and it was time to go.

Ten minutes later, they had piled everything into the van,
picnic basket, chairs and all, and were headed home. Katie
gazed out the window as they left the park behind, and
thought about what her mom had said. She thought about the
white horse, and when she closed her eyes she could almost
see it in her mind, glowing in golden rays of sunlight.

"What an amazing animal, certainly the most beautiful
creature anywhere in the whole universe, if it really existed."
A moment later a thought occurred to her that made her
smile. "I wonder where the white horse could be right now.
I bet it's guarded by angels in Heaven. The white horse and
the wonders of Heaven... Too bad Jack couldn't think about
things like that." Katie thought to herself and smiled at the
vision, then happened to open her eyes and stared in wonder.
One second later and she would have missed it. Across the
way, in a wide open pasture was a white horse, as grand and
wonderful as anything Katie could imagine.

"STOP!"

Katie yelled so loud, Dad slammed on the brakes and
woke her brother who had drifted off in the back seat. Katie
wasted no time and scrambled out of the car with her mother
close behind.

"What is it? What happened?" Jack said, rubbing his
eyes and trying to sit up. When he saw it was only a horse
and not something really interesting like a dragon or an
ogre, he grumbled and went back to sleep.

Katie and her Mom crossed the quiet country road and
went right up to the big white fence that surrounded the pasture. They stayed perfectly still as the wind rustled through
the trees. The horse stood at a distance, grazing with its long
white mane gently flowing. The animal was graceful and at
the same time filled with power. Katie held onto her
mother's arm as she watched the white horse and giggled

with excitement. When she did, the animal looked up. It looked right at them and Katie held her breath. The horse took a few curious steps in their direction. For a moment it seemed that it might actually come to them. It paused, gleaming in the sunlight, then turned and bolted away, its hooves thundering across the field. When it finally disappeared over the hillside Katie clapped and yelped for joy, then hugged her mother.

"I saw him, Mom! I saw him! That was great!"

Mom looked at Katie seriously for a moment.

"Honey, you know that's not the horse from the story." She said.

Katie smiled and felt a little silly. "I know." she said and had to remind herself that it really wasn't. It had all happened so quickly, first the story about a white horse, and then to actually see one. Mom had to admit it was quite a coincidence.

When they returned to the car, Katie peered out the window. "What do you think his name is?" she said.

"Who?" Dad asked.

"The white horse!" Katie replied eagerly.

Dad thought aloud, as he started the van.

"I don't know...Lightning? Trigger?"

Katie stared out the window as the van pulled off.

"No, that sounds too made up." Katie said.

Dad frowned and decided to keep his opinions to himself then turned his attention back to the road. Katie looked behind them, hoping to get one last glimpse of the white horse.

"I think I'll call him... Snowball." she said.

Dad glanced at Katie in the mirror then looked at Mom with a smirk.

"Snowball?" he whispered. "Good name for a rabbit."

"Good-bye, Snowball." Katie said as they drove away and the pasture disappeared among the trees.

The experience had been nothing less than enchanting. The picnic was everything Katie expected and the surprise of the white horse was a gift she would never forget. Jack, on the other hand, was miserable and hadn't gotten much sleep since Katie wouldn't stop talking about the horse for the entire ride home.

It was dark when they pulled into the driveway. Katie got the baby as Mom and Dad unpacked the car. And while everyone else was busy helping, Jack climbed out of the van and marched into the house, like a grumpy old man who couldn't be bothered. The angel stood at the front door and watched the boy as he slumped past.

After dinner, Jack still wore a frown and the fact that Katie was in a great mood didn't help matters at all. When it was time for bed, Katie was still beaming a smile and should have known better, but just couldn't help herself. She skipped down the hall to Jack's room, threw open the door and went straight inside.

Numlock and the little winged creatures dove for cover as the little girl entered the room. Jack was seated at his table, pretending not to notice her as usual, when Katie rushed up behind him, wrapped her arms around his neck and gave him a hug.

"Hey! What's the matter with you?!" Jack shouted and pushed her away as he jumped to his feet. When he turned around, Katie was standing there in her fleecy flannel nightgown, and pink bunny slippers.

"I just came to say good night." Katie said.

"Look kid, just because you saw some stupid horse, don't get all mushy on me!" He said, doing his best to be mean and utterly pig headed.

"Wasn't he wonderful?" Katie said staring off dreamily. "It was like God just put him right there, in the perfect place, so we could see him."

"What do you mean, we?" Jack said and turned his back

to her. The castle Baithenwar and its stone bridge lay in front of him and Jack was in the middle of another game. "If you think I care about that stupid horse, you're cracked." he said.

Jack placed the bronzed wizard under the stone bridge gently, and muttered to himself as he settled into his chair and considered the dragon's next move. The monster would surely follow him into the dark and when he did... Katie peeked over Jack's shoulder and tried to be polite.

"What's the matter? Didn't you..."

Jack rounded on her with fists clenched and eyes glaring.

"Can't you see I'm trying to do something here? I saw your dumb horse, okay?! And I don't care. I don't care about your stupid fairy tales or your baby stories. None of it matters to me! Now quit bothering me, all right?!"

When Katie opened her mouth to speak, Jack yelled even louder.

"Did you hear me?! I said, GO AWAY!!" he shouted then turned around and pretended she was gone, just to make it perfectly clear. Katie hung her head and turned to leave. Just ahead of her, standing in the doorway, was the seven foot angel, shining like the headlight of a freight train, and glaring straight at Jack. This was the second time the angel had witnessed the boy's ill mannered behavior. Katie paused then turned and stood in front of her invisible guardian.

"Tomorrow is church," she reminded Jack, but the boy just stayed hunched over the table with his back to her. "Good night." Katie said with a whimper. Again there was no response, but before Katie could leave, Dad came storming into the room and walked right through the angel which parted like smoke. He pushed his way past Katie and went straight for Jack. Dad had heard everything from downstairs and after Jack's rude behavior and selfish attitude all day long, he was in big trouble.

Katie turned away and sulked back to her room with the angel close behind. Dad's voice echoed down the hall as he yelled at Jack and scolded him for being so mean. When Katie climbed into bed, the angel took his position in the middle of the room, while Katie stared at the ceiling and listened. Jack was really getting an ear full now and she could hear him pleading.

"But... but she... but she was..."

From the sound of things Jack wasn't making a very good case. After a while it got quiet and Katie listened for any sound at all. A moment later there was a knock at the door. Katie sat up and was surprised to see her Dad standing in the doorway.

"Katie, Jack's got something he'd like to say to you." He said with a stern voice then reached over and pulled Jack into view. He held the boy by the back of his collar which made Jack look like a stiff necked puppet. Jack looked at Katie with a nasty scowl on his face, and his lips drawn tight. His mouth twitched and wiggled as though something was struggling to get out then...

"Sorry," he said and winced like the word had thorns.

Dad released him and Jack walked away, grumbling and filled with resentment. Suddenly Dad looked tired and worn. "This wasn't the way I wanted the day to end." he said.

Katie forced a smile. "That's okay, Daddy. It's not your fault."

Dad leaned into the room a little.

"I love you, Pumpkin. Sweet dreams." He said and blew her a kiss.

When he went to close the door, he remembered that Katie liked it open, then pushed it halfway, smiled once more, and walked away. The hallway light went out and Katie lay back in bed. The angel could feel her sadness, but knew there was no excuse for the boy's behavior. With Katie safely tucked in, the angel took one last look around the room, smiled at the little child of God then vanished in the moonlight.

As usual, Katie said her prayers. She prayed for her mom and dad. She prayed for her little sister but most of all, she prayed for Jack. Like all her prayers it was short and sweet. She prayed that God would not be angry with Jack and that God would help her brother to forget about magic. She felt like she was praying for a miracle, and had no earthly idea that she was about to get one.

With that, Katie rolled over and snuggled her cheek against the pillow and just before she closed her eyes, she happened to glance at the door. When she did, something made her smile. The door reminded her of the silly words Jack had said over and over again, when he had tried to cast his spell. She remembered the words because they made such a funny rhyme. In fact it sounded so silly Katie couldn't resist and said the words softly, so that they barely whispered from her lips.

"Dig a who… big a who… bah lah, boo gia."

Katie smirked at the ridiculous sounding words, and doubted they were even words at all. Then in the perfect stillness, she looked at her bedroom door which was half open, exactly the way her dad had left it. In the dark, the door was pointed straight at her, and had become a thin line, so that all she could see were the edge of the door and the door knobs on either side.

When she moved her head one way she could begin to see more of the front of the door. When she moved the other way she could see more of the back. Katie decided to play a little game and see if she could make it so that she could see neither the front nor back of the door at all. That would make the edge of the door look the thinnest.

With her head on the pillow, Katie moved ever so slightly until the door looked the thinnest that it possibly could. And just when she thought she must be looking right at the precise and exact edge of her bedroom door, there was an instant flash like a burst of sunlight that filled the room for a split second and was gone. Katie sprang up in bed and sat there in the darkness staring and blinking. She held her breath, and rubbed her eyes then tried to stay perfectly still, wondering what had happened and where the flash of light had come from.

"Perhaps a car had gone by, or maybe lightning…No." she thought.

She had seen headlights pass across her ceiling. She had seen lightning light up her room. This was neither of those things. Katie sat there in the dark, trembling, waiting for her heart to stop racing and tried to calm down.

After a while she tried to convince herself that she had imagined whatever it was. The only problem was the flash of light had left the faint image of a line dancing in her eyes and she could still see it. As Katie stared into the empty space in front of her, it was that faint sliver of light that reminded her of the strange phrase that accompanied the traveling spell.

"Set ye door at the Nohr World's sliver of a splinter's eye to ye dwelling place then rest ye brow at the spot."

Although Katie couldn't remember them exactly, whether she knew it or not, she could not have performed the spell any better if she tried.

"Set ye door to ye dwelling place." meant you were to point the edge of your door to the place where you slept. That's exactly what Katie's Dad had done when he left the room.

"Rest ye brow at the spot," simply meant to lie down.

"Of a splinter's eye…" was the hard part. That meant you had to look at the door, just the right way, and find the exact spot where the other world would open up after you said the magic words. And that is precisely what Katie had done by accident.

Katie wondered if she might be dreaming, but it was the flash of light that had caused her to sit up in bed and here

she was sitting up. When she had calmed down, she half suspected that the light had come from the edge of the door
itself. After all, it was in the shape of a long thin line and
that had to be more than coincidence. Katie took a deep
breath and when her heart wasn't pounding quite so hard
anymore, she decided to lie back down.

Katie placed her head on the pillow, feeling more awake
than ever as she tried to find the edge of the door again. She
moved this way and that, and felt a little silly when nothing
happened. She looked right at the door and studied its shape
just like she had when she first lay down. She moved just a
little... nothing. She moved again. The line of the door got
thinner but still nothing. She moved ever so slightly, what
seemed like the smallest fraction of the tiniest part of an inch.

The flash of light was blinding, but this time Katie didn't
move. She held stone still, squinting at the silvery light that
was once the edge of her door. It beamed brightly, but cast
no light in the room at all. With the rest of her bedroom covered in darkness, it was like looking through a narrow slit in
a wall on a bright sunny day.

"Set ye door at the Nohr World's sliver."

Was this a sliver of the Nohr World she was seeing and
where on earth was that? Katie stared at the thing, wanting
to get closer, wanting to sit up, but she dared not move; for
fear the light would disappear again. Katie watched the
thread of light beaming in the darkness and after a short
while, her neck grew tired. She had to move and shifted very
slightly, but instead of going out, the light shone bright and
steady.

Katie moved very slowly as she sat up then pulled the
covers back and climbed out of bed. She slipped on her robe
then patted the floor with her feet, till she found her slippers.
When she was ready she started forward to get a better look,
fully expecting the light to disappear at any moment. But the
closer she got, the more she thought she could make some-

thing out. With a few more steps, she could actually begin to see into the narrow space of light, and knew that what she had suspected was true. This was more than a light. It was indeed a thin sliver of a door to something, or somewhere. Katie stared right at it, as hard as she could. And although she could only see a tiny slice she suddenly knew what it was she was looking at. What's more she knew where it was.

Katie tried to stay calm as she walked closer and closer, longing to get a better look. She crept forward with her arms outstretched and teetered like a tight rope walker on a string. The closer she got, the more she feared it would all disappear. Instead the opening appeared to grow wider, as her curiosity drew her forward and she stared in wonder. When she finally crossed the dark floor, Katie was bathed in light. She could hear birds chirping and the rustling of leaves as a cool breeze blew across her face. Then standing there, she paused for the briefest of moments and tried to remind herself to tell Jack that his traveling spell actually worked. And without another thought of the past or future, she stepped through the opening and disappeared from her quiet bedroom and the world she called home.

A moment later the guardian angel returned with a flaming sword in hand, and then rushed to the magic portal only to see it close before his eyes. In an instant he became fully visible and Katie's room was suddenly ablaze with his heavenly light. The seven foot angel grabbed the edge of Katie's door, searing the paint with his touch and clenched his teeth in anger. The little girl had stepped out of this world and entered another, and now that she was gone, the powers of darkness had outsmarted him and there was nothing he could do. The warrior of God stood in the earthly realm and slowly looked toward Heaven. To follow the child would not only require the permission of God. It would call for another guardian that was far greater than he. With that, the angel lowered his head and disappeared.

When Katie stepped into the light she was standing at the edge of a pasture with a large wooden fence behind her. Beyond the fence was a narrow country road. She had seen this place before. It was the very same spot she had been to earlier that day, the place where she had seen the white horse. Only now she was standing on the other side of the fence, with the pasture stretching out in front of her.

Katie looked out from the shade of the tall trees and blinked a few times to make sure she wasn't seeing things. There, in the distance, was the white horse standing in the middle of the green pasture just as she remembered him. Katie stood silently and stared. The horse was a good ways off, nearly fifty yards. With one step then another, Katie started forward slowly and found herself tiptoeing through the grass as though she were sneaking up on a mouse. Just then, the horse raised his head and looked right at her. Katie stopped and giggled then crept forward again. If only she could get close enough, one touch was all she wanted, one gentle stroke of his white mane. If only the horse would let her, and then he bolted. With a few long strides he had doubled the distance and Katie yelled,

"Snowball! Wait!"

Amazingly, the animal paused and turned to look back. The horse seemed to know its name and Katie laughed at the thought. But her laughter turned to surprise when the beautiful white horse reared back on its hide legs then turned and galloped away.

"Wait!" she cried again and watched the horse disappear in the row of trees at the edge of the clearing. Katie ran across the pasture without a care of what lay beyond the woods, and ducked inside the forest as she chased after the white horse. She scurried around trees and hopped over tufts of tall grass as the horse weaved its way through the woods up ahead. It was all she could do to keep sight of the beautiful animal. And even though she knew it was impossible to catch him, chasing after the horse was so much fun. Katie giggled as she ran and knew she had to be dreaming. She felt lighter than air and ran till her hair flowed like silk and her slippers flit across the blades of grass and barely seemed to touch the ground.

Just one touch, just one touch, on and on she went through the maze of trees, laughing and running, but no matter how fast she went, the white horse remained at a distance. When Katie finally paused to catch her breath, she looked back and saw there was no path or trail, only the thick woods all around her and everything looked the same. Strangely, the white horse had stopped to look as well. Katie smiled at him. Surely the horse knew the way back to the big green pasture. There was no need to worry. All she had to do was keep him in sight. Suddenly the animal bolted again, and was off in a flurry of leaves and a cloud of dust.

"Wait!" Katie cried, and ran on with the horse just ahead, never getting any closer, and never getting any farther away. The white stallion ducked in and out of autumn trees that were suddenly filled with leaves of amber and scarlet. Katie kept running, and hardly noticed the trees changing colors.

Above her, gray clouds rolled across the sky, like a dark curtain drawn over the land. And as the light grew dimmer, the horse became strangely bright until he glistened like a jewel in the woods. Soon the forest was dark and the tall trees were hunched over and stooped with age. They reached down with twisted branches and when Katie looked, the lush green forest was filled with shadows, and the old trees with their knotted limbs began to melt away in the darkness until there were barely any trees left at all.

When the horse finally stopped, Katie looked around once more and the smile left her face for everything was turned to night and she was hopelessly lost. "How could this be? Where had all the trees gone?" She wondered then turned to see the animal watching her and nodding its head up and down. It seemed to be beckoning her to follow, and for the first time Katie got the impression that the horse had not merely been running, but was actually leading her some-where. She also sensed that in some strange way whatever he was leading her to, was somehow responsible for all of this. The white horse turned and walked on, leading the way more slowly.

"Wait! Please wait! Where are you taking me?!"

Katie's voice echoed into the night as she followed in earnest, looking around fearfully. The animal walked aim-lessly across the hard and rocky ground that trailed off into the night and Katie followed, trying to avoid the sharper stones beneath her feet. She spent most of her time looking down as she made her way forward, glancing up every now and then to make sure the horse was still there. She limped and stumbled in her fluffy little slippers and did her best to keep up. Then when she was sure she could go no further Katie looked, and to her surprise, the horse had stopped. She stood there panting and afraid.

"Was the horse lost? Perhaps it had come to its senses and was too afraid to venture any further …Yes," Katie thought to herself, "That was it. Now it will turn around and go back, back to that beautiful green pasture."

Waiting there in the cold gray darkness, Katie could only hope. She looked at the horse and the horse looked back at her as though it had suddenly reached its destination which appeared to be in the middle of nowhere. Katie just stared at the animal, and wished she had never followed the white horse.

"I'm so stupid." Katie heard herself say, and then paused when she realized it wasn't her voice. Indeed, she hadn't uttered a word, yet she could have sworn she heard some-thing. It was a little squeaky voice that barely sounded human.

"... All alone are we?"

There it was again. Katie hesitated then looked behind her. She saw no one and felt silly for even looking.

"All the stupid ones usually are... Alone that is... til you showed up." said the voice.

Katie looked again, and again she saw no one. She looked all around her and finally glanced down at her feet. There she found a fat little mole sitting on the rocky ground next to her left bunny slipper. Katie jumped back when the mole sat up, gave her a disapproving look and folded its tiny arms across its chest.

"He tricked you too, eh?"

Katie didn't know what to think. "Are you... talking to me?" she asked.

"I'd turn around if I were you. Coravandia is no place for the likes of you. Nor me for that matter." said the mole.

"I beg your pardon," said Katie, not sure how she should properly address a mole, especially a mole that talked. The little creature looked off into the night with a thoughtful gaze.

"Joylessness... Joylessness." he said, sounding very tired.

Katie decided to stop talking and just let the tiny creature have its say.

"Joylessness is to blame." the mole continued. "Joylessness came to our land and all was darkened. He is responsible for all this, you know. He is a curse to this place."

Katie tried not to look confused, but she couldn't help it.

"He?" she said. "Who?"

The mole looked at her as though she were crazy.

"He who?!... Joylessness! Joylessness! Haven't you been listening?" he said.

Katie drew back a little.

"I'm sorry, but I don't understand. You talk as though joylessness was a person."

The tiny mole looked at Katie and laughed.

"Hah! A person?... A person, child? You have to have a heart to be a person. He is more monster than anything else. Gellzoowin is his name and he is Joylessness himself."

The mole turned around and started to walk away.

"The throne's changed hands. It's all gone bad." He said then called over his shoulder. "Don't say I didn't warn you."

Katie just watched him and marveled as the little mole padded off into the dark. But before he got too far, he stopped and stood up on his hind legs then raised his arm and shook his tiny mole fist in the direction of the white horse.

"Rogad! You're an evil wicked sod!" the mole yelled out in his squeaky little voice, to which the horse snorted and shook its head defiantly. The mole looked back at Katie. "Beware the great brown bear. He is out of sorts now that he has lost the throne." Then with a courteous nod, the mole started off again and disappeared into the darkness.

Katie watched him go then looked at the white horse which she regarded with greater suspicion and doubt. In spite of the warning, she took a chance and stepped forward. The horse didn't move. She took another step, then another and still the horse appeared unconcerned as she drew nearer.

Katie wanted nothing more than to climb aboard the back of the animal and ride him out of the strange land. Again, it was the thought that kept her going. Soon Katie was closer than she had ever been, only ten yards away when she stopped again. She hadn't seen the huge rusted axe, with its blade buried in the ground next to the animal.

The tip of the enormous axe was firmly embedded in the rock and held the weapon with its handle pointed straight up in the air. She looked from the battered blade to the smooth ground beneath her feet. There were large gray stones, carefully set into place all around her. There were even strange designs etched into their smooth surfaces. Katie started toward the horse once more.

"How odd" she thought, "that these fine stones with their peculiar designs should be in the middle of nowhere with those great stone pillars."

At least the jagged rocks were gone and she could walk again. Katie stopped and looked around in shock.

"Great stone pillars?!"

Her eyes bulged wide. There were twelve enormous stone pillars, six on either side of her. "Where had they come from?" She wondered. "They weren't there a minute ago, or were they? Maybe I just didn't see them...Impossible!" she thought.

Whatever the case, they were there now.

Katie shook her head feeling like she was going a little crazy and kept her eyes wide open in case anything else should suddenly appear, and just then something did. There was a terrible and loud creaking sound, the earsplitting noise of ancient iron hinges pleading to be oiled. Katie expected that such a terrible noise would surely frighten the white horse. But strangely enough, the animal didn't even flinch and just stared at her with its cold dark eyes. Katie watched as an invisible door swung open in the empty space behind the horse.

A bright orange torchlight covered Katie and lit the ground around her. It glared forth and she shaded her eyes so she could see through the open doorway to the great stone entrance that lay beyond. Other things started to appear as reality shifted all around her and Katie could hardly believe it when the white horse began to change shape before her very eyes.

The animal became darker. Its smooth skin began to wrinkle, and sprout warts. It reared back on its hind legs which grew shorter and thicker, then hunched over like some terrible beast. Its neck shrunk down to a fat stump and its forelegs became huge hairy arms.

Scraps of cloth, bits of armor and animal hide, wrapped

with leather straps were suddenly draped over the creature's body and before Katie could even think, the transformation was complete. The horrible ogre, Rogad, reached down and drew his axe out of the stone which made the blade ring. He held the weapon in his massive fist and grinned. The creature was so ugly, it didn't matter that he was missing half of his teeth.

Katie would have screamed if it weren't for the tremendous structure that was still appearing behind the ogre. It loomed out of the darkness as though it had been there all along, hidden from view by some impossible source of magic. The dark castle walls stretched out on either side of her, while the castle towers seemed to go up and up and disappeared into the darkness. On either side of the great castle doors stood two giants, forty feet tall. Their hulking forms held perfectly still and peered down at the child, with dark brooding faces, that were chipped and cracked with age. The moss covered statues, were cold and lifeless and Katie was thankful of that.

When the veil of magic was lifted, Katie staggered back, her mind reeling in disbelief. The space around her was now a huge open courtyard surrounded by fortress walls, while high above, dark creatures milled about and looked down from their sentry posts. Katie stared wide eyed, trying to take it all in then jumped when the ogre moved aside. Something was coming. Light surrounded the figure that appeared in the doorway of the castle and Katie instantly knew that this was, "him," the one who was responsible for all of this. The man stood straight and tall and looked down with eyes as dark as the grave. He was draped in a long bronze robe, a lavish and regal garment that swept the ground when he walked. The material was thick and flecked with red sparkles that shimmered like polished copper, in the dim torch light. His fur lined collar covered his shoulders like a lion's mane and made him look grand and powerful.

He came forward to get a better look at Katie who stood there trembling. She watched him glance toward the sky and when his steely gaze came to rest upon her once again, his lips curled into a devilish grin and he spoke.

"How nice, how absolutely splendid. The mouse has followed the cheese. Welcome, Katie Campbell... I am Gellzoowin." he said with a voice that almost purred.

Katie stood rooted to the spot. He knew her name, and as if that weren't bad enough, she knew his name as well. When she realized where she had heard it, Katie jumped back and covered her mouth with a startled, "Eeeek!"

She hadn't recognized it when the mole had said it, but now she was sure of it. It was the same name Jack had mentioned, the name on the sheet of paper. "Gellzoowin's sorcery and house of something or other." She remembered thinking that the name was silly when she first heard it and figured that whoever had made it up could have spent a little more time thinking up a better one. She had no idea that the name was real and had a real person attached to it. But as the mole had warned her, this was not a person. The thing standing before her wasn't even human.

One look and Katie knew that this was a wizard. He looked more like a wizard than anything possibly could. Perhaps it was his narrow eyebrows that were arched beyond belief or the way he stood, poised for the moment, or his bedeviled smile. Katie couldn't tell what it was exactly but knew he looked incredibly sly. Everything about him, even his sparkling teeth looked sly, if not a little too pointy.

He was tall with hair as black as oil. Katie would have guessed he was in his forties, but in human years, he was closer to five hundred and forty. Gold and lead beads braided into his hair showed that he was a wizard of great acclaim and a master above many.

Katie tried to catch her breath as she gazed at the wizard. From the looks of everything, Jack was right. Wizards were indeed real. Katie glanced over at the terrible ogre that was still glaring at her. It appeared that ogres were real as well. And now that she had seen it all Katie wanted to run, but since her feet wouldn't move she used what little courage she had to remain standing and tried not to shake.

"The traveling spell?" she heard herself say and was surprised that she could even make her mouth work under such horrible conditions.

"Yes," smiled the wizard, "The spell is mine." He said and turned away, with his robe billowing behind him then shouted an order that made Katie jump.

"Bring her!" he said.

The horrible ogre came forward. It took huge steps and its head lolled from side to side. The creature looked clumsy with its long arms banging against its knees. Katie watched him come closer and closer, until he towered over her and his shadow covered her like an inescapable wave. Before Katie could move, the beast tossed his axe from one hand to the other, then reached out and grabbed her.

The ogre's thick leathery fingers squeezed Katie's arm tightly and held her like a vise. She pulled, kicked and struggled to break free, but only managed to flop around like a helpless doll, as the big ugly monster brought her along and dragged her inside the castle.

CHAPTER FOUR

Before Gellzoowin's Throne

*K*atie had no idea where the beast was taking her. All she could think about was the ogre's monstrous hand wrapped around her tiny wrist. The creature's skin felt like sandpaper that scratched her and made her wince as she staggered and stumbled along behind him.

"Please!" Katie cried. "Let me go!"

Rogad ignored the child and never looked back as he grunted and snorted and brought her through the stony corridors of the castle, past flaming torches and towering pillars. Soon they came upon another beastly ogre standing guard at the entrance of a large chamber. This was Slag. His lower jaw jutted out with huge yellow teeth that curled up on either side of his nose. Katie stared at the thick ugly beast that growled and watched her with great suspicion as she stumbled past and entered the dark hall. Rogad plodded forward and once they were inside, he released the girl then turned around and exited the chamber, slamming the heavy oak doors behind him.

Katie rubbed her wrist as she backed away and found herself standing in a pool of light. When she turned around, Gellzoowin was smiling down on her from atop his dark throne, while all around her, things waited in the shadows just beyond her view, strange shapes that were holding still trying not to be noticed. As her eyes adjusted she could start to see them. There were woodland creatures, large plumed peacocks, great horned deer, badgers, and wolves, all gathered around, quietly blinking at her.

Slowly, a little red bushy tailed fox came forward and took a few steps into the light, then sniffed the air and quickly returned to the shadows. The animals looked on and waited patiently as though Katie were about to say something important. Soon other things began to emerge, creatures that moved among the animals. There were trolls and elves, little people that pointed and watched and could hardly sit still, while behind them stood the darker creatures. These were worst of all and Katie tried not to look at them. There were ogres, goblins, imps and urchins, frightful creatures like lizard monkeys, winged jackals and other nameless things that only lived in nightmares. Most of them tended to stay in the shadows where they belonged, but Katie could hear them grunting and snorting, chattering among themselves, filled with curiosity. Suddenly there was something hurrying out of the shadows, but before Katie could scream, the hideous hook nosed goblin scampered up, pointed its bony finger at her and laughed.

"HAH!" he jeered with great satisfaction then quickly made his way up the throne steps and perched himself next to the wizard, like a vulture. Numlock peered down at Katie and grinned. He was happy to be back in the Nohr World and anxious to see what would become of the little girl now that she was without her precious guardian.

Another noise echoed from out of the darkness and distracted Katie from the ugly little creature. There were heavy footsteps and the sound of long claws scraping the stone floor. Katie backed away, her eyes growing wider as she watched the huge beast lumbering out of the darkness.

"Beware the great brown bear," the mole had said and the warning echoed in her mind.

The animal walked into the light and Katie froze. The bear was truly massive. His head alone was bigger than she was. His legs were the size of tree trunks. His barrel shaped body was well over a thousand pounds and his fur, glistened a deep rich red that shone like auburn. The animal moved slowly as it came forward and looked right at Katie with his golden brown eyes.

Katie wanted to faint. She wished she could faint, but she was too scared and unable to move. She feared the monstrous beast would gobble her up in one bite, but to Katie's absolute amazement the great bear walked right past her.

Katie stumbled as she forced her stiff legs to move so she could see where the beast was going. She watched the bear mount the first few steps of the throne then sit down at the wizard's feet. When Katie had calmed herself, her first thought was that the animal was the wizard's pet. But she began to think otherwise when the great bear sat up, leaned forward, and rubbed its chin as though it were studying her quite carefully. Katie stared back in utter dismay. Then as if that weren't surprising enough, the enormous beast opened its mouth and spoke.

"A child of God" he said in a deep rumbling voice and shook his head. There was a gasp from the shadows as though this was a terrible development.

"Calm yourself, my dear Bromwin. All is well, I assure you." The wizard said as if to dismiss the animal with a word.

The bear growled as he climbed down from the steps of the throne that was once his then slowly walked around the child to observe her. With his chest out and his head held high, Katie could see he was indeed a king. When the bear was done, he stood in front of Katie and gave a disapproving glance down at her bunny slippers which were a little ragged, but smiled up at Bromwin with their usual pleasant grin. Katie looked at the bear in horror.

"They're not real! I promise!... They're just my slippers!" she said, and wiggled her toes to prove it. The bunny slippers nodded as if to say it was true and, "No harm done."

The bear huffed and Katie breathed a sigh of relief when he turned away to face the wizard. Bromwin growled loud enough for everyone in the great chamber to hear.

"All is not well, wizard." Bromwin said. "She is a child of God, a bearer of light. You had no right to bring her here."

Gellzoowin peered down from his throne.

"Do not forget who is in charge, dear Bromwin. I will tell you when you are in danger and when you are not." he said.

Bromwin growled back.

"How did you do it?" he demanded but the wizard only smiled and seemed to enjoy the growing sense of confusion that surrounded the child and her arrival. Bromwin turned to Katie once more.

"Do you know where you are, child?" he asked in a voice so deep Katie could feel it grumbling inside of her.

"No sir, but I'd like to go home now... if I may." Katie said.

Bromwin stepped closer and looked her in the eyes.

"This is the Nohr World." he said. "The middle kingdom beyond the moon and the stars, past the cities of jasper and gold, beyond the earthly realm of slumber, but near to your dreams."

The bear looked on with a curious gaze and Katie just stared. She had no idea how to respond, or even if she should. The wizard smirked at her charming ignorance and Bromwin sighed.

"Indeed, you are innocent. The heavenly spheres are beyond your concern, yet here you are... So how did you get here? How did you come to be in our world?" the bear said, wondering aloud.

Katie understood very little, except for the last question.

"I came through your door, I mean my door." Katie answered. The bear looked at her questioningly.

"The side of my door." Katie added, trying to be helpful.

There was no reaction until she said, "It was a traveling spell."

The bear growled once again, and Katie could feel the sound of it go right through her. Bromwin turned to face Gellzoowin and bared his fangs at the wizard.

"More of your evil magic to defy the law. You bridge the gap between our worlds and bring God's wrath upon us all." Bromwin said.

"What I do is no concern of yours." Gellzoowin said and sat back, casually admiring one of the larger rings on his fingers. "I will use my magic as I see fit." he said.

Bromwin glared at the wizard.

"You have taken my throne and cast your spell of fear over my people, but you do not frighten me wizard. The fact remains, you have taken a child of God and placed her in harms way. In doing so you have angered all mighty God and will surely pay!"

The wizard raised an eyebrow and stared at the bear with an intensity that would have made any lesser creature wilt away, but Bromwin was not done.

"Mark my word, wizard. As sure as I stand here before you, I..."

The bear's words ceased abruptly and the hall fell silent as every living creature pulled back into the shadows. Katie waited for Bromwin to continue, and when she finally looked to see what wrong, she gasped. The great brown bear had been turned to stone.

The statue of the bear was perfect to the finest detail, from the rough stone texture of its fur, to its smooth polished claws that glistened in the dim light. Had it been carved by a master sculptor it would have been a work of art, but this was a frightful work of magic, and Katie could only stare at the lifeless creature standing before her. Still for all her fear, there was something hauntingly peaceful about the statue. It was covered in a light frost that sparkled like diamond dust. Katie summoned her courage to reach out and touch the frosted surface then pulled back and whispered. "What have you done?"

The wizard looked down and smiled as he admired his own handiwork. "I like my subjects a little more soft spoken. Remember that child. It will serve you well."

Suddenly, he paused to glance around the room then turned to Katie with a look of surprise. "My dear, it seems you have forgotten something."

Katie looked around her.

"It seems you've misplaced your guardian. I'm afraid that was not very wise. The Nohr World is a very dangerous place, especially for a human child. You really should have one, you know... a guardian that is."

The wizard mocked her with a look of concern. "Don't worry. The challenge will not go unanswered. It's all part of the plan." He said with a fiendish grin then sat back in the shadows and waited.

In a distant land known as paradise, where angels guard the twelve gates of Heaven and towering mansions pierce the clouds, the Heavenly host was assembled and an army of God stood ready. Glistening angels gathered together to see who among them would be chosen to rescue the child of God who had been spirited away into darkness.

The archangel Michael stood like a general before the assembly. There were seraphim and cherubim, the angel Gabriel, Azrael, the mighty Uriel, and a thousand gilded warriors, ready to heed the call. Then from the heavenly throne came a beam of light that shone down upon a lone warrior, an angel with the heart of a lion. The mighty guardian stepped forward from among the ranks and knelt to receive God's blessing.

In an instant, a brilliant ray burst forth from the hallowed halls and shot into the sky above the star spangled realm. It whistled from one end of the great expanse to the other in the twinkling of an eye. At the leading edge of that brilliant ray was the mighty soldier of God rocketing forward at speeds unimaginable, trailing fire for a hundred miles.

The angel plunged downward, forging through the clouds like a fiery comet and looked to the world below. Soon he was skimming the tree tops, his eyes like living lanterns searching the land as he approached; and thus God's wrath descended swiftly in the form of an angel, a rod of iron, the measure of truth, the instrument of justice that was known as, "Stadia."

Katie stood next to the stone bear and the creatures in the dark throne room stared at what remained of their goodly king. They all feared the wizard and his power, and kept their murmurings to themselves, all except one. A light flashed out of the darkness and rose above the crowd. It darted around the bear then hovered over his head, fluttering on sparkling wings. Katie shied away from the golden light until it held still long enough for her to see then stared in wonder. The little fairy was barely two inches tall, and glistened like a star, yet for one so small her tiny voice caught everyone's attention. Kitch cried out in anger. "You monster! A pox upon your lot! You double dabbed monster! How could you?!" She yelled.

Gellzoowin turned aside in disgust. "I hate fairies." he said looking toward the wall.

"That is because you have no power over us, you beast! If I could I'd cast you into the lake of fire myself."

Gellzoowin's eyes glowed like red hot coals as he glared at the fairy, and growled.

"It will take more than you, my dear, Kitch. Far more than you."

The glowing fairy was full of fire and bold as she could be as she hovered over the stone bear, her tiny wings a blur. Katie gazed at the little creature when suddenly the throne room doors burst open.

"THROOOMM!"

Before Katie could turn around, Rogad and the other ogre came tumbling in, and rolled across the stone floor until they were sprawled out flat on their faces. The two monsters laid there groaning, and were either unwilling or unable to stand. Gellzoowin and all the dark creatures looked to see what had happened when a loud voice echoed across the hall.

"Fear not!"

The words rang through the dark chamber as a tall figure of a man strode into the throne room. A long gray cloak flowed around him. It draped all the way to the floor and fully covered his brilliant armor. A gilded helmet of silver and gold was upon his head and had a luster that glowed brightly. This was the helmet of righteousness and his was the armor of God.

The angel was even bigger than the one that Katie had left behind. For now, his wings remained invisible as the soldier of God marched toward the little girl and when he removed his helmet, Katie could see his was a face etched by the hand of God. His eyes glistened like sapphires. His hair shimmered like spun gold and flowed about his shoulders. The angel was beautiful and strong. With just one look, Katie was lost in his perfect countenance and knew that he was her defender. The wizard however was not so impressed and nestled himself in the comfort of his throne.

"Speak of the angel," Gellzoowin said in a slow and lazy voice.

The angel approached with his helmet tucked under his arm and as he drew near, a sense of peace rose within Katie that told her who and what he was. When he finally stood before her, Katie tilted her head back till she was looking straight up.

"You're an angel, aren't you?" she said.

"Indeed I am, child of God." he answered softly. "I am Stadia. Are you all right?"

Katie loved the warmth of his voice and smiled till her eyes nearly shut.

"I am now." She said. "I am now."

Suddenly Gellzoowin's eyes turned black as coal, and the wizard jumped to his feet, upon hearing the angel's name.

"What is this?!" he yelled and made the creatures in attendance pull back even further. "Where is the archangel? Where is Michael?!" he roared.

Stadia smiled down on Katie and only gave the wizard a casual glance.

"This is an outrage. Speak to me, minion! Answer me!" Gellzoowin demanded.

Stadia took his time as he turned to face the wizard with a long slow gaze.

"Spare yourself. Your threats are meaningless. If it were not for almighty God who has sent me, I would have no need to grace you with an answer. The archangel is about his business. That is all you need to know."

Gellzoowin shook with rage. His face turned a darker shade of purple. His black eyes bulged. Katie squinted and took a few steps back, afraid that he might actually pop. Then as quickly as he had been risen to anger, the wizard suddenly became calm again. When he returned to normal, he took a deep breath and forced a smile.

"You're trying to bait me... aren't you? Very clever, very clever indeed." The wizard looked the angel up and down. "Perhaps I shall have great sport toying with you after all and when I am done, your Lord shall think better next time and send me a real challenge."

The angel smiled. "I shall do my best not to disappoint you." He frowned at the statue of the bear. "This is your handiwork, is it not?... Return the bear now."

The fairy Kitch flew near the angel and yelled out.

"Yes! Yes! Turn him back, you wicked toad!"

Gellzoowin leaned forward and glared at the fairy that quickly darted behind the angel and peeked out over his shoulder.

"You heard him!" She added boldly.

The angel locked eyes with the wizard. It was a direct challenge and all the creatures in attendance watched eagerly to see what would happen next. A few moments later, the wizard simply sat back on his throne and smiled.

"Of course... Of course, as you wish." The wizard said warmly.

With a flick of his wrist, the bear was back and Bromwin's booming voice echoed throughout the chamber as he finished the sentence he had started just before the spell was placed upon him.

"...I will not allow you to harm this child of God! Do you hear?! As long as there is breath within me, I will fight you!"

Everyone smiled at the bear that was completely unaware of what had happened. Bromwin turned to the angel in surprise and Stadia smiled down on him saying, "Fear not, dear king. The favor of God is upon you. I have come to help."

Bromwin bowed before the angel, humbled by his presence.

"The Lord is truly merciful. Angel of God, you are most welcomed." Bromwin rose and quickly took the opportunity to plead his case against the wizard.

"This, this creature has taken control of my kingdom. With the use of magic, the ogres and his evil horde, he has turned our land into a place of darkness. Though he has promised to leave here once he has found what he is looking for, there is no truth in him. I trust him not!"

Suddenly, a little man stepped forward, barely four feet tall. His bright red beard and dark brown eyes shimmered in the torchlight as he thrust his fist into the air.

"Here, here!" yelled Goe Garth, leader of the troll people.

Goe Garth was rugged, his skin as tan as leather, his hands as big as oven mitts. The troll was dressed in rawhide and wore high boots with a thick leather belt that held a short sword strapped to his side.

Others yelled their approval as another troll stepped forward, plump as a dumpling with a face as round as a pan. His clothes were made of the finest elk yarn and were neatly tailored. This was Gimble and Katie liked him the moment she saw him. He nodded at her and doffed his large rakish hat which had a big white feather tucked in its brim. Other trolls rallied behind the angel as well, then more and more until all of the woodland creatures and the king's loyal subjects were cheering as one. The darker creatures, ogres and goblins alike, sneered and rattled their weapons, and in the midst of the uproar, the wizard finally raised his hands.

"Wait!... Hear me! Hear me!" He shouted. "The bear has spoken correctly! I have no quarrel with you, Chronicle trolls, Woodlanders, any of you! As soon as I have found that which I seek, I swear by the fiery tongue of the Gollock, I shall leave this place."

Stadia's eyes narrowed, as he spoke.

"And what is this thing which you seek?" he asked.

The wizard paused and every living creature leaned forward, waiting to hear the answer, and would have gladly given him whatever he wanted to make him go away.

"I seek the white horse, the white horse known as Majesty."

The wizard called out in a loud voice for all to hear. At

first, there was silence, and then Katie could hear the name repeated softly, over and over again.

"Majesty. Majesty. He seeks the white horse, Majesty!"

The word spread throughout the chamber until everyone was staring anxiously. Katie was a little shocked herself. She found it peculiar that they all seemed to know about the white horse. After all, that's how she had come to be here. She was chasing what she thought was a white horse. And now, it just so happened that this wizard was looking for a white horse as well. Katie suddenly felt a knot in her stomach and suspected the answer to the mystery would not be a pleasant one.

The crowd was still murmuring and seething anxiously when there came the tiny sound of laughter. The fairy flew out from behind the angel, and the goblins and ogres gave curious glances. Kitch laughed so hard she bobbed like a feather on the air until she came to rest on the great bear's back. The tiny creature rolled around in Bromwin's fur, kicking her feet and beating her fists then held her belly, unable to control her laughter.

When she finally sat up, she looked at the wizard with a chuckle and a snort then burst out laughing again. Bromwin looked back to see the fairy slip off his shoulder with her wings a flutter and plop down onto the floor next to him. Katie couldn't help herself and smiled as she came closer and stooped down.

"What's so funny," Katie asked and had to wait a while for the fairy to settle down again.

Kitch took a deep breathe and finally climbed to her feet, exhausted. She looked up into Katie's big brown eyes and said, "The wizard is wasting his time. Everybody knows that no one knows where the white horse is."

The wizard smiled cleverly and pointed at Katie.

"Then this child, my dear fairy, is that "no one" of whom you speak... For she knows far more than you think."

Kitch stopped smiling. It was an absurd statement. The angel Stadia turned to look at the little girl, then King Bromwin, then Goe Garth, and Gimble, and suddenly everyone in the chamber was looking at the little human child. Katie stood there, scratching her leg and squinted, which is what she did when she didn't know what to do. She had no idea what the wizard was talking about and could only think of one thing to say.

"I want to go home." she whined.

The word "home, home, home" echoed throughout the chamber as all the creatures pondered what the wizard had said. It was obvious from Katie's expression that she didn't appear to know anything, but the wizard seemed quite certain of his claim. Stadia stepped forward.

"Wizard, I know not what scheme you have laid out before you, but I know this. It will not involve this innocent child. You will deal with me directly."

Gellzoowin looked down from his throne.

"You are of no use to me, angel. My interest is in your master. I seek to defeat the Lord of Glory himself," said the wizard.

With that, every creature in the throne room gasped. One troll fainted, another screamed while others stumbled and pushed their way out of the chamber, fearing a lightning bolt would surely burst through the ceiling and strike them all dead.

"Blasphemer," King Bromwin roared.

Kitch darted behind the angel again, while others stood trembling. Gellzoowin narrowed his eyes then leant forward and glared.

"I will not only defeat the Lord of Glory but I will use this child to do it, and there is nothing you can do to stop me." He hissed at the angel.

Hearing that, Stadia advanced on the wizard and marched up the stone steps, when Gellzoowin called out.

"Careful angel, lest you jeopardize this innocent child of God."

Stadia glared back.

"You have no power over her. She is under my protection." he insisted.

The wizard smiled.

"Ah, yes. But what of her brother?... Her dear, non-believing brother? What protection do you offer him?"

"What does he mean?" Katie said. "What about my brother?"

Gellzoowin sighed.

"Yes, such a problem. What to do? It appears that your brother's lack of faith has put him out, so to speak, and your mighty angel is powerless to help him. I wonder where the boy is now. I certainly hope he is safe." Gellzoowin said, and smiled.

Stadia backed away from the wizard and Katie rushed up beside him.

"I don't understand. What does he mean?" she asked, gazing up at the angel.

Stadia frowned and looked down as though he were trying to figure out his next move. A moment later, he turned to Katie.

"I must go." He said.

"No," Katie cried. "You can't leave me here! Take me with you!" she pleaded.

Stadia stooped down and put his hand on her shoulder.

"I dare not take you away. Our Lord has allowed this to happen for a reason and when I return we will find the answer. Till then, there is nothing to fear. You will hardly know that I have gone."

As Stadia spoke, Katie looked at the wizard and his goblin and all of the horrible creatures that surrounded the throne.

"You will be safe as long as you do not speak to the wizard. He is very clever, but say nothing to him. Do not talk to him until I return. Say nothing. Is that clear?"

Katie felt a little braver and nodded her head. Just then the tiny fairy zipped through the air, quick as a spark, and stood on Katie's shoulder.

"Don't worry. I'll be with her the whole time. She won't say a word." Kitch said and saluted the angel like a proud little soldier. King Bromwin, came along side to add a word of reassurance.

"We will protect her until your return." He said with a deep growl.

Stadia stood to his feet, nodded to the bear and the fairy then looked to the wizard.

"If you harm a single hair on her head, I will grind your bones to dust."

The wizard bowed politely to acknowledge the threat as the angel left the chamber; and as soon as he was gone, Rogad slammed the door shut behind him. The ogre looked at Slag who was still sprawled on the floor next to him then rubbed his aching chin and bared his jagged teeth. As far as he was concerned, the little girl had become far more trouble than she was worth.

Katie turned to face the wizard, and whatever courage she had, quickly left her. Gellzoowin smiled down from his throne with the hideous goblin by his side. Behind them, a hundred yellow eyes, glaring out of the darkness.

"It's all right child." Bromwin said, sensing her fear.

With that, Katie wrapped her arms around his neck, which was a lot like hugging a bus, and buried her face in his thick fur. The shimmering fairy fluttered just above to offer a little more light, and standing there lost in a dark world, Katie thanked God for her new found friends.

CHAPTER FIVE

Baithenwar

*J*ack was fast asleep, and although his room was dark and silent, his dream was filled with fire and magic, for in his dream he was a powerful wizard. The evening mist settled within the hills and the high tower of Castle Baithenwar gleamed dully in the moonlight. A shadow descended silently along the tower wall as a cloaked figure came to rest on the balcony. Jack peered down with his hair matted and sweat pouring from his brow; while far below where the stone bridge met the castle wall, two red eyes glistened in the dark. Ribbons of smoke curled up out of the shadows as the dragon waited and watched for the young wizard to show himself again.

Jack smiled down at the two red eyes glaring dimly up out of the darkness. With his wizard's cape half burnt, he could still feel the heat of the dragon's fiery breath on his back and knew he had narrowly escaped with his life. Then with a wave of his hand, Jack turned and flung the terrace doors open wide. Once inside, they slammed shut behind him as he threw off his smoldering cape and went to his war table. There he found his maps strewn across its surface, with a wooden goblet perched at the edge of the table. Jack quickly guzzled down its contents, then tossed the cup aside and peered down at the numerous scrolls, ready to devise another plan to meet the beast in battle.

Jack rummaged through the maps, flinging them here and there, when one of them happened to flip through the air and land at the feet of a dark foreboding figure, standing in the shadows across the room. The giant of a man was clad from head to toe in polished black armor. The dark soldier held a grim mace in his clenched fist and stared straight ahead. Amazingly, the enormous black knight was a perfect replica of the miniature toy Jack had in real life; only this one was eight feet tall, weighed a ton and could actually talk.

"How goes the battle?" echoed the deep voice from within the heavy armor, like a giant in a cave.

Jack looked up and grinned at his dark companion.

"It was close. Real close! He nearly got me!" Jack said excitedly, with sweat still dripping from his brow. "I flew under the bridge and he followed me into the dark just like I knew he would. That's when I hit him with a lightning bolt then slipped on a rock. When he came at me, there was so much fire, I didn't think I was going to make it! He got my cape! See?" Jack pointed to the cloak, still smoldering on the floor.

"Yes" said the black knight. "You are most fortunate, sire. The dragon is swift for his size. He will be difficult to defeat."

"Not if I can get him where I want him." Jack said as he unrolled one of his maps and pointed at the stream indicated below the castle. "Here! See?!" Jack said.

The black knight tilted his head down, with a noisy creak from his metal collar.

"Ah yes, of course, the element of water." The black knight's voice was slow and ponderous. "Dragons of the air hate the water... a brilliant strategy." the black knight said as

Jack began to formulate his plan.

"If I can just get him into the deeper part of the stream." Jack paused to look around. "Where're the other maps? The water charts." Jack quickly leafed through the maps on the table then stood up sharply.

"I know. They're in the cabinet." He said and whirled around so fast, he didn't see the big man standing directly behind him and slammed into him like a brick wall. Jack hit the floor hard and lay there for a few seconds then propped himself up and shook his head to clear the cobwebs. "Hey!" was all he could think to say as he stared at the solemn figure. Stadia looked down at him then slowly noticed the towering black knight, standing in the shadows. The creature was easily a foot taller, and armed for battle. Stadia gave him a cautious glance then turned to the boy as Jack climbed to his feet.

Jack rubbed his head. "How'd you get in here?" he said with a frown.

"Come with me." The angel said.

"Hey, I'm a wizard you know." Jack whined as he dusted himself off.

Stadia glanced at the black knight again.

"Listen to me. This is all an illusion. You are living in a dream and you have no powers. Now do as I say. Time is short, we must go." he said.

"I'm not going anywhere with you." Jack said and scowled, waiting for some response as Stadia walked past, but the angel never looked back.

"I'm afraid your life depends upon it." he said and sounded like he meant it. It was a threat that made Jack pause to reconsider.

"My life?... Hey!... Who are you?!" Jack called out, as the angel walked away and faded into a cloud of thin, wispy vapor. Jack quickly turned to the black knight in a fluster and spoke as though he was late to catch a bus.

"Um, okay listen! If I'm not back in one hour, you come and find me! Alright?!" he said but the suit of armor gave no response. With that Jack chased after the angel. "Wait for me!" he yelled then ran into the mist and disappeared from his dream and the castle chamber.

CHAPTER SIX

The Wizard's Table

*T*he sky over Coravandia was dark and grim but not as grim as the wizard's throne room. Many things had happened while the angel was gone. The creatures had begun to yell and argue about the angel and the human child. Most of them had never seen a child of God and the last time the trolls had seen an angel was during the wizard wars. Now there was both a child of God and an angel in the same place at the same time and that was cause for worry.

The clamor grew even louder when the ogres joined in, bellowing and howling, and making so much useless noise that Katie had to let go of Bromwin's neck to cover her ears. Enraged, the bear turned and roared.

"That is quite enough!" the great bear said and the hall fell silent. "We need not be afraid. The angel has not come to destroy us. He is our champion."

After years of ruling over his kingdom, the bear had learned to make great speeches, and now that everyone was listening, he was just warming up to it.

"What the wizard hath wrought he hath born out of his own sinful heart and brought upon himself. His own wickedness and evil deeds have found him out. He who has seized the throne with sorcery and exalted himself will be brought low this day. I tell you, the wizard is most pitiful among us, for his fate is in the hands of God and there is nothing he can do to escape judgment."

"Here, here!" the trolls yelled.

The little fairy smiled at Bromwin and admired the brave king who spoke so boldly before the wizard. At the same time, she thought it strange that the wizard had not interrupted or even uttered a single word in his own defense. And when she looked, she saw the hook nosed goblin sitting atop the throne, in the wizard's place, grinning wildly.

The fairy flew to the goblin in an instant, and zipped around the creature like a fiery dart. Numlock ducked and dodged to get out of her way as the fairy searched high and low, looking everywhere only to discover that the wizard was indeed gone. He was nowhere to be found. But even worse, the child was gone as well.

"Furthermore..." King Bromwin said.

Kitch flew to the bear, in the middle of his lengthy speech, but no matter what she did, he turned aside and kept talking. Finally she buzzed around Bromwin's muzzle so fast, the bear's whiskers caught fire. Bromwin jumped back, sputtering and shaking his head angrily then crossed his eyes to get a better look at his whiskers which were still smoldering. Gimble took one look at the cross eyed bear and giggled. Goe Garth elbowed the little troll and frowned while Bromwin turned to the fairy in anger.

"How dare you! Such impudence!" he roared, rubbing his nose with his paw.

"THEY'RE GONE! THEY'RE GONE!!" Kitch shouted, pointing to the goblin.

Bromwin looked to the throne then glanced around him.

"But, but... The child was right here! She had hold of my neck." Bromwin said.

Just then someone cried. "What of the angel?! We've lost the child of God, what do we do now?!"

The question was enough to cause a panic, as half of the creatures chose that moment to run while others yelled and screamed even louder. Bromwin did his best to calm them, but it was no use. They all feared the worst.

With that, the little fairy took to the air and knew she had to get above all the noise of all the creatures. She flew higher and higher, all the way up to the dark rafters then fluttered her wings to clear the dust and sat quietly in the shadows, with the noise of the crowd still clamoring up from below.

The little fairy plugged her ears and tried to concentrate. She focused her mind until the noise was little more than a distant echo, and when she was ready, she began to listen for the wizard. The fairy listened ever so carefully. Her tiny ears so keen, they could hear the summer leaves changing colors in autumn.

Softly, quietly she began to hear beyond the walls of the chamber and listened. The mind of the wizard was a cold dark place, filled with unspeakable horrors and the little fairy wanted no part of it. But sitting there among the shadows, she knew she had to keep listening if she was to find Katie and save the child of God.

The noise had been so loud, Katie couldn't stand it. She covered her ears and shut her eyes and wished that all of the creatures and all the yelling and all the noise would go away then all at once it did. The silence had come so quickly, Katie uncovered her ears and opened her eyes, but had to shut them again to escape the brilliant sunlight. The light of day was even more of a surprise.

She had just been in the dark throne room and hadn't moved an inch, yet she could feel the warmth of the sun on her face and could have sworn she saw trees and flowers all around her. There was the occasional chirping of birds, and a sweet fragrance in the air. Katie opened her eyes more slowly and squinted at the beauty that surrounded her.

Her heart leapt. She was no longer in the wizard's throne room. She was bathed in sunlight and sitting in a quiet meadow, with no earthly idea of how she had gotten there. There were roses and wild flowers all around. When Katie looked down she found herself seated in a beautiful high backed chair, made of the most exquisitely crafted wood she had ever seen. Dazzling gold patterns, of inlaid wood glistened like silk. The arms and legs of the chair were carved into huge ornate claws and the cushions beneath her were made of rich red velvet with lace fringe and gold tassels. The chair looked more like a throne, expertly made and flawless.

Stretching out before her was the longest, most elegant banquet table Katie had ever seen. Three large crystal vases filled with exotic flowers, luscious blooms bursting with color. Set all around them on silver platters and bowls was every kind of food and dessert imaginable, a bountiful meal fit for a king.

Everything was perfect, down to the slightest detail, and would have truly been wonderful if it were not for the evil wizard who sat at the other end of the table, sipping a cup of green tea. Just the sight of him was enough to make Katie's blood run cold. Gellzoowin smiled and waved to her. It was a little wave that said, "Hello, there again."

Katie thought about jumping out of the chair and running away, but since she didn't know where she was, she grabbed the chair arms, closed her eyes and tried to concentrate on what the angel had said.

"Say nothing. Say nothing." She repeated over and over again as though the words themselves would protect her from harm.

"Katie?" The wizard called to her gently from across the long table.

Katie's eyes popped open when she heard her name and

looked at the wizard like a frightened deer. She couldn't bear his gaze. His eyes were a pale blue and reflected the sky, but she remembered how they blazed red as fire in a fit of rage. Katie sank down behind one of the floral arrangements and the wizard called to her.

"My dear, is something wrong?" Gellzoowin said in a tone that actually sounded friendly. "I must admit, I was rather hasty and could have handled things a bit better. I'm sure you'd agree." he chuckled. "Can you ever forgive me? Now that we're alone and away from all that noise and clatter we can sit and talk."

Katie held her breath. "Say nothing. Say nothing." She said to herself.

The wizard smiled then looked on with genuine concern. "Please, you don't look at all well. Are you sure you're alright?"

Katie peeked up over the flowers.

"Yes." she said, then quickly clasped both hands over her mouth as though a bird had just escaped from her lips. "Say nothing! Say nothing!" she reminded herself.

The wizard smiled like a devilish fox.

"I was beginning to worry. I know that you have traveled a long way and thought you might like a little something to eat before you returned... home."

Katie's eyes lit up.

"Home?... I'm going home?" Katie said in surprise.

Gellzoowin grinned, "Why yes, of course you are. Surely you cannot stay here in the Nohr World. Home is where you belong. I can have the trolls take you back immediately if you like, unless of course you'd rather have something to eat first."

The clever wizard paused to let Katie look at the banquet table. There were exotic dishes wonderfully prepared, surrounded by mounds of fresh fruit. There were shrimp and lobster, steak, sausage and omelets, a whole turkey, pheasant under glass, a broiled duck smothered in mango sauce and even a roast pig, glazed with honey and covered with juicy pineapples. Then there was a world of desserts. There were cookies and donuts, puddings and pies. There were milk shakes and ice cream sundaes with toppings of all kinds. Soon Katie was smiling at all the delicious food in front of her. With all that and the promise of home, the wizard didn't seem so bad now.

Gellzoowin took another sip of his tea and let out a scrumptious moan of delight.

"Mmmmmnnn! There is nothing I like more than green tea. It is my absolute favorite." He lowered his tea cup and paused, then looked at Katie as though a thought had just occurred to him. "Tell me, child. What is your favorite food?"

Katie didn't even have to stop to think and popped up in her seat.

"Cherry cheesecake, with strawberries and whipped cream swirled on top." She blurted out. "My mom showed me how to make it. But Gramme Nannah used to make it the best, the best cherry cheesecake in all the world, but that was before…before she passed away." Katie looked down and her smile faded.

"Oh, I'm so sorry. Do tell me about your grandmother." The wizard said, trying to sound caring and did a good job considering the fact that he hated the old woman, since it was her prayers that had kept them away from the child. The wizard continued cleverly.

"I get the impression she was quite a special person."

"She was." Katie said and seemed to come to life again.

The wizard smiled. Now that the girl was talking, his plan was working nicely and he could see it all coming together, until she mentioned the Bible. That's when the wizard spit out his tea and nearly dropped his cup. The word stabbed him like a needle in his flesh and made him cringe. In fact it made him cringe every time Katie said it, and it was all he could do to sit still as she spoke.

"Nannah always read the **Bible**. She loved the **Bible**. She even knew parts of the **Bible** by heart and told us **Bible** stories."

The wizard flinched and squirmed and twitched and turned, like he was sitting on a tack while the girl rambled on.

"She had a lot of names for the **Bible** too. She called it, the **Good Book**, the **Staff of God**, the **Word of God**, her **Pillar of Strength,** but I just like to call it the plain old **Bible**."

"ENOUGH!" Gellzoowin shrieked and gave Katie a start. The wizard quickly tried to compose himself.

"I'm sorry." He said slowly, through gritted teeth. "That was a lovely story, but I'm afraid it's getting late and the food won't last forever, you know." The wizard gave a weak chuckle and Katie looked at him suspiciously.

"Tell me." he said. "Did I hear you say your grandmother made cheesecake?"

"Yes." Katie said reluctantly.

"That is very interesting because, you see I am rather fond of cakes and pastries myself. In fact, I do believe we have some cheesecake right...over...there."

Katie looked to where the wizard pointed and gazed at the huge slice of cheesecake that was practically sitting right in front of her. She couldn't image how she had missed it. Strangely the more she looked at it, the more it became just like the cherry topped cheesecake she had pictured in her mind. It was absolutely perfect. The perfect size cheesecake with a perfect swirl of whipped cream and pieces of strawberries with a perfectly plump cherry placed on top.

"Please don't be shy. Go ahead. Have a taste." The wizard said and sipped his tea.

Katie picked up her fork and when she took the first bite, the wizard could feel the white horse within his grasp and smiled at the human child who was obviously no match for his clever wizardry.

Katie ate and talked, and only pausing to wipe cream off of her chin and sip a glass of milk. It was then that the spell of enchantment took effect and Katie started to change. The transformation was ever so slow. Katie didn't feel the slightest bit different, but whether she knew it or not, with each bite she took, she was getting a little younger. Slowly the months and years fell away and by the time the spell was complete Katie was as cute as she could be and looked exactly as she did when she was only six years old. With her long hair turned to strawberry blonde curls, she was also three inches shorter and had to sit up straighter to reach the table.

The wizard watched her carefully and magically refilled his cup of tea. According to the feeble old wizard Marplot, a younger Katie, would have twice the innocence and be more likely to remember the knowledge given to her by God. The wizard sat back in his seat, ready to put his theory to the test.

"Katie? How do you feel?" The clever wizard asked, and took a sip of tea.

"Fine, thank you," Katie said.

Gellzoowin nearly gagged with laughter when he heard Katie's new voice. It was higher and squeakier than before and the fact that Katie didn't notice, made it even more amusing. Gellzoowin pretended to clear his throat and continued.

"You have been such great company" he said.

"Thank you, Mr. Zoowin," Katie said and the wizard smiled with delight. She even talked like a six year old.

"Have you enjoyed my hospitality?" He asked.

"I have." Katie said politely.

"Then perhaps you can return the favor." The wizard said, smiling graciously.

Katie frowned. "You mean the white horse, don't you?"

The wizard gave a sheepish smile as though he hoped it weren't too much to ask.

"You think I know where he is, but I don't." Katie said. "Besides that was a mean trick you played on me, turning that ogre into a horse." Now that she was smaller Katie was a little braver as well and the wizard pulled back, pretending to be surprised.

"But my dear child, how else could I have brought you here so that you could tell me about the real horse?"

Katie thought for a moment and her eyes lit up with excitement.

"The one I saw in the pasture?... You mean, Snowball?!" she said.

The wizard cringed at the thought of such a ridiculous name being assigned to the most magnificent creature in the universe. Gellzoowin sat patiently and listened as Katie rambled on and on about the white horse she had seen in the pasture, and then finally interrupted.

"Yes, yes, that is all well and good, but I want you to think and tell me about the other white horse... The one called Majesty. Where is he right now?"

"Majesty?" Katie said. Although she had never heard the name before, it seemed strangely familiar then slowly came to her. "You mean the horse from the book. The horse mommy told me about." She said in a whisper. "...I don't know." Katie replied.

The wizard leaned forward.

"Ah, but you do know!" he said glaring at her wildly.

Katie just sat there, staring as blank as a chalkboard and in her innocence, she began to feel sorry for the wizard. He wanted to find the white horse so badly but all she knew was what her mother had said, and that was hardly anything. When it became clear that the child had nothing more to say, Gellzoowin rubbed his chin and tried to think.

"I know!" he said with a look of surprise. "We'll play a

little game and pretend that you do know. You just start talking and make up a story, all right? Just tell me a story about
how to get to the white horse."

"But how will that help you if I really don't know?"
Katie asked.

"Ah, ah, ah. You let me worry about that. Just... tell me
a story." The wizard smiled reassuringly.

Katie didn't see how it would really help at all, but she
decided the least she could do was try to come up with
something. The problem was she wasn't a very good story
teller. The wizard waited while Katie thought. She was trying to think of the kind of stuff her brother would say, magical stuff, stuff that would make a good sounding story.

"Alright," she said and smiled.

This time it was the wizard who sat up in his chair, staring with eager anticipation and as Katie spoke, the wizard
hung on her every word.

"There are four kingdoms you must pass through to get
to the white horse." she began.

Gellzoowin listened like an attentive child.

"First..." Katie said, and then paused to think. She was
waiting for something interesting to pop into her head, and
then she continued. "First there is the land of the giants"
Katie said.

The wizard gasped and covered his mouth to muffle his
screams of joy. Katie had not expected that reaction. The
wizard uncovered his mouth and whispered, "The land of
great discoveries!" he exclaimed as though the place was
real and he knew exactly where it was. "Go on, child, go
on!" he insisted excitedly.

Katie smiled politely and continued.

"Then there is, ah... um..." This making up stuff was
tough going. "What would Jack say?" she thought. Then it
came to her. "There is the forest of the living trees which
protect the, uh, cloud... stones."

Those last two words didn't seem to go together. Katie smiled weakly and wanted to apologize. She felt she wasn't doing a very good job.

"YES!... Of course!" Gellzoowin shouted and made Katie jump.

"Go on! Go on!" he said as though she were about to uncover buried treasure.

Katie shifted in her seat, feeling a little uncomfortable and had to stop again. She looked up into the sky, trying to think of something else to say. And just at that very moment, the little fairy popped right out of the space in front of her nose.

Kitch swooped down and buzzed around Katie furiously.

"NO! NO! NO! Say Nothing!" she shouted, hovering in front of Katie's little round face. "Mind what the angel told you! Do not speak to the wizard! He is..." Kitch paused, and then drew back in surprise. "What...what has he done to you?!" she cried.

The fairy marveled at the little girl who was now smaller and younger than the last time she had seen her then glared at the wizard who threw his arms up in abject rage. His eyes turned red and he yelled at the sky which became black as night. Suddenly everything went dark and was gone, the bright green meadow, the beautiful banquet table with all the fine food. In an instant, it had all disappeared and changed into something else.

They were back in the castle, in another dark chamber and all that remained in front of Katie was a rickety old table covered with a canvas cloth. On it was a single candle dripping wax and a dirty dish with a chunk of rotted green cheese set before the child. Her grandmother's cheesecake had merely been an illusion. It was a piece of this horrible thing that Katie had put in her mouth instead. She could see where she had nibbled off bits of it and suddenly the sweet flavor of cinnamon sugar turned to the foul taste of sour milk in her mouth. Katie nearly gagged as she waved the little fairy aside.

"You tricked me!" She said, sputtering and spitting out the bits of stale cheese.

Suddenly the great bear and a host of trolls and woodland creatures, flooded into the darkened chamber, shouting joyfully.

"We've found her! She's here! She's here!" they cried, thankful to see the child of God alive. But Katie only glared at the wizard, for he had indeed tricked her and placed her under his wicked spell.

CHAPTER SEVEN

The Angel and the Wizard

A troop of ogres and grim goblins marched into the chamber behind the trolls, pushing everyone aside as they made their way to the wizard, and then surrounded Gellzoowin who slumped back in his chair and stared at the little girl.

"It was all going so well." he muttered.

"Scoundrel!" the bear growled and shook his paw at the wizard. Gellzoowin ignored him and sneered at the sparkling fairy fluttering in the air next to the child.

"Meddling fairies." he groaned.

Suddenly something shook the room like an earthquake and the stone wall behind the ogres buckled. The burley beasts and green goblins staggered out of the way just as the wall caved in, raining down chunks of rock and debris. When the dust settled, Stadia stepped through the gaping hole and stood atop the rubble.

"Please, do come in," said the wizard with a glance.

Katie's eyes lit up as the brave guardian approached and Jack walked in right behind him. The boy stood on the pile of rocks, looking on in amazement.

"Cooooool!" he exclaimed. "That was awesome!"

"Jack, you're here! You're here!" Katie shouted and clapped for joy, but Jack's attention was firmly riveted to the angel.

"How did you do that?!" Jack said, gazing at the big man.

But Stadia only stared at Katie, who had been shrunk down to the size of a six year old. His gaze was so intense, Jack finally turned to look at his sister.

"Hey!... What happened to you?" Jack said and laughed.

Stadia looked the little girl up and down as he marched forward then reached back and drew an enormous shield out of thin air.

"Woooah!" was all Jack could say when it miraculously appeared before them.

The shield of faith was bigger than Katie and shone like glass. A thin layer of energy seemed to float over the face of the shield and gently rippled across its surface like water. The angel placed the shield before Katie so she could see her reflection and the instant she saw herself she smiled. There was no shock or surprise only admiration for the image that stared back at her. Katie remembered what it was like to be six and recalled she rather liked that time in her life. She was "cute as a button" as Dad would say and looking at herself only brought back fond memories. Seeing this, Stadia withdrew the shield which vanished into thin air as quickly as it had appeared. Katie looked up at the angel and tried to look as sweet and innocent as she possibly could.

"I spoke to the wizard." she said rubbing one bunny slipper against the other.

Stadia looked down on her.

"I know," he said.

A moment passed and when Katie realized that was the extent of his anger, she smiled and turned to her brother, excitedly.

"Jack! Wait till you see!" she said and hurried past the angel. Katie pointed at the creatures huddled together in the shadows.

"All of the animals can talk! It's amazing!"

Jack looked around, and peered into the darkness, trying to take it all in.

"This place is great!" He said. "It's like some kinda' realistic dream!"

"It's not a dream, Jack! It was your traveling spell, remember? It brought me here! It worked! It really worked!"

"It did?" Jack said, trying not to look utterly horrified as the reality of it all began to sink in. "You're serious... You mean that... Hey, where are we?" he asked.

The fairy flew in front of Jack and the boy stepped back from her shimmering light as Kitch announced, "This is Coravandia, eastern region of the Nohr World, grand domain of the great King Bromwin born of the Fineland, who sits upon the Vandian throne." The fairy turned aside and gestured, "That is until he showed up." Kitch said and pointed behind her. The boy gazed past the glimmering fairy and peered at the dark figure seated in the shadows.

"Who's that?" Jack said in a hushed whisper.

Katie glanced over and wished he hadn't asked. "Gellzoowin," she said and winced as though someone had broken a plate in the kitchen. Jack's mouth hung open as he stared at the master wizard himself.

Gellzoowin rose to his feet, his shiny bronze robe flickering in the dim torch light as he loomed out of the darkness and started toward the angel who glared back at him.

"What have you done to her?" The angel's voice filled the room, rumbling, low and steady like distant thunder. "Is there no honor in you? No honor at all among your kind?"

There was a flash and another tremor that shook the castle. Katie backed away and turned to look out of an open portal in the stone wall. From there she could see storm clouds gathering in the night sky, as the angel spoke.

"I turn my back and like a coward you take advantage of an innocent child."

Lightning crackled in the billowing darkness and thunder shook the land. Katie looked at the angel then gazed up at the night sky. Each time he spoke, the sky reflected his anger and his words were followed by thunder. The ogres and goblins stood behind Gellzoowin then shrank away as the power of God was revealed in his messenger. But once again the wizard was unimpressed.

"You would challenge me to test your strength, but such power would raise this castle to its foundation. Look around you. Surely, you would not wish that any harm should come to these poor creatures as a result of your holy wrath poured out upon me." Gellzoowin said slyly. "As for the child, I assure you she is unharmed. Look at her. She is the picture of innocence, and you have me to thank for it."

Stadia was hardly amused and held his piercing gaze upon the wizard.

"Anyway, you are too late. She has already told me more than I needed to know."

"Then release her," Stadia demanded.

"When I am done. And now that you have been good enough to bring me the boy, you will mind what you say and be careful to use the door next time."

Stadia grabbed his sword. "You try my patience, wizard. Do not presume to tell me what to do. I have only one Lord."

The wizard beckoned the angel to come closer, and when they were face to face he spoke so softly only Stadia could hear.

"The girl will do as I say, because I possess her brother. His soul belongs to me and is mine to do with as I please. Remember, he is a non-believer and you cannot protect him."

Stadia sneered as the wizard backed away and turned to Jack.

"Welcome, Jack! I have been expecting you."

Gellzoowin reached out his hand and Jack slowly made his way forward, staring in wonder.

"Wizard's fire!" Jack said, as he gazed at the pink light radiating from Gellzoowin's hand. A moment later, Jack paused and felt something, a warm and tingly feeling bubbling up inside him. There was no discomfort only a curious sensation that made him rub his belly and when it was gone, the wizard called to him.

"Come, there is much work to be done and many things for you to see."

A slow and eager smile crept over Jack's face as his feet rose off the floor and he became aware of his new found power. Katie watched in stunned amazement as her brother took to the air.

"Katie, look! I can fly! I can fly!" Jack said and went higher and higher until he disappeared among the dark rafters above. He lingered in the shadows, looping around the wooden beams, once, twice, and then dove straight down with the confidence of a hawk. Katie watched as he swooped under the old wooden table and grabbed the canvas cloth then threw it over the tiny fairy, which fell to the floor underneath its weight.

Katie ran to uncover the fairy as Jack arced back into the air, laughing and spinning. He did cartwheels against the ceiling, then swooped down once more with the wind whipping through his hair, drew his legs underneath him and landed with expert skill right in front of the wizard.

"Coooool! That was great!" Jack said and reached out to steady himself, a little dizzy from his trip around the room.

"Yes and there is much more I can teach you," the wizard said and grinned at the angel then turned and called to everyone in the chamber. "Prepare the wagons and spread the word... We leave tonight!" the wizard said with a shout then placed his arm around Jack's shoulder and led the boy away. The two faded into thin air and the hideous procession of ogres and goblins disappeared behind them.

"Noooo!! Come back!" Katie cried and rushed to the spot where they had vanished. Kitch glowed like a candle and hovered over Katie's shoulder.

"This is most unfortunate." the fairy whispered.

Katie turned to the angel. "Can't you do something?" She pleaded.

"It is the wizard who controls him now." Stadia answered.

"But, can't you stop him?"

"Not without risking your brother's life." He said.

The tiny fairy shook her head as she flit back and forth. "Most unfortunate indeed."

The angel studied Katie with a ponderous gaze. "The wizard believes you can find the white horse, the one that is called Majesty. Is this true?"

"No!" cried Katie. "I don't know anything. I just told him a story and he believed me. I made it all up. Really, I don't know anything!"

The angel stood silently while Bromwin and the fairy and a host of trolls, watched and listened.

"Hmmmm, but you are a child of God, a bearer of light. That is certain." he said giving it some thought. "The wizard has chosen you above all others and has risked a great deal to bring you here."

"And here you stand!" said Kitch.

Katie just stared at them through her tears.

"For the moment, let us assume there is some truth to his claim."

Katie looked down in despair and a moment later she felt a hand beneath her chin then gazed up into the eyes of the angel once more.

"Fear not. It is a bold adventure which lies ahead, and you are very young, but if you are brave, I believe the opportunity will present itself to save your brother."

Katie tried to summon her courage. "Will you come with me?" she asked.

Stadia rose to his feet. "It is God's will. He has sent me to watch over you, and so I shall. Together we will learn what it is you know and uncover the wizard's plan."

Suddenly the fairy leapt in front of them like a spark from a flame. "Together!" she shouted in her tiny voice.

"Indeed!" said Bromwin. "Together!" The bear's booming voice filled the chamber.

"Together!" cried Goe Garth, who stepped forward to join them.

Katie looked around the room with growing surprise as one by one the trolls gathered around, then drew their little swords and shouted all at once.

"TOGETHER!"

"We will stand with the child of God. If you will have us." said Bromwin. The bear bowed graciously before Katie who was speechless and could only marvel at the entire group standing around her. "Y-yes... thank you... all of you." she said finally.

"It is settled then." said Goe Garth. "Come brothers. There is much work to be done."

CHAPTER EIGHT

A Dark Departure

*T*he beginning of any great adventure was a cause for celebration in the land of Coravandia and this was no exception. In fact, there was the sense that this was to be the greatest adventure ever undertaken by man or beast, king or slave.

Torches lit the castle walls and trumpets blared to signal the wizard's departure while hundreds of onlookers watched the band of travelers assembled in the stone courtyard and the preparations being made for the journey. Katie stood next to the bear in the midst of the commotion and stared in wide eyed wonder at all the strange sights around her.

There were three wagons set to make the trip, one for the trolls, one for the ogres and one for the wizard. Bromwin pointed to the largest wagon in the middle of the courtyard.

"The Rabble wagon, forty feet long, and as big as a house. It belongs to the trolls. A beauty, isn't she? Notice the fine craftsmanship, the stairs and railings leading up and down."

Katie gazed at the wagon with all of its cranks, and pulleys, and eyed the huge wooden mast at the center.

"Looks more like a boat with wheels." Katie said.

"The Rabble is the best made wagon in all the land, with the finest crew of wagoneers to drive her. I picked them myself." Bromwin said proudly.

"Look there!" he said and pointed high up on the wagon. "That's **Goe Garth** the driver and captain, a fine soldier and a good leader."

The troll stood aboard yelling orders to his men who rushed about to secure their cargo. They moved so quickly Katie could barely keep up with them, but recognized the troll with the stylish hat and a white plumed feather.

"I remember him." Katie said and pointed.

"That's **Gimble**." Bromwin said. "A good little troll and master builder, the designer of the Rabble wagon. But don't let his size fool you, he eats like a horse."

Just then a gray bearded troll popped into view, armed with a short sword and a silver hammer strapped to his side. His armor breastplate was badly dented and looked like it had seen too many wars.

"That's **Binderbec**, the old soldier and blacksmith."

But before the old troll could move, a black haired, bushy bearded troll came along side. He was bigger than all the others and carried a long spear.

"That's **Gral Tibbore**" Bromwin said. "He's a Tern troll, big and ill tempered, but Terns are good fighters and Gral is among the best of his kind."

Next came a happy little troll with rosy cheeks, and a beard as white as snow. He looked around quickly and nodded in their direction.

"Every crew needs a good priest and **Friar Jingles** is certainly the best among many." Bromwin said. "We call him Jingles because his proper name is too long and would take you breath away in the saying." Bromwin waited and soon another troll appeared. "Ah and there's **Raylin**."

Katie caught sight of the nimble little troll as he slid down the tall mast. Raylin wore a red tracker's cape and a wide brimmed hat, pulled down low which made him look mysterious. When he reached the deck, Katie could see that he was indeed smaller than all the rest.

"Raylin is our tracker, the best in all the land and a master swordsman. Lastly there is **Rumyon.**" Bromwin pointed to a fat little troll that was busily polishing a bottle of wine with his sleeve. The troll paused briefly to curl the ends of his handle bar mustache then returned to his polishing with great diligence and care.

"No crew would be complete without a cook and toastmaster and Rumyon is always ready with a grand toast for any occasion." With all present and accounted for, Bromwin nodded proudly. "The crew of the Rabble wagon, seven stout hearted trolls, tried and true."

Just behind the Rabble was another wagon, considerably smaller, nearly half the size and in terrible disrepair. It creaked and sagged in every direction and looked as though it might fall apart at any moment.

"What about that one?" Katie asked.

"That one belongs to the ogres." Bromwin growled, and no sooner had he spoken than a piece of the wagon fell off as one of the ogres happened by. The hairy beast picked up the plank, gave the wagon a brief glance, then tossed the wood aside with a grunt. Katie and Bromwin ducked as the board sailed overhead and the ogre walked off, grumbling to himself.

There were nine ogres all together. The only one Katie recognized was Rogad. He was the tallest of the beasts while Slag stood beside him with his huge pointed teeth that jutted out at either side of his nose. The other ogres were so fierce and frightening, Katie could hardly bare to look at them. There was one however that wore a silly grin, and was a constant nuisance to the rest. The ogre had teeth like a picket fence and eyes that couldn't stop dancing. This was Zarq who was an idiot, even by ogre standards.

Katie watched as four of the ogres loaded large wooden crates aboard their wagon, while Zarq took them off the other side and put them back on the ground to be loaded again. This went on for quite some time until Zarq grew tired and decided to take a break.

Four other ogres sat in a huddle, playing a game of cards with large dried leaves. They growled as they passed the leaves around and looked at each other suspiciously. Soon they were frowning and peaking at each other's leaves. Once the shoving began, the leaves went flying and a vicious fight broke out. Katie watched in horror as the ogres fought like a pack of ferocious animals while everyone else ignored the beasts and went about their way in the busy courtyard.

"Ah, here she comes." said Bromwin.

When Katie looked, she saw a tiny light coming down from the sky. It flitted about, as if searching for something then darted straight toward them. The sparkling fairy landed on Katie's shoulder and looked around with excitement.

"Well, what do you think?!" Kitch asked.

"About what?" Katie said, her face aglow with the fairy's light.

"All this!" Kitch replied. "Your new family."

Katie looked at the horrible ogres, which were snarling and wrestling on the ground in front of them. How anyone could mistake the pile of smelly beasts for her family she didn't know. The fairy pointed.

"The Weegans!" she said.

"Weegans?" said Katie, still confused.

"You know, the trolls!" said Kitch. "They're Chronicle trolls mostly, very loyal and trustworthy. They will be with you from now on until you reach the white horse and so will I!" The fairy leapt in front of Katie and glowed even brighter. "I love a grand adventure. Don't you?!"

Katie pulled back a little, and looked at her. The little fairy paused, floating on the air.

"Perhaps not." Kitch said with a little more thought. "After all you are a child of God and probably get to do this sort of thing all the time. However, I'm just a simple fairy and for me this is amazing. Quite amazing!" she exclaimed.

With a spark, and a twinkle of dust, the tiny fairy was gone, just as other lights started to flicker on across the courtyard. The trolls struck their flints and one by one, they lit the lanterns aboard their wagon. The ogres that were wrestling on the ground stopped fighting long enough to take notice then clambered to their feet and ran off to do the same. As the golden fires blazed brighter, Katie could see the flags that flew above both wagons. The larger wagon flew the flag of the trolls, which was ornate and very colorful, while the ogres' flag was nothing more than the tattered remains of an old sack that was hung on a pole and looked as though it had been recently pulled from a bucket of slop, which is precisely where it had come from.

The ogres clearly didn't understand what flags were for, and were merely copying the trolls. Even so, the dirty old rag represented the ogres quite well and was a fitting symbol for them.

The third wagon was very different from the first two and smaller still. Strangely, it carried no cargo. It was fancy, and looked like a carriage made for royalty. It was black and studded with jewels. A cloth canopy that stretched over the wagon bore the crest of a silver and black dragon which was the symbol of sorcery and magic. This was the wizard's carriage and strange things milled about in the shadows beneath it. Katie hadn't noticed them at first, for all the activity in the courtyard, but now she could see them more clearly in the flickering torchlight. The little figures were smaller than trolls and even uglier than the ogres. They wore spiky black armor and had skin as green as swamp water. These were war goblins, hand picked by the wizard and born for battle. It was hard to tell their exact size, because they were always hunched over and kept their heads hung low. Katie counted six of the horrible creatures that were busily oiling the wheel axles with buckets of grease, but none of them were as horrible as the seventh goblin which happened to be standing right next to her, sniffing her hair with his long hooked nose.

Katie jumped back and Numlock bared his crooked yellow teeth, grinning wildly. The goblin had been waiting there to frighten her and now that he had completed the task, Numlock winked his glowing green eye and scampered off to join the others when the bear caught sight of him.

"Be gone! You horrible ceature!" Bromwin growled then looked down at Katie. "Are you alright?"

Katie nodded and tried to catch her breath.

"Beware the goblins and mind yourself. We don't want to lose you before we begin." Bromwin said. Katie smiled politely as the bear looked around them.

"As you can see, everyone is very excited."

"Yes they are." Katie said. "But where are they going?"

Bromwin turned with a look of surprise.

"We're off to find Majesty, of course and you're leading the way." he said.

Katie stomped her foot and pounded her fist against her leg.

"But, I don't know where he is!" she cried.

The bear simply smiled at the little girl then came low to the ground so that his big brown eyes were just below hers.

"What you mean to say is, you don't remember."

Katie's face went blank as she stared at the bear and listened.

"My dear, you are a child of God. There is no other creature in our world as blessed as you. Has no one ever told you?"

Katie shook her head.

"God preserve your innocence." Bromwin said, and

purred as he chuckled to himself. "Our Lord gives his children special knowledge." The bear continued.

"He does?" Katie asked.

"Indeed. Because only in your innocence can you truly know God." The bear said and smiled at the mystery of it all. "As you grow older your innocence fades as does the knowledge you have been given and you must learn to think like a child once more if you are ever to find God again."

"Is that what happened to me?" Katie asked. "Is that why I can't remember, because I got older?"

"It happens to everyone, but not everyone is given the knowledge you possess."Katie thought for a moment.

"So you mean, God told me something I used to know but now I've forgotten it?" Katie said, trying hard not to be confused.

"In a manner of speaking," the bear said. "The knowledge still lives within you. It hasn't gone. All you need to do is grasp it. The truth is, what you know, you don't know you know. And what you think you don't know, you know indeed."

Katie stared at him. Now she was confused. She looked down at the ground, pausing to think then tilted her head up with a look of doubt.

"And what about my brother?"

The bear's face suddenly changed and he became very serious.

"Your brother has forgotten everything all together, and is lost." With that Bromwin turned and headed for the Rabble wagon and made it clear that he did not wish to discuss the boy at all.

A stiff wind blew through the stone courtyard, drawing sparks from the torches and bringing a chill to the air. Katie shuddered and drew her robe around her. The temperature was dropping fast and Katie looked up at the cold dark sky as the frosty night descended upon them.

"Here you are. This should help matters." Goe Garth said.

Katie turned to find the troll standing next to her with a fur cape. He draped it around her shoulders and Katie snuggled inside the warm cloak. "Thank you. Thank you very much." Katie said and looked to the sky. "It feels like winter."

"Yes, it never used to be this cold." Goe Garth said, rubbing the girl's shoulders to warm her.

"Did the wizard do this?" Katie asked, still trembling a little.

"No, he's not that powerful. The wizard is a curse to us and causes us to suffer." the troll said then looked up at the black clouds gathering in the sky. "I believe it is God himself who is trying to drive the evil wretch out of our land. It'll start to snow soon. Happens every night about this time, ever since the wizard got here. I pray we can survive another storm."

Just then there came a loud noise, the sound of chains, clinking and banging. A crowd of trolls pulled back to make way as the ogres, dragged great lengths of iron chains across the courtyard. As strong as they were, the beasts labored to load their heavy cargo onto their wagon, all the while puffing steam into the cold night air and kept about their task as it began to snow. Katie watched them with growing concern as the first flakes drifted down and Goe Garth helped her with her hood.

"What are they doing? What are the chains for?" she asked.

Goe Garth looked to the ogres, his eyes filled with regret.

"Those?...Those chains are for Majesty." he said.

Goe Garth lowered his head and walked away, leaving Katie with the snow falling around her. And as she stared at the horrible iron chains being piled aboard the ogre wagon, for the first time she wished she knew nothing of angels or Heaven and wished she had never read a word from the Bible. Maybe then, in her ignorance, the white horse would be safe. As it was she would lead the goblins, the ogres, the evil wizard and all the forces of darkness straight to the white horse and never forgive herself for what might happen.

The little mole had tried to warn her when she first entered the strange world and now his words were truer than ever. "Things were very bad indeed."

Katie watched the terrible ogres as the snow fell and sprinkled the ground with a white frost. And just then a familiar little voice spoke to her from somewhere nearby.

"Unusual weather we're having... as usual... isn't it?"

Katie looked down. The tiny mole was back, and up to his little mole knees in freshly fallen snow.

"This is not the Fineland you know. Things change here. We get old and it gets cold." he said.

"The Fineland?" Katie asked and looked at him blankly.

The mole tried again.

"The place where nothing ever changes? Never grows old?" He said as if she should recall.

Katie just stared.

"You aren't from around here are you?" he added.

"I'm sorry. Everything is so strange to me. I..."

The mole interrupted.

"I told you. You should have turned back." he said.

Katie stooped down and looked at the tiny animal very closely. He wore gold rimmed glasses and his funny little mustache collected flakes of snow. A tiny red scarf gathered around his neck warmed him against the cold.

"Who are you?" Katie asked.

"Just a woodland creature." the mole replied, squinting through his glasses. "And you, I presume are the child of God. I didn't recognize you at first. My eyes aren't what they used to be, you know... Anyway, we've been expecting you."

"You have?" Katie said with some surprise.

"Yes, well when the wizard showed up, we knew God would send someone. We just didn't know who, and here you are," he said looking up at her smartly.

Katie dropped to her knees in the snow and stared at the ogre wagon, loaded down with chains. The mole watched a single tear roll down Katie's cheek.

"I wish I had never come here." Katie said. "I'd do anything to turn back now."

"Tis too late for that, deary. But I'll give you this." the mole said in his squeaky little voice and motioned for her to come closer. Katie thought it was rather silly, since the mole's voice was too tiny to be heard above all the noise around them. No one even knew he was there. Still, Katie leant forward.

"Be encouraged, you hear?!" The mole said. "The evil one is clever, but not very smart. There's a difference you know. Besides you have an angel, and the wisdom of God to guide you."

Katie thought this was rather insightful for a mole, even one that could talk. The little creature turned to walk away then stopped and added, "That's as good a hand as any I'd say." He nodded then started off again. "I'd get some boots if I were you!" he yelled back to Katie and with the snow nearly up to his waist, he ducked under the blanket of frost and disappeared.

Katie stood up and looked down at her bunny slippers which were already covered. "Ahem!"

When Katie turned she found Gimble standing there behind her. The round little troll was wearing his large hat with the long white feather stuck in the brim, and in his hands were a pair of fur lined boots.

"For you, child of God." The troll said proudly and

stooped down. He brushed the snow from Katie's slippers then helped her slide her feet into the animal hide boots, slippers and all. The boots came all the way up to Katie's knees and wrapped her legs in thick fur.

"Thank you" Katie said when there came a shout from the troll wagon.

"Gimble, prepare the harness!" Goe Garth yelled.

Gimble smiled apologetically, doffed his large hat and bowed. When he did, the long white feather swished in front of Katie's face and tickled her nose. With that, the troll ran off to help the others as an eerie silence fell over the crowd in the courtyard.

Slowly every eye turned as something entered through one of the larger gates in the side of the castle and cast its giant shadow across the snowy ground. Katie took a step back as Binderbec, the old blacksmith approached the wagons. In one hand he carried his silver hammer. In the other he held a long leather reign like a leash. Attached to the end of it, was the biggest most gigantic horse Katie had ever seen. The giant stallion pranced like a young colt and stood twelve feet tall, glistening jet black from head to tail with hooves as big as barrel heads.

"A beauty, isn't he?" said Bromwin as he returned to Katie's side.

"He's enormous!" Katie exclaimed.

"Yes, he is." the bear replied. "His name is Nix, which means night, but we call him, Juggernaut... I think it fits. Don't you?"

Katie just nodded as the horse settled down and plodded forward with its head hung low like a gentle giant. Binderbec loped along in front of the animal and Katie felt the ground quake beneath her feet as the black stallion drew nearer. With one swipe of his head, the giant horse could have easily flung the old troll across the courtyard like a match stick. Instead he allowed Binderbec to lead him, until he stood before the Rabble wagon.

"Whoa!" the old troll said and raised his silver hammer.

As soon as the horse was in position, Gimble and the others quickly harnessed the giant horse to their wagon. When all was in place, Juggernaut raised his head and pawed the flag stones with his mighty hoof. The horse shook his silky black mane against the flurry of the snow and seemed to sense it was time.

Then came the ogres once again and the fury they brought with them was an absolute nightmare. There was kicking and biting and growling and snorting as two enormous wild boars fought against their captors. It took six of the biggest and strongest ogres to handle the ugly beasts. Each boar was as big as an ox, and had long yellow tusks that curled back on either side of its fat snout. Their huge heads were covered with wiry bristles of hair that stuck out like cactus needles while their pink eyes flitted back and forth as they wrestled against the ogres, bucking and grunting all the while.

Two of the ogres grabbed the boars around their necks, while the others fought to grab a leg or a tail. Mostly they shoved and punched the giant pigs to keep them moving.

One of the ogres made the mistake of grabbing a hind leg and the boar lashed out with a swift kick. It was Zarq who went flying with a few of his teeth trailing behind him.

When the ogres finally managed to hitch the boars to their wagon, the animals bucked and stomped all the more. They shook the ogre wagon until the chains rattled and wooden crates toppled over the side. Rogad roared and grabbed the reigns and pulled with all his might as the wild boars bucked and stomped. But the beasts were too strong and it was all Rogad could do to stay aboard.

Everyone watched as the boars raged, and another light appeared in the sky. The angel slowly descended through the snow and others backed away as he settled down next to

Katie, soft as a feather. By the time he arrived the boars were in a full rampage. They used their hind legs to punch holes in the front of the ogre wagon, kicking and bucking, splintering planks and cracking boards.

"Be still." the angel said softly.

Katie turned with some surprise and no sooner had he uttered the words than the wild boars settled into their harness and were tamed by his gentle command. The ogres blinked at each other and hardly knew what to make of anything.

"How did you do that?" Katie asked as Bromwin stepped forward.

"Thank goodness you came. Those dim witted brutes and their terrible beasts would have destroyed everything before long."

"Patience, dear king," Stadia said. "The ogres are the least of our worries."

Just then the wizard emerged from the castle dressed in his heavy wizard's cloak.

"What is all this noise!?" he shouted with his young apprentice close behind. Jack hurried along, dressed in his own wizard's robe, the wizard's robe he had always dreamt of. It was deep blue with billowing sleeves and studded with diamond gem stones across the chest and shoulders. It was the wizard's idea, "To add some sparkle." In Jack's arms were a bunch of maps which he managed not to drop.

Gellzoowin preceded to the last wagon and climbed aboard his black coach. Jack piled the maps into the carriage and Gellzoowin helped the boy up. Once Jack was aboard, he settled into his seat and leaned back in the soft cushions that were prepared for him and the wizard. He rubbed his hands along the polished brass railings and admired the comfort of the carriage, that is, until the goblins climbed aboard. Jack cringed at the sight of the ugly creatures clambering up over the sides. His first instinct was to grab something to defend himself, and then he remembered that the goblins were with the wizard, and slid back in his seat and tried not to move. The goblins took notice of the boy with their beady little eyes and growled. They could smell his fear but all it took was one glance from the wizard to silence them.

One by one the creatures made their way down into the shadows, like obedient dogs, and stayed near the floor. Numlock was the last to go. The goblin glared at the boy, but dared not risk a second glance from the wizard and finally withdrew to take his place with the others. Now that Gellzoowin had arrived, and the wagons were ready to depart. Kitch darted in front of the angel, with her light sparkling.

"Where will she ride?" Kitch asked, excitedly, pointing to Katie.

Bromwin stepped forward.

"I would be honored if the child would ride upon my back." he said.

Katie looked at the huge bear with his thick brown fur.

"Oh, could I?" she asked.

Bromwin smiled. "It would be my honor." he said softly then turned to the troll wagon. "Gimble!"

The little troll jumped to his feet and stood ready.

"Fashion me a saddle for the child, to ride on my back." said Bromwin.

With a nod, the troll grabbed his tool sack, a small bundle of wood and went to work. Tools flashed, shards of wood and saw dust flew everywhere and before Katie knew it, the job was done. It was just like Jack had said. The troll's amazing speed was matched only by his remarkable skill. Gimble brought the saddle to the bear which looked more like a little chair, finely carved and lined with sheepskin. It even had arms and handles for Katie to hold on to. With a few leather straps, Gimble quickly fashioned a harness. When all was done, the chair fit snugly onto Bromwin's back and the bear looked like a fine and fancy ride on a merry-go-round. With the saddle chair in place, Gimble paused to dust off the seat, and the bear raised his paw. Katie beamed a smile and with a grand flourish of his hat the merry little troll helped her climb aboard. Katie's boots sank into Bromwin's soft fur as she climbed up on his back then sat down in the saddle chair.

"It's perfect." she said and nestled into the fleecy wool lining until she made herself comfortable. Gellzoowin had been silent as long as he could and when Katie was finally aboard, the wizard yelled out.

"We don't have all night! Proceed!" He said then placed an arm around Jack's shoulder and motioned them on.

Bromwin looked up at Katie, "Where to, child?"

Katie turned to the angel who looked at her reassuringly, but before he could say a word, there came a shout from behind them.

"Coravandians!"

Rumyon, the toastmaster stood in the crows nest, the highest point atop the troll wagon. There, he raised his goblet then leaned back so far he nearly tottered off of his high perch. The crowd below reached out to catch him, but the little troll waved them off, signaling that he was all right. Rumyon cleared his throat and tried not to wobble. He had prepared for this moment for quite some time.

"Princes of the woods, Good king and fair creatures of the Nohr World!" he said. Gellzoowin looked on seething, with malevolent eyes.

"This is truly a joyous occasion." said Rumyon. "The time has come when the sun shall rise on a new land. A land free from evil! Free from darkness! May our kingdom return to light and prosper all its people!" The toastmaster proclaimed and the crowd cheered.

Not to be outdone, King Bromwin stepped forward, with Katie on his back, and took his place in the torchlight.

"Good citizens, we venture forth upon a brave and dangerous journey. As your king, I appoint my friend, the clever and learned fox to watch over you. He will wear the crown until such time as I return and give you the benefit of his clever council."

The little red fox was shocked by the announcement and those standing nearby patted the animal on the back. While they applauded, Gellzoowin sat and listened and hated. He hated the speeches, the cheering, the gently falling snow, but most of all he hated the waiting.

"Will you get on with it?!" The wizard shouted impatiently.

Bromwin gave the wizard a sideways glance, then turned up his nose and continued.

"Dear friends and loyal subjects, if by chance we do not return, do not mourn us. For if we perish, the wizard will perish with us and you shall be rid of him forever... Blessed be our land!"

"Here, here! Good toast!" cried Rumyon. "All except for the part about perishing with the wizard." The troll mumbled to himself, then raised his goblet for a drink.

The cheers went up again, and all were in good spirits; all but the ogres that grunted, the goblins that hissed and the wizard who sulked in his chair and waited.

And in the midst of all the noise, Bromwin turned to Katie.

"Child of God, we are ready...Which way do we go?"

All eyes were on the little girl, from the smallest troll to the largest ogre as Katie looked around and tried to think of where she was supposed to go, even though she didn't have a clue; and then she remembered what the bear had told her.

"What you know, you don't know you know."

It was a strange notion, but a comforting one and since she had no intention of leading them to the white horse, Katie decided she might as well act as though she did. So she sat up straight, looked out at the northern gate in the castle wall and without another thought, pointed through the falling snow.

"That way!" she said and looked up at Goe Garth aboard the great troll wagon. Then with one flick of the reigns and a crack of the whip, the mighty stallion, Juggernaut, pulled and pranced and pranced and pulled until the wagon wheels turned and the Rabble rolled forward. Soon the enormous troll wagon was moving steadily and on they went through the castle gates to the sound of cheers and waving onlookers. The ogres roared and Rogad brought his bull whip down on the backs of the wild boars that pulled and snorted and puffed clouds of steam until they were moving as well.

Jack watched the two wagons proceed ahead of them but when he looked at the front of the wizard's carriage, he was surprised to find there was nothing there at all, just the ground and empty space.

"Forward." the wizard commanded and with a wave of his hand the carriage lurched and Jack fell back, watching in stunned silence as the black coach rolled on its way and followed after the ogre wagon.

"Coooool!" Jack said and marveled at the wizard's power.

As the caravan pulled away, a great horn sounded in the distance and the bell towers of Coravandia began to ring, to signal their departure. When the wagons were well beyond the city gates, Katie could still hear the horn far off, and saw the torches along the castle walls flickering through the falling snow. In the dark, its towers loomed like gray shadows on the horizon. And just before they disappeared from view, Katie thought she could see the sparkle of emerald green and golden spires pointing into the night sky as the wizard's spell lifted and light returned to the land. A moment later Coravandia was lost in the swirling snow.

Katie drew her fur cape around her and squinted against

the icy wind on her face. They were well on their way now, and running into the cold dark night. The frosted ground stretched out in front of them like an endless carpet. Bromwin ran along side the great black stallion while the troll wagon plowed through the snow with its lanterns glowing. Just behind them the ogre's whip cracked and the boars leapt at the sound.

The ogre wagon rumbled and shook in a worrisome manner. Its front wheel wobbled badly and Rogad had been unable to hold a steady course ever since they began. The rickety wagon trailed behind, veering back and forth. At one point it went further and further in a different direction, till it was lost in the falling snow. When its torches reappeared in the dark, the tumble down old wagon drew nearer, rattling noisily, until it raced along side once more, and came so close the ogres nearly bumped wheels with the trolls. Goe Garth looked down and yelled.

"Give way!... Watch where you're going!"

The ogres shook their fists and shouted back while Rogad whipped the boars furiously, and headed off once again, towing the wobbly wagon in the wrong direction. The little fairy chased after them, but it was no use. The ogres didn't seem to care and Goe Garth flicked his reigns to put more distance between them.

Bromwin could hardly keep up and watched the Rabble disappeared in the swirling snow up ahead. Katie held on as the bear galloped through the icy mist then looked back. In the dark of night, she could see lights through the falling snow, flashes of blue and green, sparkling in the distance aboard the wizard's carriage. With a glance over his shoulder, Bromwin called to Katie.

"They are working magic." He growled.

Katie gazed at the light and tried not to be afraid for her brother.

Jack gazed at the wizard and watched his every move, eagerly awaiting his turn to try his hand at a spell.

"Alright, now your turn." said Gellzoowin.

Jack nodded then sat up and pulled back his sleeves.

"Flacto Miklemus." Jack said and threw his arms out in front of him. With a poof and a spark, a black winged imp appeared, the same devilish creature Jack had seen in his closet only now it was perched on his shoulder. Jack moved stiffly as he looked at its catlike face and could feel its boney fingers gripping his shoulder. The little creature flapped its wings in the breeze and tried to steady itself as the carriage rumbled through the darkness. Its yellow eyes darted here and there and only glanced down at Jack as it waited for its next command. In truth it seemed more interested in the falling snow than anything else. The wizard looked at Jack and simply motioned toward the creature.

"Your servant." he said with a smile.

Jack held as still as he could and waited for the wizard to give the signal. Gellzoowin nodded and Jack said the words in reverse, the same words he had uttered at the door of his closet to send the evil messenger away.

"Sumelkim Otcalf!"

With a command, the demonic little imp launched itself into the air and vanished in a puff of smoke that was swept up and away in the swirling snow behind them. Jack stared off into the night.

"Coooool!" he said and turned back to the wizard. "That's the spell you used to send me the letter."

The wizard nodded and Jack smiled.

"You were the one who spoke to me."

The wizard nodded again.

"You put the box in my closet." Jack said.

The wizard nodded once more and smiled graciously. Now that Jack was sitting in the wizard's company, in the comfort of his carriage, he decided that this was as good a time as any.

"The vaulted verses." Jack said. "What does it mean?"

Gellzoowin looked out across the dark snowy landscape.

"You're a clever boy. I thought surely you would have figured it out by now." he said and paused to let the boy think a moment, but Jack couldn't even begin to guess.

Gellzoowin shrugged. "The vault is the box and the spell is the verse. The spell in the box is the vaulted verse. It's really quite simple."

In fact, it was so simple, Jack felt foolish. He shook his head and frowned at his own stupidity and wished that he had been able to show the wizard how smart he was by figuring it out on his own.

"That's it?... You mean, that's all there is to it?" Jack said.

"How would you like to try something really fun?" Gellzoowin said.

Jack looked at the wizard suspiciously as Gellzoowin smiled and rubbed his chin.

"You seem fond of the word "cool"... perhaps you would like to try your hand at a simple freezing spell."

"A freezing spell?" Jack said. He listened to the wizard's instructions, and when it was his turn, he looked a little doubtful then uttered the strange words exactly the way he heard them. "Ex cambro... Leatee!"

With a wave of his arms, and a puff of green smoke, a real live pigeon appeared in Jack's hands. The goblins watched and shrank away from the boy, afraid of real magic in the hands of a human child. Jack wasted no time. Before the pigeon could fly away he yelled out the rest of the words Gellzoowin had spoken.

"Be Hava Keeeeen!" He said and when he did, the pigeon ceased to move and turned to solid ice before his eyes.

"Be Hava Keen! Be Hava Keeeeen!" Jack said again and again. Each time he said it, another layer of frost appeared

128

until the ice pigeon grew so cold he dropped the thing, which shattered like glass against the floor and sent the goblins scampering.

"Now that was WAY cool!" Jack yelled and shook his hands, to warm them after the frosty spell.

"Very good. That will do for now." Gellzoowin said.

Jack was so excited, he could barely sit still and rambled on and on as the carriage raced through the night. Gellzoowin pretended to listen as the boy told him about things from his world like airplanes and trains, popcorn and movies, video games, computers, basketball, baseball and night games. He even told him about cinnamon toasted crackers, his favorite snack, but it was all nonsense to the wizard who hardly paid attention. Gellzoowin did however show some interest when Jack mentioned "night games" and "stadium lighting." In his world there was no such thing as electricity or light bulbs; they used candles and oil lamps.

"Balls of light in the darkness." The wizard said and made note of the strange idea then with a wave of his hand, he commanded his magical carriage to go faster. Jack held on as their speed increased and the carriage was suddenly racing ahead through the wind and snow. In moments they had caught up to the bear. Bromwin pretended to ignore the black carriage racing along side and Katie held on as the bear picked up speed. Gellzoowin laughed and called down from his carriage.

"Is that the best you can do?... Surely you can go faster!" he said.

Bromwin ran on and tried not to look, but Katie couldn't help gazing up at the horseless carriage and the hideous little goblins glaring over the railings. They pointed at Katie and cackled like crows, while Jack sat there, cheering and laughing and having fun. Through it all, the wizard smiled down on Katie as if to say, "See, I have your brother, and just watch what I do next." She could almost hear his wicked voice taunting her and wanted to make him go away, when suddenly the wizard looked up at the sky.

The angel descended with his cloak billowing around him, and snow swirling and placed himself squarely between Katie and the wizard's carriage. Stadia glared down at Gellzoowin with eyes so bright, the wizard shielded his face and turned away.

"Bah!" Gellzoowin shouted then with another wave of his hand, he slowed his carriage and retreated into the night. Katie watched them drop further back, until they were lost in a tempest of snow. When the wizard was gone, Bromwin finally slowed his pace and looked up at the angel.

"Thank you." he said, as he galloped along, gasping for air.

Stadia turned to Katie with a stern look.

"Do not concern yourself with your brother. Fix your mind on things ahead." He said then sailed back into the sky. Katie watched him disappear in the snowy darkness above, and found it hard not to think about her brother, especially when he was in the company of an evil wizard and his wicked goblins. Katie pulled her hood snugly around her face, as the bear scampered through the snow then caught sight of the troll wagon, which had slowed its pace. When Katie looked, snow covered branches were passing over-head, a few at a time, then more and more.

"Bromwin, the trees! They're back! They're back!"

"Yes, I see them," he said, his thick legs kicking up a frosty mist as they entered the Northern Woods. Soon there were trees all around and they were traveling down a wind-ing path that was covered with a thick blanket of snow. Iced branches sparkled like crystal, as the silvery moon peeked through the trees.

A white horned deer, a snow cat and an artic wolf, watched the golden glow of lanterns and listened to the thundering hooves of the black stallion as the wagons approached. The clamor of the troll wagon filled the woods with wheels rumbling and pots banging. The great bear scampered along with Katie on his back and just behind, the ogre's whip lashed the air as the rickety old ogre wagon rattled past with giant boars snorting and squealing into the night. Lastly, there was the wizard and the boy aboard the wizard's carriage, which moved silently like a ghost ship, manned by a crew of goblins. And with it came the presence of magic. When they had passed, the woodland animals watched the glow of the torch lights fade into the distance, and were thankful when peace was restored to the woods.

With only a few hours left till day break, Katie looked to the sky and thought she could see the angel through the trees, circling high above. She thanked God for his watchfulness, and as her eyes grew heavy she laid back then pulled the cape around her and drifted off to sleep.

CHAPTER NINE

The Spirit of Living Fear

When Katie awoke it was daybreak and she was rocking gently, back and forth in her saddle chair. The
snow was gone and the smell of orange nectar filled the air
as Katie sat up to see the lush green grass all around.

"What happened? Where are we?" she asked.

Bromwin looked back and smiled.

"You'll to have to stay awake if you're going to keep up
with things." he said and turned to Stadia who was walking
next to him, draped in his long gray cloak.

"How long have I been asleep?" Katie asked.

"Several hours." the angel said and looked to Bromwin.
Katie watched them as they continued to talk in hushed
tones then turned her attention to the beautiful landscape.

Green filled the world around her. Katie never dreamt a
color could make her so happy and had missed it with all her
heart. The sunlit trees and golden hills were bathed in light,
while emerald shadows filled the valleys and streams below.

Katie threw off her cape and looked behind her. There
was the rest of the caravan, rumbling slowly through the
open field. The black stallion and the troll wagon moved

along smoothly, and then came the wild boars and the ogres. The ogre wagon still shook badly and the wobbly wheel was no better.

Just then, the fairy flew next to Katie, glittering gold.

"There's something up ahead!" she shouted.

Kitch darted away and Katie turned to see what it was as Bromwin came up over the hill then stopped and peered at the strange sight before them. The bear spoke in a whisper.

"The land of great discoveries."

Ahead of them stood a line of towering pillars that stretched across the horizon like a row of giant fence posts. Katie stared in amazement and couldn't believe what she was seeing. For although she didn't know where she was going, she had managed to lead them straight to the place they were looking for.

"Come" said the angel.

As the wagons made their way down to the flat land, the closer they got, the bigger the pillars became. The closest one was a hundred feet thick and rose into the sky till the top of the structure disappeared in the early morning mist. The wagons came to a stop and everyone gazed up in silence. The base of the giant column was covered with moss and ivy while higher up enormous symbols carved into the stone, looked like words of an ancient language. Goe Garth steadied the black horse and held the reigns tight, while Gimble sat next to him, with a puzzled look on his face.

"What do you suppose it means?" Gimble asked.

"Perhaps, a warning." Goe Garth whispered.

The next pillar was a mile away and just as big, as was the one beyond that and on and on, into the distance. Strangely, the only thing that connected them was their shadows. The sun rose in such a way that the tip of each shadow touched the base of the next column and, like a fence, seemed to mark the dark boundary of the strange land. As Katie stared at the giant pillars, she quickly got the sense that this was as far as they should go. In addition to their size, there was something very deliberate about their placement that made them seem all the more mysterious.

"What are they?" Katie asked. "Where did they come from?" she said then turned to the angel and found him staring at her blankly. Kitch and Bromwin and all the trolls were watching her as well.

"What's the matter?" she said.

No one answered.

"What is it?" Katie asked.

She could feel her heart begin to race and knew something terrible had happened. She was sure of it. Indeed, something told her it was this terrible thing that Stadia and Bromwin had been discussing when she awoke.

"The wizard and your brother are gone." the angel said plainly, and with little emotion.

With a look of panic, Katie jumped out of the saddle chair as quick as she could and slid down Bromwin's back. She landed in the wet grass and ran past the black horse. She dashed along side the troll wagon then came up on the wild boars which stirred and nipped at her on the way by. The ogres aboard the wagon barely noticed her at all and just sat there grumbling when Katie slid to a stop and stared out across the open plains. There was nothing behind the wobbly old wagon except wheel tracks. Katie whirled around, eyes wide with fear.

"Where are they?!" She cried.

"They have gone ahead." the angel said.

"But, but...but!" Katie sputtered, too upset to know what to say.

Bromwin stepped forward.

"They have reached the land of great discoveries before us and crossed the dark boundary. We suspect they dropped back sometime during the night and took another route."

"How do you know?" Katie pleaded.

"Where else would he go?" someone yelled from above. Binderbec the old soldier climbed down from the wagon and stood in front of Katie. His old armor breastplate and helmet were as gray as his beard and rattled when he walked.

"If I may be permitted, sire." he said respectfully and Bromwin nodded.

"If the angel is right," said Binderbec. "Gellzoowin has gone to lay a trap for us. Of that you can be sure. Make no mistake. The wizard's treacherous mind is at work even as we speak. It is wise that we be prepared to defend ourselves."

Gral Tibbore, the barbarian jumped from the wagon with wild hair flowing and landed next to Binderbec. The big troll held his spear ready.

"If I could get close enough, I'd pierce the wizard's heart and be rid of him forever." he sneered, jabbing his weapon in the air.

"Not so!" came a shout from atop the troll wagon. Raylin jumped down and took his place among the others standing before Katie. The little tracker stood boldly before the barbarian, with his cape swirling around him.

"You kill one wizard and another will only take his place. Evil is a persistent foe." Raylin said.

"Young pup!" Gral Tibbore scoffed. "What do you know of wizards?"

Raylin stood his ground before the larger troll and adjusted his sword.

"I was at Trokien and fought against the wizard clans. I lit the torches on the Maskun wall and met the Dardane hordes. I have seen my share of battles, barbarian."

Gral Tibbore looked the young troll up and down.

"You fought in the wizard wars?... I didn't see you there."

Raylin squared his shoulders.

"I was on the front lines. Where were you?"

Gral Tibbore growled and Bromwin stepped between the two trolls who locked eyes and prepared to cross swords.

"Save your strength. The enemy is out there."

Gral sneered then thrust his spear into the ground and drew a spark off a rock. "I'd still send the wizard to his grave if I had the chance." the barbarian growled.

The angel fixed his gaze upon the land beyond the great stone columns.

"I would not worry about that now. There will be enough to contend with before we meet the wizard again." He said.

Katie stood by as long as she could then grabbed the angel's cloak and tugged.

"Please! We have to find my brother!" she said.

Stadia looked down at her. "And ignore the dangers that lay ahead? That is exactly what the wizard would have us do."

"Yes." said Binderbec. "The angel is right. We must be cautious or it could be our undoing."

Stadia looked to the others. "Come gather round!" He said.

The bear came forward with the fairy by his side, while the rest of the trolls climbed down from the wagon and were quick to form a circle around Katie and the angel. The giant boars pranced about nervously, while Rogad and the ogres sat aboard their wagon like a pack of lazy vultures, and looked disinterested in anything the angel had to say. Stadia faced the great stone columns with Katie by his side, and pointed to the distant land.

"Listen carefully. The way ahead is filled with untold dangers. Beyond the pillars is the land of great discoveries where strange wonders abound, both good and evil. If we are to pass through this place we must do so with care."

The trolls huddled close as the angel continued.

"The giant pillars are the first of the great discoveries and mark the southern boundary of this land. They are the pillars of fear, which cast their shadow of doubt across the land."

Katie's eyes slowly trailed down the giant column to the enormous shadow and she wondered if the familiar expression "The shadow of doubt" had truly come from this strange world. The shadow itself was over a mile long and a hundred feet wide. Strangely, everything within the dark stretch of ground looked dry and desolate, as though it had been scorched by fire.

"A spirit dwells within the shadows, wicked and most dreadful." said the angel.

"A spirit? What kind of spirit?" Gimble asked with a doubtful look.

Stadia turned to the troll.

"The spirit of living fear." he said.

"The spirit of fear! The spirit of fear!" the trolls said to one another.

Rumyon peered at the shadow. "We have all heard the legend of foreboding, a spirit imprisoned in darkness that brings dread to all who walk in its shadow."

The angel continued.

"The spirit is a servant of evil, a tormentor that feeds on fear, ever thirsting but never fed. It guards this ill begotten land, trapped within this hopeless corridor." Stadia said.

Katie stared at the shadow. As far as she could tell there was nothing there.

"Is that true?" Katie asked in a whisper.

Stadia paused and gave Katie a cautious glance. "The truth is all I know." he said.

Katie looked up and smiled apologetically and had to remind herself that she was indeed talking to an angel.

"Sorry" she said and turned to the shadows once again.

"What do we do then?" Friar Jingles asked.

Bromwin looked out across the shadow to the sunlit ground on the other side.

"The wizard made it across. If that scoundrel could do it, there must be away." he growled.

"Not so fast." Stadia said. "Remember, strange wonders abound here, both good and evil. The shadows are rooted in evil and the wizard's spirit is akin to them. I suspect the forces of evil have given both him and the boy safe passage. We however, are the ones who are at risk, for we are an enemy to darkness." he said as he peered into the shadow.

A few yards away Rogad sat quietly, only flinching every once in a while as the angel spoke. The huge ogre was trying hard to concentrate, but found it difficult since another voice was talking to him at the same time, a voice inside his head. It was a familiar voice that was very insistent and wanted him to do something. It prodded at him and made him twitch. It grew louder, stronger, and more persistent until the ogre could hear nothing else. It was the wizard Gellzoowin urging him to speak.

Rogad jerked his head and blinked as he fought to control his brain. He squinted and trembled, trying to stop his lips from moving, but all the wizard had to do was push a little harder and then...

"RIIIEEES!!" Rogad bellowed like a crazed animal. Everyone jumped when the ogre stood up and roared from atop his wagon.

"Range... el, add!... Range... el... riieee!" The ogre's booming voice was garbled, and sounded like his mouth was filled with rocks. He stood with fists clenched and was obviously enraged about something but no one knew what he was saying and the other ogres just stared at him dumbly.

"What did he say?" Gimble asked as though anyone could possibly know.

Rogad snarled at the nagging voice, pounding like a drum in his head. The voice told the ogre to speak more clearly and insisted that Rogad try again. The ogre put his hands to his head, closed his eyes and strained as hard as he could to say the words exactly the way he heard them in his mind. Everyone pulled back as Rogad bellowed once more. "LIIEES!... Ange- el... bad! Ange- el... Lieeee!"

Suddenly all the other ogres were roaring and grunting, and shook their weapons in agreement. The trolls listened to hear what else the ogre would say, but Rogad was done and fell silent. The voice in his head was giving him different instructions now.

The ogre drew his long leather whip, swirled it around in the air, then brought it down over the boars with a mighty, "Crack!" The wild boars squealed and leapt forward, charging the crowd of onlookers. The fairy darted up as Bromwin jumped aside, and Goe Garth and the trolls scrambled to safety, which left Katie standing directly in the path of the wild beasts. Katie closed her eyes as the boars ran with hooves flying, ground shaking, and ogres roaring, when Stadia snatched her up and pulled her out of the way. The animals thundered past in a cloud of dust, with the rickety wagon racing full speed and rumbling straight toward the shadow of doubt; then with the boars at a dead run, the ogres bellowed and shouted as they left the trolls behind and plunged head long into the icy darkness. And as soon as the shadow swept over them, a cloud of dust appeared in the distance and came to life.

The spirit of fear rose out of the ground like a ghost from its grave, and grew till its monstrous form stood above the ground like a gnarled old tree. Its dead skin was milky white, cracked and dried like the parched earth, while its crimson eyes glowed in the dark and wisps of white hair swirled around its withered head like cobwebs. Once the creature was summoned forth, it moved like the wind, reaching out its long arms and spiny fingers, as it chased after the ogres then let go a terrifying scream.

When the white specter descended on the wagon, the wild boars squealed like they were branded with a hot iron and the ogres were filled with terror. One look in the face of living fear, and they clung to each other, crying and yelping like startled dogs, then clawed and climbed to get away from the hideous ghost as they sped across the dark and forsakened land. Then as if to save them from their torment, the old wagon mercifully bolted out of the shadows.

Once the ogres were back in the sunlight, the horrible spirit disappeared and they were free of its grasp. Still the ogres glared like madmen and the boars ran wild, for the terror was in their hearts and the fear was still with them. The ogre wagon bounded across the landscape: pots, pans and chains, jingling and banging. Soon the rickety wagon crested a hilltop, dropped out of sight and disappeared in a trail of dust. Once they were gone, all was silent and the trolls simply stared in shock until Gimble whispered.

"Did you see that?"

Their eyes were still gaping wide as they looked to the shadow of doubt which was quiet and peaceful once more.

"We have seen the enemy." said Stadia. "Such is the power of fear."

Goe Garth, the troll leader climbed back aboard the wagon and grabbed the reigns.

"Come lads. Let us see this enemy a bit closer."

"This be close enough." said Binderbec.

One by one they climbed back aboard and Goe Garth moved the wagon closer. Some of the trolls pointed at the tracks where the ogre wagon had crossed into the shadow, while others observed the objects that had fallen off in their flight. When they were only a stone's throw away Goe Garth stopped the Rabble wagon. The black stallion pawed the earth and Stadia watched as Bromwin came along side and peered into the darkness that loomed in front of them.

"I can feel it... It's there... waiting." Bromwin said.

Binderbec stared down from the wagon and squinted. "Where?...I don't see anything."

The trolls peered into the shadow, each one with hand on sword. They watched and waited for any sign but there was no movement, none at all, only the gentle breeze whistling through Binderbec's armor. Finally, the stillness grew unbearable and Gral Tibbore yelled.

"Are we just going to stand here like cowards?!" he shouted. "I say we go through. Take our chances and fight!"

Goe Garth shook his head.

"You can't fight a spirit!" he said.

Rumyon joined in.

"I say we go back!"

"We can't!" Jingles said and stepped forward. "We must go on! It is our duty."

Soon an argument started aboard the wagon. Goe Garth and Gral yelled back and forth, while Rumyon shouted at Raylin, Binderbec shook his silver hammer and Gimble and Jingles squabbled and squawked. Just then, Katie happened to notice the angel who did not concern himself with the trolls. Instead, he started toward the shadow of doubt and held his helmet by his side as he drew nearer. Katie watched him with growing concern and was about to call to him when he stopped.

The angel stood so close to the shadow of doubt, the toe of his shiny boot nearly touched the edge of the cold gray darkness. Slowly and carefully, he raised his helmet and put it on, then turned his gaze upward to the great stone column. When he looked down again, Katie wondered what he was doing, and at that exact moment the angel stepped forward. He entered the shadow of doubt so quickly and quietly, Katie had no chance to make a sound. Instead she pointed and could only stare in shock while the trolls continued to fight amongst themselves.

The darkness covered the angel instantly, as he strode across the grim, desolate landscape. Then, just like before, the spirit appeared suddenly and out of nowhere. Its pale ghostly form came swiftly, moving in and out of the shadows like a monster coming out of the deep and hurtled forward with white hair billowing and crimson eyes glowing in the dark. The evil spirit lashed out with its spindly arms, and wrapped them around the angel, like an octopus. Once it grabbed hold, hideous claws curled out of its fingertips then tore the angel's cloak and raked against his armor, casting yellow sparks in the dark. The monstrous spirit glared at the warrior of God, with eyes that were wild and insane with rage, but Stadia would not be turned aside as he marched through the shadow.

Just then, Friar Jingles cried out from atop the wagon.

"Look, the angel goes forth!" He yelled.

The trolls all stopped their bickering and gasped at the sight of the angel and the evil spirit already locked in battle. The spirit of living fear clawed and pulled till its arms were stretched, its eye bulged and its lips were twisted into a hideous snarl. Still, the mighty warrior of God moved forward with cold, grim determination. The evil spirit redoubled its efforts and called upon the shadows for help. Suddenly a wind rose up and swept across the ground like a tornado. It howled and roared, lifting dust into the air and turned the ground to shifting sand beneath the angel.

Then in the midst of the violent storm, the spirit of fear slowly dragged the angel down. With each step he took, Stadia sank beneath the surface and pulled against his captor which only drew him down faster. He sank to his waist and then his chest. And just when it seemed he would surely be swallowed up by the swirling sand and dust, the angel's wings suddenly appeared, glistening white in the howling storm. All at once they were there, beating furiously then with the power given to him by almighty God, he laid hold of the wicked spirit and pulled. Inch by inch, the angel rose up out of the dust and brought the wretched thing with him, until he had ripped the ghastly creature out of the ground, like a tree by its roots, and was moving forward once more.

The trolls watched as Stadia marched through the murky veil of darkness with the evil spirit in tow, only now the creature was screaming and fighting to break free. The angel's wings slowly disappeared as he strode forward and dragged the shrieking spirit behind him.

Jingles pointed to the angel and yelled, "Look how he holds the spirit captive!"

King Bromwin nodded. "Only an angel of God could bring fear to the spirit of fear itself."

With the edge of darkness only a few yards away, the monster grappled and gaped in horror till the very last second then disappeared into thin air as Stadia stepped into the light. In an instant, the wind died down, the storm ceased, and the spirit of fear was gone. The angel's cloak reappeared, perfectly draped around him, untouched and unharmed as everyone watched in silence. Although it was quiet once more and all was calm, there was no cause for celebration. The trolls had all seen the ogres driven mad by the spirit of fear, and now they were greatly concerned; for an angel gone mad was far more dangerous than a whole army of ogres. Stadia stood with his back to them and Katie held her breath, while the trolls held their swords and waited. They watched the angel look left and right, then reach up and remove his helmet. With that, Stadia tucked it under his arm and turned around.

"Trolls, mount up!" he said.

The angel's voice was calm and clear and the trolls all gave a sigh of relief.

"Bromwin." Stadia called out across the darkness. The bear stood tall and listened.

"As the sun rises, the shadows grow shorter. Take the child and travel the length of this shadow until you come to the end of it. There you will find a path, lit by the sun. It is at that point, you may cross over. Be sure to stay in the light and you will be protected. Once you are on this side, return to the spot where I am now, then follow the wagon trail. You will find me with the ogres."

The trolls said nothing. Like Katie, they just stared, filled with curiosity. Then Goe Garth finally cleared his throat and called out.

"Excuse me... But are you sure you're all right...quite all right that is?" he said.

Stadia smiled across at them.

"I assure you, I am fine... Now go." the angel said.

With the trolls back aboard their wagon they set out on their way and as they went, Gimble looked across to the other side. 'I wonder what happened to the ogres."

When the voice had spoken to Rogad, he never expected to be perched atop the ogre wagon, blinded by dust, horrified and on a path of destruction behind the thundering wild boars. Rogad pulled back on the reigns which snapped in his hands and plunged the wagon out of control. The wheels rumbled and banged over rocks and stumps, till it seemed everything would come apart. With a jolt, two of the ogres were thrown overboard. One was enormous and waved his blubbery arms in huge circles while the other was Zarq who sailed through the air, with a silly grin on his face. Zarq hit the ground first, bounced once then twice and had all but escaped serious injury when the big ogre came down with his fat rump, and plowed Zarq's head into the ground like a dirt pancake.

Down the hill, the wagon twisted and bounded with ogres screaming, wood and metal screeching and skidding. It was then that the wobbly wheel chose that moment to come loose and fly off. Without the wheel to hold it up, the front axle dropped, and stuck in the ground like a dart which sent the back of the wagon flying.

Every object, large and small, was instantly launched

into the air, boars, chains, ogres, and all. The wagon flipped end over end, spinning like a pin wheel until it plowed into the ground with a horrible explosion and smashed to pieces. Rogad was among the last to come down. The monstrous ogre flapped his hairy arms wildly, and wished with all his heart that he was just a little fairy floating on the breeze, but unfortunately he was over five hundred pounds and flew about as well as a refrigerator filled with bricks. Other things were falling as well, a wooden chair, sacks of grain, and a large iron kettle. Rogad listened for the voice of the wizard, but now that he was nearing the ground, there was only the wind whistling in his ears. And with the world rushing up to meet him, Rogad simply closed his eyes and tried not to look when he slammed into the granite boulder jutting out of the grassy hillside. The ogre crunched into the rock and stuck to it like a bug on a windshield then slid down, scraping his face against the cold hard surface. As Rogad lay there, he knew he had hurt something. The truth was he had hurt everything. The only thing that didn't hurt was the back of his head, and then...

"CLANG!"

The big iron kettle came crashing down and cracked him right on the spot. A nasty lump rose up where the pot had bounced off and now everything did indeed hurt. Rogad hugged the big rock and tried to lay still. All things considered he was glad not to be flying and wished the wizard hadn't caused him so much pain. Then just before the ogre passed out he mumbled something, five little words muttered with his face still smushed into the rock.

"...Wizard bad... wizard... very bad."

Bromwin walked behind the troll wagon and Katie rode on his back, never taking her eyes off of the long dark shadow that loomed to their right. Although she couldn't see it, the spirit of fear was near and drew ever closer, attracted by the golden glow of her precious innocence.

At one point Katie thought she glimpsed something, a smoky mist moving in the shadows, then an eye, a cold gray gristly thing peering at her from out of the dark.

The creature emerged silently, and Katie shrank back when Bromwin saw the ghost and roared.

"Don't look at it!" he said, but Katie couldn't resist. The bear roared once more.

"Don't look! Don't look!" Bromwin said, then stopped in his tracks and turned his back to the creature. But no matter which way he went Katie spun around in her chair to see the evil spirit that grew larger and larger, as it loomed toward them.

When the trolls looked back, Goe Garth finally stopped the wagon, and watched in horror as the spirit of fear stood at the edge of the shadow and a long white spindly arm slipped out of the darkness and reached into the light.

"Dear Lord!" Rumyon shouted. "It's after the child!"

"I...I thought it was supposed to stay in the shadows. What do we do now!?" Gimble yelled.

The spirit cried out with an ear piercing scream as the bright hot sunlight seared its ghostly flesh, which bubbled and boiled while its big knuckled fingers pawed the air and beckoned Katie to come closer. All the while, the spirit gained more strength from the fear of those around it and fought to resist the sunlight. Its horrible arm stretched longer and longer like a thick slithering vine, till it was nearly twelve feet long and drew ever closer to the child.

The trolls watched aboard the wagon and Gimble grabbed the railing.

"Run! Don't just stand there!" He cried.

Binderbec held the troll and pulled him back.

"For goodness sake, man! Control yourself!" he said, then with another look, the old soldier leaned over the side and cried out. "RUN FER' YE' LIIIIFE!!"

With that, the good friar Jingles leapt from the wagon, like a nimble sprite, with his troll sack slung over his shoulder then hit the ground running

"Get the wagon out of here. GO!!" He said and waved them off.

Goe Garth lashed the reigns and the wagon lurched forward while the others watched and Jingles ran to face the monster.

CHAPTER TEN

Chaos

*B*romwin could barely move as the evil spirit held him in a trance and reached for the child, its long hideous arm burning in the sunlight. Katie could hear its skin sizzle and pop, and watched in horror as its hand crept ever closer then opened wide and slid toward her neck when suddenly the little troll leapt in front of her.

"HOLD!" Jingles cried out in a loud voice, then reached inside his troll sack and pulled out a huge leather bound book. With that as his only weapon, he held it up in front of him like a shield and stood boldly before the spirit of fear.

"Foul creature! In the name of our Lord, the bright and Morning Star, I bid thee depart!" he yelled. "Be gone wicked spirit, or suffer the wrath of God!" he shouted.

The spirit's eyes blazed from within the shadow of doubt. Now that it had been challenged, it grew even larger and Jingles could see it more clearly. The lower part of the monstrous spirit was still vapor and floated on air like smoke, while the rest of it loomed above them in the dark with its gnarled and smoldering limb still dangling in the light.

"BE GONE!" Jingles commanded as the book began to glow and grew brighter, until it shone like a lantern in his arms. When the beast cast its eyes upon the light, it shuddered and the arm drew back, quick as a whip. Then all at once, the spirit disappeared and retreated into the depths of the shadows. Katie stared from atop her saddle chair, while Bromwin looked back and forth to see where the monster had gone. The two were still peering into the shadow of doubt when the little fairy flashed before of them.

"Look away! Look away!" Kitch shouted. "Both of you. Keep your eyes to the ground and don't look up again!" she said, wagging her tiny finger at Katie and the bear. The fairy turned to the trolls aboard the wagon.

"You too!" She yelled and that was all she needed to say.

Friar Jingles stood next to the bear with the book cradled in his arms. Slowly the light subsided and the book returned to its normal appearance.

"Thank you, good friar. You saved our lives." said Bromwin.

Jingles gave a brief smile and kept his eyes on the shadows.

"It is the power of the Lord the creature fears, not me." he said.

"Thank you." said Katie, still trembling.

The little troll watched the shadows. "We'd best be on our way."

"Quite right, quite right." said Bromwin.

The bear lowered his head and led the way, with Jingles along side and the troll wagon just behind them. They moved quickly, keeping the long shadow to their right and their eyes to the ground so that the evil spirit could no longer frighten them. After a while they came upon the next pillar towering into the sky.

"Look there!" Raylin shouted from his crow's nest, high atop the troll wagon.

Up ahead, near the base of the pillar was a path, a clear patch of sunlit grass that led across to the land of great discoveries. It sparkled brightly with morning dew and was just as the angel had promised. As the sun rose higher, the shadow of doubt was indeed growing shorter, and the dry barren ground it covered, was miraculously restored with thick green grass. But just as they prepared to cross over, the spirit of fear returned with white hair billowing and its wretched face twisted into a hideous grin. It rose above them as big as a tree and swayed in the darkness, moving back and forth, daring anyone to cross the sunlit path.

Gral Tibbore wasted no time and grabbed his trusty spear. The barbarian jumped from the wagon then drew his sword and sneered at the spirit of fear as he plodded across the sun drenched earth, and when he had reached the other side Gral jabbed his spear into the ground.

"Hah, vile spirit! Where is your power? Come into the light and fight me!" the barbarian shouted, brandishing his sword at the wretched creature, but the spirit remained silent and only turned to watch the others who started across.

Kitch fluttered past with wings sparkling, then came Bromwin and Katie who did their best not to look. The black stallion pulled the wagon slowly with the trolls gaping silently at the ghost that lurked in the dark. Once they were all across, Rumyon mustered his nerve then pointed and jeered at the ghastly spirit, floating before them.

"HAH!...What's this?! A dirty dishrag?... Who left their soddy laundry hanging on the line?"

Raylin and Gral Tibbore laughed and waved their arms till the trolls all joined in raucous laughter, whooping and hollering to show their bravery and make fun of the ghoulish ghost. Soon all of their fear was gone and as the sounds of joy filled the air, the horrible spirit began to shrink away, further and further until it was little more than a pathetic wisp of vapor. But just before it disappeared and sank beneath the ground, there came a frightful noise from out of the shadows.

"Yoooouuu'll beeeee saaaahhh-reeeeee!" the evil spirit hissed, then vanished.

With those haunting words, the trolls fell silent, and looked at each other. Slowly, one by one, their smiles returned and Rumyon raised his bottle for a toast.

"Lads! We have looked fear in the face and it has fled! What finer band of trolls have filled a flagon and hailed a toast to drink?!"

Binderbec raised his cup and shouted. "Aye, we fine lads stood toe to toe and chased it from the brink!"

"Here, here!" cried Rumyon. "A good toast and a good rhyme!"

While the trolls celebrated, Katie turned her attention to the base of the great stone pillar that rose into the sky before them. It was as big as the one they had left behind and the top of it was lost in the clouds. Once again, Katie marveled at the sheer size of it, as the tiny fairy fluttered around then landed on her shoulder. "What's the matter?" Kitch asked.

Katie just stared and took a while to answer.

"...It's so, big!" she said.

Kitch laughed.

"Oh that. Everything is big to me. You get used to it after a while."

Katie squinted up into the sky.

"I wonder who made them." she asked.

Kitch gave Katie a curious look as though it was a ridiculous question.

"Who made them?... Why, the giants of course. Who else?" Kitch said then darted away.

"The giants?" Katie said in a gasp. Just the mere mention of the word made her heart beat faster. With everything that had happened, Katie had forgotten where she was and wished the little fairy had not reminded her that the land of great discoveries was indeed known as the land of the giants.

"Giants," Katie thought. "Surely not real giants, how big could they be?... This is all his fault." Katie thought and wondered how she had let the wizard trick her into such a thing. What she had told him, she had simply made up, yet here she was. Then a frightening thought occurred to her. What if everything else she had told the wizard was true as well? She struggled to search her mind and remember the silly little story she had told him, when the bear suddenly called out.

"Come lads. We must find the angel."

Goe Garth nodded and with a gentle flick of the reigns, they started back the way they had come; only now they were on the other side of the shadow of doubt. The bear trotted at an easy pace then glanced up at Katie, as a gentle breeze blew across the quiet landscape.

"Peaceful isn't it?"

Katie was still trying to remember what she had told the wizard when she looked down at the bear.

"I'm sorry...What did you say?"

"Everything is so peaceful." Bromwin said.

Katie took a moment to look around.

"Yes, it is."

"It's those ungodly beasts." The bear replied.

Katie had no idea what that meant, but Bromwin was never one to leave a thought unfinished.

"The ogres." Bromwin grumbled as he trotted along behind the troll wagon. "They are nothing but trouble. We're better off without them."

When Katie stopped to think she had to agree, things were generally nicer without the ogres, but aside from a healthy fear of giants, the only thing she happened to care about at the moment was finding her brother. Minutes later they reached the tracks of the ogre wagon that went straight through the shadow of doubt, then trailed past them and went up over the rise in the distance. Goe Garth clicked his teeth then flicked the reigns again.

"That way." He said.

Bromwin watched the troll wagon trundle on its way then shook his head in disgust. "Treacherous monsters." he growled.

Kitch hovered just above. "Indeed! To be rid of the ogres is our gain. Don't you think?" she said looking down at Katie.

Katie shrugged. "I don't know... I guess so."

"Oh, now don't you waste your cares upon them, my dear. They have no concern for life. Not yours, mine or even their own." She said fluttering aloft with her hands on her hips.

Katie remembered how the ogres loaded the chains onto their wagon and grinned at the prospect of capturing Majesty. It was easy to hate them when they acted like monsters, but the last time she saw them, they were screaming like a bunch of frightened children and Katie couldn't help feeling sorry for them.

The bear made his way slowly, grunting and huffing every time they came upon an object that had been thrown from the ogre wagon, a wooden crate, "Humph!"; a sack of grain, "Ha-rumph!" Katie watched the way ahead while the bear grumbled and growled as they came up behind the troll wagon and the little troll Raylin signaled down to them. He waved then put his finger to his lips. "Shhhhh!" he said then pointed over the hillside.

Bromwin stopped then lifted his head to hear the sound of distant weapons clashing and Goe Garth shouted. "Come lads! We must join the fight."

The black horse leapt forward and Bromwin turned to Katie.

"Don't worry. No harm will come to you. Just stay aboard my back." he said then galloped after the wagon.

Katie held on as the ground rose steeply ahead and tried to be brave as Bromwin made his way up the hill, then once they reached the top she stared down at the sheer insanity that was going on below. The place where the ogres had crashed was a total disaster, as was their wagon which was smashed to bits.

The wild boars were still harnessed together, and stood under a tree off to the side with their leather reigns tangled in the branches. They snorted and grunted, swinging their heads to and fro, trying to break free while the ogres stood a ways off roaring like wild animals. There on the field of battle, the burly beasts wielded their clubs and axes, and surrounded the angel with his shimmering sword.

It was the first time Katie had seen the angelic blade drawn from its sheath, a blade forged in Heaven, the sword of the spirit, the sword of Raymah. The weapon shone bright, glistening like water and caused the ogres to shield their eyes as their old rusted axes clanged against the awesome blade and rang out like hammers against an anvil.

"Plang!... P-ting!... Clang!"

The blows rained down and sparked like white flares while up on the hill, Bromwin made his way through all the debris, when he stepped in a wooden bucket and got his paw stuck. Katie held on as the bear shook his hind leg and stumbled around, trying to free himself.

Down below, the battle raged on as the ogres lunged to the attack. Stadia met each blow with his sword pointed down and smiled as though it were all good sport. The ogres roared, heaving their huge clubs and axes in great circles and with one swipe Stadia cut Rogad's club in half. The ogre glared at the nub of wood in his hand then picked up a huge stone, and hurled it at the angel. With another slash, Stadia split the rock in two which hit the ogres on either side like a slingshot to the head. The beasts staggered back, reeling from the blow then dropped their weapons and fell face down in the dirt.

Another ogre roared and brought his axe down as the angel slashed upward and with one deft stroke the axe head was severed from its handle. The huge rusted blade went twirling through the air while the ogre stared at the wooden handle like a child whose ice cream had just fallen off the cone. The wild boars squealed and bolted when the axe head hit the tree and cut their reigns. With the boars set free, two more ogres dropped their weapons and chased after the animals, since the boars were good to eat and a hungry ogre never let a good meal get away.

Up on the hillside, Bromwin hopped around with Katie on his back and kicked his leg until the bucket finally flew off then charged down the hill. Thinking he had arrived just in time the brave bear watched as one by one the trolls lowered their weapons and smiled. The ogres had grown weary and the angel would make quick work of them. The four remaining beasts heaved their clubs and swung their axes until they stumbled about and could barely stand. Then with one last roar they fell forward as Stadia stepped aside and buried their weapons in the dirt. Katie watched then blinked when a hot spark leapt from the angel's blade and lit the ogres' pants on fire. With a hoot and a howl the beasts ran off, fanning the flames behind them, and trailing smoke in a hasty retreat.

Binderbec the old soldier jumped forward, brandishing his little sword.

"Brigands!" he yelled as they went. "May ye britches burn bright and ever light the way behind ye!"

The trolls all laughed then clapped their backs and slapped their bellies.

"Well done! Well done!" Goe Garth shouted.

"Well done, indeed." said Raylin.

The little fairy flew to the angel, full of excitement.

"Teach me how to do that!" she said.

Stadia only smiled as the trolls gathered around and marveled at his sword.

"A blade as bright as crystal" Goe Garth said and stared in wonder.

Stadia allowed them to admire the sword a little longer then slid it gently into its sheath, and drew his cloak around him. When the sword was gone they all turned to look at the horrible wreckage strewn around them. What was left of the ogre wagon was scattered over the hillside and littered the ground like so much trash. Katie was about to say something when Goe Garth yelled out.

"Step alive!" The troll leader shouted. "Don't just stand there. Let's get to work!"

The trolls were suddenly a blur of activity as they set about their task. They gathered the ogres' supplies, organized the crates, stacked the barrels, bundled and mended the sacks of grain and when everything was neat and tidy, they set about to repair the wagon. They measured, sawed and hammered. They polished things up and tightened things down and when Katie looked again, not only had the wobbly wheel been replaced, but the ogres had a fine and sturdy wagon, that was better than new. Even the angel had to smile. And as soon as they were done, Goe Garth called to his men.

"Gral, Raylin, Binderbec, go out and fetch the ogres. Bring them back if you can."

The trolls nodded and just as they were about to leave, something appeared in their midst. At first it stood there unnoticed, but now all it did was draw attention to itself.

The little creature hopped past the bear that took a few steps back and growled. The trolls, the fairy and the angel all watched in silence.

It was a little white rabbit that had arrived unannounced. On it were strange markings that shone brightly as though the animal were lit from within. Brilliant neon lines formed letters on its side that disappeared only to reappear and change colors again and again. The rabbit stood in their midst, blinking and flashing like a billboard, as its multicolored fur spelt out the words, "NO BABIES ALLOWED!" It was plain for all to see. The words meant nothing to the trolls or the bear, but Katie stared in amazement and watched the absurd little creature which sniffed the air and continued on its way. The rabbit ignored everyone as it flashed on and off then hop, hop, hop, and "Poof!" it was gone in a cloud of red smoke.

Binderbec came forward and coughed. "The foul smell of sulfur!" He said, waving his hands through the smoke then frowned at the spot where the rabbit had disappeared. "No babies? Preposterous! What does it mean?"

Katie climbed down from Bromwin's back and before the smoke could clear she heard the sound of laughter, a soft smug chuckling that came from behind them. The trolls drew their swords and turned to see the boy wizard standing there with his arms folded.

"Jack," Katie said with surprise. "I knew it was you!"

Jack arched an eyebrow and approached with a clever smirk, trying his best to look cunning like the wizard when Bromwin suddenly roared.

"GRRRAAAARRRR!!"

Jack jump back and threw his arms out in front of him, fully expecting the bear to attack. But when Bromwin only glared at him and stood his ground, the boy did his best to assume a more relaxed position and tried not to look absolutely flustered.

"Jack, your eyes," Katie said in a gasp. "They're blue!"

Jack turned to his sister. "You like'em? It's just a little trick I learned." he said boastfully as he walked through the crowd of trolls, careful to keep his distance from the bear.

"You think that's something? Check this out!" he said and raised his arms. Katie watched as he mumbled something under his breath, and the air stirred around him. Suddenly two more arms sprouted from Jack's robe and jutted out of his sides.

"TAH-DAH!!" he yelled and raised his arms, all four of them. His normal arms were still draped in the sleeves of his robe while his two new arms were completely bare up to the shoulders. Jack waved all of his arms around and Katie pulled back in horror. "GRRRRRAAAARRRR!!"

The great bear roared again and leapt forward. Jack jumped back and was so afraid, his magical arms disappeared instantly as he staggered away and nearly tripped over his own feet. Bromwin bared his fangs and snarled as Katie hugged his neck and held him tight. When Jack saw that his sister seemed to have control of the animal he spoke a little bolder.

"What's the matter with him?" he asked.

"He doesn't like magic, Jack. And neither do I."

"Thanks for the warning." Jack said then glanced around and could feel the trolls watching him with contempt. Gral Tibbore and Raylin remembered the wizard wars and the vicious young apprentices who led the battle, eager to impress their masters. They held their swords ready and watched the boy's every move as the angel came forward.

"Where have you been? Where is the wizard?" Stadia asked.

Jack folded his arms and looked up at the angel with a cocky smirk.

"Relax. Everything's fine." he said with a wink.

"I asked you a question." the angel said firmly. The power of his voice made Jack stand a little straighter, and since there was no wizard to protect him, he decided to answer the question. Jack told them everything. He told them how they had crossed through the shadow of doubt in the light of the full moon. He told them about the wizard's maps and his knowledge of the various legends that surround the strange land.

"It's like he knows everything. Once we crossed the border Gellzoowin took the goblins and sent me back. He even told me where to find you. And guess what? You're exactly where he said you'd be."

Bromwin came forward and could no longer contain himself.

"You are so filled with evil you boast of it. Have you no shame?" Bromwin growled.

Jack scowled and looked at the bear in resentment.

"I am not evil!" he yelled. "What do you know anyway?!"

Bromwin locked eyes with the boy and Jack instantly knew he had made a mistake as the bear came forward.

"What do I know?" Bromwin growled. "I will tell you what I know. I know you have been taught by the wizard Gellzoowin and you study the black arts. I know you passed through the shadow of doubt unharmed by the evil spirit that dwells within it. Tell me young apprentice, how can that be?"

The bear let the question linger. Jack blinked and thought for a moment.

"Spare your feeble mind and I will tell you. The shadow of doubt is evil and only a being who is akin to evil can escape its harm. You stand before us untouched, living proof that evil has found a place in your heart. The least you can do is admit it." The bear said then turned and walked away.

Jack hardly knew what to say and struggled to think of something.

"That doesn't prove anything!" he shouted.

The bear paused to glance over his shoulder.

"A brilliant defense." he grumbled.

"Where is the wizard now?" Stadia asked again.

Jack glared at the bear then turned to the angel and could scarcely hold back the tears. He stood there, arms folded, stewing over the bear's tongue lashing and when he was utterly fed up, he finally had to confess.

"He's with the giants." Jack said with a disgusted look on his face.

The trolls gasped, the fairy's glow went dim and Bromwin stopped in his tracks. The tide had shifted with a word and now they looked at Jack in fear.

"He told me to give you a message." Jack said as a smile crept across his face.

"What is this message?" Stadia asked.

Jack took his time. He let the wind howl through the trees and picked a bit of nothing from the sleeve of his robe. He pretended to ignore the bear and only glanced at the trolls who waited anxiously. When he was ready Jack looked up at the angel.

"He said to tell you, that you are about to meet your match." Jack sneered, his voice filled with loathing.

The fairy's eyes grew wide as she backed away from the wizard's apprentice.

"What have you done?" she gasped.

CHAPTER ELEVEN

The Thunder Cane

*T*he wizard sent the boy to deliver his message, unaware that he too would have to abandon his carriage before long. Soon the ground had become so rough and wild with vegetation, the wizard and his goblins had no choice but to continue on foot in the dead of night.

The war goblins were quick to arm themselves. Each one grabbed a dragon spear, stored in the undercarriage of the wagon. The seven foot lances were razor sharp, forged from black iron ore. Then with weapons in hand they marched into the darkness and followed the wizard into the Thunderland Forest, the forest of the giants where everything was big.

They had walked for hours, with only the stars and a faded old map to guide them, when Gellzoowin wondered if he might not be lost. It wasn't until daybreak when they came upon an apple laying on the ground that the wizard knew he was indeed going the right way. The shiny red apple was as big as a briar bush, and the worm that was wrapped around its base, was thirty feet long and thick as a serpent.

The seven goblins followed the wizard and eyed the

great worm with caution as they passed by. Numlock, was careful to stay close to the wizard, and held his spear ready to lash out at anything that looked peculiar or threatening. But since everything in the Thunderland forest was both peculiar and threatening, he was constantly pointing his spear at one thing or another. Indeed, the giant woods were filled with animals that could swallow a goblin whole and Numlock trembled at the thought.

Gellzoowin however was not the slightest bit afraid. In fact, the wizard seemed quite at ease as he walked through the giant forest, and went on his way as though it were merely a stroll in the park. This was because of the message the wizard had sent to all of the creatures within the woods. It was more of a warning, given with his mind, the same way he had spoken to the ogre. It said, "The great and all power-ful wizard Gellzoowin is coming and if you don't want to be eaten you'd better hide... if you know what's good for you."

The animals, for the most part, did what they were told and stayed out of sight. However, there were certain kinds of creatures that were too simple minded to understand any kind of message at all, even one given by an all powerful wizard; creatures like birds and insects that lived to hunt and eat. But Gellzoowin didn't seem to mind as he marched ahead.

The goblins followed close behind and Numlock looked back ever so often, to see how the war goblins were pro-gressing. They had begun the journey huddled together grumbling and complaining, but as the walk grew longer, the goblins straggled behind, marching in single file, until they were strung out along the path and there was considerable distance between each of them. At last count there were six goblins, but when Numlock looked back he only saw five.

Unfortunately, no one noticed the little gray field mouse that had been following them for the last mile. Normally a mouse would have been nothing to fear, but this was a Thunderland mouse, a giant mouse of the giant woods, a mouse as big as a bear. Still it was very quiet as it crept ever closer to the goblin that was trailing behind all the others. Then when the time was right the mouse moved, quick as a wink, and the goblin disappeared without a sound. The others marched on, rustling through the grass and no one noticed that they were now minus one.

Then there was the garden snake that blended into the dirt so well, the wizard and the goblins strolled right over its head, without a care or even a glance downward. The giant snake waited for the wizard to go by and once the wizard was gone, its yellow eye peered up out of the dirt and watched the goblins one by one. Then just as the last one marched by, the hungry snake opened its mouth, and snatched the goblin off the trail while the others kept right on going... minus two.

Up ahead, a spotted lizard hung from a vine. It watched the group walking below and when the wizard was well out of sight, it dropped on a goblin as it passed underneath then dragged the little morsel into a hole. Now the group... was minus three.

A fuzzy tailed squirrel, a tree frog, and a snapping turtle all claimed a goblin, and managed to do it without challenging the wizard's command for none of them had attacked the wizard himself. When Numlock finally looked back, there was no one left. The goblin stopped and stared in horror.

"Master, master!" he cried.

Gellzoowin paused to cast a lazy glance over his shoulder.

"What now?" The wizard groaned, as though the goblin had been a nuisance, when in truth the creature hadn't uttered a word for miles. Numlock thrust his boney finger at the path behind them.

"LOOK!" he shouted. "They're gone!"

Gellzoowin looked at the empty trail and raised an eyebrow.

"Oh, dear." he sighed, sounding more tired than upset.

Numlock had hoped for more of a reaction than that,

and tried not to look absolutely terrified when a huge shadow swept over them. His eyes darted up and Numlock trembled as Gellzoowin shook his head.

"There is always one who must test the power and be made an example." he said, sounding a bit annoyed.

The bird that circled high above was a common every-day sparrow; however this particular sparrow was the size of a small airplane. It had caught sight of the little green goblin and the sparkly bronze coated thing with the furry collar moving along the ground. The sparrow meant no harm. Like most sparrows, it was merely hungry and looking for food. Unfortunately the bird didn't understand that the little sparkly brown coated thing, next to the goblin, was indeed a tiny wizard. It did happen to think, however, that whatever it was, looked a lot tastier than the worm it had eaten, on the trail a ways back, and that was reason enough to attack.

Numlock raised his dragon spear as he stared at the winged monster circling in the sky then felt his legs go weak when the giant bird folded its wings and dove down, headed straight for them. It whistled through the air as it picked up speed, its shadow growing larger and larger. And just before it struck, the bird let out an ear piercing, "Shrieeek!"

Numlock fell to the ground, screaming in terror then with one swipe of his hand, Gellzoowin grabbed the goblin's spear. The wizard narrowed his eyes as the bird dropped out of the sky like a meteor, then muttered a spell and raised the weapon above him. Numlock never recounted exactly what happened next because his eyes were shut. Still he knew what should have happened and couldn't understand why he wasn't dead.

What the giant bird had intended was to reach out and pluck the wizard off the ground. Instead the bird burst into flames, shrank all the way down to the size of a normal sparrow, then dropped out of the sky, cooked to a golden brown, steaming hot and landed on the head of the dragon spear, ready to be eaten. Gellzoowin had warned the giant animals and in a split second, he had made good on his promise.

The wizard eyed the tender morsel, then plucked the little cooked sparrow from the tip of the spear and popped it into his mouth. He savored the flavor as he crunched on its bones, then spit out the beak and swallowed the rest of the bird in one gulp. The poor unfortunate creature was more of a snack than a meal, but Gellzoowin enjoyed it nonetheless.

"Not bad... a little salty." he said, smacking his lips like a chef tasting the soup. With that, the wizard handed the spear back to the goblin and continued on his way.

"Come along and don't dawdle. I shouldn't have you disappearing on me as well." Gellzoowin said. Since that was as much sympathy as Numlock could expect, the goblin climbed to his feet and chased after the wizard.

The goblin stayed on the wizard's heels for several miles as giant eyes watched them from the bushes. Numlock trembled as he cowered behind Gellzoowin and followed so closely that he stumbled into the back of the wizard when he came to a stop. But before the goblin could plead for his life, the wizard reached down, grabbed him by the scruff of the neck and yanked him into the air. Numlock looked down in horror and did his best to hold on as the ground trailed away beneath him and up and up they went.

"We have come thus far on foot." Said Gellzoowin. "Now we take to the air."

The wizard and the goblin flew through the low lying branches of the giant trees, fifty feet above the ground, and Numlock was just starting to get used to it when there came a rumbling far off, the sound of distant thunder. The wizard laughed aloud and the goblin trembled.

"HAH! We're in luck!" Gellzoowin shouted. "Tis the heart of the Thunderland forest, and my prize... the Thunder tree!"

The goblin dangled helplessly, still armed with his dragon

spear. "The Thunder tree, master?" he asked as Gellzoowin gazed ahead.

"Aye, the tree that lays at the center of the giant woods, a tree bigger and taller than all the rest, so big its branches touch the clouds and summons the thunder; the tree that possesses the power of lightning itself!" Gellzoowin said still peering ahead.

"We must be close!" he shouted when suddenly they began to drop. Numlock cringed and grabbed the wizard's arm.

"We're going down!" the goblin screamed.

"You Fool!" yelled the wizard." The spell is wearing off and you're too heavy!"

Numlock looked up, shocked at the notion that this was somehow all his fault.

"But you're the one who picked me up!" cried the goblin.

It was the wrong tone of voice to talk with the wizard, but Numlock did have a point, so Gellzoowin let him go.

"SAAAAH-RREEEEEE!" the goblin screamed as he plummeted like a rock and crashed to the ground in a heap.

Without the goblin's added weight Gellzoowin floated like a leaf on the wind and landed quite gently. When he was back on the ground, the wizard straightened his robe, and glanced over at Numlock who stood up rather stiffly. The goblin knew better than to say anything about nearly being killed and merely dusted himself off, then grabbed his spear and looked around suspiciously.

"Tis darker here." Numlock said which was more than obvious.

Gellzoowin raised an eyebrow. The goblin's limited powers of perception never ceased to amaze him. Still Numlock was right. Now that they were back in the giant woods it was almost as dark as night. Gellzoowin looked up through the trees and peered higher and higher until he saw the great tree towering above them in the distance. They were standing in the shadow of the Thunder Tree and the wizard shouted.

"There you are!" he said and started off again on foot.

Numlock was about to follow when he caught the scent of something. The goblin sniffed and sniffed, and just when he thought he was imaging it, he heard something stir in the woods nearby then whirled around and thrust his spear in front of him, glaring into the bushes.

"Numlock!" Gellzoowin called.

The goblin jumped at the sound of his name and chased after the wizard, but couldn't help glancing back as he went. For, even though he didn't see anything, his goblin senses told him, they were not alone.

With another hour's walk they came to what looked like the edge of the giant woods, and the wizard stared in wonder. The Thunder Tree stood high above, reaching up to the clouds, while ahead of them stretched a sea of dead leaves, a mile wide, that surrounded the giant tree trunk. The goblin suspected any number of terrible creatures could be living underneath the leafy blanket, but Gellzoowin was unafraid and plodded onward, wading into the thick dense brush, determined to reach the tree. With each step he sank deeper and deeper until he was up to his waist in dead leaves, and moving steadily forward. Numlock followed with his spear overhead, and stayed on the tips of his toes then jabbed the weapon down, here and there, to keep anything away that might attack from below.

When they had made it across, Gellzoowin marched out of the dry crackling leaves and stood at the base of the Thunder Tree. A few seconds later, Numlock emerged gasping and out of breath, with his spear in hand and eyes bulging wide.

"Master, master!" he said, pointing his spear at the leaves behind them. But the wizard only gazed up at the mammoth tree truck that stretched out like a gigantic wall before him, and towered into the air. Its monstrous branches and leafy canopy stood a mile above, and everything in its shadow was cast into darkness.

Gellzoowin watched in awe then reached out and slid his fingers along the cold, hard surface of the thunder tree, feeling every tiny bump and crease. And when he held still, he thought he felt something. In truth, the tree seemed to be humming, as though filled with some sort of energy then just when the thought occurred to him the sky lit up with a flash. The roar of thunder shook the ground and in the twinkling of an eye, the giant tree was struck by lightning. With a loud "Crack!" it absorbed the electricity, drew the surge down through its massive trunk, then flew into the wizard's hand and blew Gellzoowin right off of his feet.

The wizard flew through the air then crashed to the ground in a cloud of dust. Numlock stared dumbly as the wizard lay on the ground, gazing up at the sky with smoke curling from his lips. When he finally stirred, Gellzoowin sat up slowly then shook his head and noticed that he had been literally blown out of his pointy black shoes which were still standing at the base of the Thunder Tree.

Gellzoowin gathered himself and did his best to stand then staggered forward, with his head reeling and toes tingling, and glared at the tree. As he stood there, Numlock looked out across the sea of leaves and was sure he saw something move.

"Master!" he said.

"Not now." Gellzoowin grumbled and brushed the goblin aside. "I'll have to be more careful," he muttered angrily as he recovered his shoes and gave the tree a long hard stare. "So you would withhold from me that which I seek." the wizard said. "Well, we shall see."

Numlock watched as the wizard raised his hands and conjured up a cloud of mist that floated in the air in front of him. With a few magic words, the thick white haze slowly took shape and the wizard gazed upon the long handled axe, magically suspended in mid air. When the spell was complete, Gellzoowin reached out and held it very gently, as though he were lifting it off of a mantelpiece then marveled at the finely honed blade.

"Ah yes, this will do nicely." The wizard said.

In spite of the present danger, the goblin took a moment to observe the wizard and his axe. Although Gellzoowin was very powerful and the weapon was truly spawned out of magic, the wizard was still a ridiculous sight, standing there next the giant tree. The Thunder Tree was a monstrous thing, nearly a half mile thick and could never be chopped down by the wizard, not by himself, not in a hundred lifetimes.

The goblin watched as Gellzoowin reached out with his axe and measured the distance. Then with his feet planted, he took a firm grip on the handle and just when he was about to raise the axe into the air, the wizard froze and stood still, trying to listen. Numlock heard it too. It was a strange sound, like the sound of leaves rustling. When Gellzoowin looked, the leaves were not only moving in the distance, there was a wave coming toward them, as something big approached beneath the surface. Without a moment to lose Gellzoowin raised his axe and took a dangerous swipe downward, a glancing blow along the side of the tree.

The magical blade hit with a spark and sent a giant splinter of wood, eight feet long, flying into the air. The object arced overhead then came down like a javelin, and stuck in the ground at the goblin's feet. Numlock staggered back and Gellzoowin dropped the axe, his eyes staring wildly as he rushed forward and plucked the wooden shaft out of the ground. He had only hoped for a small piece of the tree bark, perhaps a tiny sliver that he could fashion into a wand. But this was a gift far greater than he had imagined. The wizard gazed at the length of wood; and in his hands, the long blackened splinter of the Thunder Tree, looked like a wizard's staff.

Gellzoowin glanced down to see the goblin with his eyes fixed on the ocean of leaves and the wave that was rushing straight toward them. Numlock steadied himself then pointed his spear at the deep underbrush and tried to prepare himself for whatever was about to emerge. Then without any warning, a giant ant crawled out and stared at them with its bulbous black eyes and hairy antennas twitching. The ant was the size of a large dog and its hard shell glistened red in the dim light. The creature stood still and seemed to be waiting for something. Suddenly another ant emerged behind it, then another. Both were bigger than the first. The wizard and the goblin slowly backed away as dozens more came forth, and poured out of the leaves like oil beneath the ground.

First fifty then a hundred, then two hundred of the monstrous creatures crawled out of the leaves and still they came. These were giant fire ants, the most common of all creatures in the forest. And like the robin, their tiny brains were not clever enough to heed the wizard's warning. Numlock gasped at their overwhelming number and looked for somewhere to run, while the wizard stood his ground and gave a wicked smile.

"Had you attacked a minute sooner, perhaps you would have stood a chance. But now I have this." Gellzoowin said and raised the wooden staff.

The creatures tightened their circle and the goblin backed away until he was cowering against the wizard's leg and pointing his spear this way and that, to ward off the giant insects. Gellzoowin ignored the goblin trembling by his side and could feel the power of the thunder cane growing in his hands. With that, he focused his attention on the nearest ant, a big reddish brown monster crouched directly in front of him; then lowered the tip of the wooden staff, pointed it at the ant and simply said... "Zapp!"

A bolt of lightning flew from the staff, and sliced through the ant in a flash, then surged ahead to carve its path of destruction. The crackling white light shot through the crowd of ants like a white hot cannonball through a crate of eggs and cut through six dozen ants in a blur of blinding energy. These had merely been standing behind the first ant and were fried on the spot. With one shot, seventy two ants toppled over where they stood, blackened and burnt to a crisp while the others standing nearby looked around confused. The ants had seen lightning but they had never seen it coming after them.

Gellzoowin gazed at the wooden staff in amazement. After the first burst of energy, the thunder cane was literally humming in his hands, and now he was ready to test its full power.

"Zapp!" the wizard shouted thrusting the staff forward. "Zapp! Zapp! Zapp!"

The goblin blinked with each blinding flash as bolts of electricity sprang forth and threaded their way through the ants like a fiery chain. Some ants were thrown into the air and burst into flames, others exploded on the spot, while still others were split in two, right down the middle.

The wizard laughed and fired away as the thunder cane spit lighting bolts like a machine gun. "Zapp! Zapp! Zapp!... Zapp! Zapp! Zapp!... Zapp! Zapp! Zapp! Zapp!... Zapp! Zapp! Zapp!" He shouted.

Gellzoowin zapped ants coming and going, running and standing still, and would have zapped ants all day long if he hadn't run out of ants to kill. And when it was all said and done, the ground was littered with the smoldering bodies of giant ants that were charred to a crisp. Gellzoowin grinned like a wild man as the tip of the thunder cane glowed red hot then finally cooled down. With the sound of ants sizzling around him, the wizard gave the staff an approving look and nodded.

"Not bad... Not bad at all." he said proudly. "You are my thunder cane."

Numlock finally let go of the wizard's robe and shook his fist at the dead ants.

"HAH!" he jeered and cackled. "Serves you right!"

Gellzoowin was still admiring the thunder cane and listening to the wild ranting of the goblin when, as fate would have it, a far greater threat suddenly made its presence known and snatched the wizard off the ground then tossed him against the Thunder Tree with stunning force. Numlock stumbled back and hardly knew what to do as he watched his master who was suddenly helpless and pinned to the tree. Gellzoowin stared dumbly as a blinding light filled the air before his eyes, but try as he might, he could not look away.

Gellzoowin peered into the glistening halo with its agonizing light and watched as a face slowly emerged. It seemed to grow larger and float out of thin air, coming closer and closer. Soon the face was plain for all to see. It was Marplot, the grand old sorcerer. The master wizard was presumably here to check up on him and see if he had made any progress, but it was all too much, and the pressure that pinned Gellzoowin against the tree was practically crushing him.

The doddering old wizard meant no harm; he was just trying to be helpful. But like an old man who yells when he's lost his hearing, or puts too much spice in the stew when his taste is gone, Marplot always used too much power with his magic. Gellzoowin often wondered about the feeble minded sorcerer, but now that he was pinned against the tree and could barely breathe, he just hoped the old wizard didn't kill him.

Marplot smiled gently and called from the light with his trembling old voice. "How goes it? Have you found the child?" He asked cheerfully.

Gellzoowin did all he could to strain his head forward and speak.

"Y-yes... we're... on our way!"
Gellzoowin said and managed to croak the few words as he felt his ribs begin to bow under the terrible pressure.

"To the horse? To the horse?!" Marplot added excitedly.

"...YES!!" cried the wizard.

"Oh, very good! Very well then. I won't keep you. Farewell. Farewell!"

A second later, the grand wizard was gone, bright light and all. Gellzoowin dropped from the tree like a piece of ripe fruit then slumped to his knees and gripped his chest, gasping for air then looked up to see Numlock, trembling like a puppy. The goblin reached out and handed the wizard his thunder cane which Gellzoowin snatched up with a growl and used it to lean on as he struggled to his feet. He ached and his head throbbed, but once he was standing he felt more in charge of himself.

In spite of Gellzoowin's wobbly condition, Numlock stayed well back and dared not offer any assistance. There were plenty of dead crispy ants lying around as helpful reminders of the wizard's wrath and power. When Numlock looked again he froze, afraid to move a muscle and gazed into the wizard's dark seething eyes which were staring right at him.

"Well, what are you waiting for? That will do, goblin... Come along." Gellzoowin said and limped away. Numlock sighed in relief then followed after the wizard and together they set off for the far lands beyond the Thunder Tree, the land of Gunvernia, the land of the giants.

CHAPTER TWELVE

A Speck of Magic

*T*he old wood cutter sat in his yard, stroking his white
bread and watched the smoke curling up from his pipe.
He puffed and puffed, then peered out across the valley,
from the comfortable shade of his favorite tree. The old man
and his son had lived in the quaint little cottage on the hill,
their whole lives. It was peaceful and quiet and the great
Gunvernian woods stretched out for as far as the eye could
see. Indeed these were the giant woods and the old wood
cutter was indeed a giant.

The old man stood and breathed in the fresh morning air.
Standing there in his giant leather boots, he was as big as a
five story house, nearly fifty feet tall. His son Gracus however was even bigger. With broad shoulders, nearly twenty
feet across and long brown hair that flowed like a river
stream, Gracus stood a full seventy feet tall and was easily
the biggest and strongest giant in the land. But he was also
a peaceful giant and with none to challenge him, the only
thing he truly hated in the world was "Specks."

That's what giants called the little people who lived
beyond their borders and never grew to be any bigger than

your thumb. Specks were known to be evil and dangerous creatures. Therefore, like all giants, Gracus and his father never ventured beyond the boundaries of their kingdom, and were quite content with their humble surroundings. Likewise, specks almost never set foot in the land of the giants, but when they did it was always trouble.

Gracus stood by the kitchen window, carefully placing flowers in a metal pot over the sink. The fresh flowers made the house smell sweet, and Gracus took special care in arranging them.

When he was done, he glanced out the kitchen window and saw his father sitting under the tree, with all of the wood that still had to be cut, piled around him. Gracus smiled at the familiar sight. He loved to help the old man chop wood in the yard, but these days he did most of the chopping while the old man just told stories and puffed on his pipe. Gracus called to his father.

"Hey, Ole fellow! There be plenty a'wood for the cutting. Ye workin' hard?!" he said playfully.

The old man sat back in the shade of the tree, puffed on his pipe and smiled.

"I be hardly workin' lad... Hardly workin'." He said softly as he gazed out at the woodland forest. It was the same response everyday.

Gracus smiled and grabbed his boots. He knew every tall tale by heart and wondered what clever old story his father would weave for him this day. Once his boots were on, Gracus stomped his foot on the giant planked floor which shook the house a little and headed for the door, but then something happened that he did not expect.

The old man cried out. "Stay back! I warn you! Get back I say!"

Gracus ran to the window, to see his white bearded father standing in the yard, with axe in hand. It had been a long time since Gracus had even seen the old man stack a single piece of wood, let alone raise an axe. Yet there he was with the old blade, gripped firmly in both hands, glaring down at the ground with a frightful scowl.

"What manner of evil thing are you?!" the old giant shouted.

Gracus tried to see who the old man was talking to, but the giant rose bush beneath the window, blocked his view. He could however hear a tiny little voice squeaking softly like a mouse as the old woodcutter glared at the ground.

"You dare to threaten me?!" He roared.

Then without another word, the old giant raised his axe high over his head and just when he was about to bring it down, he froze where he stood and his flesh turned to stone. Gracus stared in disbelief at the gray lifeless statue that just a moment earlier had been his father, and now was little more than a lawn ornament.

Outside, poised at the foot of the giant statue were the wizard and his goblin. Gellzoowin smiled up at the giant that loomed high above, towering fifty feet into the air. Both he and Numlock stood in the open, on the giant stone path that led through the old garden. At first Numlock was terrified, but now that giant was turned to stone, the goblin danced around and around, twirling and laughing. Gellzoowin held the thunder cane by his side and gazed up at his handiwork. The wizard had turned many things into stone, but the old wood cutter was by far the largest living thing he had ever cast a spell over. If nothing else, he could boast of the accomplishment even though it was not part of his plan.

"Oh well, no harm done. I'll just have to find another giant, that's all."

Even Numlock was starting to feel better about the journey, and didn't know why he had ever been so afraid, when suddenly the ground began to shake with the unmistakable sound of the footsteps of another giant drawing nearer. Gellzoowin braced himself against the thunder cane, while

Numlock wasted no time and jumped behind the wizard again.

The old wood cutter's son lumbered outside, with the ground quaking beneath him and stood in the path, staring at the statue of his father. When the dust settled around his giant boots, he saw a tiny little man dressed in a shiny bronze cloak, carrying a thin splinter of wood. To the giant, Gellzoowin was barely three inches tall, an insignificant little speck that he could crush with barely a thought.

"What have you done to my father, speck?" The giant growled and even the sound of his voice made the earth quake and the goblin tremble. Gellzoowin took his time and spoke calmly.

"This was your father?" the wizard said innocently. "Oh my dear giant, I am so sorry. I merely asked him for his assistance and he refused me. I regret I can see now why you are so upset. Allow me to introduce myself. I am the wizard, Gellzoowin."

To the giant's ear, the wizard squeaked and squeaked like a mouse until the sound of his annoying little voice made the giant want to squash him under his boot. But when Gracus took a step forward, the wizard raised the thunder cane and shouted.

"Hold giant!"

The bolt of lightning leapt into the air with a flash and blasted a limb off of the tree next to the seventy foot giant. The branch alone was as big as an oak tree and came down with such a thunderous roar that the goblin toppled over then glared out from behind the wizard to see what had happened. When all was quiet once more, Gracus stared at the tiny object in the wizard's hand, stunned by the amazing force of the thunder cane.

"Extraordinary, isn't it?" Gellzoowin said.

Now that he had the giant's attention, Gellzoowin pointed the thunder cane at the head of the statue and spoke with a more serious and threatening tone.

"If you truly care about your father and wish to see him alive again, you will do as I say. I am now your master and you are my humble slave."

Gracus reached out and touched the wrinkled stone face of the statue.

"Very well, I will do as you say." the giant grumbled.

Gellzoowin looked at him intently.

"Swear it... I said swear it!"

"...I swear," said the giant.

The wizard lowered the thunder cane and Numlock grinned to see the towering giant reduced to a helpless slave.

"Good!... See? We're getting along already." Gellzoowin said and smiled, then paused to look at the young giant in a ponderous manner. Even in his slouched position it was clear that Gracus was much taller than the statue of his father. In fact he stood, head and shoulders above it. The more Gellzoowin compared his size, the more he knew this was no ordinary giant, and began to think back. As a young apprentice, he had been a student of giant history and folk lore. Most of what he learned he had forgotten. But one word came back to him. Gellzoowin smiled wickedly, and spoke in a clever and crafty voice.

"Would I be correct in assuming that you are what is known as... a titan?"

The giant stared at the ground, for he was indeed a giant among giants and there was only one of his kind born in every ten generations. Gellzoowin repeated the question, this time with a more accusing tone.

"You are a titan, aren't you?"

The giant nodded, "I am."

Gellzoowin smiled at his blind good fortune. He had not only found a giant to help him in his wicked plan. He had found the most powerful giant of all.

CHAPTER THIRTEEN

The Armor of God

*K*atie rode aboard Bromwin's back, in her saddle chair, while the angel walked along side and Jack sulked a few paces behind. Further back Goe Garth drove the troll wagon with Gimble and Binderbec by his side. After the spirit of fear, the trolls were on their guard and looked for danger in every shadow they passed.

"Where are we going, now?" Gimble asked, but when no one answered he rubbed his belly and whined. "When do we eat?"

Binderbec, the old soldier peered straight ahead.

"Don't you ever think about anything other than your stomach?"

Gimble gave it some thought. "I think about food." He said.

Binderbec shook his head and turned his attention to Goe Garth.

"Where are we going?" He asked for his own curiosity.

Goe Garth kept his eyes forward. "We follow the child, but our heading is northward. If I remember the charts of this forbidden land, all of the greatest wonders lay deep within the territory. The northern passage is the most direct route and should steer us clear of danger."

Binderbec squinted into the distance and stroked his beard. "A wise choice." he said.

The wagons moved slowly, while the little fairy flit back and forth, and the ogres trailed behind. After the thrashing they received from the angel, the beasts were too battered and bruised to make trouble and chose to sit quietly aboard their new wagon.

Up ahead, Stadia kept pace with the bear and Katie watched the angel walk in the calm of the midday sun. She loved looking at him, especially the way he was now, handsome, and somber, staring straight ahead like a soldier. He looked confident and filled with strength, yet there was something sad about him, something in his gaze. Indeed the angel was a mystery, and in all her fascination Katie could hardly contain herself a moment longer and simply had to speak.

"Excuse me." she said.

"Yes, child of God."

Katie smiled at the sound of his voice while Jack sulked a few paces behind and pretended to ignore them, sure that anything they had to say was of no interest to him. Katie rocked back and forth in her saddle chair, as the bear sauntered along, and tried to speak as politely as she could.

"I just wanted to say that I'm really happy you're here."

The angel nodded. "It is my duty to serve." he said.

Katie gazed at his handsome face. "And... and I'm really glad you're all right."

The angel nodded again, but Katie couldn't keep the question bottled up a moment longer.

"I just have to know. How did you do it? How did you get through the shadow of doubt without... well, you know..."

Katie didn't want to say the words. It seemed so disrespectful, but she couldn't think of any other way to say it.

"Without going crazy." She said.

The angel looked straight ahead.

Katie scooted up to the edge of her seat. "Please you have to tell me. Everyone wants to know. That horrible monster made all the ogres go crazy but it didn't do anything to you. How did you do it?"

Bromwin and the others listened as the child spoke to the angel in a way no one else could. Indeed everyone's ear perked up as they waited for the answer, everyone including Jack. Stadia walked with a stern look and Katie was sure she had offended the warrior of God until he glanced over and smiled. The angel drew his cloak around him and looked ahead once more.

"There is no secret. The answer is… truth." He said.

Goe Garth, Gimble and Binderbec, listened and looked at each other, confused.

"When you have truth, it guards your mind from all deception, and you need not fear. God is truth and His word is my strength, my sword, my shield. I wear the full armor of God and in truth, I am protected from evil."

Katie had only glimpsed his armor, at a distance in the midst of a raging wind storm when he fought the spirit of fear. Now the angel's cloak covered him from head to toe and she wondered what the armor of God looked like up close.

Jack drew a little nearer, trying to listen as they strolled along, but remembered the bear's six inch fangs and was careful not to get too close.

"The armor of God?" Katie asked.

Riding on Bromwin's back, she was practically eye level with the angel and Stadia looked over at her.

"Yes, the armor of God. Have you never heard of it?"

"No," Katie said. "I never even knew God had armor."

Stadia smiled.

"The armor is for you, not God." He said. "Have you never read your Bible?"

Katie put her finger in her mouth and tried to think. When was the last time she had actually read from her Bible? It had indeed been a while, and she certainly never remembered reading anything about the "armor of God." Katie felt embarrassed and lowered her head. It was one thing not to have read her Bible, but now she had to admit it to an angel, and admit it to an angel of truth no less, but the answer was obvious.

"I see" said Stadia.

Katie looked up and tried to explain.

"I-I've read a little of the Bible, but mostly I had it read to me, by my grandmother. I wanted to read more, I really did. It's just that every time I tried to, it made me sleepy." Katie made a face and looked down again, wishing she hadn't said that last part.

Bromwin smiled, enjoying her honesty.

Stadia glanced at Katie as he walked.

"Sleepy?" he said, sounding surprised. "Reading your Bible should renew your mind. It should make you excited." Stadia said, pretending to be upset.

"No, it does!" Katie explained. "It's just that I get tired so easy, that's all." she said and tried to smile which was hard to do while she was lying to the angel of truth, but Stadia was merciful.

"You are young." he said. "I trust when you are older you will have more understanding, then the word of God will come to life for you and it will be as real to you as I am now. Or do I make you sleepy as well?"

Suddenly Katie was bouncing and shaking so much, she thought there was an earthquake, until she realized it was only Bromwin laughing. The great bear laughed till his huge belly shook and his back went up and down. Katie frowned and waited till it was over and Bromwin cleared his throat then pretended to look at the view around him. Once they were moving along smoothly again Katie turned to the angel.

"Oh no, you could never make me sleepy. Not you!" Katie insisted. "Really!" Katie tried to sound as sincere as she could and wished she could start all over again.

"Thank you" said the angel.

Jack continued listening, and didn't like all the chit chat. Like a good spy, he wanted to hear something he could tell the wizard that might give him an advantage.

"As for the armor of God," Stadia said, "it is a perfect defense against evil, and a perfect weapon as well."

Gimble frowned at Binderbec's old and dented armor.

"How can it be a weapon?" Gimble asked.

The angel smiled at the question and answered as he went.

"If your armor is strong enough, your enemy cannot hurt you and he will lose confidence. Sometimes he will even flee without a fight and whenever you can win the battle without lifting a hand against your enemy... that is the perfect weapon."

Hearing that, Binderbec stuck out his chest and gave his own armor a good whack with the palm of his hand.

"How about that? Good answer, eh?" Binderbec said.

Gimble smiled at the old soldier whose armor was as dented as a trash can and looked about as sturdy. "Yeah, the perfect weapon." He said and the angel continued.

"The armor of God has a purpose and each part has its own special power. My helmet is the helmet of salvation. It fills me with the knowledge of our Lord. It is my weapon against fear. And with it there can be no shadow of doubt."

The trolls nodded and listened carefully, when all of a sudden the angel stopped talking. Katie wanted to know more and said so.

"What about the rest?" she asked.

"Read your Bible." is all the angel said.

Stadia marched on ahead as though something else had drawn his attention and Bromwin smiled up at Katie.

"Perhaps you should take a nap... before you begin." The bear chuckled and Katie bounced up and down again. The trolls watched the angel walk ahead as another noise caught their ears. The sky was growing darker now. There was a distant booming and Katie looked up at the billowing clouds. Goe Garth looked to the sky as well.

"It's going to rain. We should find shelter!"

The thunderous noise was far off at first, but came again and again and seemed to grow nearer. Just then, the little fairy flew to the front of the wagon and hovered between Goe Garth and Gimble.

"I don't think that's thunder." She said.

CHAPTER FOURTEEN

In The Shadow of the Titan

*T*he small caravan approached a narrow mountain pass with steep cliffs on either side. Dark clouds rolled across the sky, churning like smoke as the thunderous noise shook the ground like the footsteps of a giant. The tiny fairy buzzed with her senses tingling when Goe Garth brought the wagon to a halt and the trolls watched the mountain pass ahead. Bromwin stopped and Katie peered into the distance, for in the eerie light they could all feel the presence of the creature before it appeared.

The giant rose up from behind the cliffs like a storm, and cast his shadow across the plain as he blocked the way ahead. With his fists clenched and his eyes set, the titan gazed out over the land, searching the shadowy hills below.

Katie took one look at the giant and held her breath, transfixed. He was terrifyingly big, bigger than she ever dreamt possible. Indeed, everything stood still, trolls, ogres, boars and wagons. For even though they were out in the open, it was just dark enough that no one dared move an inch or otherwise risk drawing the giant's attention.

The bear spoke slowly and as softly as he could,

"Don't... move," he said.

But Katie had no intention of moving and couldn't even breathe. Jack stood nearby and crouched down, staring in amazement when suddenly the wild boars began to grunt and squeal. The frightened animals had seen enough and fought to back away as fast as they could. When the giant heard the noise, he swung his head around and looked right at them. His enormous eyes were like black pools, dark and mysterious, and terrible to behold. Now that they had been seen, the trolls trembled, the ogres cringed, and the idiot Zarq fainted dead away and fell off the back of the wagon.

Cool night air swept across the rocky cliffs as the giant blew out great puffs of steam, which made the impossible creature look even more awesome and menacing.

Even Gral Tibbore, who was the bravest among the trolls could barely move, while Binderbec shook so badly his armor rattled like a tin can and the others had to hold him still, just to stop the noise.

Now that they had been spotted, the band of travelers feared for their lives and forgot about the one thing that truly stood between them and the monstrous creature that towered over them, when suddenly the giant called out.

"Which of you is Staaay- deee- ahhhh?!"

The giant's booming voice echoed through the mountain pass and on down to the flat lands beyond the trail. The angel stood before the giant, only a hundred yards off and wasted no time answering the call.

"I am Stadia, a soldier of God, an angel of the Lord. What is it you seek?"

The angel was a tiny thing standing in the shadow of the titan as the giant glared down. Everyone listened in amazement for there was no fear in the angel's voice. In fact, Katie stopped trembling long enough to look at the guardian who stood ready to defend her. "What do you want?" he asked.

"It is you I seek and there is only one thing I want." The

giant growled. "To grind you to dust beneath my boot."

Everyone trembled at his words then looked to the angel.

"I do not wish to harm you." Stadia said and approached the giant slowly.

With that, Gracus looked to the sky and laughed so hard, his hot breath punched a hole in the clouds. Then without any warning, he rushed forward, charging ahead with such speed and fury, everyone pulled back as though he would surely crush them all. Then when he was right over the angel, the titan raised his giant boot which was as big as a house and brought it down with all his might. The sound was like an explosion as it slammed into the ground with a roar and heaved the land up like a wave. With the ground rising up all around her, Katie tried to scream, but was too busy falling, and toppled off of Bromwin's back.

When she hit the ground, the big bear collapsed next to her. Half the ogres fell off their wagon as did the trolls. Those who didn't fall could only hold on until the ground stopped shaking and prayed they didn't die of fright.

When the earth and dust settled, even the boars were quiet and stood there panting. Katie looked up from the grass, to see the terrible giant glaring down, with one foot buried in a crater, ten feet deep. A few seconds later, Gracus stepped out of the hole, his great leather boot dripping with dirt and mud. Katie just stared in shock, while the trolls turned away, unable to look at the horrible sight. It had all happened so fast.

"No, it can't be." Katie said. "It can't be."

But no matter where she looked, the angel was nowhere to be found. Still she couldn't bring herself to believe what seemed to be the horrible truth. The giant had carried out his plan. He had slain the angel in the blink of an eye, and whatever was left of him lay crushed and buried in the muddy pit at the giant's feet.

Tears filled Katie's eyes as Bromwin rose up to face the

giant and all fear left him. Now there was only rage in his heart and the need for revenge. The hair stood up on Bromwin's back like bristles on a porcupine. He started forward, slowly at first, then an angry growl began to build inside of him, until the bear king opened his mouth and released a terrible ear splitting roar.

"GGGRRRRAAAAARRRR!!"

Bromwin charged the giant with fangs bared, claws raking the ground, and jaws gaping wide. Gracus watched the bear race toward him, but to the giant, Bromwin was little more than a kitten and just as harmless. When the bear leapt into the air, the giant barely raised his foot to brush him aside. The toe of the giant's boot hit the bear like a train and sent Bromwin flying. Katie watched the bear twirl, end over end as he soared through the air then crashed into a thicket of reeds at the edge of the clearing and came to rest in a giant elderberry bush. The titan stared at the grassy thicket and growled.

"I have no quarrel with you." He said then turned away and looked down at the crater in front of him. Katie watched the giant through her tears and as frightened as she was, it was suddenly obvious that the enormous creature was no longer a threat to them. Now that the angel was gone, he had turned from absolute rage to utter sadness, and looked as though he had no idea what to do next.

As everyone watched and stared, there came a sound, a sort of cackle that was immediately annoying the instant Katie heard it. It was the sound of insane laughter, which grew louder and echoed across the field like a noisy crow.

Goe Garth shook his head in disgust and muttered to himself.

"Only one as wicked as a goblin could find such pleasure in the misery of others."

The goblin Numlock appeared in the distance, leaping and dancing for joy, and the trolls moaned at the sight of him. The wizard came out of the mist behind him, looking clever and confident, with the thunder cane in his grasp. The enormous titan just hung his head and ignored them both as the wizard and the goblin approached and came to the edge of the pit. Numlock peered down into the murky darkness with eyes bulging. There was nothing left of the angel. Not the slightest trace.

When the goblin ceased his cackling, Katie could hear the heavy breathing of the giant who stood there with his hair in his face, puffing white clouds of steam. The wizard looked up from the pit and gestured to the giant standing behind him.

"Hah! Behold the titan!" He announced then grinned and looked around him. The victory over the angel was a proud moment and since there were no other wizards to share it with, Gellzoowin decided he would take the time to appreciate himself. With a flick of his wrist he produced a mirror out of thin air, then struck a regal pose with the thunder cane by his side and gazed at his own reflection. Then when the moment was done and he had praised himself sufficiently, the mirror disappeared, and Gellzoowin turned his attention toward Katie, who was still lying on the ground, sobbing.

The brave trolls rushed to surround her, and Jack nearly burst out laughing. Without their precious angel to protect them, they were a ridiculous sight standing there on their own. Jack scoffed at them once more, then rose into the air and took off like a shot. Flying as fast as he could, he forgot about his landing and would have preferred to set down in front of the wizard, with style and grace. Instead he dropped out of the air, slipped on the wet grass, bounced on his rear, then slid and smacked his head on the ground. When he stopped, he laid there a moment then looked up to see the wizard standing over him.

"You had better practice that." Gellzoowin said smugly

then walked past.

Jack frowned and pounded his fist in the dirt then looked up and saw the giant peering down at him from out of the mist. His mind reeled at the size of the titan as he lay at the giant's feet, locked in his gaze and afraid to move.

"It is said, when the eye of the giant is upon you, your soul trembles." the wizard said as he walked away, then paused to look at the boy.

"Stop gawking like a stuffed owl and come along." The wizard demanded.

Jack blinked until he was finally able to look away then got to his feet and chased after the wizard. When he caught up, he forced a smile and tried to sound more excited than afraid, with the giant still looming right over them.

"That- that was great. He squashed him like a bug!" Jack exclaimed as he scurried along, glancing up every now and then at the colossal creature.

Gellzoowin held his head high. "Yes, I know." he said.

Jack smiled at him then looked up at the giant again.

"He- he sure is big… If anything, I guess I wish it could have lasted a bit longer…the fight I mean."

Gellzoowin only smirked. "In contests of life and death it is always best to settle it quickly. I'm quite satisfied with the outcome." The wizard said and marched on like a conquering hero with the boy by his side. Rogad and the ogres sat quietly aboard their wagon, perched like gravestones on a hilltop, as they watched the evil wizard approach the trolls and the little girl.

Katie hadn't had a really good cry since she entered the Nohr World, but now that the angel was dead, the bear was gone, and she was six years old again, she burst into tears and could hardly control herself. With the child lying helpless on the ground, the trolls tightened their circle and formed a battle line to stop the wizard from reaching her.

"Stand your ground!" said Gral Tibbore as he stepped

forward and pointed his spear at the wizard.

Gellzoowin paused, clearly amused by the little troll.

"Oh yes, of course. I dare not go any farther for fear that I might kill you where you stand...Or should I say, be... hava keen."

The wizard barely muttered the magic words then came forward until his shadow covered Gral Tibbore like a cold dark specter and the troll began to shiver. Gral shook until his teeth chattered and bits of frost hardened the tips of his beard. The others watched and backed away as ice crystals crept over the troll's face and Gral turned blue in a few short seconds. Even with his life ebbing out of him, the brave troll refused to move and Gellzoowin smiled down on him.

"What's the matter troll? Is there no fire left within you, hot enough to fuel your courage? Stand aside, before I freeze your blood, solid in your veins."

Gral Tibbore stood as long as he could, then when he could no longer feel his legs, or his spear in his frozen hands, he staggered away from the wizard's shadow and collapsed in Rumyon's arms. But before Gellzoowin could step forward, Raylin drew his sword and took Gral's place.

"You'll have to freeze me too!" The little troll sneered.

Goe Garth and Gimble stepped up to block the wizard's path as well, while Jingles and Binderbec stayed close to Katie who was still sobbing on the ground. Gellzoowin shook his head, amused by their show of bravery then watched as Katie propped herself up, with tears streaming down and struggled to speak.

"W-why...why?" She cried until nothing else would come out.

The wizard looked at her with some surprise then turned away as if to ponder the question. "Why." He asked. "Why indeed?"

Gellzoowin's face was suddenly radiant. It was a good question and another perfect opportunity to reflect upon his brilliance. The wizard took his time and when he was ready, he looked down on Katie with a glint in his eye.

"It was a game... and he lost. I simply removed a pawn from the board. It cost the angel his life, but he paid the price for his arrogance." Gellzoowin said and thought about it a little more. "Yes, a simple reminder that I am not to be trifled with. Call it a lesson." The wizard said and nodded.

"And what a lesson." the goblin snickered then leapt forward and pointed at Katie.

"First, he tricked you then tricked the angel to bring the boy. Now the boy's here, the angel is gone and there's no one left to oppose us, clever from start to finish." Numlock said and grinned with his nervous eyes flitting back and forth.

The wizard stopped to look at the goblin, and decided not to zap him since the interruption was only more praise and adoration. Numlock skulked away as Gellzoowin turned to face the little girl who was still sitting on the ground crying.

"Now, you will do as I say and lead me straight to the white horse." He said with the thunder cane glowing by his side.

Katie looked up at the wizard and sobbed. With the giant looming over them, and the wizard boasting and brimming with power, everything truly seemed hopeless. But there was one thing left that was forgotten; one little thing that always managed to spoil the wizard's fun.

Concealed in the shadows at the back of the troll wagon, atop a large wooden crate was an open toolbox. Inside, just under the lid, between two troll hammers, sitting on a short handled wooden mallet was the tiny little fairy. With sparkling wings and her silvery glow, the fairy stayed hidden from the wizard and the world.

Kitch gazed up at the darkening sky. It was full of purples and pink lavenders, but there was no beauty in it for her. She mourned the death of the angel and needed a quiet place where she could think. Kitch tried to be brave and closed her eyes as she dared to look into the wizard's black heart once again. Perhaps there she could find a reason for this terrible act, a reason why the giant had killed the angel. The wizard's thoughts prowled around the fairy like demons and taunted her as she trembled in the stillness and saw every wicked thing the wizard had done. She saw the woodcutter turned to stone and the titan that grieved for his father. She watched the giant submit to Gellzoowin's wickedness to save his father's life. And now that she could see into the depths of the wizard's heart, she knew that it was all a cruel trick. The wizard had no intention of changing the woodcutter back from stone. He would use the titan to protect him from harm, and once he had braved all dangers and captured the white horse, he would kill the trolls, kill the boy, kill the child of God, and finally kill the titan himself and leave no witnesses behind. The fairy could scarcely believe the wizard's treachery nor could she bare the sorrow of it all.

Indeed her heart was so heavy she would have cried, if it weren't for the fact that fairies could not shed a tear. In the middle of that thought, Kitch felt a gentle tapping and looked down at the tiny drops of water that had splashed her white gossamer gown. It happened again and once more. Kitch looked up to see the rain, but there was not a cloud in the sky then touched her cheek and with a look of surprise she watched the sparkling teardrop, slide down her finger tip and fall on her gown. Kitch was indeed crying and the more she tried to wipe the tears, the more they came.

"This cannot be!" she cried, unaware that something even more amazing was happening as she wept. The wooden mallet upon which she sat was slowly shrinking. Indeed, while the tears streamed down her face everything was steadily getting smaller, and when she looked, to her utter dismay, even the toolbox itself was closing in around her.

"What's happening?!" Kitch gasped and look around as

a shadow swept over her and a voice whispered down from above, "The land of great discoveries."

Kitch gazed up, staring in wonder then sprang to her feet when she saw the face of the angel smiling down upon her.

"You're not dead!... Tell me I'm not dreaming!" she cried through her tears and glowed till she was nearly ablaze with light.

"Put out your light! Put out your light!" the angel said and covered her with his hands as he looked around. Kitch dimmed her light, and Stadia smiled down on her. "No I'm not dead. True enough and you have grown."

The angel watched as the tiny fairy continued to grow until she was four times her normal size and the wooden mallet beneath her shifted under her weight. When Kitch tried to stand, she wobbled then tumbled down, flapping her wings wildly. She banged around noisily, amidst the hammers and nails and was an awkward sight, climbing out of the jumble of tools. When she finally emerged, Kitch was nearly twelve inches tall and stood on the railing at the back of the wagon, frowning over her shoulder. Her little wings had hardly grown and were no more than tiny buds sprouting from her back, totally useless for a fairy that was now too large to be called a fairy any longer.

Stadia drew close to her and spoke softly.

"In your lament, your tears have caused you to grow." he said. "It would seem this land holds great discoveries, for you as well."

Kitch dried her eyes and in spite of everything, she was happy to see him.

"No greater discovery than you!" the fairy said.

Stadia put his finger to his lips and winked. Kitch gave a cautious look around, and then waved for the angel to come closer. Hidden safely from view at the back of the troll wagon she whispered into his ear and told Stadia everything she had seen in the wizard's dark mind and every evil thing he had done to the giant. And just when she finished, a light-ning bolt shot into the air with a thunderous crack and lit the grimy clouds with an eerie green glow.

After the show of strength the wizard raised his thunder cane and brought it down hard. When he let go, the cane was planted like a tent pole in the ground, and stood straight and tall. Gellzoowin raised his hands and walked around the staff as though he was the finest of all wizards and this was indeed the greatest show in all the Nohr World.

"Wasn't that grand? Wasn't that magnificent?!" he shouted.

Numlock clapped and Jack wanted to shout for joy, but felt a little awkward, since everyone else looked like they were at a funeral.

The wizard looked around him as if to say, "Well? Wasn't it?"

The goblin grinned like a trained monkey, while the trolls just waited and Katie cried. Katie had cried so much, she began to hiccup. And with all the sniffling and hiccupping, sobbing and crying, the wizard could stand it no longer.

"Stop it! Stop it! Do you hear?! I will not have you ruin this celebration!" Gellzoowin snapped. But his outburst only made Katie cry all the more and Gellzoowin finally looked away in disgust. Jack watched it all from a distance and for the first time, he felt sorry for his little sister. It was clear she had chosen the wrong side. She was one of them, the ones with no magic.

"It's not her fault. She's just a kid." Jack thought to him-self and was about to say so, when Katie raised a trembling hand and pointed at him.

"Why couldn't you believe? Why couldn't you just believe?!" Katie sobbed through her tears. "None of this would have ever happened if it weren't for you, you and your stupid magic!"

"Me?!" Jack yelled and instantly forgot about his pity. "What did I do? I didn't do anything! The angel's the one who brought me here!" he shouted.

Katie wiped her eyes and stood to her feet.

"No Jack... No, you did this. You wanted to come here. You're the one who put the spell on my door. Where did you think it came from? Where do you think it went? It brought me here. The angel only brought you, because he cared. He did it to protect you, but now I wish he hadn't."

Jack shot back.

"Oh yeah? Well I didn't ask for his help! And as far as your angel is concerned, it served him right. He got what he deserved and so did that know-it-all bear! So don't blame me. It's not my fault the angel took on the giant and got squished!"

Jack glared at his sister and Gellzoowin smiled.

"Well said, well spoken my dear apprentice. I could not have put it better myself." Numlock stood back then turned to the ogres with a giggle and pointed to the hole in the ground. "Squished to jelly... squished to jam!" he said.

The ogres jeered and laughed and shook their big hairy fists.

"That's right!" Gellzoowin said, boasting joyfully then turned to Katie and grinned. "Squished to dust and gone for g..." The word stuck in his throat and the wizard's eyes bulged. Jack looked and stared; as did the trolls and ogres and everyone fell silent.

When Katie finally turned around, she saw a young girl coming out of the shadows from behind the wagon. She came slowly and when she stepped into the light Katie could see it was really a little woman, dainty, barely five feet tall and surrounded by a golden light that made her skin sparkle as though she were dusted with fine glitter.

"Who is she? Where did she come from?" The trolls whispered to one another.

The woman was so radiant and exquisitely beautiful, even the wizard was surprised by her appearance and didn't recognize her. Strangely however, the more Katie looked at the woman; the more familiar she seemed. Then with a shy and gentle smile, the woman looked up and Katie suddenly knew. The last time she had seen that face, it was the size of her pinkie nail.

"It's the fairy!" Gimble said and blinked as though his eyes were playing tricks.

Binderbec stood there, smiling at her beauty. "...That's one big fairy!" he said as he gazed up at her, for Kitch was indeed taller than any of the trolls. Rumyon stepped forward and glared at her suspiciously.

"Impossible!... What happened to you? What manner of sorcery is this?" the troll said and turned to the wizard.

Gellzoowin said nothing and just stood there watching, until another figure stepped out of the shadows, a figure much larger and more powerful, draped in a long gray cloak. The goblin screamed, the trolls gasped and the wizard stared in amazement as the angel stepped forward. Indeed no two expressions were alike. When Katie saw the angel she reached out for him, with tears in her eyes while Binderbec cried out. "It's a ghost, a spirit!" he said, brandishing his sword and staring in horror.

Friar Jingles stepped forward and pat the old troll on the back. "Calm yourself. He has always been spirit, made flesh by God. Tis the angel himself, that stands before you."

"Oh," Rumyon said. "Well done, very clever."

Rogad and the ogres didn't know what to make of the angel and simply waited to see what would happen next, while Jack took a few steps back with his mouth dropped open and the wizard tried to mask his shock with an awkward smirk.

"You're alive." Gellzoowin grumbled. "How wonderfully disappointing."

Katie tried to speak but was so choked with tears; she could barely make a sound. Stadia came forward, watching her with some concern as the trolls moved aside to let him pass, their faces beaming.

"Are you all right?" He asked and Katie laughed through her tears. She wanted to ask him the same question but just nodded instead. Satisfied that she was unharmed, the angel turned his full attention on the wizard. "You were saying."

Gellzoowin smirked. "You are more clever than I anticipated, but I should not be your greatest concern right now. You still have him... to contend with." He said then pointed straight up and smiled while the titan glared down from the darkness above.

CHAPTER FIFTEEN

A Crushing Defeat

*T*he giant's rage returned as he peered down through the fading light with steam billowing from his nostrils. "I swear on my father's life you will not live to see the sun again." he growled.

Stadia glanced up at the giant. "I'll be right with you." he said.

The wizard and the boy backed away as the angel marched toward them, then walked right past and went to the back of the ogre wagon, while Rogad and the other monsters watched with some curiosity. The angel rummaged around until he found what he was looking for, then hauled one of the thick coils of iron chain off the back of the wagon. Its heavy links hit the ground and rattled noisily as the angel returned to Katie, dragging the chain behind him.

Stadia paused for a moment to remove his cloak. When it fell to the ground, he stood before them covered from head to toe in armor that sparkled like polished silver.

Katie gazed at the full armor of God. Every piece was flawlessly crafted and trimmed with white gold filigree. So wonderful and elegant was the angel's armor, the trolls marveled at its perfection and knew that no weapon formed against it would prosper.

The breastplate of righteousness and the helmet of Salvation shone the brightest. The belt of truth shimmered gold and girded the angel's waist while the rest of his armor glistened like platinum. All together the angel's armor was stronger than folded steel and covered in light. The trolls watched quietly as the angel unfastened the sword of the spirit, still encased in its golden sheath, and drew his shield out of thin air. These he placed on the ground before Katie, and the beautiful fairy.

"Safeguard these and make sure that the wizard does not touch them." Stadia said.

Gellzoowin sneered at the comment than looked away. With that the angel turned and went off to do battle with the giant, armed only with the length of chain trailing behind him. Kitch held the sparkling shield and knelt beside Katie who wrapped her arms around the angel's sword and watched as he strode past the wizard.

"I'll deal with you later." Stadia said and Gellzoowin grumbled as he watched the guardian and looked forward to his destruction. Stadia marched across the open field with the length of chain rattling behind him then stood before the giant once more and shouted.

"Titan, I come in the name of the Lord and there is none greater."

The giant looked with surprise. Unlike before, the angel did not squeak like a mouse. Indeed his voice was suddenly louder and stronger than when he first heard it. Gracus glared down. "You speak like a giant!" he bellowed.

"I am a messenger of God" Stadia replied.

"That means nothing to me! You are my enemy and I am your destroyer." the giant said then hunched down and came forward.

"Hear me!" said the angel and thrust out his hand.

Gracus paused.

"I know that you serve the wizard. He has tricked you and holds your father's life in the balance. I can save him."

The giant leaned in closer, unsure of what to make of the angel.

"You have the power to change him back from stone?" he asked.

Stadia gave the giant a firm look. "No, but I..."

Before he could finish, the giant opened his mouth and roared.

"YOU LIIIEEE!" the giant shouted. "You lie to save your life!"

Gracus bellowed once more with hot steam pouring from his mouth. "I bring your doom, angel. And you can take that message back to your God!... Prepare to die." With that, Gracus drew his knife and held it out before him. The blade alone was as big as a cathedral door, five feet wide and twelve feet long, and glistened in the fading light.

The giant thundered ahead and Stadia watched him advance with the length of chain stretched full out behind him. Then with the chain in one hand, Stadia reared back and swung the full length of it over his head. The five hundred pounds of iron linked chain swept huge circles, and sliced through the air as the mighty angel wielded it like a giant sling. The other hand he held out to steady himself as the chain whirled round and round.

WHOOSH, WHOOSH, WHOOSH, it went like a giant propeller. Gracus paused and frowned when the angel of God called to him above the sound of the whirring noise.

"The time for talk is ended. Come ahead if you must."

The titan sneered at the challenge and rocked back and forth as he watched the chain, and prepared to attack. Stadia narrowed his eyes and waited.

Katie stood with the others near the troll wagon, and as she clutched the angel's sword a thought came to her. The whirring chain reminded her of the brave little shepherd with his slingshot and the ancient battle with the Philistine giant. Only now the fight was between an angel and a real giant that was big enough to topple a mountain.

The wizard smiled, his eyes glowing with excitement, while Jack stood nearby grinning, filled with eager anticipation. He had wanted to see the fight go longer and now he would get his wish.

"This is it. This is it!" Jack said then glanced around before the fight started and decided to make himself comfortable. Jack spread his arms and floated into the air then with a few magic words and a simple conjuring spell, he laid back as dad's leather sofa recliner appeared beneath him, or at least one that looked just like it. With a swish of his hand, a box of popcorn and a large soda, complete with plastic lid and straw, appeared next to him. When everything was just right, he sank into the thick comfy cushions and took a sip of his drink then sat it back on top of nothing, where the cup magically refilled itself. Now everything was indeed perfect, with one exception. Night had come quickly and the light was fading fast. There was the occasional glint of the angel's armor, and a flash of the silver chain that circled round and round.

"Too bad there's not more light." Jack said, stuffing popcorn in his mouth.

Gellzoowin looked to the sky and pulled back his sleeves. It was something Jack said earlier, that gave him the idea. The wizard muttered under his breath, and a faint glow appeared in the distance that slowly grew brighter. Katie huddled against the fairy and Kitch held her tight and the trolls watched and wondered.

With a poof and a puff of smoke came a cluster of lights, another puff and another cluster, then another and another, until all around huge floodlights appeared on the cliff sides and every hilltop, as a dozen more popped out of nowhere.

Jack sat up in his chair.

"Wooooaaw!... Stadium lighting!" he cried, his mouth half full of popcorn.

But these were not like any lights Jack had ever seen. Gellzoowin had merely conjured up magical spheres of energy and suspended them in mid air with his powers. There were no poles or wires or plugs or anything, just balls of light that floated above and only pretended to be light bulbs. Soon the entire battlefield was lit as bright as day and the two combatants paused to look around, equally surprised by the light. Jack yelled out, and pumped his fist in the air.

"YEAH!!" he said, and spilled more popcorn. "That's what I'm talkin' about!"

Jack adjusted his chair, sat forward eagerly, then conjured up more popcorn and kept stuffing his face. With the lights shining brightly, Katie could see everything now and the titan looked even larger. The giant's forearms were as big as school buses. His face was younger, and not quite as mean as she originally thought, but all things considered, he was still an angry giant and that was more than frightening enough.

The angel however, sparkled and flashed like a polished jewel and seemed even smaller by comparison. But now that the giant could see him clearly, he growled with his monstrous teeth clenched tight.

"You made me miss once, but I won't miss again." Gracus snarled, rocking back and forth as the angel swung the chain, round and round.

"WHOOSH, WHOOSH, WHOOSH!"

The giant jabbed his knife at the angel, but Stadia hardly moved, swinging the chain at an even and steady pace.

"WHOOSH, WHOOSH, WHOOSH!"

The giant went slowly to his right, and turned the knife over so that the blade was pointed down. Stadia moved, step by step, to keep the titan in front of him and with only fifty feet between them, Gracus inched closer and closer, like he was sneaking up on a fly.

"Why doesn't he move? Why doesn't he do something?!" Kitch whispered. Katie trembled in the fairy's arms and couldn't bear to look, but managed to peek through her fingers with squinty eyes. Now that the fairy and the child were holding each other, the angel's weapons were lying on the ground unattended and while everyone watched the giant, the wizard gave Numlock the signal. The goblin crawled on his belly as quiet as a spider, moving like a shadow across the ground. Slowly and steadily he drew closer and looked around to make sure he was not seen. Then quiet as a cat, he came up behind the fairy and crouched over the weapons then gazed upon them with his eyes aglow. The wizard watched and could almost feel the angel's sword in his grasp when the goblin reached for the shimmering sword and... "PZAAATT!"

A fiery spark leapt from the blade and plunged into Numlock's hand like a white hot needle. With a yelp, the goblin jumped in the air and did a backward flip to get away from the thing then scurried off, holding and shaking his hand in mind numbing pain. Gellzoowin frowned at the clever sword which seemed perfectly able to guard itself then turned his attention back to the giant on the battlefield.

WHOOSH, WHOOSH, WHOOSH!

The chain went round and round as the giant crept closer, timing the swing, and waited for his chance to attack. Indeed everyone waited and watched breathlessly, rocking with each whirl of the chain, and just when they thought the giant would surely pounce, there was a horrible crash and everyone turned to see the ridiculous ogres in a violent brawl aboard their wagon. The beasts bellowed and roared, with their huge fists flying in a fitful rage. The trolls scowled and the wizard shook his head. No one knew how it started or could even be bothered. All that mattered was the angel, and the giant who was about to attack and just when Katie turned around, he did.

"WHOOSH, WHOOSH,... THUDDD!"

The angel drew back as the giant came down with his knife like a thundering avalanche. Gracus blinked at the spark of the blade and drove his knife down with such stunning force, it plowed through the dirt and the hilt of the weapon struck the ground like a hammer.

Everything happened so fast, once again it seemed like the battle was over before it began. Katie and the fairy stared while the trolls gasped. A moment later Jack cheered and the wizard shouted as the dust swirled.

"Done!" Gellzoowin said with a sneer. "You're finished. I got you!...I..."

But once again his words were cut short, when the giant suddenly bolted upright and grabbed his throat, leaving his knife buried in the ground. Gellzoowin stared with a curious look and like everyone else, wondered what was happening.

The giant twisted and turned. He wrenched his body this way and that, with sudden jolts and jerks, all the while clutching his neck. The trolls were equally baffled by his behavior until the titan's face turned red as a beet and it looked like he was being strangled. The problem was he was standing all alone and appeared to be doing it to himself.

Raylin climbed aboard the troll wagon and scurried up to the crows nest as quick as he could to get a better look. Then from atop the high perch, the keen eyed tracker pointed and shouted. "Look! Around his neck!"

Just then Katie thought she saw a glint of something beneath the giant's chin. At the same time, the good friar Jingles thrust his fist into the air and cried out.

"It's the angel!"

Gracus did his best to get his fingers around the iron chain wrapped around his neck, but his giant fingers were far too big and thick to grab hold. Then while he stood there clawing at his throat, he suddenly remembered the light, the bright flash that he saw. The glint that he thought was the blade of his knife was the angel in his silver armor that jumped like a spark, and wrapped the chain around his neck before he knew what was happening. And now the angel was on his back and he was being strangled.

Stadia crouched between the titan's shoulders, with the chain pulled tight and rode the giant like a monstrous bull. He pulled and groaned with all his strength as Gracus reached back blindly, trying to grab hold of him. The giant spit and sputtered and ripped out great black clumps of his own hair as he clawed the air behind him then dropped to his knees, and pounded the earth with both fists in a fit of rage that shook the ground. He roared and bellowed till he made so much useless noise, he almost got the attention of the ogres who were still fighting aboard their wagon.

With his energy spent, the giant collapsed, sending clouds of dust spewing into the air. But the titan was far from done. He rolled onto his back then arched his body and dropped down hard, again and again. The land shuddered and quaked, but try as he might to crush the angel, the chain stayed tight around his neck.

Finally Gracus struggled to his knees and crawled to the edge of the woods, where he ripped two giant bushes out of the ground, each one the size of a forty foot oak. The titan rose up and swung the trees into the air, then brought them down on his back, with dirt and grass flying. Tree limbs exploded and branches splintered and cracked like kindling as blow after blow rained down on the mighty angel. But Stadia's will was as strong as iron and the armor of God, was even stronger.

When it was done, the bushes were smashed to pieces until all that remained were two jagged stumps clutched in the giant's fists and his hair was a massive tangle of branches with giant splinters lodged in his back like planks of lumber. With no air left, the titan staggered to his feet and grabbed his throat once more. His hands were rubbery and weak and only pawed at his neck as his face turned blue and he stumbled.

Everyone gazed up in horror and watched as the seventy foot giant fought to find his balance. Kitch wasted no time and grabbed Katie by the hand.

"Where is the angel? I don't see him!" Katie said.

"Not now!" Kitch yelled and ran with Katie in tow.

Goe Garth took one look then scampered up to his seat at the front of the troll wagon and grabbed the reigns as the other trolls climbed aboard. The troll leader cracked his whip and Juggernaut pranced as he turned aside, and brought the huge wagon about.

The titan's eyes were nearly swollen shut as he swayed forward. Jack jumped out of his comfy chair and staggered back in horror, feeling his way behind him then finally turned to run, and sped past the wizard who stood there staring up in disbelief. With a few more steps, the giant rocked back on his heels, then teetered forward, and down he came.

"Hurry, Goe Garth! Hurry!" Gimble shouted.

"I know, I know!" Goe Garth said, and cracked his whip.

The black horse lunged forward with the huge wagon rumbling behind him. Kitch was still running when Katie looked back.

"He's falling!" She cried, her eyes gaping wide as the titan toppled over like a giant tree.

"RUN!!" Binderbec yelled, from the back of the wagon and reached out for them.

Jingles, and Rumyon joined the old soldier, and stretched out their arms as Kitch scooped Katie off the ground.

"Take her!" she cried and tossed Katie into the air.

Binderbec caught the child and nearly went over the side, when Jingles grabbed him from behind and together they pulled Katie into the wagon. Then with one desperate leap, Kitch dove for the back of the wagon as it pulled away and Rumyon and Gral grabbed her arms. "GOOOOO!!" They yelled and lifted her aboard.

"Wait for me!" Jack cried when all of a sudden the eighty ton giant crashed to his knees with the sound of thunder. The explosion threw Jack into the air with his legs kicking and arms wheeling, when Jack suddenly remembered he could fly. With his head pointed down he launched himself into the dirt then arched his back and tried to pull up. But with no time to stop or look back, Jack closed his eyes and slammed into the ground with his arms flailing, and feet dragging as he shot through the grass, like a torpedo through water.

By the time Gellzoowin turned to run, the shadow of the titan had already swept over him. As quick as he could, the wizard flew to the thunder cane, then plucked it out of the ground, and looked to the ogres. The dumb brutes were still brawling and fighting aboard their wagon and it wasn't until one of the wild boars gnawed through its leather harness then broke free, that the ogres looked up. And as Rogad jumped to save his life, just before the giant fell, he thought he saw the wizard standing nearby, smiling as though the total destruction that was about to happen was of no concern to him, at which time the wizard melted away into thin air.

The giant came crashing down with a roar and this time the land rose up like a tidal wave that hurled a wall of rocks and debris forty feet into the air like a monstrous curtain rushing forth across the land. Goe Garth held on as the troll wagon pitched forward, and the violent quake sent the crew sprawling. Trees toppled and the cliffs shook as the shower of rocks and dust billowed out further and further until it covered the Rabble wagon, blinding them in their desperate flight to escape. Then with the quake rumbling into the distance and the dust settling, Goe Garth called to the horse and pulled back on the reigns. "Whoooaa, boy! Whoa!" he said then looked around to see where he was.

Katie and the trolls rose up one by one and dusted themselves off as they peered over the side of the wagon. In the quiet stillness, everything was dark again. All of the magical lights, conjured up by the wizard were gone, and the titan lay face down between the shadowy cliffs, perfectly still like a man mountain sprawled out across the land. In fact, laying there in the dark, with the dirt piled all around him and the enormous mound of brush and branches sticking out of his back, it was hard to tell where the giant stopped and the ground began.

Somewhere in the darkness Jack climbed to his feet, covered in dirt and spitting grass from his teeth. He coughed to clear his throat then looked around. Only twenty feet behind him, was the awesome and immense head of the fallen giant, which 'was face down in the dirt and lay totally still. As Jack stood there looking up, he could hear the sound of heavy breathing close by then turned to see the wild boar standing next to him, looking up as well. The beast panted through its thick hairy snout and was shaking terribly, which was more than could be said for its companion. The other boar was crushed and buried somewhere beneath the giant. When it was a little less shaky, the monstrous pig looked at Jack, snorted at him, then turned and trotted off into the night, wagging its stubby tail. Jack watched until the animal disappeared in the dark and there came another sound, the sound of something stirring somewhere above. He looked up at the giant and the tangled mass of branches piled on top of him. Indeed, there was enough wood stuck in the giant's back to build a small house.

As the sound grew louder, Jack squinted into the darkness. Something was struggling underneath the dense thick brush, and breaking through tree limbs as it fought to make its way to the surface. A moment later, a hand rose up out of the debris, and the angel emerged, tall and unscathed. His armor shimmered as he looked to the sky and the dismal clouds above, then reached back and dragged the heavy iron chain out of the murky underbrush beneath him.

Jack peered up at the angel as he gathered the thick coils of chain together and looped them over his shoulder. There was no boasting or pride in the guardian. In fact, in his moment of glory, Stadia showed no emotion at all as he stood atop the fallen giant, then slowly looked down and cast his watchful gaze upon the boy. Jack staggered back, fearing the angel more than ever then tripped and stumbled into the wizard who was suddenly standing right behind him.

Gellzoowin pushed the boy aside with a sneer, then raised the thunder cane and thrust it into the ground to make his own challenge before the angel. Gellzoowin glared at the sword of Raymah strapped to the angel's side, the weapon he had sent the goblin to steal, the weapon which was never truly out of the angel's reach.

"I suppose you think that was clever." Gellzoowin sneered. "Well I have a few tricks of my own!" He said and gripped the thunder cane firmly.

Stadia smiled as if amused by the threat then tossed the huge length of chain into the air. Jack watched it spiral toward them then jumped back when it crashed to the ground at the wizard's feet, with a horrible clatter.

"Confounded angel!" Gellzoowin snarled. "Is there no end to you?"

Just then, something stirred in the dark, off to the side and Jack jumped again. When he looked he saw Rogad, half buried in dirt and leaning against the giant's enormous ear. But the ogre was in a state of shock and barely moved. The noise was coming from somewhere next to him. It was the ogre Slag who was just now, clawing and scratching his way through the rock and dirt, trying to dig out from under the giant's massive shoulder. The ogre could have used some help, but with a fair amount of grunting and groaning, he finally freed himself then rolled onto his back, and stared blankly at the sky. The two brutes, Rogad and Slag were all that was left of the ogre clan. Their wagon and supplies, weapons and food, comrades and companions, were all crushed and buried under the giant, gone for good. When Rogad finally came around, the two ogres stood to their feet, battered and bruised, and looked at the immense giant that had nearly killed them. Aside from a grunt and a wince of pain, there was no reaction. Now that the others were gone, Rogad and Slag simply looked exhausted.

The Rabble wagon trundled out of the darkness and the trolls stared in awe. Stadia stood atop the giant who looked twice the size, now that he was lying down and seemed to go on forever. Goe Garth called out.

"We have a champion!"

"Here, here!" cried Rumyon.

"Here, here!" the others yelled. The trolls applauded as the angel leapt from the giant's back then touched down light as a feather in front of the wagon. A moment later he drew his cloak out of thin air and wrapped it around himself as Katie looked down from the wagon above, beaming a smile from ear to ear and clapped her hands.

"Oh, you're alright!" she said.

Stadia looked up with a playful smile.

"You weren't worried were you?" He asked.

Kitch came along side Katie and gave her a reassuring hug.

"Not for a moment." she said then looked a little less certain. "Well maybe just a little."

Binderbec joined the others at the front of the wagon to celebrate the angel's victory and happened to notice Jack standing off to the side. The boy kept his distance, looking timid and afraid.

"Hey boy!" Binderbec shouted and waved. "Pretty good

show, eh? A comfy couch, a nice little snack and WHAP! A giant falls on yer' head!"

The trolls burst out laughing and Jack just watched, content to sulk as they cheered and had their fun.

"Well done, angel. Well done!" Rumyon said then cried out. "A toast! A toast!"

"A TOAST!" said the trolls.

Each one produced a cup, a flask or goblet and the toast-master poured the wine.

"To the angel!... Our champion! Our protector!"

"HERE! HERE!" they yelled. "HERE! HERE!" "HERE! HERE!" With three cheers and three drinks the toast was done and Goe Garth beckoned to the angel.

"Stadia! What do we do now?" he asked then looked at the wizard. "What do we do with him?" the troll said with a frown.

"He is my concern. Continue on," Stadia said. "The child of God will lead you. Travel through the night and I will find you by day break. In the mean time I will tend to the wizard and his young apprentice."

"What are you going to do?" Katie asked.

Goe Garth gathered the reigns and the trolls turned away from Jack with a look of regret as they went back to their places aboard the wagon. Katie looked back and forth at the angel and her brother, when the wagon lurched forward and she called out again.

"What are you going to do?!"

But Stadia remained silent and standing there in his long gray cloak he looked more like an executioner than an angel of mercy.

As the wagon got under way, the two hulking ogres, Rogad and Slag, clambered aboard and flopped down on the deck. The beasts made enough noise that the trolls came running. Gimble was first to draw his sword and stood before the ogres. "Get off my wagon! This be no place for the likes of you!" he said.

"Who invited you?!" Gral sneered with sword and spear in hand.

Slag glared at the troll and looked him up and down.

"I eat you for snack!" Slag growled with his yellow teeth glistening in the dark, to which Gral shoved his spear under the ogre's nose, till Slag was looking cross eyed at the tip of his blade. "Not before you taste this!" Gral said with a grin.

Jingles stepped forward and took Gral by the arm. "Leave them, brother. They've been through enough. We have room. Let them be."

Gral Tibbore withdrew the spear, with a grunt and the trolls walked away to light the lanterns. Gimble stayed behind and watched the ogres as the orange lights flickered on around them. The beasts ignored the little troll as they made themselves comfortable and huddled in a corner then pulled a thick canvas tarp over themselves like a blanket. Gimble frowned and pointed his sword.

"Now you listen to me!" he said. "If you are to stay, you will do as you're told and attend to your share of the work. Your shiftless ways will gain you nothing. One slip, and over you go! Is that clear?"

The ogres pulled the covers over their heads with a grunt which was as much a response as the troll could hope for and Gimble marched off to join the others.

Now that they were leaving, the trolls watched as the wagon rumbled past the fallen giant and the torch lights lit the man mountain. They passed the giant's knife, still buried in the ground with its polished wooden handle glistening in the dark. The muddy pit was a deep black hole where the titan had driven his boot into the ground. Then on they went across the open plain toward the mountain pass below the shadowy cliffs. With the fairy's arms to comfort her, Katie looked back filled with worry for her brother and gazed across the darkness until she could see him no longer.

Jack watched the lantern lights fade as the troll wagon headed off into the night. When out of the stillness came a faint little noise, a plea to the angel.

"Don't hurt him!... him...him..." Katie said, her tiny voice echoing in the distance and then they were gone.

When Jack turned around the angel was glaring down at him and Jack backed away slowly. He looked around then moved toward the wizard and was about to slip behind Gellzoowin when he was suddenly shoved back into the open. The hideous hook nosed goblin stuck his head out and glared at Jack. "Go find your own hiding place." he hissed from behind the wizard then peeked at the angel and ducked out of sight.

Now that they were face to face, Gellzoowin held his thunder cane which was still planted in the ground and smiled with a devilish grin.

"Tell me, angel. Are you faster than lightning?" He said then gave the thunder cane a tug. The wizard smiled and pulled, then smiled and pulled again. With another smile and a pull, Gellzoowin grabbed the wooden staff with both hands and gave it a good yank.

"Zap him master, zap him!" the goblin whispered in his nervous little voice, and wondered what was taking so long.

Gellzoowin yanked and pulled, again and again until he was fighting with the thing that refused to budge. Stadia observed the wizard's strange behavior with a curious smirk. It was obvious that Gellzoowin meant to use the thing as some sort of weapon, but he wondered what the wizard could have possibly hoped to accomplish by tugging on the little sprig of a tree. When Gellzoowin finally looked, the staff had sprouted leaves and was indeed rooted to the spot. Gellzoowin glared at the budding little tree in disbelief.

"How in the world?!" He gasped, then released the staff and staggered back. "I am cursed, truly cursed." The wizard said in astonishment.

"The land of great discoveries" Stadia said, as he came forward.

The wizard was not amused nor was he prepared to fight the angel without an advantage. Now that his thunder cane was gone, Gellzoowin stared in a sulk and just when Stadia was about to grab him, something made the angel pause. It was a stale smell, a noxious odor in the air.

Stadia backed away as a faint mist began to seep out of the wizard's skin and roll down his body, until a thick green cloud poured out from under his robe. It rippled across the ground, and bubbled and boiled. The foul mist turned the grass brown and scorched the earth where the wizard stood. Numlock clapped his little green hands joyfully as the angel slowly backed away and retreated to a safer distance, while the essence of evil flowed out of and surrounded the wizard like a shield.

The horrible stench smelled like rotten eggs but not to Jack. He took deep breaths, one after another and filled his nostrils with it. To him, the green vapor was as sweet as honey and orange blossom nectar. Jack gazed at the strange green mist churning like cauldron smoke around his legs and smiled at the clever wizard who had stopped the angel in his tracks.

The wizard smiled cleverly. "What's the matter, angel? Is it something I said? Please come closer."

Stadia held his ground as Gellzoowin put his hands on Jack's shoulders and placed the boy in front of him, like a prized possession. "Have you nothing to say?" the wizard asked.

Stadia's eyes narrowed. "Coward." He growled.

"Me?" said the wizard in surprise. "No, it is you who stands at a distance. I have nothing to fear, unlike you, for at least I am not a murderer." The wizard said, pointing an accusing finger at the giant laying face down in the dirt.

"You have killed an innocent being, angel, killed him in

cold blood. Where is your mercy now? You misused your powers and for that you will pay. Your so called god of mercy, whom you serve, will now have no choice but to punish you. He will pour out his wrath upon you, strip you of your power and cast you down, like the tyrant that he is. Then you will be condemned for all eternity! So you see, angel. You have lost and I...have won."

No sooner had Gellzoowin finished, than a loud monstrous noise broke the silence. It came from out of the dark and was so deep and so loud that it shook the ground and echoed into the night. Jack and the goblin looked at each other with eyes bulging. When it grew quiet again, they slowly turned their gaze to the dark mountainous figure that was stretched out before them. The sound was unmistakable. It was the long anguished moan of a giant, a giant that was merely unconscious and very much alive.

With only the slightest movement of his head, the titan sent a wall of dirt cascading down. Jack and the goblin jumped back while Gellzoowin just stood there, looking thoroughly disgusted as the dirt settled at his feet. The angel fixed his eyes on the wizard.

"God is merciful and in turn I have shown mercy on the giant and he lives. You are the tyrant, wizard. You are the one who lives by wrath and seeks to condemn. You turned the giant's father to stone... Now you will turn him back."

"...And if I don't," said Gellzoowin.

"Then I pray that God will save you." The angel replied.

"Hah! Save me?... Save me from what?" Gellzoowin scoffed.

Stadia glared at the evil wizard. "Save you, from me." said the angel.

Slowly the wizard's smile turned to a frown and Jack watched the green smoke disappear from around them as quickly as it had come.

"Done," said the wizard with a scornful sneer then took

Jack by the hand. "Come, boy. Let us leave this awful place and find somewhere more hospitable to rest."

Jack gave an awkward smile as he trotted off and headed into the night, with the wizard and the goblin hurrying along behind. Numlock glanced back every now and then, and just before he disappeared in the dark with his green eyes glowing, he shook his fist at the angel then turned and chased after his master.

When they had gone, Stadia looked up at the giant that was laid out before him and heard another sound in the darkness as something stirred at the edge of the field. The great brown bear climbed out of the bushes with bits of elderberries stuck to his fur and had no memory of how he had gotten there. A few fragments of wood still clung to his back, the splintered remains of Katie's saddle chair. Bromwin shook himself, till all of the wood had fallen away, and winced at the terrible pain in his side. The bear limped across the open field and took his time as he made his way to the angel, then looked up and down the length of the enormous giant.

"Hmmmmm... What did I miss?" he asked.

The angel watched as the giant stirred and the wall of dirt shifted again.

"Nothing really," he said then turned and smiled at the bear. "Come, my friend. The others have gone ahead. We must catch up to them before day break."

Stadia moved slowly and the bear limped along side while together they followed the dusty trail and left the sleeping giant behind.

By morning the titan would awaken to see his father, with fluffy white beard and rosy red cheeks, smiling down on him. He would be surrounded by a crowd of friends and the old wood cutter would be curious to know how his son had wandered so far outside of their kingdom, but Gracus would remember little and consider it all a dream. With that, the old woodcutter would give a hearty laugh, gather up his son, and head back to the high country where he and the other giants would be safe; away from angels and wizards, and the world of troublesome little specks.

CHAPTER SIXTEEN

What's a Gollock?

*A*lthough darkness had settled on the land, there was still a faint half light from the moon; and the keen eyed tracker called down to the crew of the troll wagon.

"Wagoneers - yooh! We have reached the Eastland border!" He shouted from his crow's nest and pointed ahead. Katie moved to the front of the Rabble wagon and peered over Goe Garth's shoulder.

"What about my brother? Shouldn't we wait for him to catch up? " She said.

"I would not worry about him now." Goe Garth said then pointed west toward the black mountains on the horizon.

"The land of great discoveries now lies to the west and south of us. We skirt north along its eastern border and have done well to stay clear of its many… mysteries." The troll's voice trailed off as though he were suddenly distracted.

"Farewell." He said. "Tis a shame and a pity that we should leave this land and never know what discoveries lay beyond the misty mountains." The troll said with a heavy heart.

Gimble sat beside him with a somber look and gazed

into the night.

"I feel it too." Gimble said. Katie looked at the little troll who gazed in a trance. "For unknown mysteries tug at my heart as well."

"And mine too!" said Gral Tibbore. The big troll clutched his spear and looked into the night.

Friar Jingles cradled his troll sack and the book within. "Courage lads! The land beckons to us. But we must not listen. We must not heed its call."

Rumyon came along side the little friar. "The land?" He said.

Jingles nodded as he tried to resist its power. "It doesn't want us to leave." He said and turned his eyes away. "It is a trick of the mind. I have read of this place. It is here we find the last of the great discoveries which dwells along this lonely border. Guard your minds well, for now that we are leaving, we glimpse ourselves in the longing of our own hearts. Mystery, the dark enchantress is upon us."

Rumyon peered into the night and was already trapped in its spell.

"Mystery," he whispered, lost in his own imaginings.

Soon the wagon began to slow and Jingles turned to see Goe Garth pulling back on the reigns with his eyes fixed on the dark mountains. The good friar shouted.

"Goe Garth!... Let go of the reigns! Let them go!" he said.

The troll loosened his grip and let the reigns fall as he and Gimble listened to a faint voice in the wind. The black stallion moved on and followed the trail as the enchanted spirit called to the trolls.

Jingles tried not to look, but slowly his eyes turned and his mind began to wander. "How many have been lured into the shadowy hills, by things real or imagined, only to meet their fate in a barren wasteland?"

Raylin gazed out across the night. "She speaks on the wind, gentle fables like a mother whispering to her child in slumber."

Aye lads." Said Rumyon. "Haunted dreams fill my mind, dreams of treasure. Dare we not claim them?" He muttered softly.

One after another, images came to them all, images of legends and wondrous things that stirred their hearts and amazed them.

Like a vision before his eyes, Raylin saw the "Cloak of Invisibility," hidden in the white cliffs beyond Gunvernia. With it one could pass through stone and vanish from sight completely.

Rumyon's lips were suddenly parched and he thirst for "The Amber Passion";

a plant that produced nectar which shone red like the setting sun and held the power of healing.

Goe Garth reached out, longing to touch the legendary "Brindle Stone" which lay deep within the Thunderland forest. The magical stone, well guarded by giant animals, could conjure up anything imaginable.

Jingles dreamt of the "The Garden of Angels," hidden away in a quiet glen and could see himself in the tranquil woods, seated on a white stone bench, in the midst of winged seraphim, radiant and luminous beings sent down from heaven.

Binderbec could almost feel "Vesper's Wind," a spirit so beautiful she took men's breath away. While Gral Tibbore saw deep within uncharted mountains, an unknown cave, filled with treasures and a lake of gold.

What Katie saw was most special to her. A stone threshold known as the "Door of Thesle" stood in the ancient ruins of an old city. Its stone walls were invisible by day and could only be seen in the light of the full moon. The magic door lay at the heart of the ruin, a mystic portal that could take you anywhere you wanted to go. For Katie, it was a doorway home. In her mind's eye, she could see her Mom and Dad standing in the mist just beyond the door, waiting for her with open arms and smiling faces. Katie gazed at the image of her parents and longed to be back home.

Then there was Gimble. The hungry troll smacked his lips and rubbed his belly as he observed a sandwich, a magnificent sandwich, twenty feet long. Beyond it was a giant's banquet filled with food, enough food for a hundred Gimbles, for a hundred years, which was regretfully more than a hundred miles away.

"I can't take it! I can't take it!" Gimble cried out, sobbing like a baby. The trolls gathered around to comfort him and shared in his sorrow, each one longing to touch the secrets they would sadly leave behind. But as the black stallion drew them farther and farther away, the images became fainter, and soon the whispering wind of the far hills fell silent and the land of great discoveries faded from their minds.

Jack and the wizard walked for hours in the dark, and soon Jack was so tired he could barely keep up. His blue wizard's robe felt heavy and cumbersome and made the going difficult; while the wizard marched at a brisk pace, with a scowl on his face and seemed determined to leave the boy behind.

"Hey, wait! What's the rush?" Jack shouted. "Gelly!... Wait for me!"

With a word, the wizard stopped in his tracks and whirled around like he had just been hit in the head with a snowball. Jack slowed to a walk and peered at the wizard's eyes that were suddenly glowing bright red, like two hot coals in the dark. Numlock stood well back, and was glad not to be the focus of the wizard's attention for a change.

Gellzoowin spoke slowly; his voice trembling with rage. "My name is not... Gelly!" he said. "It is Gellzoowin Octor Payliantis, and if you call me that once more, I will..."

The wizard was so furious he just glared at the boy until his glowing red eyes faded in the darkness then without another word he turned and walked away. Jack stood there in shock as Gellzoowin marched on and had no way of knowing that in the wizard's language, "gelly" was a horrible word which plainly translated meant, "the utter most hind part of a wart hog's backside."

Still, all things considered, being called a pig's rear end was the least of the wizard's problems. Gellzoowin peered into the night, across the dark open plain and seethed to himself as he walked and pondered his situation.

"It all started out so well." The wizard hissed.

And now everything had suddenly gone wrong. He had lost his goblins, lost his thunder cane. He had lost his ogres when the giant fell on them. He had even lost his giant who had lost the fight with the angel. And now that the angel, who was supposed to be dead was still alive, he felt he was losing control of the situation. On top of his injured pride, they had been hiking for miles and his feet ached terribly. But in spite of it all, the wizard was reassured to know that help was on its way. He had summoned his carriage which they had abandoned, miles away at the edge of the giant forest. Under his magic power, the carriage would make its way to him, and stop at nothing to get there, even if it arrived in splinters. Gellzoowin peered into the night as he walked, hoping to get a glimpse of something and listened for the sound of wagon wheels in the dark, but there was nothing, only the howl of the wind.

"Confounded carriage. Where are you?!" The wizard shouted, and seemed to grow angrier with each step.

Numlock loped along at a distance. He had seen the wizard at his worst and now there was no telling what he might do. Gellzoowin walked and schemed, walked and schemed, trying to think of a plan to destroy the angel, if only to keep his mind off his aching feet.

"Think, think, think," he said to himself, but the more he thought, the madder he became. The madder he became, the less he could think, until he finally stopped with fists clenched, looked up at the dark sky, and screamed till his eyes turned black and the veins bulged in his neck.

"AAAAAARRRRGGHH!!"

Jack backed away as a dark cloud poured out of the wizard's mouth. At first he thought it was smoke that was spewing into the air, which was strange enough, until he heard the weird squeaking sound and the cloud grew larger and larger. By the time Jack thought to run, it was too late. The thick black swarm of tiny bats, no bigger than bugs, filled the air and covered Jack. Their teeny wings fluttered across Jack's face as they flew in his hair and tried to go up his nose. Jack sputtered and swatted at them, trying to keep them away, and would have screamed but didn't dare open his mouth. They swarmed around the goblin, who whimpered and jumped and flailed at the horrible creatures.

"Go away! Go away!" he cried.

The tiny bats squeaked and flitted about frantically until they finally figured out which way was up then rose into the night sky and disappeared. When it was over and Jack had barely caught his breath, he looked at the wizard who was much calmer now and staring off into the darkness.

"What was that?!" Jack yelled.

"It was necessary." Gellzoowin said quietly.

"Necessary?" Jack said then jumped with a start when the last of the tiny bug bats flew out of his hair. "GROSS!!" he shouted, swatting at his head then stood there glaring at the wizard. "You could have at least warned me before you gacked and spewed bugs all over me!" he said and was still shaking when he heard a noise and whirled around. Something was coming straight toward them out of the dark and he could hear it crushing rocks on the path behind them. Jack squinted then backed away as the horseless carriage rolled out of the dark like a ghost ship coming out of the fog. With a yelp for joy, the goblin rushed past him.

"Master, your wagon! We're saved!" he shouted.

"Aaahh! Here you are, finally." Gellzoowin said as it came to a stop, right in front of him. The carriage had indeed arrived but had obviously suffered some abuses in the course of its travels. The cloth canopy was torn and the sides of the carriage were raked with monstrous claw marks, as though it had been attacked by giant wild animals. In addition, there were large clumps of bushes and branches caught in the wheel spokes and the undercarriage of the wagon. Without further inspection the wizard climbed aboard like a king ascending the throne, then turned to Jack and the goblin who were about to join him.

"Clear that off." he demanded, pointing at the wheels.

Numlock hurried to obey and after what Jack had just been through, the last thing he wanted was to upset the wizard. Both he and the goblin quickly went from wheel to wheel, clearing off the brush as fast as they could while Gellzoowin peered up at the sky.

"Come along. We don't have all night." he said impatiently.

When the job was done, the goblin hopped aboard and perched himself atop the carriage railing. Then as soon as Jack climbed in, they were off, with a wave of the wizard's hand. Now that Gellzoowin was back aboard his wagon he fell silent once more and stared straight ahead, guiding the coach with his magic. Jack watched and waited, afraid of what else might hop out of the wizard's mouth, should he lose his temper.

"The angel was supposed to be dead." Gellzoowin grumbled. "But now that he is alive, how shall I proceed… How shall I proceed?" he said thinking aloud.

Numlock blurted out, "It will come, master. It will come. Good ideas take time."

The wizard turned slowly and Numlock hopped down from the railing.

"Please don't kill me." he said and shrank back into the shadows near the floor.

Gellzoowin turned away and sulked. "The angel must be dealt with before we find the white horse, but how?... If only I had a dragon." Gellzoowin thought, even though there were no dragons in the region.

Dragons were found only in the high mountains and black swamps of the kingdoms to the south and they were headed north. The wizard shook his head.

"NO! NO! NO!" he yelled, then threw his head back and looked to the sky. The goblin cringed and Jack shied away. When he did, the wizard happened to glance over to see the boy huddled in his corner of the carriage. Numlock was no less afraid, but was at least smart enough to hide in the shadows where he could not be seen.

The wizard scowled at Jack who was clearly afraid. But as Gellzoowin watched, he noticed something. The wizard couldn't say what it was exactly, but in some way, the boy reminded him of himself when he was but a lad. Perhaps it was his youthful curiosity. Or maybe it was the fear in the boy's eyes, fear of the wizard's untold powers.

Gellzoowin knew that fear, the fear of being at the mercy of someone more powerful than yourself. As the carriage rumbled on, Gellzoowin thought back and remembered his old master, the great and evil sorcerer, Protem.

Protem was one of the more accomplished wizards of his time and very fond of making up his own spells. In fact he had devised a spell that gave him the power to see through solid objects and pass through walls. It was that spell that turned his eyes as white as snow. But even with those frightful eyes, Protem was far worse than he looked.

Gellzoowin was only twelve when he had become an apprentice to the old sorcerer and as a youth, Gellzoowin had never known anyone more wicked than Protem. It was the old sorcerer who used to zap him with electric shocks whenever he felt it necessary, or else just for the sheer fun of it. Protem would always wait till the boy wasn't looking. Sometimes he would even leave the room, then reach back through the wall; and with a snap of his finger, a silvery thread of light would leap from his hand and hit the boy like a hot lash across his back. And if that wasn't bad enough, there was the terrible sound of the wizard's laughter. It was like the whine of a sick cat and Gellzoowin hated that almost more than the pain of the lash.

When Protem was granted the high unholy status of grand sorcerer, things got even worse. Gellzoowin got zapped all the more and each time, he would look into the wizard's white eyes for some explanation, but there was none, only the cruel satisfaction the wizard got from his pain and suffering. Gellzoowin remembered the day when the torture ended. The old sorcerer was about to conduct an experiment of teleportation when he pointed his bony finger at Gellzoowin, gave specific instructions about how he wanted his dinner cooked, then "poofed" himself into another world. Unfortunately, he had forgotten to take the return spell with him and wherever he was, the evil sorcerer was trapped and stuck there forever, never to be heard from again. And none of his magic tricks or even his white eyes could ever bring him back. At least that's the way Gellzoowin liked to remember the story.

The truth was Protem had indeed taken a return spell. It was just the wrong one.

Gellzoowin had switched them. The spell that Protem had taken was a spell for bugs. With it you could make insects appear and disappear and send them anywhere you wanted them to go.

Gellzoowin knew the clever old sorcerer would try to find a way to bring himself back, and as the sorcerer's apprentice, he had thought it out quite carefully. The only way the wizard could use the spell to return was to change himself into a bug and that simply wasn't done. To change from wizard to bug was not only gross, it was foolish since bugs were stupid; which meant that once you had a bug brain you would not only forget how to change back, you would forget everything entirely and then you'd be stuck as a bug.

Gellzoowin remembered how he laughed when Protem disappeared. It was the happiest day of his young life and he hadn't seen the old sorcerer since. But that wasn't quite the end of it. Shortly after he left, Protem started using bugs to send messages. Gellzoowin recalled when a rather large black beetle appeared on his dining room table, with tiny white letters written on its back.

It read, "Send me the proper spell you silly little dolt!"

Gellzoowin smiled and tossed the bug out the window. There were more bugs, more messages, more pleadings for help. Gellzoowin ignored them all. Eventually the bugs stopped coming all together and that was that. When years had passed and Protem was forgotten, Gellzoowin took over the castle and had become an accomplished wizard in his own right, with powers to surpass the old sorcerer. He smiled at the thought.

This made Jack a little uncomfortable since the wizard was looking right at him with a strange grin on his face. Gellzoowin's eyes drifted very slightly and he appeared to be off in a dream, lost for the moment, in his happy thoughts. And although his eyes were open, Jack started to wonder if the wizard was even awake when suddenly Gellzoowin blinked and he was back.

Jack could tell the wizard was back, because he was being frowned at again. The wizard scowled at the boy, who still looked afraid. Gellzoowin thought about giving Jack an electric shock and rather fancied the idea. Jack backed away sensing danger.

"One good shock couldn't hurt," the wizard told himself. "Well, actually it could hurt quite a bit." He thought. Still, it would give the boy something to think about. Gellzoowin tossed the idea around for a while then decided that all things considered, he'd better not. If nothing else, he needed the boy to help keep the girl in line, especially if he was going to find the white horse.

"Yes, Majesty of course...of course." Gellzoowin reminded himself then turned away. With the wizard looking elsewhere, Jack breathed a sigh of relief.

The carriage rolled on, until it came to a dry river bed then gradually dipped forward as it started down the embankment. The dried stream was full of rocks, some stones as big as a troll's fist.

The wizard's carriage swayed back and forth as they started across, the wheels rumbling over the rocks which made a great clatter as they went. Jack and the goblin held on as Gellzoowin glared over the side and watched the rocks churning beneath the wheels then all at once his face changed and he looked at Jack.

"Rocks!" the wizard shouted and nearly leapt out of his seat as the carriage made its way up the other side of the dried river bed. As soon as they were across, the wizard clapped his hands and laughed aloud. Both Jack and the goblin watched him suspiciously.

Gellzoowin smiled at his own blind folly. He had been trying to think of a plan and with the problem of the angel to deal with, and all the many disappointments, he forgot he already had one.

Once the carriage was back on level ground and moving smoothly again, the wizard reached into his pocket and turned to Jack, who was looking at him with serious doubts.

"Are you all right?" The wizard asked.

Jack glanced down as the wizard pulled something out

of his robe.

"Sure." he said, trying to look calm.

Gellzoowin opened his hand slowly and when Jack looked, he saw a little blue stone lying in the wizard's palm. It was smaller than a robin's egg, and had tiny white flecks all over it. Numlock crept out of the shadows, his eyes wide and glowing green. The goblin immediately recognized the stone, for he was there in the Thunderland forest, when they had found it. Gellzoowin cupped his hands and held it carefully, but as far as Jack could tell there was nothing particularly interesting about the little stone, at least nothing that he could see.

"Do you know what this is, boy?"

Jack squinted, with a pained look on his face and wished the wizard hadn't asked.

"A rock?" he said, and forced a weak smile.

Gellzoowin drew back in surprise. "Not just any rock, dear boy. It is the only one of its kind. This is the magic Brindle Stone, which contains instant magical power, the greatest and most amazing of all wonders in all the Land of Great Discoveries!"

Gellzoowin announced it like it was the main event, and indeed it was. For with all the dangers and all the dreams of all the ages, no one had ever been able to fetch the legendary Brindle Stone from the Thunderland Forest, and those who had tried were no longer living. But then, none of them had ever enlisted the help of a seventy foot titan to do it. Jack looked at the puny stone in the wizard's hand and smirked.

"Looks like just a rock to me." he said.

"By the flaming tongue of the Gollock!" The wizard exclaimed as he sat forward, and held the rock closer for Jack to see. "This is far more than a rock, boy. This stone can conjure up anything you can think of."

"Really?" Jack said. "Anything?"

"Indeed... Anything." the wizard said then held the

bright blue stone under Jack's nose and watched as the boy's eyes lit up with excitement. Gellzoowin smiled, for in his cunning he was far too cautious to use the magic stone himself and devised a simple plan to test it. Since the magic stone could conjure up anything you could imagine, and what he needed was a dragon to kill the angel, he would use Jack to make the wish. The only trick was getting the boy to wish for the right thing.

Gellzoowin gazed into Jack's eyes, trying to plant the image of a dragon into his mind then spoke softly.

"Anything you can think of, anything at all, even... a dragon." Gellzoowin said, trying to nudge Jack with a casual suggestion, but the boy was not as feeble minded as an ogre. Instead, his thoughts were a jumble of ideas that rushed through his head in a blur and were impossible to see clearly.

"Think...think!" Gellzoowin said, staring intently as he tried to read his mind.

Soon a faint smile crept over Jack's face and images began to rise out of the boy's mind, like fish coming to the surface of a pond. But what the wizard saw did not impress him.

It seemed that Jack was hungry and most of what he was thinking about had to do with cheese. There were cheese pizzas, grilled cheese sandwiches, a cheese burger, macaroni and cheese, cheese on crackers, cheese flavored popcorn and something called cheese wiz, which the wizard found offensive even though he didn't know what it was.

Then there were the non-cheesy items, electronic things like video games, a wide screen TV and all sorts of remote control toys. Just then a peanut butter and jelly sandwich popped into Jack's mind then disappeared, only to be replaced by a Norton 500 dirt bike with huge knobby wheels. The wizard frowned at all of the strange images and knew that the boy was utterly incapable of deciding what to wish for.

"Dragon, dragon, dragon!" the wizard said with his mind, trying to force the idea into the boy's head. But Jack just tapped his cheek as he gazed up at the sky, and gave no sign that he was anywhere near making a decision. Unable to wait any longer, Gellzoowin decided on a more direct approach.

"Perhaps a dragon!" the wizard shouted and made the boy jump. Gellzoowin cleared his throat then assumed a gentler tone.

"Wouldn't you like to see a dragon, a real live dragon in real life?" Gellzoowin said expectantly, as though that would be the most perfect thing ever. Jack thought about it a while.

"There're a lot of things I'd like to see," Jack said. "I can't make up my mind."

"Ah yes, well that is a problem. Isn't it?" the wizard said, more cleverly than a crooked used car salesman.

Jack gave him a curious look. "What do you mean?"

"Well, you see there is one thing, one very important thing you should know," the wizard said.

"What? What is it?" Jack inquired with greater interest.

Now that Gellzoowin had the boy's attention, he was more aloof and appeared somewhat disinterested. "Well, whatever you decide, you must be careful and choose wisely, for although the stone has great power, it is limited." The wizard said then gazed down at the stone. It was a pause of the utmost eloquence which caused Jack to ask. "Limited how? In what way?"

Gellzoowin could almost see the dragon materializing before his eyes as he continued. "I'm sorry to say, but it is widely known that the magic of the stone will only work once. It can only grant one spell for each person who uses it."

Jack sat back and suddenly looked disinterested all over again.

"What good is that?" he said, and instead of seeing the one wish as incredibly precious, he now saw the stone as utterly useless.

The wizard hardly knew what to say and suddenly the carriage was picking up more speed, which Jack noticed immediately. Then with his anger growing and the wind howling around them, Gellzoowin glared at Jack and finally shouted.

"By the six legs of the fiery Gollock! This is the Magic Brindle Stone, boy! It possesses the power of absolute magic! There is nothing it cannot produce! Nothing! The only limit is that of your imagination. Only a fool would question its power!"

Jack quickly withdrew to his corner of the carriage, frightened by the outburst. The goblin who had shown some interest in the matter, quickly decided he didn't want to be turned into a toad and retreated back to the shadows. Gellzoowin sat back and took a deep breath and the carriage slowed its pace as he tried to compose himself.

"Forgive me. Obviously you are too young to fully grasp the significance of such a gift as this. And with only one wish, I understand, you need more time."

The wizard's eyes glinted as he tried to force a little kindness into them. Jack watched him carefully as he continued.

"To help you decide, I would be happy to answer any questions you might have. Please feel free to ask me anything. I am only here to help you. Think of me as your humble servant... really."

After the wizard's behavior, Jack nearly laughed at the suggestion, but managed a polite smile. The carriage rumbled on and there was a long pause as the boy appeared to be considering the wizard's offer. Jack thought and thought while the wizard waited. After a while Gellzoowin gritted his teeth and pretended to smile.

"Well?" he said, and tried not to look like he was about to explode. Numlock shrank back into the shadows, even further. Just then the wizard thought he saw something. He thought he saw the boy's lips move, ever so slightly and leaned forward.

"What's that?!" the wizard said sharply. "What did you say?!" he asked then turned his head sideways and strained to hear.

Jack tried to find the courage but could only bring himself to utter the words in a timid little voice.

"...What's a Gollock?" he whispered.

Gellzoowin was sure he hadn't heard the boy correctly.

"What was that?" the wizard said, half smiling with a ridiculous look on his face.

Jack cleared his throat and tried to speak up. "I said, what's a Gollock?"

Gellzoowin pulled back and tried to keep his eyes from twitching. The question had absolutely nothing to do with the discussion, and was totally unexpected. Now it was the wizard's turn to mutter. Gellzoowin began to nod and mumble to himself until his face trembled and his lips sputtered like the lid on a kettle about to boil.

'He's gonna blow!" Jack thought and tried to think of something to say.

"I'm sorry. I was just curious. I heard you say it, and you mentioned it several times..." Jack said trying to calm the wizard, or at least get his attention.

The wizard kept muttering all the while. And although it was obvious that no amount of apologies could possibly help, Jack simply couldn't stop himself from talking.

"Look, I'm sorry, all right? I only wanted to know what it was, that's all. I thought maybe you could show me."

"Show you?!" Gellzoowin snapped.

"Yeah," Jack said and shrugged. "I just thought that maybe, since I didn't know what it was, you could tell me about it or show me. What's the big deal?"

But the wizard just kept gibbering on and on, occasionally

shaking his head in disgust. Eventually, his ranting grew louder until he spoke in a high pitched voice, and sounded silly. Jack frowned as the wizard made fun of him, saying the same sentence over and over again.

"What's a Gollock? What's a Gollock? Show me a Gollock," Gellzoowin said, mocking the boy and trying to sound as silly and childish as possible. Then as Jack looked on, the wizard gazed upward and shouted to the sky.

"What in the realm of the Nohr World does that have to do with...?" But before he could finish, there was a pop and a spark. Gellzoowin looked down and gasped when he saw the magic stone in the palm of his hand and realized what he had done. "Show me a Gollock," and with those four words he had made his wish.

"No wait!" The wizard said as he felt the power of the magic stone coming to life.

"NO!... NO! A dragon! A dragon!" He shouted desperately since he already knew what a Gollock was and had no desire to waste his only wish on the silly whims of a stupid little boy. But liked it or not, the deed was done. Still he would fight it if he could.

Jack had no idea what was happening when the wizard wrapped his arms around his stomach, and Gellzoowin's face turned as red as a cherry. The more the wizard strained to hold back the magic power, the more the pressure built up inside of him. It swelled and pressed hard against his insides until he groaned then hunched over, and clenched his teeth as he fought the thing with all his might.

"No!... No!... Don't come out!" he croaked. "It's... not... my...wish!"

The wizard shook and trembled, with his head down and lips pulled back in a terrible snarl, then just when it seemed he would surely pop, he looked up in horror and stared through his watery eyes. And just like that, it was done. The wish was gone and had escaped into the world to do his bidding.

Jack gave the wizard a doubtful smirk.

"What was that all about?" he asked.

There was no answer. Gellzoowin only looked past him with an empty expression. Now that he was ignoring the boy once again, Jack simply didn't know what to make of it. First he was mad, then he was happy, then mad again, now he was nothing. The wizard was empty of all emotion and simply stared into the night like he was waiting for a bus.

"What did you do to him?" said a squeaky little voice behind Jack.

Numlock crawled out from under the seat and approached the wizard slowly.

"I didn't do anything." Jack said, as he turned to look at the little creature, then stared at him intently. Sitting there, he couldn't believe he was actually talking to a goblin. In fact when he stopped to think of it, it was the first words he had spoken to the creature.

"You're a goblin, aren't you?" Jack said, like he wanted his autograph. Numlock stared past the boy, his eyes fixed on the wizard who still had no reaction.

"Master?...Master?" he said as he stepped closer and dared to wave his hand in front of Gellzoowin's face. But the goblin might as well have been invisible. Numlock turned and gave Jack a sly look.

"You put a spell over him, didn't you? How did you do it?" he asked warily.

"I didn't to anything!" Jack insisted. "All I said was what's a Gollock? Then he started acting all weird."

Numlock glanced down at the magic Brindle Stone, which was still cupped loosely in the wizard's hand, then looked at the boy with a fright. The goblin quickly turned and began to sniff with his big hooked nose pointed into the air.

Jack watched the ugly little creature run back and forth, up and down the length of the carriage, then jump up onto the railing. Numlock sniffed the air once more then stared out into the darkness.

"What's the matter with you?" Jack said, then looked at the wizard, who was still hunched over and clutching his stomach while the goblin gazed off into the night. Jack watched them and wondered if they hadn't both gone slightly mad when it occurred to him, "What of the carriage?" They were still rumbling along at a good pace, and without the wizard to guide them, they would likely crash into anything at any moment.

Jack peered over the side to see the ground rushing beneath them then turned to the goblin who looked somewhat panic stricken, and wondered if the same thought hadn't occurred to him. But Numlock only stared off across the dark landscape and seemed concerned with little else. Jack was still struggling with the problem of what to do about the wagon when the goblin scurried along the rail, to the back of the carriage and pointed.

"LOOK! They're coming!" He shouted.

There on the horizon was a faint orange glow in the darkness behind them, like something ablaze in the distance.

"What's that?" Jack said.

Numlock turned like an angry cat and hissed.

"You're a foolish boy! A very foolish boy!"

Suddenly the wizard stirred and seemed to awaken.

"You said you wanted to know...and so you shall." He whispered, staring aimlessly, too tired to look at the distant fire. "What's done is done. And now that it is on its way, there is no stopping it." Gellzoowin murmured and looked up at Jack.

"It is the Gollock" He said. "...It is the Gollock."

CHAPTER SEVENTEEN

Locust of Fire

*T*he Rabble wagon traveled all through the night, while the trolls worked in shifts and took turns keeping watch. With the sun rising over the eastern mountains, Raylin kept a sharp look out from the crow's nest.

"Wagoneers hooo! Sunrise on the morn!" he yelled, down to the others.

Katie slept on the deck, wrapped in her fur cape and only just stirred at the look out's call. Binderbec, the old soldier sat close by. As gritty and full of bluster as he was, the old gray beard smiled down on Katie like an adoring grandfather, then waved to the others. One by one, they gathered around to look upon the child of God as she slept. Katie awoke with a start, to see the six little men crowded around her.

"Please, don't get up! We were just watching you sleep." friar Jingles said cheerfully. The troll had a pleasant smile and was the only one with a snowy white beard. With his round belly, rosy cheeks and sparkling blue eyes, had he been dressed in red, instead of his brown leather vest and woolen work clothes, the troll would have looked exactly like Santa Claus.

243

Jingles bowed with a chuckle, cleared his throat then gave his proper name, "Good day, child. I am Bartooleenee Euweezeenee Ephernat but you may call me Jingles. Everyone else does."

Katie recalled what the bear had said about his long name and smiled at the sound of it. The nickname suited him as well, since tiny little bells adorned his clothes instead of buttons. There were twelve bells all together, some brass, some silver and each one beautifully crafted to make the tiniest ting jingle.

"These are my little angels." Jingles said, pointing to the row of bells on his chest.

"Each one represents an angel I have met through the course of my life. And as you can see I have met quite a few."

Jingles pointed to a little silver bell that was shiny and new, sewn on the cuff of his sleeve.

"This one is for your guardian, the angel Stadia." Jingles said proudly.

"Where did you get them all?" Katie asked.

"I made them myself," said Jingles. "I am a bell maker by trade."

"Really," Katie said then noticed the large book sticking out of his troll sack. It was the same book Jingles had used to save them from the spirit of fear.

"And what's that?" she asked, pointing to the sack. A few of the other trolls looked at each other, and prepared themselves for what was about to come.

"This?" Jingles smiled, then reached inside and pulled out the old leather bound book. He held it carefully and in such a way, Katie could tell it was very dear and very special to him. The troll spoke slowly and with great pride.

"This is my constant companion and my source of strength. It is the book of faith, the Word of God." He said, smiling warmly.

"Some say he's a better preacher than a bell maker." Rumyon added.

The good friar chuckled at the remark. "And a finer compliment I couldn't receive from me' own mother." He boasted happily and bowed to Katie. "Would you care to pray with us?" He asked.

Katie gave a nervous smile as did some of the trolls, who began to fidget and grumble.

"Don't mind them, child. Most of them haven't uttered a prayer since they were wee little Weegans and wouldn't know where to start. That's why I'm here. It is my job to offer up prayers to God so that His blessings will be upon us all along the way."

"I didn't know that trolls prayed." Katie said.

Jingles smiled again. "Not all of us do, only those who believe and have seen the goodness of God. Still I pray for everyone, even those who don't have sense enough to pray for themselves." Jingles said, and glanced over his shoulder at Gral Tibbore and Rumyon who looked like they wanted nothing to do with the little priest and his lecture. "Anyway I shall pray for you." Jingles added and nodded graciously.

"Could you pray for my brother as well?" Katie asked.

"Why of course! The lads and I would be happy to." Jingles said, but when he looked, the trolls had turned away at the mention of the wizard's apprentice and were already leaving to return to their chores. Jingles watched them go until he and Katie were standing alone, and did his best to force a smile.

"Forgive them. They are mostly soldiers who have a heart for war, and not God. I will surely pray for your brother. That I promise you." Jingles said reassuringly, then nodded and went on his way to fetch Rumyon and prepare for breakfast.

Katie was about to lay back down, but now that she was no longer surrounded by the trolls, she could see the huddled figure of a little girl, much smaller than she was, crouched against the wall on the other side of the wagon. The girl was very pretty and very thin; barely three feet tall with tiny arms and legs and a little face that almost looked miniature. Katie watched the child who stared back at her. Strangely, no one else seemed to notice her or pay any attention. Katie smiled to be courteous and the girl smiled back then waved politely as if to say, "Hello there again."

Katie was about to wave when the little girl turned slightly to make herself more comfortable, and when she did, Katie saw the two tiny wings sprouting from her back.

"Kitch!" Katie said in amazement, "What happened to you? First you were big and now you're getting small again." she said.

Kitch grinned. "Isn't it great?! The land of great discoveries made me big and now that its magic is wearing off..." The fairy leapt to her feet. "I'm shrinking all the time. See?!"

Kitch held her arms out so that Katie could look at her. Katie nodded and smiled. The fairy was indeed shrinking, but far too slowly to see and since it was all a mystery to both of them, the two just sat and chatted.

Goe Garth flicked the reigns as the sun peeked over distant mountains and dawn arrived. When Katie looked across the open plains, golden rays streaked the sky and the land was covered with flowers. A wonderful tapestry filled the lust green meadows with every color imaginable and stretched in all directions as far as the eye could see. Katie marveled at the beauty of it all.

"Where are we?" she asked. "Everything is so...so perfect."

"You ought to know the answer to that question." Goe Garth smiled as he drove the wagon. "After all, it is you who are leading us and not the other way around."

Katie frowned at the troll and was reminded of what the

bear had said.

"What you know you don't know you know." With that thought she looked around and decided to take a guess.

"I would say that land this beautiful would have to be… God's country." she said.

The fairy smiled and clapped her hands, "That's correct!"

"It is?!" Katie said in surprise.

Goe Garth flicked the reigns. "Of course it is. What did you think?" said the troll leader as they rode along.

Katie climbed up to the driver's bench at the front of the wagon, and poked her head over Goe Garth's shoulder. From there she could see the way ahead, a bright green field, speckled with blue Morning Glories and white Oleander, with the beautiful black stallion, glistening in the morning sun.

The little troll Gimble came up behind Katie. "They call this place the Sacred Finelands." he said, then took a deep breathe and smiled at the sweet smell of Lilac and Fineland Sage.

"The Fineland?" Katie asked. The term seemed strangely familiar and then she remembered. "There was a mole, a little mole that spoke to me. What did he say?... the place where nothing- nothing ever grows old. That was it."

Gimble looked at Katie and nodded, "Old Borgle Goodfellow, chatty sort, strange sense of humor."

"Yes, yes indeed," said Goe Garth. "The little sprout was right. This land stands exactly as it did when the hand of God first touched it."

Gimble smiled, "The land is eternal."

"It's like the robe of Christ," said friar Jingles as he made his way to the front of the wagon. Katie turned around with a look of astonishment.

"You know about, Christ?" Katie said, her eyes staring.

Jingles smiled as he stood before Katie. "Yes, well in a manner of speaking. I have heard of Him. What I know I learned from a chance meeting, really," he said. "Years ago when I met a young man, he was from your world and on a pilgrimage. As we traveled through this sacred land I told him of its wonders, and so impressed was he, that he shared with me, a poem."

Katie watched the little troll rub his white beard thoughtfully as he tried to remember.

"Ah yes, now I recall." Jingles said, then struck a lofty pose, cleared his throat and recited the poem with as much vigor and robust energy as he could muster.

"This spotless robe the same appears, when ruin's nature sinks in years. No age can change its glorious hue. The robe of Christ... is ever new. And when he takes our pain and fears they too will sink in to the years. And oh what thanks will be his due when we become forever new." Jingles doffed his hat and Katie clapped her hands excitedly.

"That was wonderful! Wonderful!" She exclaimed.

"Thank you." Jingles said. "I rather liked it myself...And now if you will excuse me."

With that the troll reached into a leather pouch that was tied to his belt and pulled out a small metal object. Katie watched with some curiosity as he bent down, and poked the shiny tool into a hole in the floor. When she looked more closely, she could see the thing was a little brass handle of some kind. Then with one quick pull, the troll opened a small trap door, removed the handle and ducked down inside. In a blink, the troll was gone and once the door slammed shut, it fit snugly into the wooden floor and disappeared as well. When he was gone, Katie rushed to the spot where the troll had stood then stomped on the floor and was still looking down when Goe Garth continued.

"Yes, everything changes, wherever you go, except here. This land is ageless, untouched by time. It is indeed as the good friar said, forever new."

"What did you say?" Katie asked, finally looking up

from the floor.

"Forever new... I said the Fineland is forever new. It is ageless, beyond the grasp of time." Said Goe Garth.

"Touched by the hand of God and made forever new." Katie said as she looked across the countryside and pondered the miraculous nature of it all.

"Indeed there is a power here, a power that surrounds us," said Kitch as she fluttered into the air. When Katie looked, the fairy was shrinking faster and was barely twelve inches tall, floating on her gossamer wings.

"My wings, they work!... They work!" Kitch yelled and was so happy she lit upon the wooden railing to let the wind sweep through her hair. With the sunrise over her shoulder and the beauty of the blue Fineland valley behind the sparkling fairy, Katie knew that God's hand was truly upon this place. And as they went, a sense of peace filled her heart and grew stronger as she looked out across the land.

Just then the trap door opened and Jingles reappeared, dressed from head to toe in a red and gold vestment; a robe that went all the way to the floor and made him look like the priest that he was. Jingles came along side Katie who was suddenly smiling with tears in her eyes.

"What is it child? Is something wrong?" Jingles asked.

With that Katie flung her arms open wide till she was overflowing with happiness and shouted as loud as she could. "I love you, Lord!... I love you!" she shouted to the perfectly blue sky.

Everyone except Jingles stared while Katie stood there, smiling with eyes closed and arms outstretched. Gimble turned to friar Jingles with a look of concern and whispered, "Is she alright?"

Jingles spoke casually, "A Child of God... You know" he said.

"Oh yes, of course, of course." Gimble replied, and nodded as though he understood perfectly and waited till Katie was done.

A few minutes later Jingles pronounced the blessing and breakfast was served. Hearty bowls of wheat cream porridge were passed among the crew along with fruit, nuts and nectarine punch. And while they ate, the trolls enjoyed the view. The gently rolling hills of the Finelands and the quiet glens were the perfect backdrop for a breakfast feast.

After a delicious bowl of sweet porridge, Katie was stuffed. With her stomach full and the trolls back about their business and nothing much to do, Katie decided to rest and lay back down. The deck of the Rabble wagon was cool in the morning shade as she made herself comfortable on the fur cape and listened to the rumbling of the wagon wheels. Katie stared up at the pink clouds as a morning breeze blew through her hair and she watched a flock of birds trail across the sky. They floated peacefully, high above and Katie smiled in the stillness of the day completely calm and undisturbed when suddenly a loud shriek broke the silence and an enormous eagle swooped down over the deck. The large bird of prey came so desperately close, it fanned Katie's face with the tip of its wing and was gone, in a blur, as fast as it appeared. Katie touched her cheek and held her breath as she stared at the empty space above her, shocked by whatever it was that had come and gone so quickly.

She blinked once then twice and was about to sit up, when a shadow covered the wagon and a rush of wind forced her back down. All at once, there was a terrible noise of screeching and flapping and the air was filled with birds, thousands of birds; birds of all kinds, crows and ravens, vultures, hawks and eagles, all rushing past, shrieking wildly.

"STAY DOWN!" Someone yelled.

Katie covered her head, and tried to stay as close to the floor as possible. Then as quickly as they came, the birds were suddenly gone, streaking into the distance. When the shadow of the birds had gone and the sunlight returned, a single white swan flew overhead, a strange and peaceful sight, compared to the flock of frenzy that had just hurtled past.

Katie held still a while longer, trying to catch her breath, when there came a rumbling. At first she thought it was the wagon, then sat up as the noise grew louder and soon became a tremor that shook the ground beneath them. Suddenly the trolls were yelling to each other. Rumyon and Binderbec hurried past. A cry from above made Katie look up. Raylin the keen eyed tracker, was high in his perch, pointing behind them and shouted.

"STAMPEDE!!"

Katie struggled to her feet as the ground began to shake in earnest. She stumbled across the deck of the wagon, reaching for the side rail then flopped against it and held on. When Katie looked, she gazed at the sea of animals pouring up over the hillside behind them. They were everywhere, coming straight toward them, roaring and bellowing and running for their lives. Rumyon fell against the railing next to Katie, along with Gral Tibbore.

"Look at them all!" Rumyon gasped. "Where did they come from?"

Gral gripped the rail and yelled, "Hold on!"

The leading edge of the herd hit like a wave. Animals slammed into the back of the wagon while others careened around it and charged past. Antelope and deer, darted this way and that and leapt into the air, jumping over foxes, wolves and wildcat cougars, running through the tall grass. The smaller creatures like rabbits and squirrels raced underneath the wagon, maneuvering around the wheels, and the thundering hooves of the black stallion.

Goe Garth fought to control the horse and kept him on a straight path amidst the frenzy and swirling dust. The frightful noise of the stampede was deafening and grew even louder when the larger animals overtook the wagon. Thick hooved rhinos, big horned elk and bull elephants, wildebeest, and woolly bison, all churned up the earth and caused the wagon to shake even more.

Katie held on the best she could and watched as the animals bunched together, shoulder to shoulder, head to tail, charging across the open plain with the earth quaking beneath them. When Katie looked down, an elk was racing along side the wagon. The enormous animal ran with its head down and scooped up a fox and a wolf then tossed them aside with its massive rack of antlers.

"Out of my way you fools!" He shouted then stumbled and down he went. Katie turned away as the herd of rhinos and elephants charged over him and trampled the elk underfoot. With the ground shaking all around her, Katie was thankful for the protection of the sturdy troll wagon and the black stallion that had managed to hold his direction in the crushing fury of the sea of beasts. Just then a voice cried out, a deep booming voice, filled with fear.

"HURRY! Don't look back! They're coming! They're coming!"

Just behind them, came the great brown bear, running as fast as he could to catch the wagon. Katie leaned over the side.

"BROMWIN! You're alive!" she shouted.

"Indeed, I am... And I dare say... I'd like to stay that way!" the bear panted, as he ran. Then with a great gust, the angel swooped down from above.

"Goe Garth! Get them out of here, now!" Stadia shouted then looked to the sky and climbed back into the air. Like a good soldier, the troll leader was quick to heed the call, and snatched his hat off of his head, tucked it into his belt, then gripped the reigns.

"Hang on!" He yelled.

"Whose coming?! What's happening?!" Katie shouted into the wind.

Quick as he could, Goe Garth whirled his whip, up and

around, then cracked it hard in the air. The sound of the lash spurred the horse and Juggernaut lengthened his stride. Then with some slack to the reigns he leaned forward and shouted, "Fly, Juggernaut!... Fly!"

With a command the horse lunged forward and it was all Katie could do to hold on. Like a freight train picking up speed, she could feel them going faster and faster.

Goe Garth lashed the reigns once more.

"Come on, boy! Quicker'n light, let'er fly!" he cried, but Juggernaut was more than up to the task, even with the huge wagon harnessed to his back.

Gimble held onto his wide brimmed hat and looked over the side to see the wagon wheels spinning furiously beneath them as they surged ahead and picked up more speed. He turned to Goe Garth with the wind in his face and tried to sound calm as he yelled above the noise. "It occurs to me that when I built the wagon, I never tested it for speed!" He shouted.

Goe Garth stared straight ahead with the reigns in his hands, the wagon wheels rumbling then glanced over and yelled. "Today's the day! I wish you luck!"

The horse had just begun to run and was already weaving its way through the herd. Its sheer size and power caused the other animals to move aside as he charged up behind them with his hooves pounding the ground like a drum.

The rhinos, woolly bison and wildebeest, all gave way and only glimpsed the horse and the troll wagon as they rumbled passed. Beyond them were the wildcats. The black stallion gained ground on the leaders with every stride and moved through their ranks with ease. Juggernaut surged past the cougars and spotted cats, leopards, jaguars and the fleet footed cheetah, but even they could not keep up and fell behind in the swirling dust.

The black horse picked up more speed and with his tail flying and long mane lashed by the wind, he maneuvered his way through the wild herd of antelope and gazelles. Katie held on and stared in amazement when she caught sight of something running among the herd, an animal, golden brown with a single spiral horn rising out of its head.

"A unicorn!" Katie cried and pointed through the whirling dust and wind.

The magnificent creature leapt like a deer then charged down the far side of the hill and was gone in the blink of an eye. The rush of animals flowed like water over the land with other mythical creatures caught up in the raging torrent. Just ahead, an awkward looking beast loped along while the smaller faster creatures ran around it and charged past. Katie marveled at the thing which looked like it was made of metal. The creature had the head and wings of an eagle with the body of a lion and was gigantic, as big as the black stallion but slow and ungainly. It half ran and half flew, bounding into the air only to come down again and gallop a few steps before it took to the sky once more. Goe Garth wished the animal would make up its mind.

"Fly or move!" He shouted.

Juggernaut closed in fast and as they drew nearer, Katie could see that the animal was not metal at all. Its short fur was steely gray and only shone like metal in the sunlight. When they were nearly on top of it and it seemed like they would surely crash, Katie covered her eyes and Binderbec shouted.

"Watch out for the griffin!"

With a screech, the beast leapt into the air with its wings opened wide and the black stallion dashed underneath and raced through the griffin's shadow. Raylin peered up as the animal sailed over the crow's nest, so close he could reach out and touch its steely gray talons then looked back as the griffin come down once again on its huge paws, bounding along behind them like a giant cat. Soon it was lost in the dust like the others as Goe Garth lashed the reigns and

Juggernaut looked for open ground.

They were approaching the front of the stampede and now with the land animals safely behind them, there were only the birds to challenge them. Katie watched as the stallion lengthened his stride and once again the giant flock filled the air around her and darkened the sky. The birds swerved aside to make way as the horse thundered past with his head down and black mane flowing. Katie covered her ears and crouched near the floor with eagles and crows screeching all around her and watched in disbelief. A moment ago she was basking in the pleasure of the Fineland and now she was surrounded by huge birds, terrified and racing for their lives, ahead of the fury of a wild and raging stampede.

Goe Garth grinned wildly as he ducked under the last eagle then looked back.

"We're in the lead! We're in the lead!" he shouted.

Gimble held on and looked at the troll like he was mad.

"Are you insane?! He yelled. "What about them?!" He cried and jabbed his thumb over his shoulder. Goe Garth lashed the reigns and gave Gimble a puzzled look.

"The stampede!" Gimble shouted. "The birds so low in the sky! Why are they here? Why is this happening?!" It was a good question, one that Goe Garth hadn't considered. He was just happy that the wheels had not fallen off then glanced down to see a jack rabbit, racing along side with its ears tucked back and legs a blur. The swift little creature had outdistanced the herd as well, but when the massive stallion thundered by like a freight train in a cloud of dust, the rabbit looked up in horror, kicked up its heels and veered off like a missile in another direction.

Now that they were ahead of the stampede, the trolls began to cheer, thinking the worst was over, until the black stallion found open ground, and bolted like a meteor. Again the trolls held on for dear life as the huge wagon bounded behind the horse, like a rock on a pond. Rumyon the toastmaster, was so scared, he wrapped his arms around his precious wine bottle and cried out to Goe Garth.

"Slow down! For heaven's sake, slow down!" He pleaded.

But Goe Garth could barely hold onto the reigns, let alone pull hard enough to slow the animal. The wheels spun and sparked and screeched, while the trolls cried out and the wagon threatened to come apart.

"What's happening?" Katie cried, above the howl of the wind, when suddenly Gral Tibbore shouted and pointed to the sky behind them. "LOOK!" he yelled.

Katie turned with her hair whipping in her face and watched as a black cloud darkened the sky and grew ever closer. Below it was the wizard's carriage, racing through the flock of birds, propelled by Gellzoowin's magic. The wizard cast his spell like a whip to conjure up more speed as Jack gaped at the darkness that was descending upon them.

"Jack!" Katie cried.

The trolls gathered around and Binderbec gazed with his mouth dropped open then whispered in a gasp. "Dear Lord! It's the Gollock!"

"The Gollock!" Rumyon shouted with surprise then turned to Goe Garth and yelled. "Faster, man! For heaven's sake, go faster!"

At first Katie thought it was a billowing cloud of churning black smoke, but as it drew closer she could see the hundreds and thousands of winged creatures flying in a giant swarm. Katie gazed at their unimaginable numbers and with the wind and the air lashing around her, she climbed to a higher spot aboard the wagon.

From there she watched the monstrous swarm descend over the land as an orange glow appeared in the belly of the cloud that suddenly burst into flames and showered the land with fire. All at once hundreds of animals were rising off the ground to be carried up into the cloud. From the smallest deer to the largest elephant, they were swept up like bits of dust caught in a whirlwind. And as they rose higher, the animals sparked like fiery embers turned to ash and disappeared inside the swarm.

"Get down from there!"

Katie looked back to see Binderbec climbing up behind her. The troll reached out and grabbed her arm, then looked out in the distance. Together they listened to the cries of the animals and watched the swarm of flying monsters as they blocked out the sun and filled the sky above them. The stout hearted troll drew Katie closer when one of the creatures swooped down with wings buzzing and Katie trembled at the sight of the beast.

Looking at it, she could see the Gollock was nothing more than an insect, a hideous beast that looked like a grasshopper, but this was an insect from the Thunderland forest, and that meant it was a giant. Most of the horrible creatures were as large as tigers. The smaller ones were runts, as big as dogs, and when they swarmed; their monstrous wings beat the air with a deafening roar. Not only were the Gollock big and fierce, they were as clear as glass. Their scaly skin was like clouded crystal, as well as their bones and innards, which were all transparent; except for the milky white blood that flowed through their veins. And when they ate, the hungry Gollock glowed like a furnace, glistening orange and yellow then burned their food and sucked in the smoke until it churned and billowed inside of them, and turned the insects black.

"Everyone below!" Binderbec yelled, as the first wave of the horrible monsters approached.

Before they could move, Goe Garth shouted, "Who will protect the wagon?!"

"I will!" cried Gral Tibbore with his spear held ready.

"I will!" cried Raylin from his crows nest above.

"And I'll mourn you when you're gone!" Rumyon

yelled. "There's too many of them! I say we run!"

"What about my brother?!" Katie cried and pointed to the wizard's carriage charging through the dust behind them. Binderbec grabbed Katie by the shoulder.

"Your safety first child! Now get below!" the troll demanded.

But Katie struggled and pulled away, "No! I won't leave my brother!"

"The child is right!" Goe Garth shouted. "There is no where to run. And if we go below, the monsters will burn the wagon! Our only choice is to fight!"

Suddenly Raylin yelled down to them. "On your guard! Their comin' in!" He cried and drew his sword as the sound of the Gollock grew louder and the monsters dropped out of the sky like bombs. Without another word Binderbec dragged Katie down to the deck, shoved her into a corner then looked to the sky as the beasts descended.

"Stay down and don't move!" he said then drew his sword and took a position higher up. Katie huddled on the floor and gazed up just as the tiny fairy flashed before her. Kitch was back to her normal size and sparkled like a diamond.

"They're coming!" she yelled, then spun around to face the swarm above. Soon the light of the fairy grew bright as a star and Katie shielded her eyes.

"What are you doing?" she yelled.

"I'm talking to them!" said the fairy.

"Tell them to go away!" Katie cried.

Kitch closed her eyes and with her shining light, she spoke of terrible magic that could destroy the Gollock, magic that would bring their doom. But although the Gollock knew nothing of magic, the fairy's shimmering light told them there was heat and where there was heat, there was food. For now the Gollock would wait and watch with wings roaring and keep pace with the light that spoke to them from below.

Binderbec glared at the flying monsters. "Ugly beasts! What are they waiting for?!"

Gral Tibbore jabbed his spear at the sky, "Come taste me steel, ye hell born creed!"

When Jingles looked to Katie huddled in the corner, he saw the fairy glowing brightly before her and shook his sword. "Pixie! Ye powers won't work on these monsters. Tis the light that draws them to us!" He said as the Gollock soared above and the deafening sound of their wings grew louder.

Gral Tibbore turned with a shout. "Put out that infernal light!" He roared.

Gimble leapt forward with his hat raised, but just before he could cover the fairy, Jingles yelled.

"Wait!" he said holding out his hand. "It's working!"

The trolls peered up at the belly of the swarm as the fairy's glow sent her message to every living monster that was flying far and near.

"Stay away...Stay away." She said. "There is nothing here for you."

The Gollock hung from their terrible wings, fanning the air wildly, neither attacking nor turning away; as still more gathered and followed the fairy's light like a beacon, while off in the distance the rest of the monsters spewed their fire across the Fineland and the animals that were running for their lives.

The stampede scattered in a wild panic as the hideous monsters swept across the land, breathing fire over every living thing. But unlike before, the stampeding herd miraculously ran straight through the wall of flame unharmed. The Gollock came down, again and again, but aside from giving the animals a terrible fright, there was not a mark on them, for the creatures that remained in the herds were of the Fineland woods and like the land around them, they were eternal and could not be harmed by fire.

The animals that had been consumed were animals from outside the Fineland woods, caught in the stampede, but now all that was left were the Fineland creatures and among them was the great bear king. Bromwin charged through the searing heat and roared as the Gollock swooped down, showering the land with a tempest of flames. When they were done the monsters searched for the slightest hint of smoke, their glassy eyes flitting back and forth. But the animals and the hallowed ground were like a desert to them. Then all at once, the Gollock turned to the wagons that were fleeing across the plains ahead; for unlike the rushing stampede, the wooden wagons were not of this land and could indeed be burned.

The growing swarm gathered above the Rabble wagon and churned up a fierce dust storm as the trolls raced for their lives. Soon it was nearly impossible for Goe Garth to see in front of them, still he lashed the horse and Juggernaut thundered on, charging through the dust and darkness, with his hooves sparking like flint rock against the ground. The wagon raced with the monsters flying above and Katie turned her gaze to the fairy whose bright and sparkling light was slowly beginning to fade.

"Your light!" Katie cried. "It's going out!"

Kitch held on as long as she could, but the swarm was too great and she could feel herself growing weaker.

"I'm sorry…I'm sorry!" she said.

The fairy's voice trembled as she struggled to keep her light going. Soon it grew so faint, that it was only a glimmer. Then, like the final flicker of a lamp in a storm, it went out and the tiny fairy fell into Katie's hands like a cold ember.

For an instant, everything seemed to go silent as a thousand glowing eyes glared down from above. The monsters hovered on giant wing with mouths dripping fire and Katie cried out with a shrill, piercing scream as the beasts came down all around them.

Raylin watched from his crow's nest as one massive beast fell straight toward him, and just before the monster slammed into the perch, the nimble little troll jumped and slid down the mast; then dropped to the deck just as the huge Gollock ripped the fiery crow's nest off of the wooden pole and rose back into the sky with more of the hideous creatures chasing after the trail of smoke.

Goe Garth lashed the reigns as another Gollock swooped down over the black stallion, breathing fire. But with Juggernaut running at full speed, as soon as the flames shot from the creature's mouth, the Gollock dropped out of sight as quickly as it had come. The next Gollock that came down did the same and fell back till the monster and its flames were lost in the swirling dust.

Goe Garth laughed, "HAH! Ye can fly but you can't breathe fire at the same time!"

Gimble looked back at the monsters chasing after them. "Aye, they can!" he shouted. "Just not at speed! We're too fast for them!"

Goe Garth laughed again. "HA-HAH! They can't touch us!" He shouted then called to the black steed.

"Run, me beauty, run! Fast as the night...RUUU-UNNN!!!"

Truly none of the Gollock could overtake the flying stallion. But the beasts would not be denied and knew that if they could not breathe fire on the black stallion, they would bring it down with teeth and claws. Slowly they came, flying closer and closer,

and the trolls watched in horror as the Gollock threatened to land right on top of them. Goe Garth threw the reigns to Gimble and yelled, "Drive!"

The troll fumbled with the tangle of leather straps and could barely keep his wits about him, as he grabbed hold of the reigns. Goe Garth raised his sword and tried to stand to meet the attackers, but fell back in his seat when something hit them from behind.

A monstrous Gollock clambered up the side of the wagon and clung to the railing with its long hooked claws then glanced around and opened its mouth ready to breathe fire. In the blink of an eye, Gral Tibbore jumped in front of the beast, and hacked off the Gollock's fiery snout with a swipe of his sword then jabbed the monster with his spear and shoved it over the side. The creature tumbled backward with an arc of fire spouting from its gaping muzzle and disappeared in the dust below.

When Katie looked, two more of the winged beasts were climbing up behind her. Binderbec and Raylin leapt forward and met them with swords drawn and leaned into the attack, cutting and hacking away at the monsters, until white steam poured from their scaly flesh and the beasts dove from the wagon to escape. Suddenly there was screaming and Katie whirled around.

"FIRE!" cried Rumyon. "We're on fire!" He said, pointing at the thick black smoke trailing behind the wagon. Suddenly the monstrous swarm fell back, eager and hungry to chug down all the smoke they could swallow. Binderbec raced to the back of the wagon and looked over the side.

"Where's it coming from?!" Goe Garth shouted.

The old soldier pointed and yelled, "It's down below!"

"Come with me!" cried Jingles. Gral Tibbore took up his sword and spear and little Raylin chased after them. Jingles looked like a little general, dressed in his red and gold vestment as he opened the trap door and shook his sword to the sky.

"Ye unholy blatherskites!" He shouted then, dropped through the floor of the wagon with Gral Tibbore and Raylin right behind.

At six hundred pounds, the Gollock that clung to the underside of the wagon was truly a monster, fifteen feet long with its seven inch claws sunk into the hard wood planking. With one blast of fire it had set the boards ablaze, then chugged and chugged and chugged, until it filled itself with smoke. Soon the hideous beast was jet black with its two eyes shining like lumps of coal. Now that it had tasted the precious smoke, the beast was frenzied, and tore its way up through the bottom of the wagon to set the rest of the Rabble on fire.

The three trolls made their way down a narrow staircase, until they reached the cargo hold in the belly of the wagon. When Jingles flung the door open, the room was thick with smoke and although it was impossible to see, the brave little friar ran forward. "Show yourself!" Jingles cried.

"WAIT!" Gral shouted, but no sooner did the troll disappear in the churning smoke than a terrible crash came from within and Jingles cried out for help. The barbarian growled at the troll's insane bravery, then hefted his spear and chased after him. With the smoke billowing around, Gral found Jingles laying at the center of the room, kicking and screaming with a hairy claw clamped to his boot. The monster had punched a hole through the floor and held onto the little troll as it made its way up.

Gral Tibbore dove forward and went sprawling as he grabbed Jingles by the arm. But before Gral could pull him back, two more claws punched through the floor, splintering and cracking the wood apart until there was a gaping hole and smoke poured out through the bottom of the wagon. When the smoke cleared, the hideous beast poked its head up and glared at the trolls. With clicking claws and teeth gnashing, the horrible Gollock dragged them closer. Gral held on, but like Jingles, he had dropped his spear when he fell and both he and the friar were helpless before the beast. The monster glared down with its hot breath pouring across their faces and just when the brave trolls thought they would surely die, Raylin lunged forward with Gral's spear in hand.

The nimble troll leapt over the hole, flipped through the air, and landed on the other side with the monstrous Gollock staring up at him. Gral and Jingles watched the fearless little tracker, as he twirled the six foot spear over his head, glared down at the beast and plunged the twelve inch blade into the Gollock's glowing abdomen. With a fierce "Screech," the monster released the trolls then dropped from sight taking Gral Tibbore's spear clattering down through the hole with it.

Jingles and Gral stood to their feet, legs trembling.

"Well done." Said Gral. "Where did you learn to do that?"

Raylin only smiled. There was still the matter of the floor boards which were on fire. Jingles turned aside and grabbed an axe from the wall. With three good whacks he had laid open the side of one of the huge barrels of water, stored along the wall. The huge container emptied itself onto the floor and soaked the planks of wood. Once the fire was out, the three trolls were slipping and sliding as the wagon pitched from side to side.

"What now?!" cried Gral as the three made their way back up the stairs to join the others above.

When they reached the deck, the trolls made their way forward as the black stallion veered from side to side. Just above the horse was a monster, sleek and fast, and narrow as a fence post. The Gollock darted back and forth with its hooked claws dangling. But even with the huge wagon harnessed to the black stallion, Juggernaut was still fleet of foot and hard to catch. With a sideways glance, the black stallion veered away from the beast only to have five more monsters come down and like a swarm of hornets, surrounding him on all sides

"They'll bring him down for sure if we don't do something!" Gimble yelled with the wind in his face. Before he could move Goe Garth reached down and grabbed his bull-whip, then without a moment to lose and a deft flick of the wrist the whip swirled through the air and, "CRACK!" The sound of it made everyone duck and look to the troll.

"Get down!" Goe Garth yelled and brought the whip around again, this time with better aim and, "CRACK!" The huge leather whip lashed the monster that was right over the horse and, like a knife, sliced off half of the Gollock's wing. Suddenly the creature was out of control and spiraling through the air like a top, then veered away and slammed into another Gollock and burst into flames.

When Katie looked up, there were ten more of the horrible beasts coming down to replace the one that had flown away. Goe Garth raised his whip and fought to lash the terrible creatures, as more of them closed in around the horse, but there were too many and the monsters would not be frightened away, by the troll and his whip.

"Faster!" cried Rumyon.

Gimble flicked the reigns as hard as he could. "That's all he's got!" He yelled.

Rumyon looked to the swarm. "We're done for!" he said with sword in hand, just as a thin, sleek Gollock dropped out of the sky and landed right on top of the horse. Juggernaut was so thickly muscled, he could have withstood the lash of any whip, but the Gollock's six inch claws were like daggers and the horse shrieked with the thing clinging to his back. Now that the animal was in its grasp, the monster puffed and chuffed till its throat was white hot, then opened its mouth to breathe fire and burn the horse alive. But with the horse running at full speed, the Gollock didn't consider the fierce winds and the torrent of flames blew back into the creature's face and blinded it instead.

Katie and the others ducked as the fire rushed past them, then watched as the Gollock tried again, spewing more flames, and again tasted the heat of its own fire. With its head blackened and its wings scorched the hideous Gollock was enraged. It wagged its head back and forth, and roared as it dug its claws in deeper. Then like a meteor whistling through the air, another Gollock dropped out of the sky, plummeting straight down and missed the horse by inches, and plunged underneath the wagon. With a bump and a crunch it was gone, but the desperate attempt to bring the stallion down had only just begun as Juggernaut slowed down with the monster on its back and the Gollock closed in around them. Just then there came a shout. "Goe Garth! Get down!"

The troll was still lashing his whip when a blur shot past his head and the monster that was clinging to the horse howled with an arrow buried between its shoulders. When Katie looked back, Raylin held a wooden bow with another arrow, feathered and ready to fire. The second shot pierced the creature's side and the Gollock burst into flames. In an instant the fiery Gollock leapt into the air and was attacked by others that snatched it up and carried it off for food. With the monster gone, Juggernaut snorted then lengthened his stride and found more speed.

Goe Garth stared at Raylin with the Gollock chasing after them once more and Raylin gave a little smile. He had made the perfect shot with two arrows, fired from a distance and not only had both the arrows narrowly missed Goe Garth by inches, but since trolls were not known to be good archers, Goe Garth knew he was lucky to be alive. Still there was no time to waste. The swarm was gathering again and the worst was yet to come.

In the midst of the horrible commotion one of the ogres stirred at the back of the wagon. Slag threw the canvas tarp off and growled at having been awakened. With his eyes still shut, the ogre moaned and stretched and just when he raised his long arm into the air, a monstrous Gollock dropped down and snatched the ogre off the deck like a plump ripe apple. The ogre bellowed and roared as he rose into the air, then opened his eyes to see all the monsters flying around him.

Slag gazed in horror as they gathered around with wings a blur, eyes glaring and hideous snouts dripping fire. Higher and higher they went into the darkness of the swarm while down below, Rogad peered up at the sky and watched as Slag disappeared in the fury of the winged creatures above. And when he was sure the ogre was doomed and there was no possible hope of ever seeing him again, Rogad pulled the cover over his head and hid himself from the creatures.

Slag hung by his arm, screaming for his life as the monsters closed in with claws ready and jaws gaping. But before the Gollock could breathe their fire, a flash of light sliced through the air and the ogre was falling, tumbling end over end, down through the swarm of creatures swirling all around. Slag flailed his arms wildly, crying out in horror then crashed back down onto the deck of the wagon and nearly cracked his head on the hard oak flooring.

When the fat ugly ogre was able to take stock of himself, he saw the Gollock's severed claw still clamped firmly to his arm. Slag whimpered and struggled to free himself from its grip and threw the hideous stump overboard. Then before he could catch his breath, he shoved Rogad to one side, scurried back under the tarp, and trembled like a frightened child.

Several of the trolls had seen the ogre fall, but it was Binderbec who saw the light shimmering in the gathering swarm. The old soldier thrust his silver hammer toward the sky and shouted, "RAYMAH!!

The sword of the spirit shone brightly as Stadia descended out of the darkness, and grew even brighter when he dropped to the deck of the Rabble wagon. Katie gazed up at him as the angel stood over her with his armor all aglow and shouted to Gimble who held the reigns of the black stallion.

"Drive!... Don't look, just drive!" the angel commanded.

Gimble gripped the reigns and simply held on as the stallion ran with all his might and they plunged across the open plain. With a heavy thump, another Gollock hit the side of the wagon, a lumpy, bearded thing that was as big as a lion with twice as many teeth. Katie turned to see the beast crawling up beside her, and then with a flash of the angel's sword, she blinked and half of the Gollock was gone. What was left of the creature, twitched and gurgled, then quickly dropped out of sight, presumably to join the other half.

The angel looked to the sky, his sword ablaze and his face set like stone. It was the same expression he had given the giant, only now there was no mercy in him.

"Turn back or die!" Stadia shouted.

The monsters hovered like vultures, sharpening their claws against their bellies and snorting flames. But in their defiance, they heard only one voice; the voice of the monarch, the leader of the locust, the master of the terrible horde hidden deep within the swarm; the jewel eyed creature known as the Guttin. For like a queen bee, wherever the Guttin went the Gollock would follow and with the gleam of her golden eyes she commanded them all to attack.

The Gollock descended like a storm, but never had they met the power and fury of an angel unleashed to wreak havoc upon them. Stadia drew back with his armor aglow then leapt into the air like a fiery missile and plunged inside the cloud of monsters. Katie shielded her eyes as the angel and the white blade whirled in arcs of light that flashed like lightning and drew the attention of all the monsters. High up in the dreaded darkness, the creatures shrieked and howled as the flaming sword cleaved straight through them and the Gollock met their doom. Some burst into flames, while others were cut to pieces and came apart in midair. Still others the angel snatched out of the sky and hurled at the multitude flying around him. The Gollock exploded like bombs and brought dozens more spiraling to the ground. Then with the swarm closing in around him the angel became a whirling blur and cut the beasts to shreds until they were bathed in their own fire and the flames poured down like rain. Still the more he slew, the fiercer the angel of God became, dealing death to all that came near, until the terrible swarm had had enough and pulled back from the Rabble wagon.

Down below, the band of trolls tightened their circle around Katie and gazed up in amazement, thanking God for the angel who shone like a star above them.

The wizard's carriage however enjoyed no such protection. When Katie thought to look, she saw the black carriage veer off and fall further back, with a column of black smoke billowing out behind it. There were so many of the fire breathing monsters chasing after the wizard's carriage, the air was thick with them.

"NOOOO!!" Katie cried then called to Stadia.

"Save them!" She pleaded, but with the swarm still flying above, Stadia stood vigilant. "I will not leave you!" he shouted.

Katie watched as the wizard's carriage burned, then screamed for her brother's life. "JAACCKK!!"

The wizard's carriage raced across the land, with the canopy ablaze and its wheels on fire. Jack watched with eyes gaping, as the Gollock chased after them and Gellzoowin stood to face the monsters. The wizard's hands were all aglow as he glared at the creatures, searching for the leader of the locust, searching for the Guttin.

With that, Gellzoowin raised his hands to summon the beast from out of the swarm, but the monsters were everywhere and there was no time. Jack slid down in his seat and cowered near the floor, while Numlock stayed well hidden in the shadows behind him.

"This is the end!" The goblin hissed, his eyes glaring out of the dark.

The wizard summoned his power as he gazed up and prepared to meet the Gollock. But before he defended himself there was another danger the wizard had to consider.

There was the "Q," the first rule of wizardry. Gellzoowin cursed the powers that presided over him especially at a time like this, but it could not be avoided. The danger was real. The "Q" referred to "the wizard's quiver" or "the seven deadly arrows," a reference to the letters A, R, R, O, W, S, which stood for "Average Recommended Rate of Wizard Spells." It was basically a speed limit. The number of spells a wizard could safely cast per minute was seven, determined by the Supreme Council and established to prevent wizards from going stark raving mad; a condition that was commonly known as "A hatter's frenzy." Strangely, if a frenzy didn't kill a wizard, it could actually make him stronger, but with no time left to think the wizard's eyes turned black and he stood ready to inflict as much destruction upon them he could conjure up with his magic.

The monsters dove to the attack and the wizard stabbed at the air with both hands, ripping the Gollock out of the sky and casting them aside. The most he could grab with one spell was ten or twelve at a time. Ten fell to one side, twelve to the other, and as soon as they were gone, more rushed in. Gellzoowin cast spell after spell, but with so many creatures coming at him, he was already up to twenty spells in only one minute, nearly three times the "Q."

Gellzoowin changed spells, as they waded in. With a flash and a "Poof," the Gollock turned to stone and dropped out of the sky. They whistled toward the ground and exploded, punching ugly craters into the hillsides. But as soon as they fell, the dirt closed in around them, and the land instantly returned to its normal appearance. Such was the eternal power of the Fineland.

Still the monsters came, flooding in upon the wizard. Gellzoowin snarled then lashed out and instead of turning the beasts to stone, hundreds of the Gollock were suddenly shrunk down to the size of normal grasshoppers. Confused and bewildered, the little insects fluttered around helplessly, till they were gobbled up by the giant Gollock and Gellzoowin laughed as the creatures helped to destroy each other.

Jack held on as the wizard changed spells yet again and hurled fireballs into the air. The streams of light fanned out and lit the sky as they exploded amidst the swarm, but the fire only brought more monsters to feed on the smoke.

With the Gollock closing in, Gellzoowin switched to compositional spells which were faster and easier to perform. These were spells that would change what the Gollock were made of, and the wizard could do it with a thought.

Suddenly the monsters that streaked out of the sky, were made of paper that was whipped up by the wind and blown away. Others turned to dust, which blew apart and fell to the ground in clumps. There were Gollock turned to bubbles that popped and stung the eyes of the others around them.

Jack watched in amazement as suddenly there were Gollock made of fine crystal that tumbled through the air then crashed into each other and shattered to a million pieces. There were Gollock made of rope that tangled the wings of other Gollock and brought more of the monsters down in a spiraling rampage. There were Gollock made of leaves and twigs, Gollock made of bread and cheese. There were even Gollock made of cinnamon crackers that looked like giant cookies which crumbled and fell apart in mid air.

The wizard had never actually seen a cinnamon cracker. The thought had merely popped into his mind. There were Gollock made of everything and anything Gellzoowin could think of, but the wizard was quickly running out of ideas. With his hands cramping and heart pounding, Gellzoowin switched to transformation spells and suddenly the Gollock were no longer made of different things, suddenly they were different things all together.

There were Gollock turned to frogs, Gollock turned to lizards, Gollock turned to cups and saucers, wicker baskets, bunches of grapes, apples and oranges. Jack's eyes danced in his head as objects flew past, objects of every shape, size, and color; objects that used to be giant winged monsters, now changed to harmless or otherwise useless things. The wizard changed them so fast Jack couldn't keep up. There were Gollock turned to pots and pan, spoons and dishes, pencils, books, hats and hinges, Gollock turned to bunnies, cats, and caterpillars. Every horrible creature that came at them got changed into something else, and as they kept coming Gellzoowin slipped deeper and deeper into a terrible and irreversible frenzy.

Soon the sheer torrent of magic drew on his will, and he grinned like a madman then turned the Gollock into stranger things. They were bizarre things, like clumps of braided hair wrapped in wire and coils of braided wire wrapped in hair. There were Gollock stripped to spindly bones that toppled out of the sky like kindling. There were Gollock turned to spiders, worms, and fuzzy winged beetles. Gellzoowin hurled spell after spell, with eyes glaring wildly and just by chance happened to look down and see the sickly old monster clinging to the carriage in front of him. The shriveled old Gollock huffed and puffed trying to set the wagon on fire, when Gellzoowin turned the creature into a bundle of straw, lit it ablaze with a glance, then kicked it over the side.

On and on he went, "Poofing" things into other things, at his frenzied pace. Still in the back of Gellzoowin's twisted mind, was the Guttin, hiding somewhere in the black swarm above.

"Come to me! Come to me!" Gellzoowin cried aloud as more of the Gollock swooped down to feed on the smoke of the blazing canopy that trailed behind the wagon. Dozens of the Gollock flew behind them, trying to feed on the smoke as the canvas cloth flapped wildly. Then with the spells flying from his fingertips and his will bent by magic, the wizard cried out.

"Cut the canopy!"

Jack watched from under his chair as the wizard cast his spells into the sky when the goblin shoved him from behind.

"Go! You silly wonk!" Numlock snarled from the shadows then retreated back under the seat.

The wizard yelled once more, "Cut the canopy!"

Jack shook his head, "No!" then jumped when a tiny thread of light hit him in the leg, like the crack of a whip.

"Alright!" Jack yelped and crawled from the shadows. No sooner did he look up from his crouched position, than a Gollock swooped down to grab him and was turned to a biddy chicken. Jack watched the fat little bird twirl through the air, then bounce off the brass railing with a squawk and tumble over the side.

Two more Gollock were right behind with fire dripping from their mouths and Jack ducked as one turned into a shoe and the other into a marble. The shoe hit the floor and slid into the shadows, where it lay quietly twitching till the last bit of life had drained out of it, while the marble hit Jack in the head and sent him reeling.

"Ouch!!" he cried, then staggered back and held his hands up in case something else came flying. Just then Numlock, popped out of the shadows, holding the conjured old shoe like a smelly diaper, then tossed it over the side with a frown and ducked back into his hiding place.

When Jack looked up, the two poles at the front of the wagon were smashed to bits, while the two at the rear held the blazing canopy with the Gollock chasing after the smoke. Once Jack understood why the canopy had to be cut, he glanced down and found a large hunting knife, stuck in the floor between his feet, right where the wizard had conjured it.

With a few twists, Jack worked the knife free, then went to one of the poles and climbed up onto the railing. He steadied himself and reached up with the knife, trying to ignore the monsters that filled the sky above. With one quick slash, the material flew to the other side of the carriage and with only one rope left to hold it, the flaming canopy flapped violently and threatened to snap the pole.

Jack jumped down, feeling very brave, but before he could cross the wagon to cut the other rope, he was suddenly being pelted by what appeared to be walnuts and buttons. Jack covered his head and looked as the wizard changed the Gollock before his eyes. The beasts came down in fire and rage and with a thought they were turned to tiny objects that rained down with a terrible clatter. Jack turned to run as nuts and buttons showered the floor then slipped and fell. He slid across the carriage on his back, and was still flailing at the sky when a very tasteful and elegant spice rack flew past his head. The spice rack was another bit of the wizard's magic and held twelve little monsters, each one shrunken down, freeze dried, neatly packaged and carefully tucked inside its own bottle.

It was a strange object to see flying through the air but no stranger than the shower of buttons and nuts that were raining down on them. Jack shielded his face as the spice rack hit the wall of the carriage and exploded. Then before anything else could come his way, he jumped to his feet and ran to cut the rope. Quick as he could, he climbed up on the rail and held on as the black carriage raced across the land like a runaway train. Then with the wagon rumbling and a sudden bump, he slipped and nearly dropped the knife. Jack clung to the pole, afraid to look down, and found the railing with the toe of his boot. With his heart pounding and body shaking, he reached up before anything else could happen, and with one good swipe of the knife, he sliced the rope above. In an instant, the canopy was gone, whipped up by the wind like a kite in a storm, then came down with a hundred Gollock swarming over it, in a seething mass of claws and wings. Soon the creatures were lost in the distance and a thousand more Gollock filled the air behind them.

Jack jumped down from the railing then dove back to his hiding place. Once he was under his seat, he watched the magic spells flow from the wizard's hands in a blurring stream. Then in the midst of it all Gellzoowin shouted.

"COME TO MEEEEEE!... SHOW YOURSELF, COWARD!"

At first Jack thought the wizard was talking to him and was about to answer, when something heavy hit the chair above him and cracked the wooden seat. Jack drew back and looked up at the long hooked claws gripping the edge of the chair. With the creature right above them, the goblin shuddered in the darkness while Jack tried to remain as still as he could.

The Gollock that clung to the chair was a runt, no bigger than a dog, but no less ferocious. The monster glared at the wizard whose back was turned. Jack wanted to cry out when he looked and saw what was coming down from the sky. Off in the distance the swarm of giant insects parted to make way for a much larger creature that was headed straight toward them. The monster descended out of the darkness and as it drew nearer Gellzoowin could see that this was truly a brutish beast, as big as a rhino and nearly three times the size of any other Gollock. Its hideous armor plated head dangled down with teeth gnashing and fire spilling from its mouth. The monster's wings buzzed with a deafening roar, and barely bore the weight of the hulking creature as it approached. Gellzoowin watched the thing as it grew nearer and his eyes lit up.

The Guttin!" He gasped.

Gellzoowin struggled to fix his twitching eyes on the beast, with his head throbbing and his arms numbed with pain from his frenzied state.

"Now I have you. Come to me. Come to me!" He said, reaching out to summon it.

The monster leveled out and hurtled forward, with jaws

gaping and fire trailing from its nostrils.

"Yes, that's it. Come to me." Gellzoowin said, willing the creature forward, and waited for his moment of revenge. The wizard grinned. Before he destroyed the beast, he would make the Guttin suffer, and drew on all of his powers to devise in his mind the most evil and fiendish spell he could imagine. Then with arms outstretched he released a burst of magic so terrible that it shot forth like a thunderclap and shook the carriage. With that, the wizard slumped forward. Now that the Hatter's Frenzy had taken its toll, and he was racked with pain Gellzoowin fought to stay conscious long enough to see the Guttin destroyed then peered out over the railing as his spell hit the horrible beast and took effect.

First the Gollock's wings, shrank to the size of a bumble bee's and the creature dropped out of the air like a rock. By the time the Gollock hit the ground its hard shell splintered then softened and turned to a sticky, bloated mass that rolled across the ground, picking up leaves, twigs and grass like a giant wad of gum.

It tumbled along in a lopsided ruckus as things began to pop out of it, long slithering tentacles that wrapped around it, squeezing and twisting it into a mass of sloshy goop, that shaped and reshaped itself until it was utterly unrecognizable. The hideous monstrosity bounded across the landscape in a whirling blur and the wizard cried out.

"HAH!! I win!" Gellzoowin cheered and winced in pain. With one last effort he lifted his trembling hand and turned the thing to stone; then paused at the blunder and muttered to himself. "Uh-oh!"

Once the deed was done, the monster became a boulder that barreled along, flipping end over end, and punching holes in the ground until it cracked and broke apart. Pieces of the rock sailed off harmlessly while the largest fragment hurtled straight toward the wizard's wagon and "...BLAAMMM!!"

The rock hit the carriage like a cannonball and shattered

the back end, turning it into splintered debris. Upon impact, both Jack and the goblin were tossed across the carriage floor, while Gellzoowin was launched into the air and thrown over the side. With his body flung upside down, the wizard banged his head, then hooked his arm around the railing and slammed against the side of the carriage. Jarred by the fall, Gellzoowin held on as best he could then blinked and blinked until the frenzy was gone and he returned to his right mind. The wizard looked around him.

"Where am I? How did I get here?" He said with his head throbbing and ears ringing with pain. He looked down at the flaming wheels, spinning wildly next him then craned his neck back to see the thousands of Gollock that filled the sky, ready to devour him.

Gellzoowin grumbled and swore and wanted to blame the angel for his bad fortune, but there was no time. His hands were slipping and a ferocious one eyed Gollock was swooping down to kill him. Then just when he decided he had had enough and was about to fall, the wizard used his last resort and melted into thin air.

"As for the boy?" the wizard thought, "He was a useful pawn but hardly worth dying for. He would simply have to fend for himself."

An instant later, the one eyed beast crashed into the side of the carriage then fell under the wagon and was crushed by the flaming wheel. Once again, Gellzoowin had timed his exit perfectly and disappeared at the precise point of disaster.

Jack looked around in dismay as the carriage barreled out of control and saw the goblin laying next to him, staring up at the Gollock that was still crouched in the chair. The black winged creature peered down, its golden eyes watching them with great suspicion, for this was the Guttin, the true leader of the locust, the master of the swarm. Now that the wizard had been dealt with, the monster perched itself on top of the chair and grinned with its eyes aglow.

Before Jack could move, the Guttin pounced on him and slammed him against the floor. Numlock scampered away and watched in horror as the six legged beast hooked its front claws into Jack's robe, and flapped its hideous wings to hold the boy steady. Unable to move, Jack could feel the weight of the monster pressing down on his chest and the heat of the ungodly creature as it puffed smoke like a demon.

Jack finally cried out. "HELP!!"

But there was only the goblin trembling in the shadows.

Slowly the Guttin's mouth gaped open and Jack peered down the monster's glassy throat and saw a bubbling cauldron of fire, ready to spill out and burn him to a crisp. Staring up into the face of death he struggled to think of what to do and finally shouted. "Ex cambro... Leatee!"

Suddenly a little gray pigeon appeared next to Jack. The Guttin turned sharply and looked at the thing, wondering where it had come from. It was indeed the wrong spell, but the only one Jack could think of at the moment. The pigeon glanced around, equally confused, then turned and launched itself into the air. Unfortunately the air was filled with fire breathing monsters and the pigeon was turned to ashes as quickly as it had come.

The Guttin turned to Jack once more, heat pouring from its nostrils. Jack wriggled and squirmed as he looked through the creature's glassy skin and watched it's belly fill with liquid fire. Up and up it came like glowing lava, till it pooled in the Guttin's throat, then with a horrible belch the beast drew open its mouth and Jack shouted.

"Bee Hava Keen! Bee Hava Keen!" he cried, his eyes clenched shut.

Any moment, Jack would feel the liquid fire pour over him, and he yelled out again.

"Bee Hava Keen! Bee Hava Keeeeeeeen!"

Jack waited, but instead of fire and heat, he felt his face and chest grow cold.

"Bee Hava Keen, Bee Hava Keen." he whimpered, sobbing through his tears.

A few seconds later Jack dared to open his eyes and stared in wonder. The freezing spell had worked instantly. The Gollock stood on Jack's chest with its mouth stuck open, in a hideous gaping yawn and was frozen solid. Jack muttered the magic words again and again, in a breathless whisper, and suddenly everything went dark.

The wizard's carriage was still traveling as fast as it could go, when it plunged into a shadowy forest. Now it was rumbling and bounding over gnarled tree roots and large tufts of grass. The wagon rocked and bounced, and with one good bump the frozen Guttin tumbled off of Jack's chest, and shattered into a hundred pieces.

The monster's head slid across the carriage floor and spun round and round, until it came to rest and stared at the frightened goblin huddled in the corner. Its frozen eyes gaped at Numlock as if to say, "What are you looking at?"

Jack wiped his tears and tried to sit up, his heart still pounding, when he looked around and saw that the swarm of monsters was gone. Instead of chasing them, the Gollock had sailed up over the trees and disappeared above.

"They're gone!" Jack cried. "They're gone!"

Numlock peeked out to see if it was true then stood up and was about to shout for joy, when a tree branch slapped him across the face like a whip, and reminded him where he was. The wizard's carriage bounded along recklessly, racing through the shadowy woods at break neck speed, missing trees by mere inches.

"We're going to crash!" Jack yelled.

With a roar, the carriage smashed through branches and thick underbrush, tossing the boy and the goblin back and forth. And before they could grab hold of anything, the entire wagon pitched sideways, flipped over and launched them into the air. Jack tumbled head over heels with arms outstretched, reaching for the sky and then the ground. Objects all sailed past, chairs, maps, wooden posts, and flaming wheels. Among them was the goblin, who flew by with an annoyed expression on his face.

"Now look what you've done." he said with a frown.

When Jack came down, he crashed through a thicket of branches and landed between two trees and gasped, with the air knocked out of him.

The hellish noise of the Gollock seemed far off now as Jack lay on his back with the whole world spinning. When he opened his eyes, the trees were swaying gently above and everything was strangely calm. Indeed, he was glad for the silence in the midst of his pain. After what he had seen and all he had been through, he was happy to be alive and glad that the beasts were gone, or at least not chasing after him.

When Jack finally tried to sit up, everything hurt so much, he set his head back down in the soft cool grass; and with the shade of the trees on his face, and his fears slowly fading, he decided to pass out instead.

CHAPTER EIGHTEEN

The Living Trees

Goe Garth took the reigns and lashed the black stallion as they raced to the edge of the open plains and ran for the cover of the dark forest. The trolls held on as they plunged inside the murky woods then watched as the black swarm of flying monsters rose into the air and swept over the forest like a wave.

"They're leaving!" said Gimble. "The Monsters are leaving!"

When Katie looked, the Gollock were gone and she breathed a sigh of relief, until Goe Garth yelled and everyone looked ahead.

"WHOA!!" the troll cried.

In their path stood a row of the largest trees Katie had ever seen and the narrow spaces between them were far too small for the troll wagon to pass through. Goe Garth pulled the reigns with all his might and was practically standing up on his seat, before Juggernaut felt the tug and drew back his head. The stallion drummed its hooves to stop, but the moss covered ground was too soft and the weight of the wagon was too great.

"We're not stopping!" cried Rumyon.

With no time to spare, Binderbec dove between Goe Garth and Gimble. The old soldier climbed down onto the rigging beam which held the horse to the wagon, then raised his hammer.

"What are you doing?!" Gimble yelled as Binderbec steadied himself and glared down at the linchpin. With two hard whacks, the harness came loose, and Binderbec jumped back onto the wagon then pointed at the horse with his hammer.

"If we crash, we don't take him with us!" He said.

Juggernaut veered aside with bridal, reigns and harness, trailing behind him. With the horse out of the way, the troll wagon barreled ahead, out of control and headed straight for the towering trees

"Hold on!" Goe Garth yelled then reached down and grabbed a wooden lever beside him. With teeth clenched and chin tucked to his chest, Goe Garth pulled up on the stick as hard as he could till the brakes squealed and the wheels locked. Everyone aboard lurched forward, as the Rabble wagon skidded across the grassy hillocks, kicking up dirt then veered left and snapped the brake. With the wheels turning once more they twisted right and the wagon tilted sideways. Goe Garth fell back with the broken brake lever in his hand.

We're going over!" cried Gimble.

Katie held on as Binderbec and Rumyon tumbled down and rolled past her. Binderbec hit the side of the wagon with a clang and put another dent in his armor, while the little toastmaster flew over the side with a holler and dropped out of sight. Pots and pans slid across the wooden deck and the trolls prepared to jump.

"Sweet mother of pearl, this is the end!" cried Binderbec, just as Rumyon came flying back over the side, like a fish jumping back into the boat and plopped down on the deck beside him. The old soldier looked at Rumyon with surprise.

"I thought you were dead!" he exclaimed.

"So did I." Rumyon gasped and looked over his shoulder as Stadia, rose up behind them. The angel pushed against the side of the wagon until they were upright again and the wheels slammed against the ground, casting sparks and spinning wildly. Although Katie was glad to see the angel, the wagon was still rumbling forward and they were still headed for the trees. With disaster closer than ever, the angel's wings appeared and Katie's eyes gaped open wide. Both wings were twelve feet long, white as alabaster and shimmering brightly in the shade of the forest. They flowed gracefully, filled with power and light and made the angel appear larger, beautiful and more menacing at the same time. Now that Katie could see him for what he really was, a supernatural creature born of the air, a true messenger of God, she watched him in awe.

Stadia braced his hands against the front of the wagon with his wings beating the air in a large sweeping motion until the wind howled and the wagon began to slow. Still they were rushing forward, with the trees nearly upon them, when Goe Garth turned to Gimble.

"Good-bye, old friend." he said.

"It's been a good ride." said Gimble.

With that, the trolls leaned back as Stadia drove his heels into the ground then with another thrust of his wings, the wagon moaned and creaked in protest as his feet plowed long furrows through the rocky soil. Goe Garth and Gimble closed their eyes as the trees rushed toward them, then with one last effort Stadia shoved the front of the wagon down and drove its wheels into the dirt until the twelve ton wagon was forced to a screeching halt. When the dust settled, the front of the Rabble wagon rested gently against the trunk of a massive oak tree that towered over them in the quiet woods.

"That was close," said Goe Garth.

"Close indeed, the breadth of a fairy's wings," said Gimble and blinked as he stared at the tree above. Goe Garth stood up and patted the oak like an old friend.

With another bump the wagon lurched back, and everyone held on as the angel lifted the wagon wheels out of the trench and set them back on the ground. When all were accounted for, the trolls patted Goe Garth on the back, "Well done! Well done!" they said then jumped down from the wagon, cheering joyfully. Gral Tibbore hooted, Raylin laughed and Binderbec howled, while Rumyon and Gimble kissed the ground and Jingles danced a jig. Now that they were safe from harm, thanks turned to bragging, bragging turned to boasts and then came the speeches.

"A toast!" cried Rumyon.

"A toast!" shouted Gral.

The trolls quieted themselves as Rumyon struck a lofty pose.

"A toast! A toast, a toast to us all! The finest of daring adventurers, the likes of which have never been seen!"

"Here! Here!" They cried.

Katie sat aboard the wagon with Kitch hovering next to her. The little fairy frowned and shook her head, for there was no thanks to the angel who had just saved their lives. Rumyon continued.

"Indeed, to embark upon such a brave and wondrous voyage in the company of this august crew is the greatest honor I could..."

Suddenly Gimble cried out, "LOOK!"

Katie expected to see a Gollock or some other horrible creature lurking in their midst, but Gimble was only pointing at Raylin, and staring at the little troll with a look of horror. Rumyon was upset to have been interrupted, but when he looked, he nearly turned as white as Jingle's beard. Soon all were staring, with the same surprise and formed a circle around the little troll.

Raylin looked at them then slowly reached up and touched his head. It seemed that somewhere along the way, the little troll had lost his hat, and now that it was gone everyone could clearly see his ears which were rather large and very definitely pointed.

"What's the matter?" Katie whispered, and had no idea what was happening.

Kitch looked on with equal surprise and flicked her hand at the little troll.

"His ears!" She said and just stared.

Katie hadn't noticed them until she mentioned it, but as Raylin stood there it soon became obvious that his pointy ears were not the only surprise. Raylin lowered his head then reached under his cape and produced a rather large pillow. As soon as he removed it, his little round belly went flat as a board and the trolls all gasped. Raylin reached behind him and drew out another pillow. There was padding in his arms and legs as well and when he was done, everyone could see that Raylin was as slender as a child. Then with all of his stuffing on the ground, he began to shed his dark baggy clothing until he stood before them smartly dressed like a soldier, spit and polished all the way down to his knee high boots and belt buckles.

Binderbec cried out, "By the beard of Zindendorf! What's this?!"

Gral Tibbore pointed his sword at the boyish little creature standing before them.

"He's an elf!" cried the barbarian.

"An elf?!" Rumyon said and was so shocked that he was nearly at a loss for words. "...Why, why, the nerve!... The outrage!"

There was a fair amount of groaning and grumbling among the other trolls at the realization, then all grew silent when Goe Garth, jumped from the wagon and approached with a wooden bow in hand. It was the same bow Raylin had used to shoot the Gollock. Goe Garth, who was taller and larger, stood before the little elf.

"So, Raylin is it?..." Goe Garth said in a slow and serious voice.

"Yes, sir." the elf replied softly. "Raylin of Forix Linder."

"Forix Linder, a soldier's lineage, a noble clan." Goe Garth said and raised the bow, then broke it over his knee and tossed the pieces to the ground.

"Do you expect us to believe you?" Goe Garth said with a scowl. "First you enlist under false pretenses. You disguise yourself, pretending to be a troll. Then you violated the trust of the crew and jeopardized the safety of us all. You even lied to the king. These are grave offenses according to our code of honor... the troll code, that is."

Binderbec joined in. "I say we give him the sack!"

Rumyon glared at Raylin and strutted around like a proud peacock as he looked the elf up and down.

"Hah!" the toastmaster began. "Elf, you may have caught the others unaware, but I've had my eye on you from the beginning," Rumyon said, with his thumbs tucked in his vest and his belly bouncing.

"You dared to impersonate a troll! You worked among us yet you stayed to yourself. We shared our food but you did not eat with us. You even padded your clothes so that you would look fat."

Rumyon paused, and put his face next to the elf.

"That was low." he hissed.

Raylin kept his eyes to the ground as Rumyon continued.

"Who did you think you were fooling? You move too slow to be a troll."

The point was arguable, since elves were both fast and nimble, but the elf was in no position to quarrel and remained silent. Rumyon took a few steps back.

"An elf!" he announced again in mock disbelief then jabbed his finger at the accused.

"You sir, are a liar and a deceiver. You are a disgrace to your own kind and have dishonored our esteemed brethren."

There was general agreement among all the trolls who grumbled back and forth when a voice yelled out. "You don't speak for me."

Raylin looked up as Jingle approached and the faithful friar stepped into the circle. Rumyon frowned at the little priest and waved him off.

"Good friar this is no time for your lofty mind-edness. I speak of the law. This elf..."

Jingles interrupted. "This elf saved my life!" he said. "He saved me from the grip of the Gollock! Without his brave assistance you would be morning me, instead of judging him."

Jingles turned to the others gathered around.

"Saved my life he did, and risked his own in the doing!"

The news caused a murmur, but the toastmaster spoke quickly.

"I can appreciate your sentiments, good friar. Your words are duly noted, even so your fair sensibilities are misplaced and of no account. Now let the law..."

"He saved me too!"

Gral Tibbore entered the circle then stood next to Jingles and even Rumyon couldn't hide his shock. The barbarian looked every troll in the eye as he spoke.

"I was there in the cargo hold and if it were not for this elf, both the good friar and I would be ashes in the belly of the Gollock right now."

Gral turned to Rumyon. "Whatever you do to him, you must do to me as well."

Friar Jingles smiled at Gral and stood shoulder to shoulder with the rugged troll who folded his arms and frowned in defiance. The elf looked up at his two new friends and stood a little taller but his accuser was not done. Rumyon shook his head in disbelief, then sputtered and fumbled for the words.

"But…but…but elves are bad luck! You know that!" He shouted.

The words cut like a knife and Raylin lowered his head again.

"See? Even he knows it." said Rumyon, then turned to the others standing around. "I have said nothing wrong. I am merely speaking the truth to uphold the law. I have nothing against this elf. In fact I have known many an elf in my day." He added, in his own defense.

Gimble smiled. "Indeed, your sister is married to one."

Even Gral Tibbore chuckled at the comment.

"That is not the point!" Rumyon shouted. "Everyone knows that elves bring bad luck upon a journey. Look at what has just befallen us. The Gollock never leave their dwelling yet they sought us out, all the way across the Sacred Fineland where there is no food for them! Why?!" Rumyon pointed an accusing finger at the little elf.

"That is why!" he said.

"Indeed! There's your proof!" Binderbec shouted.

Gral Tibbore arched an eyebrow and gave the elf a suspicious look while the trolls grumbled and nodded.

"Wait, wait…listen!" Jingles said.

"No, you listen!" said Binderbec. "Rumyon is right!"

The trolls all joined in, shouting in agreement as Jingles tried to speak.

Katie watched from atop the wagon with the fairy by her side and couldn't understand why the elf had become such an issue. Standing there with his head down, he looked absolutely harmless.

"An elf! I never would have suspected." Kitch said, her eyes gleaming.

Katie shook her head. "I don't get it. Why are they so

angry?"

"Can you blame them?" Kitch said. "It's true. Elves are never welcomed on a journey, with anyone, ever. Everyone knows they're bad luck!"

Katie sat there and thought about the comment for a while then asked. "Do they ever take trips? I mean together, with each other. Do elves bring each other bad luck as well?"

The fairy looked at her blankly. It was a question she had never thought of. It was also a question that made her feel a little ridiculous, and since she had no answer, Kitch gave a smirk then turned away to watch the trolls as Binderbec stepped forward to add his opinion.

"If we are to succeed, we must leave him here. Abandon him with all his belongings, and anything he has touched. We must bathe and purify ourselves from his elvishness, break from bad luck and break from his bad fortune. It is the only way!"

Rumyon agreed and nodded to the others then paused as the angel stepped forward. Stadia frowned at the angry little trolls who suddenly tried to look calmer and more reasonable, in his presence.

"You superstitious little men. What is luck?" He said. "Has God not created you all? Both troll and elves alike?" He paused to let the question sink into their prideful hearts. "Have you forgotten the true enemy who seeks to devour you all? I assure you it is well with the evil one this day. Your bickering is like sweet wine on his table and your silly fears, serve him well."

The trolls glanced at each other and tried not to look at the angel as he spoke.

"Your stiff necks and hard hearts have dulled your senses. If this elf had brought the Gollock, why then did he not cast them out when they were tearing your wagon apart and threatened his own life as well? Who here truly believes the elf has such power? Let him speak."

The trolls looked back and forth in a sheepish manner.

"We battle the powers of darkness that lay in wait for us at every turn. We chase the wizard, a sorcerer who has the power of magic and plots our doom. So tell me. Who is the greater concern, the wizard or this elf? Who is the greater threat?!"

The angel glared down on the trolls. "Luck..." he said and scoffed. "Only a fool places his faith in luck when he has the power of God to protect him."

The trolls hung their heads like children and stood in shame before the elf. Still the angel was not finished and gave each one a stern look.

"If luck be your master then serve him. As for me, I will serve the Lord..." Stadia said, then reached out and put his hand on the little elf's shoulder.

"This noble one stands with me!... Who else will join us?" Stadia said and looked around. "Who else?"

One by one they came, until Rumyon stood alone then with his head down, the stubborn little troll shuffled forward. When they were all together, Stadia stood before them and made his declaration.

"Let it be known henceforth, that we are bound together by faith and are one under God. Let us vow to keep the enemy outside our ranks, and leave fear to those who would come against us."

The trolls all watched as Rumyon looked to the elf then reached out and the two shook hands.

"Noble Raylin is it?... Noble Raylin, indeed." said Rumyon then smiled and leaned in toward the little elf. "You still could stand to gain a few pounds, you know... for health sake." Rumyon said and winked. Raylin nodded and patted the troll's fat belly.

"Thank you friend, but I don't think I could ever be as healthy as you."

Rumyon agreed and the trolls all laughed at the elf's good humor.

Katie turned to the little fairy that was still fluttering beside her.

"I guess elves are good luck now." she said smiling then looked past the fairy as the huge black horse came through the shadow of the trees beyond the wagon. The giant stallion glistened with sweat as he took a few cautious steps into the light. His muscles flinched and trembled, exhausted from the long run. The mighty stallion snorted then shook his head and looked up. There was trouble in the air and the smell of smoke.

High above, the Gollock settled in the trees and now that they were beyond the Fineland border, they spewed their terrible flames and quietly fed on the trees that burned. The monsters gorged themselves and turned black as they filled with smoke then hunched their lumpy backs and used their claws to hold the trees and burn more wood.

Down below the trolls watched and listened as a strange sound filled the air, the mournful sound of a thousand voices crying out in pain. It echoed through the woods and seemed to come from everywhere at once. The trolls all looked around.

"These woods be haunted!" Binderbec gasped. And as the sound grew louder, Katie suddenly remembered where they were and stood atop the wagon, staring up in disbelief.

"The land of the living trees." she whispered as the trees cried out.

Katie covered her ears and turned this way and that, as bits of burning embers began to fall.

"The trees are alive!" Goe Garth yelled.

High above a tree limb broke with a horrible "Crack!" and the trolls scattered as the branch plunged through the smoke like a flaming torch and crashed to the ground, with a rain of sparks trailing behind it. Clinging to the branch was a monstrous Gollock. The giant insect was jet black and filled with smoke. It scampered to its feet, with soot billowing from its nostrils and eyes glaring. But before anyone could move, the hideous creature launched itself into the air with a grunt then disappeared in the trees above. Soon sparks and embers were falling all around as the fire raged above and Garth jumped aboard the wagon.

"Hitch the horse!" he shouted. "We've got to get out of here!"

Binderbec, ran to the stallion amidst a rain of fire while Juggernaut pranced and thumped the ground with his hooves.

"Easy, boy. Easy." Binderbec said then grabbed the reigns and just as he drew the animal forward the angel shouted. "No! Don't move! Anyone!"

Stadia watched the trees and the glowing embers raining down.

"What are we waiting for?! The forest is burning down around us!" Rumyon cried as the screams of torment echoed through the woods and Stadia gazed up at the trees.

"Something terrible is about to happen." He said.

"About to happen!" Rumyon yelled, amidst the fiery sparks swirling in the air. "What could be worse than this?!"

Soon the sky was filled with thick black smoke as the forest burned and the monsters ate their fill. Then all at once, the trees began to sway as if blown by the wind, but there was not so much as a breeze, and before the beasts could move, the burning branches came to life and grabbed them. They grabbed the Gollock by their legs then wrapped around their necks and waists and wings. In a matter of seconds, thousands were caught, while thousands more took to the air and vines lashed out to catch them. Once again the trees dragged the beasts down and the Gollock fought to break free, biting and snapping and clawing with their wings buzzing. Then when the trees had caught as many as they could hold, another noise filled the air, a horrible screeching that grew louder and louder.

"What's that?!" cried Rumyon.

"The Gollock," Stadia said calmly. "The trees are fighting back."

The panicked screams of the Gollock grew until the trolls could hardly stand it and pieces of the monsters were suddenly falling from the trees, from tiny parts to large horrible chunks.

"They're ripping them to pieces! Seek shelter!" cried Goe Garth.

"Hurry, hurry!" Kitch shouted, swirling around and around as Katie climbed down from the troll wagon and everyone ducked underneath to find cover.

Pthumpf! Crunch! Whack! Thud! Bang!

Pieces of legs, scaly claws, monster wings, and gnarled parts that no one could even recognize came crashing down and smashed atop the wagon. Katie huddled next to the angel when something large struck the wheel behind her, then bounced off and hit the ground with a heavy thud. When Katie looked, the Gollock was staring right at her. It lay in the grass on its side, with its hideous mouth working feverishly as though it were trying to speak. Katie screamed and Stadia pulled her away.

Raylin and Binderbec drew their swords and jumped in front of the child, then lowered their weapons in disgust when they saw that it was only half a Gollock. The back of the thing was gone, and Katie could hardly bear to look as the half creature dragged itself away with slimy gobs of goop trailing behind it. All across the forest the Gollock rained down in parts and pieces, until the trees had spent their rage and there was nothing left of monsters, then as quickly as it all began, it was done and all that remained was the sound of the crackling fire.

With the forest ablaze the trees wasted no time and sank

their roots deep in the soil, summoning water up from underground springs and streams. The moisture flowed into the trees, then with a gurgle and a hiss, water seeped from the branches all across the great forest until it showered down like rain. In minutes, every last fire had been put out and the water subsided. When it was done the rain turned to mist and settled on the grass like morning dew. With the battle ended, Rumyon peeked out from under the Rabble wagon. "It's over. It's all over." Rumyon said.

The trolls looked up with nervous smiles then stepped out into the open and lowered their swords. Katie came out of the shadows behind them, staring at the pieces of dead Gollock littering the ground all around them.

"Gross!" she exclaimed.

"Gross, indeed!" Friar Jingles agreed with a disgusted look on his face.

Kitch darted out as the angel stepped into the open and the little fairy gazed up at the trees.

"They're gone." Kitch said with a sigh of relief. "This time they're really gone."

"Yes, but how did they get here?" Rumyon said then glanced over at Raylin. The elf frowned and yelled at him.

"Don't look at me! I didn't do it!" He said, when suddenly a voice called out.

"How did they get here, indeed?" came a deep familiar growl.

"Bromwin?" Katie said and turned around to see the great brown bear limping toward them. He came through the trees slowly and stepped over the grim remains of the dead Gollock that littered the ground. The bear was exhausted as he made his way to them, then sat down in front of Katie and fell against the wagon wheel.

"I missed you," she said, as she reached out and stroked his fur then pressed her face against his.

"There, there, we are all together now... safe, for the

time being." Bromwin sighed, then looked around at the remains of the monsters that were strewn everywhere. "This was an evil and unnatural thing that should never have happened. The Gollock should not be here and would never have come this far of their own free will."

Friar Jingles stepped forward. "Yes, my king. On that we can agree, but it remains to be seen. How did they get here?"

The bear swung his huge head around to look at the troll.

"I believe the Gollock were summoned." He said. There was a long pause as the trolls all looked at each other and the answer came to them at once, "The wizard."

But before anyone could speak, the black horse was prancing around again, nervously looking here and there at the grass that surrounded it.

"What's the matter, boy?" Goe Garth said then peered at the ground that had suddenly come to life. The trolls looked around with fleeting glances, eyes wide with fear and when Katie looked down, she saw the grass coming to life beneath her feet as well. At first she hopped around and hardly knew where to stand then grabbed hold of Bromwin's fur and climbed up on his back. Goe Garth and the others stood with weapons ready and watched plants, vines, knotted weeds and thick tree roots all came to life and begin to move with a purpose, creeping and crawling everywhere around them.

"Do not be afraid," said the angel. "They have not come for you."

"Who…who then?!" said Rumyon, his voice a tremble.

The trolls struggled to stay perfectly still, as a muddy tree root rose up out of the ground nearby, and wrapped itself around the horrible remains of a dead Gollock. Once it had the thing in its grasp the tree root dragged the carcass down with a slurp and disappeared underground. The trolls looked as roots, weeds and snaking vines set about the job of cleaning up and disposing of the ugly carcasses that littered the forest floor. From the largest chunks to the tiniest pieces, soon every last bit was dragged under the ground until the task was quickly accomplished. And when the soil had swallowed it all up and there was nothing left of the hideous creatures, the grass smoothed itself over then lay perfectly still as though it had never been disturbed.

"It's okay, it's okay." Bromwin said when things returned to normal.

Katie climbed down from the bear very slowly and stared at the ground that had quickly and quietly gobbled up the monsters. Goe Garth peered up at the trees as well then waved to his men and gathered the trolls together. Once they were in a huddle he whispered quietly

"We're in a spot lads." He said.

"Aye!" said Gimble. "Tis the trees that ripped the Gollock to pieces."

Goe Garth nodded. "And disposed of them like so much rubbish."

"The trees be more fierce than the Gollock!" said Gral Tibbore.

"Aye!" said Rumyon.

Binderbec glanced around then leaned in even closer. "I believe they have us surrounded." He said. "So what do we do now?"

Before anyone could answer, there came a voice from the quiet woods, a deep and airy whispering on the wind.

"Whoooooo aaaaahhh yooooou?" The distant sound echoed from the trees, which spoke as one. "Whoooo are you, and what evil do you bring?" The trees whispered again as the trolls stared in wide eyed wonder.

Stadia came forward and stood next to Katie.

"Fear not, great forest. I am Stadia, guardian of..."

"Weeeeee know whoooooo you aaaaahhh... angel." The trees interrupted. "The presence of the Lord is with you."

Upon hearing that, Katie and the trolls looked at each other with some relief. It was nice to know that the living trees knew an angel of the Lord when they saw one.

The trees spoke again. "It is not you to whom we speak. It is the little one...

the human child."

The trolls turned to Katie who just stood there blinking.

"It is she who has brought this evil upon us. Who is she? And why is she here?" the trees demanded.

Katie drew closer to the angel and grabbed his cloak.

"It's not true. Tell them it's not true!"

The angel glanced down at her, "Be still." he said then looked to the trees.

"This child is innocent. The one you seek wields magic from the mischief of his own heart and lays somewhere else in the forest."

Stadia held his hand out to Katie. "This human child bears you no harm. She is a true child of God. And as such you must give her free passage."

There was a long pause, and while everyone watched and waited, something else stirred aboard the wagon. The ogres Rogad and Slag, peered out from under the tarp. They looked around and were greatly relieved that the wagon had stopped and the Gollock were gone. But when a nearby tree lifted its roots, like the tentacles of an octopus and lowered its branches into the light to get a closer look, Slag and Rogad retreated back under the tarp, satisfied that they were still very much in danger.

Finally the trees responded to the angel, their voices echoing on the wind.

"Yoooooou bring destruction. We have seen it. Turn back. Leave us in peeeeeeace."

Stadia stepped forward, "You <u>must</u> give us safe passage!" he demanded.

He waited again and Katie gave the angel a nervous glance.

"Is this an order from God?!" The trees asked sternly.

Stadia thought for a moment, then replied.

"In truth, it is not," he said.

"Then yooooou must goooo!"

Katie tugged Stadia's cloak trying to get his attention and spoke softly. "That's okay. Let's just go. Let's go!"

"Hear me!" the angel persisted. "I have been given charge of this child whose mission is one of mercy. It is the wizard and his forces who oppose us now. If you stop us, you serve the wizard and are in league with the powers of darkness which is against your very nature."

The forest stood silent to ponder his words and when they had given it some thought they responded, this time more softly.

"What is this mission?... Tell us."

Stadia looked up, with his head held high.

"We seek the one that is known as Majesty." the angel said.

All at once there was a roar like a mighty wind that blew through the trees and lifted their branches toward the sky. Katie held onto the angel as the towering oaks arched backward, till they looked as though they would surely topple over, then swung forward like giant bows, bending. Down and down they came till their uppermost branches swept the ground and touched the grassy floor. The band of trolls stood there watching in stunned amazement, as the trees held their lowly position. Katie watched and blinked at the wondrous sight. The living trees had literally bowed down before them at the mere mention of the name, "Majesty."

Then with another roar, the wind rose and the trees arched back into the air, till they were standing straight and tall once more. The trees whispered again, this time in softer and gentler tones.

"Truly you are sent by God, for only one gifted with His knowledge would undertake such a journey."

Katie smiled and felt more relieved.

"But, if we may ask. Why do you wish to find the sacred horse? What pains you so deeply that you would strive to risk so much?"

The angel said nothing for the longest time and when Katie looked, she was surprised to find Stadia smiling down at her. It was a look that simply said, "Well?"

Katie just stared back at him as if to say, "Well what?"

"They're talking to you." he said. "They want to know why you seek the white horse."

The forest of living trees watched and waited silently as Katie looked up at the angel with her mouth hung open and scarcely knew what to say.

"They need to hear it from your lips... Tell them." he said.

Katie just stared at the impossible demand and the angel gave her a gentle nudge with his smile. "Tell them," he said. "They will understand."

Katie reached back as he inched her forward, then turned to the bear, who raised his paw and gestured for her to go on. When she looked to the trolls, they smiled and waved like proud parents.

"Be brave. All is well." said friar Jingles.

The troll's words were kind, but Katie didn't feel brave standing there with the entire forest gazing down at her. In fact she was shaking in her little boots when the tiny fairy flew to her in a haze of light and smiled reassuringly.

"It's okay." she said. "Just pretend you're not afraid and tell them about your brother."

Before Katie could blink, the tiny fairy was gone to join the others.

"Pretend I'm not afraid...." Katie thought to herself.

That was easy enough if you were a fairy from the Nohr World and had special powers. Katie muttered and grumbled.

"Pretend I'm not afraid.... But I am afraid. I'm just a little girl, and I want to go home."

Then like a flash, the words came to her, the words she had said in the hallway, in front of Jack's room. "God is more important than magic." It was a bold declaration, followed by an oath sworn from her heart. "Whatever it takes to make him understand," She said. "No matter what."

The trees were still waiting when Katie took a deep breath and tried to stand straight and gather up her courage.

"Hello," she said.

"Greetings, child of God." the forest said in a proud and resounding voice. Katie was a little surprised by their hearty response then smiled to herself. They didn't have trees like this back at home.

Now that she had said, "hello," she felt rather pleased and stood there smiling, when it occurred to her that the trees were still waiting.

"If...if you please," she said looking left and right, not sure where to look exactly since the trees were all around her and the whole forest was listening. "I have to find the white horse, because the wizard has my brother." Katie said then bowed very slightly, and stepped back. She turned and smiled at the angel with a sense of satisfaction.

"There, I did it. That wasn't so bad," she thought then breathed a sigh of relief and waited... and waited and looked around and waited some more until she wondered if the trees had even heard what she said. Then it occurred to her that although what she said was true, it probably didn't make very much sense. Katie summoned her nerve and stepped forward again.

"The wizard is very bad. And the white horse is very good." Katie explained, but still there was no response. She sighed and knew she would have to explain her explanation, and tried again.

"I'm not the one who wants to find the white horse. It's the wizard. He's the one who...who..." Katie glared at the trees that hadn't made a sound, then stomped her foot, and smacked her fist against her leg.

"Are you even listening?! My brother is with the wizard. But the wizard doesn't even like him. He's just using Jack to make me do what he wants. I'm sure the white horse is great and everything, but all I want is for my brother to know about God. I don't care about magic, wizards or any of that stuff. I don't even care about what happens to me. I just want God to save my brother... That's all." Katie said, and was a little calmer by the time she had finished.

Katie looked up at the trees, and listened to their leaves rustling in the wind, then lowered her head. She had done her very best and just when she thought it was all completely hopeless, there came an answer.

"Well said, child of God," the voices whispered on the wind.

Katie looked up in amazement as they continued. "There is no love greater than one who would risk their life for another. The grace of God is upon you." The trees were silent for a while longer then called out, "Angel!... You must find the wizard and deal with him before he can do any further harm."

Stadia stepped forward.

"I would gladly, but I do not know where he is." He said.

The trees spoke loudly for all to hear. "We know where the wizard abides and will lead you to him and his apprentice. Travel due west through the woods, you will find them both there."

With a nod of his head, the angel started for the wagon. Katie trailed behind, then paused and looked up at the trees.

"I'm sorry about the giant grasshoppers." she said.

"It was not your fault. All has been put to right." The trees replied as the bear came up to her and the trolls all gathered around.

"Well done, child of God. Well done, indeed." said

Bromwin.

Once the stallion was hitched to the wagon, and they were settled aboard, the trees pulled back and a path appeared through the woods to show the way. Stadia rose into the air, with his cloak billowing.

"Follow me," he said. And off they went, deeper into the forest, in search of the wizard and his young apprentice.

CHAPTER NINETEEN

Captured

When Jack awoke he was laying in the grass, flat on his back, with something like a table leg lying across his chest. He shook his head then peered down at the object, through his blurry eyes. The gray scaly thing looked as though it were made of glass and had two hooked claws. It was a leg of the Guttin which had broken off when the monster was smashed to pieces. Jack jumped at the sight of the thing then tried to brush it aside. The hideous leg clung to his robe, dangling by the thorny hooks that covered its scaly flesh. When it didn't let go, Jack screamed and swatted at the leg, with the huge sleeves of his wizard's robe flapping wildly, until he finally managed to break free.

As soon as the leg fell to the ground, the grass came to life and reached up, like strands of living hair, to grab hold of the leg then quickly pulled it under the wet soil, with a sloshy gulp. As soon as it was gone, Jack scampered to his feet, staring in shock, unable to believe his eyes.

"Amazing, isn't it?" came a voice.

Jack whirled around to see the wizard. He was standing nearby and appeared to be in good spirits. He was also back

303

to his senses and very much in control of himself. Jack looked the wizard up and down. There was something different about him. He seemed somehow larger than Jack remembered. Even his bronze robe looked fancier. It was now flecked with gold instead of bronze, and sparkled a bit brighter.

The hatter's frenzy had indeed worked in Gellzoowin's favor. The wizard was stronger and more clever and well aware of the change, but continued to speak casually as though nothing unusual had happened and smiled down on the boy.

"Yes, I myself had forgotten where we were. It wasn't until the trees had begun to defend themselves, that I remembered."

"The trees?" Jack said, still flustered and rather shaky.

"Yes, they killed the Gollock, you know. Well, not all of them, but enough to convince the beasts to leave us alone. They took them by surprise and literally ripped them apart, limb from limb. A ghastly sight I must say, but an impressive show of strength, nonetheless. Oh but you were asleep for all of that. I would have awakened you, but you looked so peaceful." The wizard smiled again then looked up at the trees with a ponderous gaze.

"Ironic, isn't it? That such tranquil and peaceful creatures as these should possess such utterly destructive power." Gellzoowin looked at Jack who was now reluctantly gazing up at the trees, not quite willing to accept what the wizard was saying.

"The trees?" Jack said again. Just the idea that these wooden giants were alive and could move at will was more than a frightening thought.

"Yes, dear boy. The trees." the wizard said softly. "Don't let them fool you. They are very much alive and very cunning. I told you, they killed the Gollock, poor creatures... It was a bit of a massacre."

Gellzoowin looked down in mock sympathy and Jack fixed his eyes on the place where the leg of the Gollock had disappeared underground. The wizard sighed.

"As ferocious as they were, they never stood a chance, not really, not against... all this." The wizard gestured around them. "Yes, my boy, not just the trees. The entire forest is alive, the trees, plants, the rocks, everything."

Jack looked all around him until his eyes settled on the towering oaks again and the wizard could feel the fear building inside him as he continued.

"In a way, the entire thing is like one gigantic living breathing organism, but worst of all, it can think... and it can even talk."

Jack turned to the wizard with a frightful stare.

"T-t-talk?" He stammered, his voice starting to tremble a bit.

"Yes. I heard them while you were asleep." the wizard said casually as Jack looked around him.

"Do you know what they were saying?" Gellzoowin asked. Jack shook his head so hard, his eyes nearly rattled in their sockets.

"They were talking about us, but more importantly, they were talking about you." Gellzoowin said and Jack's face went white.

"It seems the trees are well aware that you brought the Gollock, and they are quite angry about the unfortunate skirmish that happened as a result of it. Many of the trees were burnt, and since they are alive, I suppose that would be of some importance to them, burning that is. Why they should be mad at me I don't know. I was fleeing for my life like everyone else. After all bringing the Gollock wasn't my idea."

It was a perfect lie, spoken perfectly before the trees that were listening to every word, and Jack knew Gellzoowin was only trying to save his own skin by making the trees think he was innocent.

Jack tried to speak but only managed to sputter. "But, but I didn't... All I said was... I mean, you're the one who..." he said, too upset to think straight.

"Ah, ah, ah." said the wizard. "I know, I know. You didn't mean to do it, but that's all water under the bridge now. We must think about what lies ahead."

Jack just stared at the clever wizard with his mouth dropped open. Gellzoowin smiled, knowing he had falsely accused the boy and appeared strangely content, standing there, in the middle of the enchanted forest.

Jack peered up at the trees and all of his senses told him to, "RUN!" He wanted to scream, or shout or do something, but since the trees were all around him; Jack stood still and tried to remain calm, his eyes pleading for the wizard to tell him what to do.

"Don't worry. They won't harm you. They are really quite civilized." Gellzoowin said calmly.

Jack watched the giant oaks, with their thick trunks and massive branches arching overhead, and wasn't at all convinced.

"Are you sure?" he said, trying not to panic.

"Yes quite." said the wizard brushing a few leaves and twigs from his sleeve.

"As long as you remain still and pose them no threat, you will be fine." The wizard said with a smile. Jack nodded nervously and then more vigorously as if to reassure himself that it was true. Once he was a little calmer, Jack turned his attention to the wizard and tried to change the subject, if only to take his mind off of the trees.

"You...you seem... bigger," Jack said, somewhat hesitantly.

The wizard was indeed taller and generally larger all around. Gellzoowin looked surprised and reacted as though someone had just complimented him on his suit.

"Oh, this! It was quite unexpected, really. But, oh well, here I am." He said, filled with false modesty. Still it was very peculiar, and Jack was curious.

"How did it happen?" he asked.

The wizard suddenly looked puzzled and somewhat annoyed. The one thing the hatter's frenzy did not do, was increase Gellzoowin's patience and he frowned at the boy.

He was not about to explain the complex theories of magical absurdity, or the various aspects of mystical reality as it related to absolute blind luck. As far as he was concerned, Jack was a simple minded human, with the total brain capacity of a squirrel. Gellzoowin simply smiled and said, "Call it a growth spurt."

Jack looked the wizard up and down nonetheless, this time with a little more concern. "Will it happen again?"

The wizard marveled at the boy's ignorance. For him to get any bigger, would take a second hatter's frenzy, and everyone knew that surviving a second frenzy was impossible. No one in the history of the Nohr World had ever survived two frenzies, at least no one on record and certainly no one in his lifetime. The last one to try was the amazing Precklesmorf, master wizard of the 3rd century, dating back to the 1st dark age.

Although this had no bearing on the situation at hand, Gellzoowin was now indeed a "frenzied wizard," and since he was in no rush and needed some time to think, he decided it could do no harm to reflect upon the matter.

As Gellzoowin recalled, Precklesmorf had experienced his first hatter's frenzy when he was but a lad, a young and brilliant wizard in a duel with a master sorcerer. To defeat the old sorcerer, the young Precklesmorf had sent himself into a total frenzy, and as a result, doubled his powers. Needless to say, the young wizard won the duel and made a name for himself, which was the beginning of his stellar career.

Before the great Precklesmorf attempted his second frenzy he had become the most famous wizard of his time. He had already written several books on sorcery and magic to include his own methods; and held the high position of "grand professor" at the prestigious Illin Barfdung University of Nohr World Magicians where he taught advanced theory. He had been awarded the alchemist's medal, five times for most hideous transformation of a wizard into something disgusting, shocking, or otherwise repulsive.

Indeed, Precklesmorf far exceeded all other wizards of his time and had accomplished every magical feat imaginable, all except for a second hatter's frenzy. By the time he was ready to attempt it, he was very old, and at the peak of his magical ability.

Gellzoowin remembered the account of the elder wizards who spoke of the time the great sorcerer's council gathered together, to see Precklesmorf attempt the unimaginable. They said that in the first five minutes, the sheer amount of magic Precklesmorf displayed was both spectacular and impressive. At a hundred and twelve spells per minute he had shattered the old record. Then, as history records, everyone watched as the amazing Precklesmorf, for the second time in his life, reached a state of total and absolute "Frenzy" and without any warning, or special fanfare, he simply popped. Some say he imploded. Either way, he shrank down to the size of a dried prune then burst like a bubble. As legend recalled the end of the great wizard was somewhat less than remarkable. Still, when Precklesmorf vanished in a cloud of tiny prune bits, it had been clearly demonstrated that no one could survive a second Hatter's Frenzy. It simply couldn't be done.

Jack watched the wizard, who seemed deep in thought, and wondered if he should come back later, when Gellzoowin turned to him and forced a gracious smile.

"No, dear boy. I doubt I will be getting any bigger." He

said and Jack let it rest at that. Just then, something stirred behind the wizard. Gellzoowin pretended not to notice and merely looked away, but the sound was unmistakable. There was obviously something there, but the look on the wizard's face simply said, "I don't think you want to see this."

Jack frowned then took a few uneasy steps to the side and when he looked, there was the goblin Numlock thrashing all around in the grass, or rather it was the grass that was thrashing all around him. The goblin wrestled for his life, with thick vines wrapped around his neck, arms and mouth. They pried his hands behind his back and swirled around every part of his body until Numlock was pinned down and it was impossible for him to move at all. Other than gurgling and staring at Jack with bulging eyes, he was utterly helpless.

Then just beyond the goblin, something else stirred in the thick brush. It was much larger and its black shell glistened in the shadows of the trees as the thing strained against the vines and branches that held it down. Jack kept his distance, afraid that it might be some kind of creature, ensnared by the forest, a rather large and sleek looking creature. But when he looked closer, he stared in amazement.

"Well, what do you think?" Gellzoowin asked, totally ignoring the goblin who was still wrapped up in vines, and fighting for his life at their feet. Jack was too bewildered to answer and just stared at what appeared to be the wizard's carriage, his new and improved carriage. The beautiful craft had been freshly conjured up out of the wizard's mind, and with his added powers Gellzoowin had managed quite a few improvements on the old model.

The new carriage was a lot trimmer than the old wooden, boxy design. It was jet black and made of polished metal that was smooth as glass. The carriage itself, was longer, and sleeker, pointed at the front and lined with velvet cushions. It had a new canopy, made of metal that would protect the passengers from the wind and the rain and even the fire breathing Gollock.

Strangely, the carriage had no wheels which made it looked more like a sled. It hovered off the ground, or at least tried to, while knotted vines and thick clumps of weeds wrapped around its hull, and struggled to keep it from going anywhere. The goblin lay, bound and gagged next to the sleek black vessel, which was presumably what Numlock had been trying to climb into when both he and the carriage were captured by the vines.

Then just when it seemed the magical craft would surely break free, an enormous tree root, snaked up out of the wet earth, and grabbed the nose of the carriage, splashing mud across its surface. Jack squinted in disgust and could barely watch as the thick fleshy limb, coiled itself around the carriage, then dragged it down hard, until the belly of the ship slammed to the ground. Once it was firmly anchored, the carriage ceased to move all together. Completely unnerved, Jack turned to the wizard, who showed little emotion.

"It would seem, they do not want us to leave." Gellzoowin said with a shrug.

"Well that's too bad. Becau..." Jack had barely opened his mouth when he took two steps and something grabbed him from behind, then yanked him off the ground and placed him right back where he was. He whirled around, fully expecting to see someone standing there, but there was no one, only a thirty foot oak. The tree was perfectly still and Jack looked at it suspiciously as he backed away and stumbled up against a thorn bush.

"Ouch!" Jack cried out, and held his hand. The black thorn that was stuck in his finger was the size of a sewing needle. He pulled it out quickly, put his finger in his mouth then glared at the bush, wondering how he could have missed such a large and dangerous thing sitting right behind him. In truth, the bush had just arrived. It had slumped along like a lazy porcupine while Jack was still looking at the tree.

Then as he stood there, nursing his sore finger, another thorn bush approached, then another and another. They scampered toward him like anxious children, and when he was surrounded they began to grow. The sound they made was like a crackling fire, as branches crinkled and popped, sprouting new thorns at an alarming rate.

Jack turned around and around, as the bushes grew fatter and taller and in a matter of seconds, they had built a hedge, seven feet high, that surrounded him on all sides and was still growing.

"Oh no you don't!" Jack cried and leapt into the air, but had barely gotten off the ground when a little vine wrapped around his boot and refused to let him go. Jack kicked and tried to fly away as he dangled in the air like a kite. Then with a fair bit of grunting and a few more jerks of his leg, the stubborn little vine began to slip. But as if to settle the matter, a thicker and stronger root lashed up out of the ground and wrapped itself around Jack's boot.

"Let go! Let go of me!" Jack cried.

The wet slimy root pulled Jack down, kicking and screaming, until he was set back on the ground, in the middle of his thorny prison. Then as quick as it appeared, the root slithered back down beneath the dirt. When Jack looked, the thorn bushes were nine feet tall with tendrils and branches that crisscrossed over his head and grew thick with leaves and thorns until they blocked out the sun and Jack was covered in shadow. With the prison complete, Jack found a tiny space in the thorns and branches and peered out at the wizard, his eyes wide with fear.

"Help me!" Jack cried. "Do something!" he said.

It was then that Gellzoowin reached down and lifted his robe to reveal the muddy roots that wrapped around his ankles like prison shackles and held him firmly to the spot.

"As I said, it would seem they do not want us to leave." Gellzoowin said calmly.

"Get me out of here!" Jack yelled, his voice more shrill and on the verge of panic.

Gellzoowin scowled at him and raised both hands. "What would you have me do? Disappear from this spot only to reappear over there, or over there? Look around you." he said. "The forest is alive, the whole forest. There is no escape."

Then as if to resign himself to the situation, Gellzoowin turned his attention to the distant trees and sighed. "A pity that I who have only just reached the height of my power should arrive here, only to glimpse my end. An unfitting fate of a life filled with such great promise."

Jack stared in desperation. "There's got to be something we can do!" he pleaded.

Gellzoowin simply raised an eyebrow and smiled. "When you think of it, do let me know, will you?" he said then looked away.

Jack couldn't believe his utter lack of concern and glared from within his thorny prison. Suddenly, the wizard was shouting, for no particular reason, other than to let the trees hear what he had to say.

"No my boy, we are in a most pitiful state indeed, much like the mouse in the belly of a lion. The time for planning is over. Our fate is sealed, and we will meet our end together, here in this dreaded forest."

Gellzoowin stood there, and after a while he could begin to hear the boy whimpering within the giant hedge of thorns, and a slow shifty smile crept across the wizard's face. In truth, he was far from helpless, but would let the living trees and the silly little boy think whatever they wanted while he formed his plan of escape.

CHAPTER TWENTY

Return of the Black Knight

*T*he setting sun poked through the trees and lit the way ahead as the angel traveled deep within the living forest, riding the wind like a wave, with a flurry of golden leaves in his wake. Juggernaut galloped along the winding path and kept pace as Goe Garth and Gimble drove the wagon with Katie and the others aboard, while Bromwin sauntered along at a more leisurely pace through the peaceful woods. With the leaves glowing like a thousand emeralds in the fading light above, the bear was in no particular hurry to find the wizard or his annoying little apprentice.

The trail meandered along until the troll wagon reached a fork in the road and a giant maple tree swung a huge branch across the path to point the way. Another mile or so, it happened again. With the help of the trees, they made their way silently and with great care, for fear that by some source of magic, the evil wizard might be listening.

Stadia peered into the distant forest as he slipped through the trees, gliding on air. Katie sat aboard the wagon and watched him soar through the woods rising high above then swooping low till he nearly touched the ground.

Suddenly the little fairy darted next to her, then disappeared through the trees only to return, bobbing playfully around the wagon. The fairy's wings buzzed like a bumble bee as she flung her arms open wide and yelled.

"Oh, to be small again! I can hardly stand still!" she said hovering on glittering wings. The fairy put a hand on her hip and pointed at Katie. "I never want to be big again as long as I live. I don't see how you can stand it." The fairy said and dashed off like a silvery streak through the woods. Katie was glad to see her so happy then gazed at the woods ahead with equal fascination as low hanging branches rose up out of their way and thick roots that stood above the dirt sank beneath the earth and made the ground smooth to let them pass. The towering elms, maples, and giant cypress trees, all moved to clear the path ahead. Even the stones rolled aside. From pebbles that swept back like rippling streams along the sides of the trail, to giant boulders the size of houses that made the earth rumble and quake when they moved. As they rode by, Katie noticed one of the larger rocks and a long jagged crack that ran across its face. At first she thought it was the weight of the boulder which caused it to split apart as it moved, until they came upon another huge stone.

The gigantic granite boulder that sat in the middle of the path, was nearly as big as the troll wagon and blocking their way ahead. Katie watched it shift its tremendous weight back and forth until the huge boulder was able to unearth itself and roll aside. It shook the ground as it went end over end, wobbling like a giant egg and after a great deal of effort, the stone came to rest against the side of a hill where it would be content to sit for another hundred years. Then just like every stone and boulder they passed, a crack appeared in the wide face of the rock till it stretched all the way across, then slowly curled upward at both ends. Katie gave the boulder a curious look and found herself waving. Indeed there could be no mistake. The rock was smiling at her, as had all the other rocks before it and Katie smiled back.

"Thank you." she said.

The trolls aboard the wagon watched the path ahead as the trees continued to part for them.

"We're almost there." Stadia said, and leaned into the wind with the black horse bounding down the trail and the troll wagon racing behind. From the front of the wagon, Katie could see the woods further on then called to Goe Garth.

"Do you think he'll be alright?"

"Who?" asked Goe Garth.

The wind whipped around them and Katie brushed the hair from her face. "My brother." She said. "I hope they haven't hurt him."

Gral Tibbore, the gruff barbarian, heard the little girl then turned to young Raylin and grumbled under his breath.

"If they wring his little neck, it'll serve him right." he sneered.

A mile away, twelve mighty oaks stood watch over the wizard and the boy. With Gellzoowin held down by his ankles and Jack trapped within the thorny hedges, there was no chance of escape, and Jack's constant struggling had only managed to make matters worse. Now in addition to his thorny prison, there was a rather sizable tree branch wrapped around his waist like a giant python, a thick and monstrous thing that had pushed its way through the wall of thorns and held him to the ground, simply to protect him from hurting himself. Jack wrestled in the shadows, clawing with broken fingernails, till his hands were bruised and bleeding and his body was covered with sweat as he groaned and strained to break free. Then with a moan he slumped forward and was about to give up when he suddenly remembered and looked at the branch with a devilish grin. His mind had been so clouded with fear and anger he had almost forgotten.

"Bee... hava... keen." Jack said the words carefully and

deliberately, and glared down at the branch. A moment later, the tree shuddered and Jack said it again. This time with a lilt in his voice, and almost sang the words. "Bee-hava keee- een."

Jack could feel the tree limb getting colder through the heavy material of his wizard's robe, when the branch began to freeze. The tree tried to let go, but the spell worked too quickly as the magic frost swept across the branch till it was frozen solid.

The wizard stood outside the hedge of thorns and watched the old oak with some interest. He had seen the branch reach through the hedge and suspected it had grabbed the boy, but what followed was a surprise to both him and the tree. The ring of frost crawled up the tree limb, like a silvery fire rushing toward the heart of the tree. Again the tree quivered and shook, distressed by the cold. Then just before the frost could reach the thick trunk and its roots, another branch came down like a giant hammer and with one blow, shattered the frozen limb and severed it from the rest of the tree in a desperate attempt to save its own life.

The living tree drew back with an agonizing groan while Jack stood within the hedge of thorns and smiled down on the broken chunk of branch still wrapped around his waist. With a touch of his hand, the frosted wood crumbled like brittle bread and fell to the ground in a sparkling cloud of crystals.

Slowly, the young wizard turned his gaze upon the thorn bushes and was about to deal with them when he noticed the little vine wrapped around the ankle of his boot. The thing quickly unraveled itself then shrank back into the ground, with a hasty retreat.

When Jack looked up, the sunlight reappeared as the thorn bushes drew back as quickly as they could to make way for him to pass.

"That's right. You'd better move." Jack said, feeling

smug and dangerous as he strolled out of his prison.

Gellzoowin gave a little smirk and lifted his robe to see the knotted tree roots unwind from around his ankles and sink back beneath the ground. Then came the wizard's newly fashioned carriage that hovered off the ground, and awaited its next command. The moment the green goblin was freed, he scampered across the grass, like they were hot coals, and jumped into the wizard's carriage as quick as he could, afraid to show his face again.

Jack swaggered toward the wizard, proud and puffed up, then stood in front of him with arms crossed, wagging his head and wearing a snobbish grin. After getting the trees to set them free, Jack was prepared for an apology, a humble word of thanks.

"I owe you my life." or "How can I ever repay you?" would be good for starters, he thought. Instead, the wizard simply looked past him and walked away. Jack turned and watched in utter disbelief as he went by.

"You ungrateful, selfish, arrogant, stubborn pig-headed..." Jack muttered under his breath then paused when he felt the gust of wind on his face and the mighty angel came through the woods, gliding on air with his thick gray cloak billowing around him. Behind him was the black stallion and the troll wagon, the shimmering fairy, and the great brown bear lumbering out of the woods. The angel set down, and approached on foot, his stern gaze fixed on the wizard.

Gellzoowin smiled at his enemy. "Ah, here comes our rescuer now." he said then turned to Jack and pointed at the angel "That's why they let you go, not your silly little magic spell."

Jack shrank away as the angel drew nearer, feeling small and insignificant once again. The wizard grinned. "Oh, come now boy, surely you realized that your sister would plead for your life, the angel and the trees would form an alliance and they would come to find you. You really must try to be more clever." Gellzoowin said as he walked back to Jack and whispered softly in his ear. "Now what do you say, we have some fun." The wizard said and placed something in his hand. When Jack looked down, there was the little blue stone cradled in his palm, the Magic Brindle Stone. Gellzoowin glanced at the angel then gave Jack a wink.

"Time to make a wish." he said.

Although the wizard had spent his own wish on the Gollock, the full power of the magic stone was still available to the boy and with Jack's fear of the angel to consider, he was sure that even if the boy did not conjure up a dragon, whatever he wished for would surely be big enough and terrible enough to deal with the guardian. Gellzoowin smiled at his own clever wickedness.

The angel marched forward and Jack tried to think, but with all the fear whirling in his mind, all he knew was that he wanted the angel to stop, and just then he did. Jack blinked and watched the angel who only waited in the tall grass and stared back. He watched him intently and wondered what had happened, completely unaware that he had indeed made a wish and a very powerful wish at that, the kind born out of fear and desperation.

"Very good, very good!" said the wizard and sounded like he had just tasted something delicious. Jack made the mistake of thinking Gellzoowin was talking to him and looked up to see the wizard gazing at the thing that was standing behind them. When Jack turned around, he jumped back and nearly tripped over himself when he saw what the magic Brindle Stone had summoned. Jack stood in the shadow of the dark brooding menace that loomed over them and gazed up at the black knight.

A smile crept over Jack's face as he marveled at the metal clad giant that had, only just now, been conjured up out of nothing. The dark ominous figure stood motionless as sparkling bits of magical dust drifted down his shining armor then disappeared when the spell was complete. The soldier stood eight feet tall with his black armor glistening red in the glow of the setting sun and was truly a giant of a man. With his helmet on and the visor down, the black knight towered over Jack and the wizard and looked like a monstrous metal robot. The mysterious knight held his battle hammer, in one hand. The head of the weapon was big as a cannonball studded with iron spikes, and as black as coal. The other hand he kept balled in a fist, a huge metal fist that was big enough to topple a brick wall.

The black knight stared across at the angel and Jack smiled. He felt much braver now, with the enormous warrior standing behind him, then raised an eyebrow and grinned, "Well? What are you waiting for? Come and get me." He whispered.

Bromwin watched from a distance and moved forward through the tall grass until he came along side the angel then glared at the enemy.

"What new evil is this?" Bromwin growled then glanced back to the wagon and kept his voice low so that Katie would not hear.

"Leave them.... Leave them and let the forest have them. It would be a fitting end for the boy and the wizard."

But Stadia only stared straight ahead.

"I promised I would remove the wizard and his apprentice. And so I shall."

The trolls sat aboard the wagon and watched with growing concern, alarmed by the black knight's sudden appearance.

"Where did he come from?" Goe Garth whispered to Gimble then moved aside as Katie climbed up between them.

"It's the black knight!" she gasped, with her eyes gaping wide.

Binderbec, the old soldier, gave her a peculiar look and frowned.

"Well, we can all see that." he said.

"No." Katie said. "I've seen him before."

The trolls all looked with surprise. "Where child?" Binderbec asked.

Katie stared straight ahead. "At home, where I come from. Jack has a toy that looks just like that."

"Some toy." said Goe Garth.

Gimble peered out across the field. "Is he good or is he evil?"

The trolls glared at him and Gral Tibbore growled. "Are ye daffed in the head? Just look at him! Does he look good to you?" he said and pointed.

Just then the angel started forward and Bromwin watched him nervously then called out. "Beware the wizard's magic!" was all he could think to say.

The angel called back over his shoulder. "This is the boy's doing." he said, his voice filled with grim determination.

"...How nice." Bromwin grumbled, as he watched Stadia advance.

Jack's confidence quickly melted away as the angel drew nearer, while the wizard watched with great interest to see what the black knight would do. He stood there, glancing back and forth at the angel and the huge soldier.

"Attack! Attack!" the wizard mumbled but the dark warrior only stared ahead, like a stone cold statue, until the angel was only a few feet away and standing before him. Jack and the wizard backed away as the angel and the black knight came face to face. Now that they were standing together, Jack marveled at the true size of the soldier, for at eight feet tall, the black knight dwarfed the angel, like a man standing before a child. His shoulders were wider, his chest was massive and the huge iron mace he held by his side made the angel's sword look like a toy.

Back aboard the wagon, the trolls watched anxiously as Stadia stood before the dark warrior with barely the length of a sword to separate them.

"What's happening?" Said Rumyon. "Do you suppose they've exchanged words?"

"Perhaps an introduction." Binderbec said, squinting across the distance.

"Or a warning." Gral Tibbore added.

"Nay," said Raylin. "Nary a word has passed between the two."

The keen eyed elf watched from a spot higher up on the wagon then pointed. "Wait, look!" he said at the first sign of movement. The others watched nervously as the angel began to circle around the enormous soldier. Stadia moved slowly and deliberately, like a general inspecting his troops and to everyone's amazement, the black knight remained perfectly still, never moving a muscle. His polished black helmet faced forward, never turning, as though the angel were little more than a curious insect that was hardly worth his attention.

At least that's the way it looked to Jack. To him the black knight was brave and defiant, and showed no fear, but to the wizard, the black knight's lack of response made him wonder if there was even anything inside the suit of armor at all. In truth, it hadn't move an inch since it appeared.

When the angel had completed his inspection and stood in front of the black knight once more, he turned his back to the soldier and faced the wizard.

Gellzoowin glanced up at the black knight then smiled at the angel as though he were an unexpected guest. "So… You're looking well." He said with a weak smile.

"I see you have grown," Stadia said and showed no concern for the thing standing behind him.

"Ah, yes. I have gained a bit in stature," the wizard said then quickly turned the focus back to the ominous creature standing behind the angel.

"Please allow me to introduce our new friend... The Black Knight, I presume." The wizard gestured toward the giant soldier, hoping he would at least flinch or nod or do something. But once again he hardly moved and Stadia just stared at the wizard and would not be deflected.

"I will deal with both you and that, later." he said, with hardly a glance over his shoulder. Stadia turned to the boy and Gellzoowin sneered at being dismissed so easily.

"Give me the stone," the angel said and reached out his hand.

Jack looked at the wizard, but Gellzoowin was too busy seething over the insult to offer any help, while the black knight simply remained motionless and seemed totally unconcerned with anything that was happening around him. Jack peered up at the angel.

"H-how did you know?" he asked in a meek little voice.

"I can feel its power... The same power which was used to summon the Gollock."

Jack clutched the stone tighter and thrust his fist behind him.

"But, I didn't do it! It was..."

"I know." the angel said. "Only the wizard would know of the wretched creatures and be so careless as to summon them here."

Again, Gellzoowin stood there, glaring at the insult as the angel continued.

"When the stone was of no further use to him, he gave it to you to conjure up more mischief. In this you have succeeded. Now give me the stone. It is of no further use to you." he said.

With one final look at the wizard, Jack reached out and handed the magic stone to Stadia then hung his head, as though he had given away his life's possessions and had no idea what to do next. But once the stone was in the angel's grasp, Gellzoowin's eyes lit up as the idea struck him like a thunderbolt and he wondered why he hadn't thought of it sooner. The magic stone was as great a threat to the angel as any dragon, and possibly even greater. For with its magic power came temptation and that could destroy the angel with only just one wish.

"Could it be so easy?" the wizard smirked, trying to hide his excitement as he watched the angel carefully. He looked for any sign of weakness, the slightest hint of want or desire. With that, the bond between Master and servant could be broken as the angel's faith withdrew from God and was placed in a tool of magic. Gellzoowin grinned, his own heart burning to see the angel so easily ensnared.

"Yes... do it.! Just one wish!" he said, as the angel gazed down at the stone then without any further hesitation the guardian closed his fist around the rock and squeezed. In an instant, the wizard's look turned to horror.

"No! Wait! Don't! You can't! You mustn't!" he cried, as the angel frowned and his fist shook, and then... "Crr-runch!"

Gellzoowin winched at the sound then watched as a thin green cloud sifted out between the angel's fingers and rose into the air.

"What have you done?" He gasped.

When Stadia opened his hand, there was only a fine blue powder that was gently picked up and swept away by the wind. The wizard watched as the great stone was lost in the breeze, on a current of air, along with the chance to destroy the angel.

"The great Brindle Stone," Gellzoowin growled. "The wonder of the seven worlds ...gone...forever. You will pay for that!" he said, his eyes burning like fire and filled with a renewed sense of vengeance.

Stadia glared back. "Save your threats for your minions." He said then finally turned his attention back to the black knight. The huge figure still had not moved an inch and with its visor down, it indeed appeared lifeless.

Stadia called to Jack as he gazed up at the knight. "Come here boy." he said.

Jack slumped along until he stood next to the angel and Stadia looked down on him. "What is this thing you have conjured up?" he asked.

Jack looked up at the huge hulking form of the black knight and didn't quite know what to say, since the figure was fashioned after a toy and had literally appeared suddenly, and out of nowhere.

"He's just my companion. You saw him in the castle, remember?" Jack said.

Stadia fixed his eyes on the black knight. "This is not the same creature." He answered sternly and waited for a better explanation.

"It's not?" Jack said with some surprise and began to look a little suspicious himself, as he peered up at the black knight. He leaned forward and squinted, trying to see if there was any visible difference between this black knight and the one he had left in the castle. As far as he could tell, everything about it looked the same. But then, the thing in the tower was only a whim of his imagination, something he had conjured up in his dream. Yet standing there in the middle of the field, looking up at the giant of a man wrapped in armor, Jack could hardly deny that this black knight was anything other then real, or at least appeared to be.

"Amazing," Jack said softly, still gazing upward, unsure of what to believe. "Well anyway, he looks just like it... just like the black knight."

It was only a thought spoken softly, the first time the boy had uttered the name, and without any warning there came a deep voice that echoed from within the black armor. "I am here, my master."

Jack staggered back in surprise and Stadia put his hand to his sword.

"He's alive!" Gellzoowin cried. "Fancy that, fancy that!

What else can he do, I wonder." he hissed, his eyes glaring.

Stadia took a step back and called to the boy, "Hear me!" he said, but Jack could hardly look away from the black knight.

"You do not know this creature or what lies within." Stadia said. "Leave this thing behind and forget you ever saw it!"

Jack gazed up at the black knight. "It called me master!" he whispered almost in a trance.

"Indeed he did." the wizard said then turned to the angel. "Come now. Let the boy have his fun. The excitement is just beginning."

Once again Jack spoke like he was in a dream. "This is the most incredible thing I could have ever wished for." He turned to the angel with a sheepish look.

"Do I really have to get rid of him?" he asked.

"Yes!" The angel replied sharply.

"No!" said Gellzoowin.

The wizard stood behind Jack and grabbed him by the shoulders. "The angel has no power over you. Don't be afraid of him. The black knight is yours to command and there is nothing the angel can do to stop you." The wizard spoke into the boy's ear like a serpent whispering in the garden.

Jack assumed a more defiant pose. "What if I don't want to?" he said to the angel, trying to sound more confident than he really was. Stadia replied with a calm that was both quiet and unsettling.

"The choice is yours... and so is your fate." he said, and left it at that, when suddenly there came a loud chorus of voices, shouting from above.

"Oh, sorcerer, you vile and wicked viper!"

Jack and the wizard looked around and suddenly remembered where they were, as the trees spoke and their voices echoed through the woods.

"You prey on innocence, and destroy the weak. Your end

will be justly deserved." Gellzoowin sneered at the trees, "Cursed magic forest." he said.

Jack's eyes darted back and forth. "I don't like it here." He said.

"Steady boy." Gellzoowin replied. "They don't like us here either."

"Take them away." The living trees said. "They are a blight to us and poison the very ground they walk on. We can tolerate their presence no longer."

Gellzoowin turned to the angel and smiled, with cunning eyes. "Well angel, what say you? We are yours for the taking. Lead on. Take us out of this wretched place, and be quick about it. The sooner we leave the better."

Stadia could only frown at the wizard and the black knight then looked down at Jack. "Beware the company you keep, boy. It will surely be your undoing." He said, then turned and walked away.

The wizard scoffed then with a wave of his hand the sleek magic carriage came forward and held its position a few yards off. As soon as it stopped, the green goblin that was hidden aboard stuck his head up to look around. Once he was sure he would not be attacked by the local plant life, Numlock rushed to the steps of the carriage to greet his master.

"All is in readiness." He said eagerly then with a flourish of his hand, he gestured toward the wizard's seat, and bowed graciously as the wizard climbed aboard.

Stadia returned to the troll wagon, and the great bear growled as he approached.

"Look at them, the evil wizard and his foolish apprentice, so puffed up and proud, yet both of them wicked to the very core."

The bear had only just muttered the words, when a little voice called out.

"He's still my brother!"

The bear turned around to see Katie peering down from

the troll wagon and frowning at him.

"I only spoke what was in my heart." The bear said, then turned away with a look of regret and said nothing further. But as Katie watched her brother board the black carriage, there could be no denying. The wizard's hold was indeed growing stronger.

"Come on... Come on." Jack said, and waved his hand, coaxing the black knight like a pet. "That's it! This way."

The huge knight took his first few steps, walking stiff legged, his armor creaking and clanking as he went with the grim mace still clenched in his fist. The trolls all watched with suspicious eyes and were filled with curiosity as the black knight made his way slowly toward the wizard's carriage, moving like a fragile old man.

With a slow and deliberate motion he grabbed the side of the carriage, then climbed aboard, and when he did the carriage sank to the ground with a, "Thud!"

"My, aren't we a big lad." said the wizard as he looked the black knight up and down then with a wave of his hand the carriage stirred and rose aloft once more.

Jack nestled into his chair and marveled at his new prized possession then with the trolls aboard the Rabble wagon, and everything in readiness, the wizard signaled to the angel.

"Lead on!" he said with a shout, and glared at the living trees.

CHAPTER TWENTY ONE

A Desperate Escape

*T*he setting sun cast long shadows through the woods as the trees led them on through the living forest. Katie glanced back occasionally. The wizard's carriage moved silently, barely stirring the grass beneath it as it floated behind the troll wagon. The black knight stood aboard the carriage, gliding in and out of the shadows, like a spirit looming in the darkness. Jingles and Binderbec stood at the back of the troll wagon, peering at the black knight and kept a close watch.

"Look at him just standin' there, like some god forsaken ghost, haunting our trail." said Jingles. "I don't like it, I tell you. He gives me the Gaggle-lilies."

Binderbec leaned on his silver hammer and nodded in agreement. "Aye', he gives me the colly wobbles."

"Then why don't you two quit your gawkin' and tend to your business?" Rumyon scoffed as he passed by then paused to look at the grim figure of the black knight gliding toward them on the wind of the wizard's carriage. Rumyon stared, unable to look away from the eerie sight, and Binderbec smiled at the toastmaster.

"Is that the business you'll be tendin' to, or would ye be gawkin' as well?"

"Bah!" Rumyon said then stormed off in a huff.

Night came quickly and the torch lights aboard the troll wagon lit the path ahead. Enormous trees stood on either side of the trail like towering giants, their thick trunks strangely colored, were unlike any other trees of the woods. They were black and silver, and glittered in the moonlight as though covered with a frosted dust that shimmered. The trolls looked on in silence while Katie climbed higher aboard the troll wagon and the little elf crouched next to her.

"The elder woods, the deepest, darkest part of the forest," he said as Katie gazed up at the trees. "Silver oaks, wisest and strongest of all in the living forest, he said. "Greatly respected above all others, these are known as "the Judges."

"Wagoneers whooooah!" Goe Garth shouted and brought the troll wagon to a halt. The angel stopped in the trail up ahead and looked back.

"What is it?" he asked, gliding toward them on the air, his face bathed in the glow of the lanterns.

"We are not all immortal as you are." said Goe Garth. "My men need rest."

Stadia turned to Katie whose eyes were already half shut then called out to the trolls, "We will stay here and make camp for the night."

With that, the wizard's carriage leapt forward and Gellzoowin sprang to his feet.

"REST?! The hags with rest!" he said, his eyes red and ablaze. "What need have I for rest? We must press on and make haste till we have left this place behind, and are gone from these wretched woods!"

The angel only stared back.

"Be still wizard, You are in no position to give orders."

Gellzoowin glanced up at the shadowy trees that loomed around him then sat down in a sulk as his fiery eyes turned cold and gray as the tomb. When all was silent, the voices of the trees rose gently above the howl of the wind.

"Weeee have heard and grant you one night's rest, with one provision." said the elder woods.

Jack sat next to the wizard, listening anxiously as the trees continued.

"Yoooou must bind the wizard and the boy. Bind them hand and foot. Bind them with ropes and chain then lay them on the ground where we will lay hold of them as well with root and vine. Then if they dare move, or use their foul magic to try and escape, we will dispose of them ourselves. Is that clear?"

Stadia answered, "Yes, abundantly."

Gellzoowin glanced across the carriage. One look at Jack and he could see the terror in his eyes, and knew the boy would never stand for it and would surely get them killed if he didn't act now. With one swipe of his hand, the magic carriage leapt forward and Jack fell back against his seat. The sleek new carriage jumped so suddenly, it swerved around the angel and flew right out from under the black knight, who rocked back on his heels, stiff as a board, and flipped over the rail. Jack looked back in horror, but the wizard only smiled, for without the black knight, the carriage was lighter and faster.

As quick as the carriage jumped, the trees reached out, their branches knifing through the darkness as the wizard plunged ahead, trying to escape capture like a fox through the hounds.

Jack yelled to the wizard. "Wait! What about the...?!" But his words were cut off when Numlock pounced on him and slapped his green hand over the boy's mouth just as a thick tree limb whacked the back of the carriage and knocked them sideways. Jack and the goblin fell to the floor as the carriage fishtailed wildly, then banged against another tree, straightened out, and lunged ahead. There was no stopping now, and as they tilted back and the carriage swept higher into the air, Numlock grabbed Jack by the collar and glared into his eyes.

"Not a sound, boy!" the goblin hissed. "Not a sound!" he said then gazed ahead as they slipped through a sea of branches that moved like serpents, coiling and bending all around them, clutching at thin air.

Jack held on as the carriage ducked and darted, clever as a sparrow, swerving away from one tree, hurtling toward the next, only to miss it by inches and kept on going in a mad dash to freedom. Suddenly the carriage dipped sharply, and made a right hand turn, which slammed Jack against the wall. A second later the wizard's carriage dove out over a black pond then banked to one side. Jack grabbed the railing to keep from falling out then looked down in amazement. The water below was as smooth as glass and black as the sky above, but there was no reflection of the carriage, none at all, only the twinkling of the stars above. Somewhere along the way, the wizard had made the carriage and everything aboard invisible. Jack wasn't sure when it had happened, and could only hold on as they sped across the pond and dove into the woods on the other side.

The trees flailed about wildly as the invisible carriage darted through the woods, but try as they might, they simply couldn't catch what they couldn't see. Gellzoowin glared ahead as he maneuvered his way through the forest with skill and daring. Suddenly they were slowing down and just when Jack thought it might be over, both he and the goblin were thrown to the floor as the carriage went into a steep climb, rocketing toward the sky.

Jack struggled to pull himself up as they climbed at an alarming rate then was flung in the air when the vessel dropped sharply. Jack grabbed his chair, which was thankfully bolted to the floor, as the wizard's carriage dove down and ducked under branches then leapt up and dropped again in a series of giant dips and arcs that lifted Jack out of his chair then slammed him down again, and again.

In an instant, they were climbing once more, then rolling in a corkscrew motion as the trees came at them from all sides. Jack slid down in his seat and fought to hold on. But with everything swirled around him, his feet flew up and tossed his robe over his head which was just as well, since the sight of the forest rolling over and over, was making him sick to his stomach.

Jack sank in his seat as the air pushed him back and the wizard's carriage shot out over the treetops like an arrow. Once they were beyond reach, the carriage leveled out at a hundred feet above the ground and became visible. Jack was still clutching the arms of his chair with his robe over his head when he finally sat up, straightened himself out and glared at the wizard.

"Are you crazy!?" Jack shouted and tried to look angry, but with his eyes still dancing around in his head from all the flying and twirling, he looked more insane with fear; which gave entirely the wrong impression. Now that they were safely away, the wizard gazed down at the trees with a clever smirk. When Jack was sure he was being ignored he shouted again.

"What about the black knight?! You're not just going to leave him down there! He'll be torn apart!"

Gellzoowin laughed in Jack's face. "HAH! Hang the black knight! The useless wonk, a lot of good he was, nothing but dead weight, and so much scrap metal."

With that the wizard leaned over the railing and laughed. He laughed at the trees below then laughed at the sky above. The wizard laughed at the whole world. And now that he had escaped the living forest, he would revel in his freedom and his laughter echoed into the night. The goblin grinned at Jack with a gleam in his boggy green eyes, as Jack sat with his arms folded, hating the wizard, hating the world, and pouted till his lower lip nearly touched his chest.

Numlock giggled at the boy's misfortune, then chuckled until the pleasure of it all bubbled up inside of him and became a full blown, gut wrenching, knee slapping whack of laughter. Numlock cackled wildly and now that he and the wizard were both laughing, Jack blinked like a sad puppy, with tears welling up in his eyes, which only made Numlock point and laugh even harder. The goblin jeered openly.

"Hang the black knight! Hang the black knight!" he taunted, and laughed.

"And why not?" Numlock thought. Goblins were supposed to be cruel and with the wizard laughing as well, he felt perfectly safe mocking the boy. That's why it came as a complete shock when Gellzoowin picked the goblin up with a spell, dangled him by the scruff of his neck, and without so much as a word, hurled him over the side. With that, Numlock was gone in an instant.

"Insolent beast. Go find yourself some manners." the wizard said, then turned away without a care. Jack rushed to the side of the carriage and looked down in horror as the goblin plunged out of sight.

"Where was I?" the wizard said, looking off into the distance. "Ah yes, our escape. It's all going so well. Don't you think?" he said and chuckled, obviously pleased with himself. Jack stared with his mouth hung open. Although he had no love for the goblin, to see the creature hurled to his death, was another matter all together.

Indeed, never had a goblin fallen so far, for so long and lived to tell the tale. Numlock flailed his arms wildly as he toppled through the air then hit the treetops like a lumpy sack, tumbling end over end, smashing and crashing through the tangle of branches. The trees caught by surprise, swatted at him like a cockroach dropped into their midst, beating and thrashing the goblin all the way to the ground where he finally crashed in a heap. Numlock laid there moaning and groaning, and dared not move, for all the pain. Now that he was visible again and resting at the foot of an old oak, the forest was strangely silent and watched to see what else would fall out of the sky. Then in the stillness, a tree branch came down, like a long wooden finger, and rolled the goblin over. Once Numlock was on his back, he summoned the courage to open a swollen eye and saw the trees rising above him. Then with every part of his body bruised and battered, the goblin groaned once more, then closed his eye, and quietly passed out.

The wizard's carriage soared through the night sky and as much as Jack hated the little goblin he still couldn't believe what the wizard had done. Gellzoowin, however, was puzzled by his reaction. After all, he had thrown away a perfectly good goblin, to defend the boy's honor, and thought Jack could have been more grateful. But now that it was done, there were more pressing issues to deal with, like their loss of altitude and the flying spell which was quickly wearing off.

Jack hadn't noticed at first, but now that they were falling faster, he found himself clutching the arms of his chair once more, and staring down at the dark forest as the nose of the carriage went into a steep dive.

"Remember, boy. Not a sound!"

Jack leaned back in his seat and hardly heard anything the wizard said as the carriage fell like a rock and the living trees reached up to ensnare them. The black metal hull was hard to see against the cold dark sky, but when it disappeared all together, the trees were helpless as the invisible carriage plunged below the treetops, untouched, unharmed and quiet as a whisper.

Although the wizard had indeed made a clean getaway, the trolls would not give up so easily. They banded together to form a search party with their lanterns in hand and swords drawn, when Stadia stepped forward.

"Leave them!" he said. "Let them go. They will not venture far without the girl. She is more valuable to the wizard than his own freedom."

Suddenly the trees stirred and whispered from the shadows that surrounded them.

"Rest for now." They said. "But beware the soldier of doom, for he has not yet awakened."

The trolls looked at each other.

"Soldier of doom? Rumyon asked then turned to see the dark figure laying in the path behind them. The black knight was stretched out, flat on his back where he had fallen, with the grim mace still clenched in his metal fist.

"Soldier of doom." said Raylin, pondering the name.

The fairy flitted about on the night air. "What do they mean, awakened?" she asked.

"Yes, what indeed?" said Binderbec.

The old soldier raised his lantern and crept forward with Raylin, and Gral Tibbore right behind.

"Careful!... Be careful, now! He's a crafty one, he is!" Rumyon warned.

Gral looked back over his shoulder. "Be still... He hasn't moved an inch." He grumbled.

Binderbec held his lantern a bit higher, and as they drew nearer, the black knight's armor glowed yellow and orange in the flickering lamp light. Then when they were close enough, the old soldier reached out with his little sword and poked the black knight in the shoulder. His blade "clinked" against the armor, and the troll jumped back. When nothing happened, he stepped forward again and tapped the black knight, this time a little harder. "Clank!" He poked him twice more. "Tink! Tink!" And still nothing. Binderbec frowned then finally brought the flat of his sword down hard against the black knight's helmet. "KA-PLAAANNG!

Finally, the angel cried out. "Come away from there!"

The three trolls backed away and Binderbec turned to the angel.

"He's dead as a doddle!" said the old soldier.

"Your curious prodding will gain you nothing. The black knight is my concern. Leave him to me," Stadia said. "Now go your way and make camp."

The trolls returned to their wagon with cautious looks back at the huge figure lying in the shadows. Then with everyone aboard, Goe Garth flicked the reigns and the stallion moved on. Soon the trail behind them was shrouded in darkness and the black knight faded from view.

"Good riddance!" said Gimble.

Binderbec held his lantern above his head. "Aye, good riddance indeed!" said the old soldier, with a squinty eye peering into the night.

The troll wagon meandered through the forest, until they came to a clearing, a circle of trees surrounding a quiet glen. Above them, a galaxy of stars filled the sky.

"This will do." said the angel.

As soon as the wagon came to a halt, the great bear nodded to Goe Garth then slipped into the shadows beneath the wagon.

"Wake me in case of battle. Otherwise let daybreak find me fast asleep, for I am most weary."

Then with a huge yawn, Bromwin curled up on the ground and promptly went to sleep. Without a moment to lose Goe Garth jumped from the wagon and secured the Rabble wheels with wooden blocks, while Binderbec unbridled the horse and set a heaping bucket of oats in front of him. The rest of the trolls went about the task of preparing the wagon to bed down for the night.

"Excuse me. Pardon me. Careful. Watch yourself."

Katie moved aside as the trolls rushed in all directions and took up their positions. With a turn of large wooden cranks, an enormous tarp was raised over the wagon, suspended by the lantern poles and stretched tight like a tent. Then with a pull of iron levers, there was a rumbling of gears from somewhere below as the floor began to move. Katie quickly ran to the front of the wagon and watched in amazement as portions of the lower deck rose up out of the floor in the shape of large wooden cupboards. They line up on either side of the ship, while the middle of the deck sank down at the same time until a wide center isle traveled the length of the wagon, like a galley, with the cupboard walls on either side. Along the walls were large wooden panels that looked like doors. Katie watched closely as the trolls went to each one and with a gentle push and a "click," the panels slid open like a dresser drawer to reveal a bed, neatly fitted with cotton sheets, a down pillow and warm blankets. The trolls plumped pillows and lit scented candles which filled the wagon with light and the fragrance of flowers. In no time, everything was charming and quaint, from brass candle holders to leather bound books on bedside tables. If there was one thing the trolls loved, it was the warmth of home, and the Rabble wagon was well equipped with every comfort they would need.

In the meantime there was more activity in the campsite below. Goe Garth and Binderbec had already started a fire, and set up a kettle for cooking. There were wooden stools and benches set around a table, and a large iron pot already bubbling with black bean stew. Then came the aroma of baked bread wafting in the cool night air, and with one sniff, Katie could nearly taste it.

Just then Rumyon popped up from behind the huge iron pot. The troll was wrapped in an apron, and carrying a large wooden platter with four baking tins filled with hot steaming loaves of fresh Plumpkin bread, cooked to a golden brown.

"Come and get it!" Rumyon yelled.

"It's about time!" Binderbec shouted.

Katie hurried down the ladder to join the trolls and smiled, since the bread hardly took any time at all to bake. When prayers were said and dinner was served, Katie settled down next to Jingles with a dish of stew and took a bite of her bread which tasted more like cake and was sweet as a pastry. One bite and she could see why the trolls were so fat. The hungry trolls ate and ate, then after the hearty meal, Katie watched Gimble heap more food on his plate.

"Eat to your full potential, is what me ole' mom used to say." Gimble beamed as he piled on more bread. After dinner, the trolls sat around the fire to relax and shared tall tales of conquest. And as the yarns grew longer and the tales grew taller, they puffed on cobble cone pipes and tilted goblets filled with green grape wine.

After a while, friar Jingles tapped out his pipe, then jumped up with his wooden stool tucked under his arm like a drum. With a bend of his knee and a tap of his toe, he banged the stool and hopped around, to dance a jig before his friends.

"Come, lads! A good meal requires good music and dance to help the digestion!"

Binderbec the old soldier rubbed his belly. "You have your dance, I prefer peace and quiet, thank you."

"HAH!" Jingles laughed. "You bunch of old larks! I challenge you to a dance. Or are your bottoms too heavy to rise up off your stools?!" he said hopping and banging his drum. "Last one dancin' wins!"

With a wink, Gimble sprang up from his stack of food, with a fiddle in hand, and stomped his foot to a giddy old beat. His little troll fingers were nimble and quick and strummed across the strings to play a fast and fancy tune. Joyous music filled the camp and Katie laughed as one troll dared to dance, then another and another until they were all hopping and dancing around the camp fire.

The cheerful little trolls slapped their knees and kicked their heels and danced to the fiddle and drum. But the best by far was Raylin who could spin, and jump and flip over backwards without missing a beat. Katie clapped and clapped as she watched the elf. Then with one big jump, he leapt clear over the fire and back again, just for the fun of it.

"Oh you think that's fancy? Watch this!" Jingles said, and backed up a few steps. The little troll spit in his hands, hitched up his britches and took a running start. With his little legs moving and his big belly bouncing he jumped over the flame and came down on the other side with his pants on fire.

Everyone laughed, when the troll slapped his rump to put out the flames and one by one, they kicked up their feet and spanked their bottoms to mock the troll, until Jingles finally sat in a bucket of water and the fire went out with a hiss.

Old Binderbec laughed so hard he stumbled over Goe Garth who fell over Gimble and knocked over Raylin, and on and on until the trolls were piled on the ground in a heap. And while they were laughing, Jingles jumped up with his pants soaking wet, then kicked up his heels and winked. As the last one standing, the dance was over and Jingles had won. The others took one look, then scrambled to their feet and chased after him, running round and round the fire. Then when they had caught the funny little troll, they gathered him up, tossed him into the air and ended the dance with a shout. "HEY!"

Katie giggled and laughed and clapped her hands.

"Do it again! Do it again!" she said.

With a nod from Gimble and a strum of his fiddle, off they went to dance another tune. Katie watched and cheered and forgot her cares, as the funny little trolls danced by the light of the fire, and did their best to make her happy, if only for the moment.

Meanwhile the two hulking ogres, Rogad and Slag sat

on a log, eating a piece of roasted wild beast. The ogres gnawed and chomped at their food which they had managed to steal for themselves and seemed perfectly content, until Slag reached across and grabbed the last leg of beast sitting in front of Rogad.

Rogad grunted and tried to grab it out of the ogre's hairy paw but Slag shoved him aside. Enraged, Rogad slapped the thick headed ogre and snatched the meat away which drew a ferocious growl. When the sluggish brute reached for the food again, Rogad gripped Slag by the throat and roared, then shoved him off the log.

Thinking it was over, Rogad turned to his morsel of food, then happened to glance over his shoulder, just in time to see an axe coming at him. Rogad toppled over backwards and watched the blade go sailing by, missing him by inches. The rusty blade came down and stuck in the log with a "THUMP," and Slag growled at his bad luck. He struggled to get it out again but not before Rogad charged him like a bull and hit him with enough force to knock the axe free. The ogres tumbled to the ground, clawing and scratching and fighting for the weapon then rolled behind a clump of bushes. After a great deal of snorting and grunting and thrashing about, a hairy hand appeared with a rock in its fist, then plunged down with a nasty crunch and a thud, and with that the bushes were perfectly still once more. The only movement was the flickering light of campfire and the shadows of the merry little trolls dancing through the trees.

After a while, the bushes stirred and Rogad emerged, dragging the axe behind him. As it was, Slag would have no further use for it. Rogad tossed the weapon aside then sat down with a growl and found the half eaten leg of roast beast, lying in the dirt.

"Food mine!" Rogad grumbled then gnawed off a piece of meat with bits of leaves and twigs stuck to it. Now the he was the last and only ogre, that was all that mattered.

The music played on, and with Slag gone it would be hours before anyone noticed that the ogre was missing, but it would be even longer before anyone realized that the angel was gone as well.

The glistening guardian swept through the air and traveled deeper into the woods, somber and alone. The living trees seemed to sense the angel's troubled spirit and watched in silence as he set down at the edge of a clearing, then walked into the moonlight and threw off his cloak. There in the quiet stillness, the angel's wings suddenly appeared, dazzling white. They sparkled and cast their light all around as Stadia stretched them full out, then folded them once more, silently behind him. He stood there a moment, listening to the wind then looked to the sky with a sorrow in his eyes, as though he held the weight of the world on his shoulders. Then like a shadow passing before a flame, something changed and the angel cried out.

"Lord, hear me!... Evil surrounds me and I am filled with rage!" he shouted toward heaven with his hands raised.

At the same time a little creature stirred in the shadows not far off. It had not been laying there long, at the base of the old oak, and only opened its eyes a slit when the angel began to speak. The goblin stirred then winced at the excessive amount of light that was suddenly shining on him and thought he saw an angel looking toward heaven, crying out to God.

"I must be dead." Numlock thought, as he peered at the guardian, glistening brightly before him then paused to reconsider, since this wasn't the kind of vision an evil goblin was likely to see in the dark underworld. Yet, laying there in the grass, it was all becoming perfectly clear to him now. Not only had he survived the fall, but it was obvious to him that the wizard had placed him there, however recklessly, to spy on the angel who he knew would come to that very spot to pray. The goblin smiled at Gellzoowin's brilliance, even though in truth it was simply a matter of blind luck.

Laying out in the open, Numlock rolled onto his belly with a good deal of pain and effort, and dragged himself behind a bush to get a better look at the angel. But as soon as he arrived, the little bush moved away, for even the shrubs of the living forest would have nothing to do with wicked goblins. Numlock cursed the bush for its stubborn good nature and tried to hold perfectly still, while the trees looked down from above and would have cried out, but dared not interrupt the angel who was still in the midst of prayer.

"My Lord, the search for Majesty endangers the lives of many. The way ahead grows more perilous and the child of God is at risk. There is not only the wizard and the goblin to contend with. The boy now poses a greater threat which only grows worse as his power increases. I weary of the game, Lord. Free my hand and I will stop this. Otherwise, speak now and let me know your plan... If not to save the child from danger, then what?! Tell me why I am here! " Stadia pleaded.

Numlock listened as the angel's voice rose toward heaven.

"Speak to me, Lord! I implore you! Tell me what you would have me do!" Stadia said, searching the sky above. He watched as storm clouds gathered overhead then suddenly the angel seemed weaker and filled with regret.

"I fear I can no longer hear your voice... I submit myself before you." He said then dropped to his knees. Numlock strained to hear as Stadia spoke more softly.

"T'was pride that caused Lucifer to be cast down, purge me of evil and cleanse my soul, oh Lord, for I dare not suffer the same fate."

A distant rumbling made Numlock look up, and before the last words could fall from the angel's lips, a column of fire fell from heaven like a bolt of lightning. Numlock shrank back as the brilliant ray lit the forest and shook the ground. The goblin did his best to look, but the air was so hot, he turned his head and shielded his eyes against the light and heat. Within the radiant beam, the angel glowed bright as a star as the fire of God poured down and scorched the earth. And just when it seemed the forest would surely explode from the sheer power raining down from Heaven, the angel and the light were gone in the twinkling of an eye. Then in the stillness of the forest, all that was left was the distant sound of rolling thunder.

Numlock lay in the darkness of the woods, gazing at the smoldering ground, where the angel had stood and a slow smile crept across his face.

"The angel... is gone!" he squeaked. "Disappeared before my eyes! Can it be?" Numlock said and winced from the pain. He clutched his side which was still smarting from the fall then struggled to his feet. The goblin looked around him and grinned.

"He's dead, he's dead. Tis' very plenty true! He's dead, he's dead. There's nothing more to do!" Numlock whispered and sang with a giggle and was just beginning to enjoy himself when a thick green vine leapt off the ground, and cracked like a whip against the goblin's rear.

"YEOW!" Numlock cried then hurried on his way, limping and hobbling as fast as he could, to go find his master and tell him the good news.

CHAPTER TWENTY TWO

The Monster in the Dark

*T*he light of the camp fire cast an eerie glow on the
woods while the trolls slept in the comfort of their little draw beds and the living forest kept watch over them.
Katie rested comfortably, asleep in her own bed with the
trolls all around her, each one with his sword lying across
his chest, which was customary when there was no look out
to stand watch. Indeed, with all the wine and dancing there
was no one left awake. Even the gentle fairy lay fast asleep
under the wagon, nestled in Bromwin's fur and snugly
tucked behind his ear.

With only the sound of the crackling fire to stir the
silence, Katie fell into a deep sleep, and as she slept, there
came to her a vision in a dream. Now that she was younger
and more innocent, the knowledge of God grew clearer
within her mind and once again, it was about to reveal something she didn't know she already knew.

In her dream, Katie stood at the edge of a cliff staring out
over the mist. There she saw five people, three young women
and two men. These were five legendary beings, teachers of
great renown, floating in the air above a wide and yawning

345

chasm, with only the distant canyon floor looming hundreds of feet below them. They stood there staring calmly, with kind and gentle faces. The three women were sisters and the men were their elder brothers. The women were dressed in long green gowns made of flowing velvet that shimmered in the light.

Each gown had a beautiful pattern woven into it, a tapestry of trees and mountains with swirls of lace that resembled clouds. And as their gowns moved, the designs seemed to come to life and were filled with color.

The women smiled down with wisdom and kindness and as Katie admired their glowing faces, a thought came to her. It was as though the twinkle in their eyes had spoken softly, whispering in Katie's mind and without a word being uttered, she suddenly knew their names.

Katie stared in wonder and pointed to each one and called their names aloud. The sisters were Cassia, Mistral, and Terrin. Their brothers were Anthium, and Conig.

"How do you do?" Katie said.

Each one of the great teachers gave a courteous nod. Mistral and Terrin were the two older sisters, while Cassia was the youngest and carried a shimmering bowl. The bowl was made of silver and Cassia held it with both hands, out-stretched. As Katie watched, sparkling water seemed to well up from out of the bowl and poured over its edges in a never ending stream. Strangely, Cassia never seemed to notice the cascade of water that disappeared like rain in the mist beneath her feet.

Mistral was taller and looked down as wisps of clouds swirled around her. Her flowing braids danced above her shoulders and her gown was swept by the wind as Mistral beamed, radiant in the midst of the gathering tempest.

Terrin was a spectacle to behold as her face was constantly changing. It was something you didn't notice right away, like the changing face of a clock. At first, Terrin was lovely and plain. Her face was round, with silky blonde hair that hung around her neck in ringlets and curls. Then slowly her features became more narrow, her face slender and more exotic with almond shaped eyes. Her golden hair turned black as ebony, and grew longer and longer until it flowed down her back. Katie watched as the woman's gown changed as well. Thick ribbons of gold and silver appeared, woven into the beautiful green tapestry of her garment. And then like everything else about the beautiful woman, the designs faded and Terrin's face changed again.

It was all a strange sight in a strange dream. The five teachers remained perfectly still as Katie stood there, gazing at them, filled with curiosity.

The two brothers, Anthium, and Conig were twins. They were much larger than their three sisters and stood behind them waiting patiently. Anthium's eyes shone like crystal and his robe was studded with jewels, while Conig's eyes were cold and gray, his chin covered with a long flowing beard. He appeared rigid, hard and filled with strength. The brothers were noble and handsome. Their robes had the same graceful patterns as their sisters, patterns of the sky and the land woven into them.

Katie watched as little white flecks moved in and out of Conig's beard. At first she thought it was dust, but when she looked closer Katie drew back, repulsed by the tiny things that were alive and flying all about. Strangely, there was something gentle and elegant, about their motion. They moved more slowly and arced gracefully through the air, like a flock of birds flying far off. Katie took a step closer, and when she could see them more clearly, she marveled at the gentle little creatures gliding on the wind, fleecy white birds, as white as snowflakes and just as tiny.

When she looked up, Conig was nodding his head as if to say, "That's right. Now you're getting it."

Katie wasn't sure what it was she was supposed to get.

They were all so strange and wonderful, with their amazing eyes peering down at her. Still, there was something about them that made Katie feel small and afraid. From the moment she had seen the five teachers she knew they held great powers, but she also knew there was something more, something they were afraid to show her, or perhaps something she was afraid to see.

"It's all right," Katie said. "I'm not afraid."

The five teachers smiled and whispered softly, "Very well."

In that instant, all five of them began to change. Katie stepped back as the earth quaked beneath her feet and the five teachers grew at an alarming rate. They grew so fast their heads were above the clouds in seconds and soon they were enormous beyond belief.

Katie remembered the giant, but even the seventy foot titan was nothing more than a speck compared to these wondrous beings and would be lost in the palm of their hands. Still, the five teachers kept growing and Katie's mind reeled at the sight of them. They grew till the cup in Cassia's hands was the size of a lake and the water that cascaded down was a raging waterfall. They grew till Mistral's wind was a hurricane, and Terrin's changing faces rumbled with the noise of a distant tremor that shook mountains.

The two brothers were even larger, colossal giants with arms that stretched across the sky. When they were done and all was calm once more, Katie stood on her cliff and yelled to them.

"Who are you?" she asked.

They all smiled and spoke without uttering a word.

"You know who we are." They answered.

Now that Katie could see them in their true form, the mystery was even greater.

"I know your names, but nothing else!" she yelled. Their answer came softly and rolled across the sky.

"Fear not. We will lead you and give you safe passage." they said.

"Fear not." The angel had said those words as well.

"Are you angels?" Katie asked, gazing up at the five beings in wonder.

The five teachers stared at her from beyond the clouds and were strangely silent."Can you help me?" Katie asked. "Can you help me save my brother?"

Conig spoke and his voice rumbled across the valleys.

"Beware the soldier of doom who is filled with darkness," he said.

Katie gave him a puzzled look, for Conig's words were all the more mysterious.

The air swirled across the chasm and Katie called out.

"The soldier of doom?" She said and remembered the words spoken by the living trees. "You mean the black knight, don't you?" Katie asked. "Who is he? Please tell me!" she demanded.

The three sisters responded as one.

"Beware the minion. He is Nemesis, the soldier of darkness, the soldier of doom."

Their words came down like a warning from heaven.

"Nemesis," Katie whispered. "But, who is Nemesis?" she wondered, and was just about to ask, when there came a terrible noise; a raspy gritty growl, like someone sawing wood with a dull blade. With that, the five teachers suddenly faded into the distant skies and disappeared.

"Wait!" she cried. "You haven't told me..."

But before she could say another word Katie awoke from her dream. The words were still on her lips when the horrible noise made her sit up in bed and look around as the mournful sound filled the camp and echoed into the woods. Katie fully expected to see some evil monster shackled in chains, roaming through the camp, but there was nothing, only Gimble, snoring peacefully and quite loudly, next to her.

The troll lay in his bed, fast asleep, breathing in with a raspy roar and wheezing out with a whistle. His wide brimmed hat covered his eyes, and the long white feather, tucked in its brim dangled down over his lips. Katie rubbed her eyes and watched Gimble and the feather with some fascination. Each time the troll inhaled, the feather dipped gently into his mouth, like a bird peeking into a hole, and stayed there until he breathed out again. Then when the troll's lips fluttered together, the feather drew back and waited until Gimble opened his mouth once more, then returned like a curious friend. Katie giggled as the feather went up and down, time and time again, without ever disturbing the sleeping troll.

Aside from Gimble's loud snoring and the occasional snort, it was all quiet aboard the wagon. Katie peered into the stillness of the forest and thought about the strange dream as the campfire cast its light beyond the trees. She thought about the teachers and what they had said; but most of all, she thought about the black knight.

"Who is he and why had the teachers mentioned him?"

She recalled how Jack looked at the black knight as though he were precious to him. "What makes him so important?" She wondered then sat up straight and peered into the dark woods, her eyes suddenly filled with fear. She remembered the land of great discoveries and Jack who had traveled under the cover of darkness; alone and unafraid. Sitting there, staring into the woods, she wondered if he would dare return to reclaim the black knight. Because if he did... Katie hated to even think about it, but the thinking was already done. She told herself she must be crazy, and agreed. Still her mind was made up. "If Jack comes back..." she thought. "I want to be there to catch him." She whispered as she peered into the night.

A gentle breeze stirred the campfire and the dwindling light barely found its way to the edge of the clearing. The shifting shadows ducked behind trees and peaked out, waiting for her to brave the darkness. With a glance around her, Katie considered the trolls. But since Jack had made a fine enemy of them all, all things considered, she knew she'd be better off without them and turned away to face the woods alone. Katie struggled against her better judgment.

"This is crazy. It's too dark." she told herself as she crawled out of her bed, in her flannel robe and night gown. Katie looked around again, waiting for someone to stop her, but there was no one awake to do it, as she pulled the thick hide boots over her pink bunny slippers.

Slowly and carefully, Katie picked up the candle on her bedside table. The brass candle holder was covered in dried wax and the single candle barely burned brightly enough to show the way as she started down the dark isle between the troll beds. Katie walked softly, looking on either side of her, careful not to wake the sleeping trolls. When she reached the back of the wagon she climbed down the ladder, which was difficult enough, with the candle holder in one hand and the darkness all around her. The moment she touched the ground she heard a growl, and in the candle light, saw the huge bear curled up and asleep underneath the wagon. As for the sparkling fairy tucked behind Bromwin's ear, all Kitch heard was the noise of the bear and the two were lost in their dreams.

Katie started toward the woods and tip toed with the grass crinkling beneath her boots. She squinted and winced with each step, but no one stirred as she crept away.

Once she reached the edge of the clearing, Katie raised her candle and stared down the dark path. There were the tracks of the Rabble wagon, trailing off into the night.

"Beware the soldier of doom." The words from her dream echoed in Katie's mind and she tried to ignore them. She was already frightened enough, peering into the darkness of the living forest. Still the last time the trees had spoken to her, they had been friendly enough, and she wasn't quite as afraid of them anymore. She only hoped the great trees would recognize her in the cold dark of the night.

"Whatever it takes... whatever it takes." She whispered in a quivering voice.

Katie looked back at the troll wagon then with her mind made up and her candle held high, she turned and stepped into the shadowy woods. The moment she left the clearing, darkness closed in around her, as she started down the trail. The tiny flame flickered and only managed to light the path in front of her feet. Katie held the candle higher as she walked and gave fearful glances at every little sound she heard, the snap of a twig, the howl of the wind.

The tall trees stood above her and somewhere in the darkness, they stooped down and bent over, creaking and moaning like grand old giants of the forest. Their branches waved just beyond the light of her candle as if to warn her to turn back but the trees dared not speak for the child was frightened enough as it was. Katie walked on in the flickering light of her candle and tried to focus on the way ahead. The trip was longer than she remembered, much longer and walking through the pitch blackness, Katie yearned to turn back. She could feel her nerves slipping, and struggled to keep her feet moving forward when suddenly... "WHOOOOOOOOOoooooo!"

The long deep haunting sound floated through the trees and stopped Katie in her tracks. She listened and tried to keep herself from shaking, but all she could hear was the sound of her own heart, pounding in her chest.

"Whooo! Whooo!" The noise came again and was a bit more familiar. Katie thought for a moment. This wasn't the sound of a monster lurking in the dark. It was just an owl.

"Silly old owl." She said, with a sigh of relief then smiled at her childish fears. She started forward again and kept walking. It would take a lot more than the hoot of an old owl to make her turn back now. She had already been captured by an ogre, made friends with a bear, dined with an evil wizard, looked into the eyes of a giant, and been attacked by fire breathing monsters. But above all that, it was the presence of the guardian angel that gave her courage. Just knowing he was out there somewhere was comfort enough. Then a brief little thought flickered through her mind and made her stop to look around. "But what if he was gone?"

Katie shuddered at the thought and told herself, "Don't be so ridiculous. After all, what's the point of having a guardian angel if he's not there to guard you?... Still if he could just appear." She wished with all her heart and kept walking with only the tiny candle and the thought of the angel to comfort her, when suddenly the circle of light came upon two enormous black boots laying on the ground ahead. Katie froze where she was and tried to hold the candle steady. She had found the black knight lying in exactly the same spot where they had left him. She wanted to call out to the angel, as the black boots glistened in the candlelight, but was too afraid to make a sound.

"It's not too late." She told herself. "You can still turn back." Katie stared intently at the shadowy figure and raised the candle higher then took a few steps forward, with the light flickering in the darkness. She could see the black knight's legs and the grim mace lying in the grass next to his body. The studded battle hammer lay half buried in the ground, still clutched tightly in his gloved fist. Katie stopped again.

"That's odd, that he should still be holding onto the weapon after the fall." she thought as she crept forward and could see more of the black knight glistening in the dim candle light. The huge suit of armor remained perfectly still and seemed to have no life in it at all. She kept moving, taking little baby steps, forcing her feet to inch forward. The closer she got, the bigger the soldier became. When she finally stopped she was standing next to the black knight's shoulder and was close enough to kick him. It was then that Katie could feel the bitterly cold air that settled around his enormous body.

A supernatural force surrounded the dark warrior. It chilled the night air and turned Katie's breathe to steam. Not only was it cold, but it frosted the grass around the dark creature and made Katie tremble. This was the closest she had ever been to the black knight and he was even bigger than she imagined. Katie wished she could stop her hands from shaking and tried to hold the candle steady as she leaned forward.

The black knight was no longer polished and perfect. He was covered in dust and looked old and forgotten. Katie held the flickering flame lower until it was over his helmet which was as big as a potbellied stove. From where she stood, she could see the metal slits in his visor and the darkness within. She took another step and held the candle a bit closer to look through the narrow openings and see if she could get a glimpse of his sleeping face, or perhaps his closed eyelids set inside the darkness.

Katie came closer still, until she was bent over and the candle was only a hand's width away from the black knight's helmet. Still she could see nothing then tilted the candle down and lent forward to shine more light in through the visor and when she did, hot wax poured inside the opening.

"Psssssssssstt!"

The scalding hot wax hissed when it dropped through the visor and Katie scurried back, with eyes gaping wide. She stood several yards away, unable to believe what she had done and gave a quick glance at the trail behind her, then looked at the dark figure laying on the ground. She stood there, ready to make her escape and wanting to scream at herself for being so careless but dared not make a sound. Instead she watched and waited. After a whole minute had gone by, the black knight remained perfectly still. As far as Katie could tell, he hadn't even flinched. She squinted at him then frowned.

"Surely he must have felt that." she thought to herself then remembered what the living trees had said.

"The soldier of doom has not yet awakened." Katie had no idea what it meant, but knew that if someone had dripped hot wax on her face, not only would she have awakened, but she would have screamed loud enough to wake the living trees.

Still she was thankful that the huge figure of the knight had not moved in the least and appeared to still be asleep.

Katie summoned her courage and moved toward the black knight once more. Step by step, she came closer and closer. And when she had returned to the spot, she stepped over the black knight's arm, which was like stepping over a log, and stood right next to his side. Now she was even closer than before. This time, she leaned over him and brought the light as close as she could, careful not to tilt the candle and spill any more wax. Katie peered down through the dark slit in his dusty helmet, with her hand trembling and the candle light shining through the black visor. Still all she saw was darkness and knew that if she was going to risk her life to save her brother, she simply had to see who was inside the knight's armor. But to do that meant she would have to lift the visor and open the helmet.

Katie stiffened at the thought. Looking at the black knight was one thing, but touching him was another. Still, if what the trees had said was true, and the soldier of doom had not yet awakened, she could easily take a quick peek and be gone long before anything happened. Katie stared at the black helmet and tried to find the strength to reach down and lift the visor.

"The longer you wait, the sooner he'll wake up." She told herself.

"Okay, okay. I'm going!" she said and bit her lip as she

tried to be brave. Katie reached down and watched the black knight for any sign of life at all, any sign of the slightest movement, as her hand drew closer.

"You can do it. You can do it." she whispered silently. Slowly, carefully, she slid her fingertips underneath the metal visor. The thing was indeed as cold as ice, but Katie didn't dare pull away or draw back. With her heart pounding and the candle shaking, she shifted her position slightly and gave the visor a gentle tug.

She had expected it to be heavy, but the visor moved easily and gave the tiniest little squeak. Katie held her breath, her eyes gaping wide open as she stared down at the black knight and waited, but again there was no movement. He had not budged an inch, and neither did Katie. She stood there holding the squeaky visor, afraid to move or make another sound.

"Just put it down!" she thought. "Just put it down!"

"No! You can't stop now."

Katie hated herself for being so stubborn and lowered the candle a bit closer then lifted the visor very slowly. To her relief, the hinges slide smoothly and silently as she raised it higher. Then with one gentle motion, she watched the visor swing up over the top of the helmet and thought she felt something move behind her, but with the black knight's face about to be revealed, she could scarcely look away. Once the visor went all the way up, it stopped with a, "click" and Katie stood there staring. She could see inside the dark helmet, but that was all she could see. At first she thought the black knight's face was hidden in the shadows or that the candle was going out, but the light was steady and burned brightly enough. Still Katie could not see the face of the knight. She then lowered the candle until it was nearly inside the helmet, and to her utter shock and horror, there was no face. Not only was there no face, there was no head. There was nothing. The black knight's helmet was empty.

Katie gawked with her mouth wide open. The five teachers had warned her. The soldier of doom was filled with darkness and now she was staring right at it; a living empty darkness that filled the suit of armor with its evil.

Katie pulled back and when she did, she bumped into something then stood frozen as the black knight's hand closed around her shoulder and gripped her tight. The black knight had indeed awakened and without any warning. Katie watched as the empty suit of armor slowly sat upright and the open helmet turned toward her with a frightful squeak. Katie gazed at the headless knight as the flickering candle lit wisps of cob webs in the darkness where his face should have been then standing there before the ghastly creature Katie finally screamed, "STAAADIAAAA!!"

She cried out for the angel until tears streamed down her face, and she was numb with fear then gaped at the empty helmet that was staring right at her. Then with the massive metal hand clenched around her shoulder, Katie screamed again. This time it was a shrill, high pitched squeal that echoed into the night and made her ears ring. She screamed until she trembled and had nothing left in her then stood there, wide eyed gasping for air, while the black knight's helmet gaped open like a huge yawning mouth that seemed to mimic Katie's terrified expression. The two held still and were a ridiculous sight, facing each other in the pool of candle light.

Slowly the black knight raised his other hand and Katie fixed her eyes on the huge war hammer as the dark warrior lifted it higher and higher. Katie pulled and tugged and struggled to break free as the empty helmet stared down, and with the visor swung open the thing almost looked hungry. Then with that thought, Katie did the only thing she could think of and tossed her candle into the black knight's helmet. The candle sparked when it dropped through the opening, cast a brief glow as it went down, then clattered around noisily in the belly of the armor and went out. She had hoped the tiny flame would hurt the black knight in some way, but all she had managed to do was throw away her only source of light and stood there in the dark, regretting the idea the second the light was gone.

Without the candle the ghostly knight looked even scarier as Katie gazed up at the war hammer above her head. Just then, a ring of smoke curled up in front of her face. When it grew thicker, she saw that it was indeed coming from the black knight's helmet. Soon it billowed black and came in an endless stream like smoke pouring out of a chimney, making far more smoke than the tiny candle could have ever produced. The flame indeed had an ill effect on whatever was inside the armor and Katie gaped at the black knight when a terrible noise echoed up from out of its iron belly. It was a horrible hacking cough like the rattle of rusted chains against a dungeon wall that shook the black knight from head to toe. Katie stumbled this way and that, when the black knight flinched and jerked his arm, shoving her back and forth until his grip weakened. And when his metal fingers hung open just enough, Katie pulled then staggered back, amazed to find that she was free.

She stood there a moment, not sure of what to do and when she thought to run, she turned and saw a glowing figure standing in the trail behind her, a tall and slender woman who had appeared out of nowhere, without a sound or a whisper. Katie watched her rise off the ground till she floated on air like a silver ghost in the moonlight then gazed down with glistening eyes that had shone through the ages. Her face was as pale as parchment and transparent like glass, but beautiful and radiant at the same time. Her glowing gown, was draped with ribbons of lace that floated on air like the mist. Katie stared up in a trance as the radiant face of the spirit smiled down on her.

"Gramme Nannah?... Is that you?" Katie asked.

The ghostly form answered slowly. "I am Aro Yal... an

elder spirit of

Lant Imoni, the living woods."

The words sang from her lips and filled Katie with wonder as she stared at her glowing form. The gracious tree
spirit paused and her shimmering eyes slowly looked
beyond the child as the black knight rose to his feet. With
the smoke gone, the dreaded creature stood to its full height
then shut his visor and started forward. At eight feet tall, the
massive brute moved with a stiff and jerky motion at first,
but soon his arms and legs swung more freely as he
marched forward with his huge metal boots clanking and
his grim mace held ready. Katie backed away, and was
about to run when the tree spirit lifted her voice and called
out to the forest.

"Maidens of the oaks come forth."

With that, two more glistening spirits emerged from the
trees nearby, one to the left, the other to the right. They were
smaller and younger than the elder spirit. Katie watched as
others appeared in the distant woods, their pale blue light
shimmering among the trees as they came quickly and
silently through the forest. The beautiful spirits came from
all directions to answer the call and soon there was a small
band of them, gathered in the clearing before Katie. There
were ten of them all together, each one small and frail compared to the enormous soldier and his war hammer. Still they
were fearless and stood their ground.

The black knight only paused a moment to observe
them, then advanced as though the shimmering spirits posed
no threat to him at all. Without a word, the brave maidens
rushed forward reaching out to grab the dark menace. Even
their gowns reached out, alive with power and bound their
flowing ribbons around the black knight's arms and legs and
held him tight. But for all their power, the dark warrior plodded forward, bringing the shimmering tree spirits with him.
Katie backed away, her eyes gaping wider, just as the elder

tree spirit spoke.

"Leave him." she said calmly.

With a wave of her hand, the maiden spirits released the black knight and as he drew nearer, Aro Yal thrust her arm forward.

"Hold! Dark minion!" She commanded.

Katie felt the air move as something rushed past and struck the black knight so hard, he staggered backward. Katie blinked, and wasn't sure what had happened. The soldier of doom turned to look at Aro Yal as though he had just noticed her for the first time, but it was the word of truth, spoken by the elder tree spirit that had sent him reeling.

The black knight started forward once more and raised his grim mace. Aro Yal looked on and with another wave of her hand the old oak standing behind her came to life. Quick as a whip, a branch swooped out of the darkness and wrapped itself around the handle of the black mace, refusing to let go. The black knight looked up, seemingly with surprise, then yanked and tugged like a spoiled child, trying desperately to pull free. With that, the elder tree spirit stepped forward, her words echoing forth.

"You... wicked... brute!" she said as her words struck the black knight like a hammer and rang out in the night. "Clang!...Bang!...Clang!"

"You dare... to attack... a child... of God?"

Her words slammed into the black knight's helmet, once again like a back handed slap across the face, jerking his head from side to side. Still he held onto his weapon and struggled to break free as he was battered about. Aro Yal spoke once more and her words rained down like an avalanche.

"Don't... you... know? ...You have no power here! ...Be gone and take the stench of evil with you!" she said. The blows rang out like a dozen hammers against the black knight's armor and the soldier of doom staggered back once more. But in spite of the fierce attack, his hulking form stood tall and defiant. Katie watched as the black knight continued to struggle against the tree limb, which held the war hammer above his head, and redouble his efforts. He pulled and strained until his armor creaked and the wood began to splinter then… "CRAAACK!!"

Aro Yal cried out, and gripped her arm in pain, then glared at the monster as a much larger tree limb was summoned forth then swooped down and swatted the black knight off of his feet with a mighty, "WACK!!" The blow slammed the black knight into another tree which grabbed him and threw him down in a heap. The tree spirit looked upon her enemy and became more radiant as she swore an oath of battle in her native tongue.

"Kia lien, lo beth la main!"

Her words echoed forth into the woods and summoned the living power of the forest. Soon her sister maidens were ablaze with light and all the woods came to life around them. Katie stood near to the elder spirit and watched as the silver oaks lifted their roots, and cut deep furrows in the soft earth as they lumbered out of the dark. The ground shook beneath them and when all were assembled, the massive trees stood behind the beautiful maidens as a second line of defense and a devastating show of strength.

Finally the black knight rose to his feet with the mace by his side and looked at the giant trees that had formed a barrier between him and the child. Slowly and silently, he reached up and raised his visor just a crack. It was a peculiar gesture, like a salute and Katie jumped back when two small objects flew out of the dark opening. The first hit the ground and rolled to a stop in front of the tree spirits. The second object landed in the grass with a thud. It was Katie's candle and the brass candle holder. The black knight spit them out then lowered his visor, seemingly in a final act of defiance.

With the maidens of the woods glaring and the trees towering over him, the black knight turned and marched off into the darkness, clinking and clanking as he went and faded into the shadows of the living forest. It was a slow and noisy retreat, but a retreat nonetheless. Katie watched the soldier of doom disappear from view and when he was gone, the tree spirits turned to her and stood silent. Some gave curious glances while others looked on admiringly.

"You are the first child of God to grace our presence, the first we had ever seen." Aro Yal said.

Katie hardly knew what to say and only smiled as one by one the beautiful maidens withdrew, gleaming with a joyful twinkle in their eyes. When they were gone, Katie stood all alone with the elder tree spirit and felt guilty for all the trouble she had caused. But the wise old spirit only gazed down, with her eyes of silver, then turned with her gown flowing, and beckoned for Katie to follow.

"This way." She said. "Follow me.

CHAPTER TWENTY THREE

Concerning Good and Evil

*I*t was a long walk back to the camp and the shimmering tree spirit lit the way like a glowing lantern. Katie walked along side, trying not to stare. She glanced up every now and then, wanting to say something, but the tree spirit was so graceful and dignified, Katie struggled to find the courage to speak.

"Thank you for saving my life," Katie said.

Aro Yal looked down upon her warmly.

"Not at all." She answerd, and bowed graciously. It was a gesture that made Katie smile even though she was trying to be serious and polite.

"I'm sorry for all the trouble I caused." Katie added as they walked along.

"Searching out the black knight was a foolish thing, a very foolish thing." said the wise old spirit.

Katie looked down, "I know," she said.

"What did you hope to gain by looking into the creature's face?" Aro Yal asked.

"I don't know," Katie answered. "He seemed so important to my brother, I guess I just wanted to see who he was."

Katie said and then lowered her head as she walked.

Aro Yal nodded. "You are very brave and very innocent, a genuine child of God."

Katie just smiled. "Thank you." she said, thinking it was a nice compliment.

The tree spirit stopped and looked at Katie.

"Do you not know what that means?" she asked.

Katie paused when she remembered what Bromwin had said.

"I think that maybe God told me a long time ago, but now I guess I've forgotten."

Aro Yal smiled down on her.

"You who are born of flesh and blood are changed, born anew, made precious in His sight, for God has received you as His own. You are of noble birth, a child of the King, a true princess of the saintly realm."

"Me? A princess?!" Katie asked.

The tree spirit smiled.

"Of course, but that is only the beginning. Indeed as a child of God you are related to the king of Kings, endowed with riches and beauty beyond all wealth or treasure. For you are an heir to the kingdom of Heaven itself. It is the promise of our Lord and the full inheritance of every child of God."

Katie stared in wide eyed wonder. "The kingdom of Heaven... Really?"

She paused again to consider what the tree spirit had said, then added, "And what about my brother?" Katie asked. "If I am a princess, doesn't that make him a prince? He's a child of God too, isn't he?"

The tree spirit paused and the joy slowly faded from her.

"I'm afraid it is not your relationship to your brother that matters. Instead, it is his relationship to God. As it is, he serves another master now."

Katie's heart sank as the tree spirit continued,

"I am sorry, but the truth must be known. Your brother has given up his inheritance to seek his own fortune, a fortune rooted in magic and has aligned himself with the darker forces and done so of his own free will."

Katie shook her head. "I don't understand," she said. "You make all magic sound evil."

The tree spirit gazed into Katie's eyes.

"Is that so strange? What makes you think it is good?" she asked.

Katie stopped to think as the shimmering tree spirit hovered silently before her.

"What about magicians?" Katie asked. "The ones who do card tricks and pull rabbits out of hats, what about them? Are they evil too?"

Aro Yal had never seen a magician and only knew about wizards and sorcerers.

"Tricks?" She said. "You mean fakery. Things which only appear to be magic yet are not? Why would anyone pretend such a thing?" Aro Yal asked with a ponderous gaze then continued. "Still, such acts as these, in and of themselves are not evil. Yet if they were to turn one's affections toward that which is mysterious and born out of true magic, then it too serves an evil purpose."

Katie turned away and no longer wanted to hear what the tree spirit had to say.

"Is that an offense to you?" Aro Yal asked. "I must warn you. Magic is alluring to the goodness in us all, but there is no such thing as good magic."

Katie looked at the tree spirit questioningly, and Aro Yal could see the doubt in her eyes. She thought for a moment. "Come let us continue and I will tell you the story of the birth of magic."

"The birth of magic?" Katie said with renewed interest and together they continued down the dark path through the enchanted woods.

"There was once a race of people, beloved by God, known as the Clarion," she said. "They were created to watch over the Nohr World and given authority over all the land and all that was within it. They were the human folk, the mankind of our world. In that time, all the world was blessed, until the Clarion were tempted by the Serpent King."

Katie interrupted, "The Serpent king?"

"Yes, he was once a servant of God, an angel entrusted with great power, then cast down for his wickedness and betrayal. In revenge, the Serpent King declared war against God and tempted the Clarion race with a power they could not resist, the power of magic, the power to be like God. So they exchanged the peace of God for the power of God, only to suffer in the bargain. That which they thought was a blessing quickly became a curse, for they could not control the power which was given to them.

Instead of creating grand and wonderful things with their magic, they called forth ogres and goblins, and other creatures born out of the darkness within their own hearts. In time their magic darkened the world itself and overcame them, pitting one against another in a battle for power that was the source of endless strife and division.

The Serpent King laughed at their folly, for in the end the Clarion became bitter and blamed God for their misfortune, and in so doing they embraced magic all the more, only to grow farther away from their God who truly loved them most.

Katie scratched her head. "What does this have to do with my brother?" she asked.

Aro Yal continued, "The Clarion are the race of wizards. The serpent king tricked them and tempted them with a power that could only destroy them. He has tricked your brother as well."

Aro Yal gazed down at Katie with a look of regret then after a long while, Katie looked up. "This Serpent King sounds a lot like Satan." She said.

The tree spirit nodded. 'They are one and the same."

Katie looked up at the elder tree spirit, her eyes once again wide with wonder. "They are?!" she exclaimed.

"Indeed." replied Aro Yal. "God is the creator of all worlds and Satan is the destroyer, who is himself doomed to destruction. Still he has his part to play, and before he is vanquished, he will seek to destroy all that God has created, both in your world and mine."

Katie blinked and simply couldn't believe what she was hearing. "B-but if magic is a tool of the Serpent King, then magic is a tool of..." Her words were a gasp.

Aro Yal smiled down on Katie.

"The truth is revealed. And now you know. It is Lucifer the fallen angel, who seeks to destroy us all."

Katie's eyes searched the ground as the shimmering spirit stood before her and the reality of it all flooded in and only led to more questions. Katie looked up at the tree spirit suspiciously. "How do you know about Lucifer?" she asked.

"We elders are gifted with the power to know evil in all its true forms, in both our worlds. That is why we are called the judges."

Katie stepped back to observe the shimmering tree spirit floating before her, then put her hands on her hips and squinted with a doubtful smirk.

"All of its true forms?" Katie asked then looked around her. "Your world is filled with magic, magical fairies, flying monsters, animals that can talk, trees that walk. Look at you! This whole forest is magical. If all magic is evil doesn't that make you evil, too?"

The wise old tree spirit laughed aloud.

"Perhaps it would indeed, if I were in your world." she said. "Such things would be strange and peculiar in the earthly realm. But in this world, flying fairies, talking animals and trees that walk are common place. It is how God made us."

Katie just listened with a hesitant look as the tree spirit floated before her and spoke to her softly.

"In your world, is it magic that the tides rise and fall, that fish breathe in water, that the trees change colors, that birds fly? These are natural things to you that go unquestioned. But they are all God's creation and no less filled with wonder."

After a while longer and a bit more thought Katie nodded and simply said, "Oh."

The tree spirit stood silently while Katie lowered her head and stared at the ground. "My brother is in more trouble than I thought." she said then asked. "Who is, Nemesis?"

The tree spirit drew back at the mention of the name.

"Nemesis?!... Where did you hear that name, child?"

Katie stood there looking a little timid.

"I... I heard it in a dream." she said.

Aro Yal leant down close to Katie and spoke in a whisper.

"What else did you hear in this dream?" she said slowly.

"That's all. There were these people that called the black knight, Nemesis. What does it mean?"

The tree spirit stood tall and looked in the direction where the black knight had gone, then whispered to herself.

"Nemesis... we knew he was filled with darkness. We could sense the evil within, but we never suspected <u>he</u> would return here. Nemesis means enemy... It means... vengeance." Aro Yal said, watching the woods with grave concern then turned to Katie sharply. "Tell me child, why did your brother call upon the black knight?" she demanded.

"I don't know. I guess he just made him up from a toy he had in his room." Katie said.

"No child. There is not enough magic in the world to create such a thing. I see now why you were led to look inside the creature's armor. Remember what I told you about the wizards and their creations? Your brother has proven me right. Whatever his intentions, he has given an ancient evil, a new way to enter our world."

"I still don't understand. Who is he?" Katie asked, looking more confused than ever.

The tree spirit turned to her and spoke quickly.

"Listen carefully. You must find your brother. The black knight is not what he appears to be. Something wicked grows within, the soul of one who has been asleep for ages. He who was once held captive is now released by your brother's hand. It is the demon, the demon Nemesis."

"A demon," Katie whispered.

Just then, a rumbling shook the forest floor and made the tree spirit look away to the distant woods. When Katie turned she saw a faint glow far off, beyond the trees as another explosion rocked the land and then another.

"What's happening?!" Katie gasped.

Aro Yal gazed through the woods.

"It has begun. He has truly awakened and gained strength." She said. "The forest now knows of the demon that walks among them and has chosen to fight."

Another explosion, lit the sky and Aro Yal stared into the distance as though she could see the battle before her.

"His hammer is a merciless weapon. Many will fall before it."

Suddenly the mighty oaks grew restless and moaned in anguish all around them, until the distant roar of the conflict faded and the forest became strangely silent once more. Katie peered into the dark woods.

"This night the war has been waged and the light of dawn will bring great suffering." the tree spirit said, still looking far off.

"What do we do now?" Katie asked. "What if he comes back?"

Aro Yal gazed down upon Katie. "There is no hope of that." She said, her eyes filled with fear and regret.

Katie took a step closer. "What is it?" she asked.

"I am sorry, my child. The black knight does not share power and will let no one stand in his way. He will soon pass beyond our border and I pray that God is truly with you, for you are your brother's only hope."

Katie listened and could feel her heart pounding as she grew more desperate, wanting to understand everything the tree spirit was telling her.

"Listen to me. The demon warrior has but one goal now, to free himself from the prison that your brother has placed him in."

Katie tried to speak, but the tree spirit would not be interrupted.

"Once he has gained his freedom he will seek to rule all who dwells within this world. But first, he will have to escape the suit of armor that binds him and holds him captive. To do that he must destroy the one who created it. Nemesis will destroy your brother."

"What do I do?" Katie pleaded and could hardly stand still.

"This is the dilemma." said Aro Yal. "To save himself, your brother must renounce his power over the black knight and give him his freedom. If not, the black knight will surely kill him to take it. But if your brother releases the black knight to save himself, he will set the demon loose upon our world, and we shall all be at his mercy."

Katie looked at the elder spirit in hopeless confusion.

"What should I do?!" Katie cried.

Aro Yal looked into her eyes. "This burden rests upon your shoulders and you alone must decide. But know this. Whatever you do, you must do it before sunrise."

"Sunrise?!... Why sunrise?"

"Nemesis will surely reach your brother by then." Aro Yal said.

Katie looked to the east and saw the purple light of dawn poking through the shadows of the trees. "But, that's only a few hours away!"

Aro Yal shook her head. "You do not have much time. The fate of us all rests in your hands."

Just then, the sound of yelling rose in the distance and Katie turned to see the faint glow of torches.

"It's the trolls. They've found me." she said, then spoke as fast as she could.

"What about the angel? What about, Stadia? Can't he help us?"

Aro Yal looked down on her. "Alas, the angel is gone."

The words of the elder spirit shook Katie to her soul.

"What do you mean?! Where is he?!" she pleaded.

"Where he has gone, I know not, but I pray he returns for the sake of us all."

Aro Yal glanced to the side at the sound of the trolls rushing through the woods. And as they drew nearer there came a roar.

"This way lads! Over here!"

Bromwin barreled ahead and lead the way, making enough noise to alert the whole forest of his approach. With that, the shimmering tree spirit backed away from the path and faded silently into the giant oak looming behind her.

"Wait," cried Katie. "Can't you help me?"

The glistening eyes of the spirit were the last to disappear inside the tree as her voice echoed from within. "It is all beyond my control."

"But I can't do this alone! What do I do?" Katie pleaded to the giant oak who whispered to her on the wind.

"You are a child of God. Trust in the Lord and He will make your way straight." The gentle words had just faded on the night air when the great bear charged out of the darkness.

"I've found her! She's here!" Bromwin roared, then skidded to a halt, with Goe Garth and the others close behind, their torch lights bobbing down the path.

"Thank God I found you," Bromwin said and swung his

head around, looking for any sign of danger. "We heard your scream and thought we had lost you."

"I...I..." Katie stammered and didn't know what to say or where to begin. Bromwin sensed her fear and confusion.

"Are you all right? What's the matter, child?" he asked.

"A tree spirit..." Katie tried to begin. "She was standing right there. And she, she..."

Bromwin turned to see the black oak with its silvery bark sparkling in the moonlight.

"Amazing!" Bromwin said looking it up and down.. "A tree spirit, eh?... When I was but a young pup my father told me of how they roamed these woods at night. I have never seen one myself. They don't appear to everyone you know, only the blessed."

Katie could tell Bromwin was warming up for another one of his long winded speeches.

"My brother is in trouble!" she blurted out just as the trolls arrived.

"Over here! We've found her!" They shouted.

Goe Garth and Raylin were first to arrive with swords drawn and torches ablaze to light the way, then came Gral Tibbore, Rumyon and friar Jingles. The little fairy came quickly, darting through the trees in a haze of sparkling dust.

"Thank God you're all right!" Kitch said in a fluster.

Bromwin roared. "Calm yourselves and be quiet!" he said then turned to Katie. "Go on child."

The trolls stood by anxiously waiting for her to speak. They waited and waited as Katie looked at each expectant face and thought about the demon that Jack had brought into their world.

"Well?..." said Goe Garth.

Katie stood in the torchlight staring, and knew she had no choice. She would have to tell the trolls and trust God for their help.

"We have until sunrise to find my brother." Katie started

slowly.

"Why? What's the matter?" said Goe Garth.

"The black knight is going to kill him."

"Kill him? Nonsense!" said Gral Tibbore. "The bumbling oaf can hardly walk! Besides, they're in league together."

"No, no he's changed." Katie said. "He, he's turned into something different."

Gral leaned in toward her and glared warily.

"Changed how?... Turned into what?" he growled.

Everyone listened as Katie told them what the tree spirit had said. She warned them of the danger, and the demon Nemesis who lurked within the black knight's armor.

"Hold on." said Rumyon. "A demon is no small matter. If we find your brother and he renounces his power over this black knight, this demon, then what?"

"Then my brother will be safe." Katie said and tried to smile.

Rumyon looked at Katie suspiciously.

"And what then?" he asked.

Katie could hardly bring herself to say it.

"Then... the demon will be set free." she said.

"Set free?!" Rumyon glared and pointed an accusing finger. "You mean set loose upon our world, don't you?"

Now that it was revealed, the trolls stared in disbelief as Goe Garth, their leader stepped forward.

"Why should we save your brother, only to endanger our own lives, our own families, our own world?" he asked, peering intently.

Katie looked at the trolls, who glared back at her, their faces cold and strange. They were distant and unfamiliar to her now, all except for Jingles who stepped forward. The good friar jumped up on a moss covered stump and raised his torch overhead so that his light shone on all who were gathered around.

"None of us knew what dangers we would face when we agreed to take this journey, yet we swore an oath." He said. "A troll's oath, given freely, and now that we face real danger your faces grow long and your hearts faint. An oath is an oath no matter what. Our word is our bond, even unto death."

The trolls remained silent as Jingles turned to Katie.

"My sword is yours, my child." he said.

"And mine." Raylin twirled his blade, and thrust it into its sheath.

"Hah!" Gral Tibbore jeered. "And when the demon reigns, the skies turns black and terror befalls us, who will stand on that dark day? Will your swords still be as ready to fight?"

"Indeed!" said friar Jingles. "All the more ready."

Gral grumbled at the response as Bromwin stepped forward.

"Besides, the angel will be there to fight as well." he added.

"Indeed!" shouted Jingles, "We have Stadia!"

Just the mention of his name made the trolls grow braver. One by one they gathered around Katie to show their support, but her smile was faint and halfhearted, for she knew the angel was gone, and could not bring herself to tell them.

"Quick!" Bromwin shouted. "We have given the enemy a head start! We must find the boy before it's too late. Come child, climb on!"

The bear lowered himself and waited till she was safely aboard and Katie leant down to whisper in his ear. "Thank you."

"What I do, I do for you, child of God." Bromwin said softly then turned to the others. "Back to the wagon! If you are with us, let us join the fight and place our fate in the hands of God. We go to save the boy!" he shouted.

With that, Bromwin turned and started back through the

woods. Jingles and Raylin chased after him, with the others close behind, while two stayed back and seemed reluctant to follow. Rumyon held his torch high and Gral stood next to him.

"We go to save the boy, to save the wizard's apprentice who would kill us if he had the chance." Gral Tibbore growled.

Rumyon nodded. "Our mission grows more clouded with each passing moment."

"My thoughts exactly, brother, my thoughts exactly." Gral said as the two started back together and with a glance and a nod, a dark and secret partnership was formed. Bromwin ran ahead, racing through the woods with Katie holding on tight, and when they were far enough, the bear called to her on the run. "Child!" He said.

Katie leaned forward and listened with the wind rushing through her hair.

"The angel is gone, isn't he?"

A tear rolled down Katie's cheek as they ran into the night.

"How did you know?"

""I could see it on your face." said Bromwin. "Is that what the tree spirits told you?"

"Yes." Katie said, weak and afraid. "What are we going to do?"

Bromwin kept a steady pace as he galloped on.

"For now, it is our secret, but I fear we shall have need of him soon enough." He said. "Pray that he returns."

Katie stared ahead and whispered, "He didn't even say good-bye."

Bromwin slowed his pace and Katie could see the glow of the campsite ahead. Just then Kitch flew past them like a fiery spark through the trees.

"Lets Go! Lets Go!" she yelled and flew to the trolls who were guarding the wagon. "Wake up! There is no time to waste! We must be on our way!" She said.

Binderbec, the old soldier jumped to his feet while Gimble nearly fell off his stool when the fairy flew under his nose and filled his face with light.

"But I'm hungry." Gimble grumbled half asleep and brushed the fairy aside.

"No time! No time!" the fairy said. "There's more to attend to in the world than your stomach."

The troll opened one eye as he got to his feet and stretched. "Perhaps," he said. "But the world is full and my stomach is empty."

When all the beds were stowed and Juggernaut was hitched to the wagon, something stirred at the back of the wagon. Gral and Binderbec drew their swords as a huge hairy arm reached out from under the canvas tarp and Rogad emerged. The monstrous ogre yawned and looked around while Gral and Raylin poked the canvas to see where the other ogre was hiding.

"Where's your ugly friend?" Gral said with an angry scowl.

"Slag, gone..." he said, still groggy and half asleep as he scratched his scruffy beard.

Binderbec raised an eyebrow and frowned.

"I see." the old soldier said then brandished his hammer in the face of the ogre.

"Well, you mind your manners and behave yourself or I'll see to it that you'll be gone as well?"

Rogad sneered at the troll then grabbed the canvas tarp and covered himself over again.

With a crack of the whip, the black stallion quickened his pace. Katie drew her fur cape around her shoulders and nestled in her seat behind Goe Garth as the wagon rumbled through the forest of the living trees. Now that they were on their way, all the trolls were strangely silent. With night fleeting and the early light of dawn approaching, the black knight weighed heavily on everyone's mind.

Although Katie was surrounded by friends, the brave band of trolls, the nimble elf, the bear king and the sparkling fairy, Katie never felt more frightened and alone.

"Wait to worry and start to pray... Start to pray."

Her grandmother's words came to her on the wind and Katie looked to the night sky. She prayed for God's help. She prayed for strength and courage. But most of all she prayed they would find Jack before any harm could come to him. And when she was done, she finished with a whisper.

"... Stadia, we need you...come back."

Katie drew the fur cape snugly against her cheeks as the night air swirled around her and the black stallion raced through the dark enchanted woods. And while she gazed at the horse something stirred inside her; a precious ray of hope, like a sudden answer to prayer. "What of the white horse? The white stallion called Majesty. Perhaps it could be of some help." She thought.

The sacred animal had proved to be a great mystery to all, but now it was suddenly much more than that to her. Indeed, the white horse was a source of comfort and hope and all that Katie could cling to as she looked to the dawn and the light of the rising sun.

End of book one

Printed in the United States
54758LVS00002B/1